Blackberry Winter

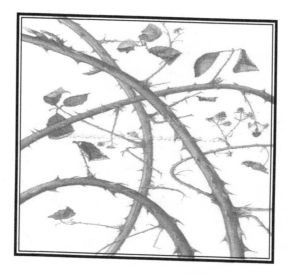

Dormant Vines

BRENDA HEINRICH HIGGINS

ISBN 978-1-64670-726-3 (Paperback)
ISBN 978-1-64670-727-0 (Digital)

Covenant Books, Inc.
11661 Hwy 707
Murrells Inlet, SC 29576
www.covenantbooks.com

Blackberry winter can fall anywhere between the third week of May to mid-June, just as the flowers start to bloom on the berry bushes. It lasts but a week, maybe two, and it's the final cold snap before summer begins. But just as sure as the winds drop off at sunset, blackberry winter leaves with summer riding in on its tail. Special, but sometimes bittersweet things can happen during blackberry winter. Just ask the old folks, they'll tell you it's so.

Isaac Deremer is a God-fearing, law-abiding man who makes his living farming his land. At age thirty-two, he is happily married to the love of his life, Mariah. The couple, through the past twelve years, have brought seven children into this world: four sons and three daughters. Isaac's proud heritage and love for this country began when his great-grandfather, for whom he was named, arrived in New Amsterdam ninety-seven years earlier. The elder Deremer came to the new world to freely worship God and enjoy a better life. Life in America has been difficult and certainly a challenge, but with strong faith the Deremer family has in the Lord, it was their belief that all things were possible. Those that dared to venture to America were met with many unforeseen happenings yet were able to carve out a new existence for themselves and their family. But now, in the late fall of 1774, life is becoming more and more difficult. King George of England who rules the colonies is unhappy with the people of America wanting their independence. Trouble is festering and anger is beginning to become a daily uncontrolled occurrence. Colonists no longer want to be ruled by a king. The king wants total control over the colonists. This toxic mix is soon to boil over. If freedom is given to the people of America, how will they survive without their mother country? Can a land of mixed nationalities and classes of people who can't even understand or speak each other's language come together and create a more perfect union? Only time will tell.

The Journal of Isaac Deremer

October 25, 1774–
April 24, 1776

CHAPTER 1

Times are changing, and war is brewing; one can just feel it in the air. The redcoats are everywhere. We seldom, if ever, saw the British Army in the northern part of New Jersey, and especially here in Mansfield township. A group of redcoats visited a neighboring farm a few days ago. Today on my trip to the gristmill in town, I overheard that old Jake Beerman, whose farm was visited, is a Tory! There is talk of tar 'n feathering Jake should he ever venture to town under the cover of darkness. I never took Jake for a Tory; heck, he can hardly speak English, let alone try being one! I guess it's the quiet ones we have to mind our manners around; don't want old King George to know that I detest his mere existence. Tariffs on this and tariffs on that; gosh, the cost of just our basic comforts like tea and sugar is almost out of reach for most of us folks. Something has to give, and although I do not relish such a thing as war, we Americans need our freedom. Don't get me wrong, I sincerely appreciate all that Mariah and I have built together, but a family needs the ability to look to the future with more certainty and the hope of a chance to keep what our blood, sweat, and tears have created for our own prosperity.

It was near dusk when I arrive back at my farm. I just finished stabling our horse Nellie when Mariah called out to me to say that supper was almost on the table. Our boys, Pieter and Albert, had just finished tending to the afternoon chores, milked our cows, and fed the animals. After we washed up, we went inside and sat down with the rest of the family at the kitchen table to enjoy the fine cooking my wife always prepared for us. We joined hands and bowed our heads in prayer, thanking the Lord for all the goodness that he has provided to us.

While placing supper on the table, Mariah asked how my trip to town went. After taking a deep breath to enjoy the aroma of my meal, I began to relay what I had learned earlier, "Looks like old Jake Beerman has found himself in some hot water, or maybe I should say tar 'n feathers. Talk has it that the redcoats paid a visit to his farm, and Jeremiah Smith has labeled him a Tory." The words I just spoke caused the older children to look at me with big eyes and mouths wide open. "A Tory, a Tory! Jake Beerman is in the haystack with the redcoats? Oh my goodness, how he can do something like that?" said Mariah as she took her seat at the end of the table in total disbelief.

In between bites of my mincemeat pie, I shook my head. "Not everyone thinks rule under King George is a bad thing. I guess they are afraid of what we will have if we are left to set up our own government. After all, our army is no match to Britain's, so we have no way to defend ourselves from the tyranny. Actually, just talking like this could probably get us in trouble with the redcoats."

I now saw fire in her eyes. "What do you mean we shouldn't be talking like this! This is our home, not the redcoat's home, not the king of England's home, our home, period!" After a few seconds of silence, I decided it was best to move on to more pleasant things and continue our discussion after the children were later tucked into their beds. No need to fill their innocent heads with troublesome details. Our table talk turned into a happy conversation for everyone to share in and enjoy.

After supper, the older children helped their mother clear the table and do the dishes. I remained in my seat working out details for next year's crops, all the while thinking about old Jake and what the future had in store for me and my family. The little ones played by the fire with their collection of pretty stones.

A short time later, Mariah began her nightly one-on-one reading lessons with our three older children, Pieter, Albert, and Elizabeth. With only a choice of one book in our home, the Holy Bible, tonight each read aloud scripture from the book of Numbers. Mariah and I were blessed with the ability to read and write. Years ago, our parents had us read the scripture from the Holy Book and taught us penmanship as best they could. We both agreed that we would do the same for our brood. Power comes from knowledge; knowledge comes from the ability to read and write, allowing one to handle their own affairs. Everyday lessons in arithmetic are gleamed from household and farm chores. We feel confident that we are providing our children with the best learning skills that we can give them. Few folks around us read or write well, if at all.

Bedtime was at about seven o'clock. All were sleeping soundly after Mariah told them one of her great bedtime stories. We briefly picked up where we left off with our earlier conversation. Sadly, we both agreed that things were looking rather gloomy and hoped for better times.

CHAPTER 2

The past few days have been extra busy here on the farm. The children helped with the final harvest, and our lofts are almost full. We took full advantage of the harvest moon, and all of us worked well into the night to complete the cutting and tying of the shucks with ears of corn still attached. We then neatly created shuck stacks out of the bundles, standing them on end to be gathered later when the ears of corn have fully dried. I guess it was past midnight when we tied and up ended the last of the shuck stacks and called it quits. The full moon was shining brightly down upon us, and the field took on the appearance of an Indian village with the shuck stacks looking like their cone-shaped wigwams.

In a few weeks, we will gather the dried ears of corn, bring them back to the barn and work as a team to remove the corn from the cob. By rubbing two cobs together, the kernels will fall into our baskets. After picking out remnants of corn husks and silk, the baskets will be stored to await their trip to the gristmill. Some of the cornmeal will be sold for profit; some Mariah will use throughout the next year to make biscuits, breads, and corn cakes. A portion of the corn still on the cob will be stored so our animals will be well provided for during this quickly approaching cold season. The corn husks will be saved and used in the outhouse throughout the coming year for our personal cleanliness.

I have been chopping and stacking many cords of firewood in whatever spare time I had throughout the past several months. The demand for wood to cook our food, and also to keep us warm during the impending winter months, is a huge endeavor in itself. Keeping the house warm is a difficult task. Earlier this summer, we made a mortar out of lime, ash, horse hair, and water and generously applied it between the logs that our house is constructed from. The mortar helps to keep cold winter winds from getting into the house and causing drafts. Every so often, we need to apply a new coat of mortar as Mother Nature's elements cause it to dry, crack, and wear away.

Today is a bright and beautiful day; we are a little over a week away from the Harvest Festival where many in our community will attend church and praise God for the bountiful harvest. But first things first. Yesterday, Pieter, Albert, and I slaughtered our three biggest pigs, dressed them out, and hung them high in the trees to bleed out away from the reach of prowling animals. Today, we will skin and butcher the animals. These pigs will provide us with a generous supply of meat. We will salt the hides, roll them, and the next time I go into town, I'll drop them off at the tannery for Eliot Warne to process. Late next summer, I'll trade these hides and a few others already tanned and order shoes to be made by Mr. Kinney. Each year, Mr. Kinney makes a pair of shoes for each family member, if needed, to be worn during the fall, through the winter and the spring. As soon as the ground warms, we go barefoot wearing shoes only to attend church, social outings, or on very special occasions.

The iron cauldron has been suspended over the outside firepit, and the fire is blazing. The smokehouse has been prepared, and soon ham hocks, ribs, roasts, and bacon will fill the shelves. In the cauldron, we will melt the pig's fat and turn it into lard, processing it for use over the next year. I can almost taste the flaky pie crust that Mariah will make using the lard. After that project, the cauldron will be filled with all leftover scrapes from the pigs, which we will turn into scrapple and souse, giving us many hearty meals to enjoy during this long cold season ahead of us. Nothing will go to waste.

As the day moved along, everyone pitched in to lend a helping hand. Even three-year-old Abigail hauled firewood and helped her mother carry meat to the smokehouse. It is such a joy to see our twin boys step up and do their part too. At five years of age, Joseph and James are now given the responsibility of collecting the eggs daily from the henhouse. Their older sister Elizabeth puts down the chicken feed, while younger Catherina helps keep the nesting boxes clean and fluffed. Pieter and Albert help with the cows, pigs, sheep, our mule Moses, and Nellie our horse. The three of us do the milking, and the boys help to clean the barn and spread the feed for the animals. There is always more than enough work to go around. Late fall into winter is our easy time: no planting, tending fields or harvest, if there is really an easy time on a farm.

As we neared the end of our workday, we managed to complete our meat processing. The lard was moved to the springhouse along with the scrapple and souse where it will remain cool, no matter the temperature. Eventually, the smoked meat will be stored safely there as well. The brook that runs through our farm has provided us with ample water. We built the springhouse into the bank where the water bubbles out of the hillside. The water flows from beneath the building forming the brook. The springhouse provides us with a place in the warm weather to keep our food cooler and in the winter keep it from freezing. Made of stone, this is a safe place for us to store our food, protecting it from any wild animal that comes roaming about in search of food. The springhouse is only a few yards from our house, so carrying buckets of water into our home is less of a chore.

Everyone was exhausted and ready to go to bed after we supped on corn bread and beef stew. Mariah even prepared a special treat for all of us—bowls of warm apple sauce for dessert.

While Catherina helped the younger children wash and dress for bed, the older three had a shorter-than-normal reading lesson. It was only seven o'clock, and all seven had washed away the dust and dirt from their tired bodies (proof of a busy day of toil), dressed in their nightclothes and were tucked into their beds. Shortly thereafter, Mariah and I followed and retired for the evening. A hard day's work and a full belly made one long to retire early and enjoy sleeping the darkness away. Nodding off with the knowledge that our lofts, smokehouse, and springhouse were beginning to be filled to the brim gave me great satisfaction. Hard work does pay off, and the fruits of labor will be enjoyed during the pending cold season. Living near the edge of the frontier, most of what we need to survive we have to provide for ourselves. What we can't make ourselves, we may have to do without. The stage comes through three times a week, weather permitting, and we do depend on it to deliver the occasional letter from our families in the Philadelphia area, or special items such as medicine. We buy only the most essential needs.

The small store in town carries bricks of tea, limited supplies of sugar and molasses, wicks for our candles that we use to light our home, linen fabric, and sewing needs. Most of the store's other inventory comes from local farmers who sell to the store owner—things like cornmeal, flour, and limited fresh fruit and vegetables while in season. Folks visit farms to get their milk and eggs. We occasionally sell to the local butcher a pig or lamb. Several times a year, he will buy chickens too, but being a small community, the supply and demand is not there. Most families provide for themselves by hunting squirrels, rabbits, birds, elk, and deer. Our creek also boasts a bountiful supply of trout, bass, catfish, eel, and turtles, just a few among other fine tasty fish there for the taking.

CHAPTER 3

The holiday season passed quickly. We were able to spend time with my brother Eli, his wife, Sarah, and their children. Eli and I purchased property side-by-side, each now owning about one hundred acres of land. We both have built sturdy log homes, barns and enjoy working the land. My brother and I have always been close with just a year in age separating us. I am older and have always tended to look out for my brother, as he was born with a lame leg. Through the years, Eli has more than mastered how to fend for himself and his family; he and Sarah have six children: two sons and four daughters. Our brood and his children love being together and get along well. For the most part, Eli keeps us supplied with beef, and we pay him back by giving him pork. This arrangement seems to work out well for both families.

Yesterday was Sunday, and both our families attended church services at the Mansfield Woodhouse Presbyterian Church along Cemetery Road. The church is but a mile, no more than two, as the crow flies; the trouble is we aren't crows! By wagon, I'm guessing it to be three miles at most. The children love riding in the wagon and enjoying the scenery, and as long as the weather is decent, we attend each Sunday. This past week, everyone needed to bundle up, and even Nellie wore a blanket when we tied her up during the service. Summer can't come soon enough.

After church, we had a potluck lunch. Mariah brought along pork and sauerkraut. By the time the service was done, everyone could smell the wonderful array of foods warming over the wood fire. After a few hours of enjoying our friend's company, we packed up the children and headed home, making sure we arrived well before dark, the cows needed milking, and the animals needed to be fed. Farmers never have a day off, even Sunday, God's proclaimed day of rest for the weary.

Eli stopped by today and relayed that Herbert Cooper's brother, who resides outside of Belvidere, wants to purchase a pair of Eli's calves. Eli asked me if I would accompany him when he delivers the animals. This will probably happen when the weather breaks and the muddy roads start to dry up. I, of course, told my brother that I would be happy to travel with him. The trip will take the better part of the day. I'm guessing in about two weeks, things should be looking up to travel. The calves will be loaded into a wagon; keeping them calm, well, I guess that will be my job.

The weather has made a complete change from yesterday and is mild and pleasant. After Eli left, Pieter, Albert, and I worked in the orchard pruning the fruit trees. We continued our cutting by pruning the grapes on the arbor by the outhouse. Last season, we got a bumper crop of apples. In fact, we are still enjoying them as they are holding up well in our root cellar. The peaches did rather well, but the pears, I am not so sure the pears are even worth the effort. When I'm in the company of Jacob Weller, I'll have to ask him for some good advice on how to produce a good harvest of pears. Jacob's pears have to be the best in the entire valley. He takes baskets full of his pears across the Delaware and sells them in Easton for a reasonable price at the town's weekly market. Jacob keeps asking me to peddle some of my scrapple, bacon, and eggs. Right now, I am just concerned with keeping my seven children, my wife, and myself well-fed. When we have extra, we share with Eli and his family. A trip to sell goods at the Easton town market requires a full day, from sunup to sundown, and right now I feel I just can't afford to spare the time. As the boys get older, perhaps I can send them to do my business for me. Maybe someday, but not until I am convinced that the boys are old enough to safely handle a long gun.

Tonight, after supper was cleared and everything put away, Mariah added a new member to her nightly reading lessons. Catherina, who just turned eight, has joined the group. She is pleased as punch and eager to catch up with the others. A parent couldn't be more pleased; in fact, I am pleased with all of my children as they appear to be thriving.

Our parents were not pleased when we decided to move away from our families. Even less happy when Eli joined in our endeavor. Life in the Philadelphia area is exciting, and the children would be attending some type of schooling or training for a career if we remained near the city. But both Mariah and I believed that a slower pace would be better for all of us. I have also learned from reading the letters we get from back home that the redcoats seem to have taken over Philadelphia. The city has turned into a haven for Tories. Judge Shippen and his family are high on the social ladder, and several family members are not ashamed to be Tories. I sincerely hope that their poisonous ideas stay in Philadelphia. The Shippen family owns the iron mine in Oxford, which is just seven miles from us. We sure don't need any Tory family telling the people of Oxford how to run their mine. So far, this isn't happening, but with family connections, one never knows how far the crown will stretch. This is more than enough of a reason to get out of the Philadelphia area.

It is best that we not relay to Mama that Eli and I will be soon taking a trip beyond Belvidere to deliver the calves. Belvidere is the last town before the frontier begins. Thanks to William Penn's son, Thomas, who got the Indians angry by cheating them of their land along the Pennsylvania side of the river, forts had to be constructed along the Delaware above Belvidere as these massacres were taking place on a daily basis. Thomas Penn claimed to have found a lost treaty from 1686 made between his father William and the Delaware Indians. The treaty stated that the Indians granted all the land as far as a man could walk in one and a half days, or about forty miles. This deal with the Indians was called the Walking Purchase.

On September 19, 1737, three of the fastest walkers in the colony hired by Thomas ran instead of walked and caused the Indians to lose about 1,200 square miles of excellent land along the banks of the Lehigh and Delaware Rivers. Stealing this land from the Indians caused so many problems that in 1758, a portion was returned to the Delaware Nation, the rightful owners, but attacks against the white man continued, as it was too little, too late. The folks from

Pennsylvania crossed the river to seek safety here on the Jersey side, and now we have had to provide protection for our own people too. The New Jersey Frontier Guards are doing a great job of protecting people, but they can only do so much.

Above Belvidere, it is not safe to go out after dark; in fact, even in daylight, one has to be extra careful. These Indians could care less who they scalp, as they will kill anyone, whether it be a man, a woman, or an innocent child. But we feel safe living eight miles south of the Belvidere area. All the Lenape Indians here are friendly and couldn't be nicer. In fact, when the pears appeared to be ripening too quickly, Eli and I offered them to the Indians so as not to waste the fruit, and they graciously accepted them. This gesture of gratefulness made us happy too, so I guess it was a win-win for all of us.

CHAPTER 4

The weather has been pleasant as we are seeing the beauty of spring everywhere. Easter couldn't have been any later this year. But then, Easter is always the first Sunday, after the first full moon, after the first day of spring. None of my complaining will ever change any of that.

I said that I would be at Eli's farm by seven o'clock this morning. Mariah packed me a wonderful lunch with lots of extra food just in case we got delayed, with some cookies to share. As I walked along the dirt lane that connects our two farms, I couldn't help but take in the serenity of my surroundings. This area is so beautiful and peaceful.

When I arrived, Eli had the draft horse hitched to the wagon and only needed to load the calves. My nephew Edward had spread a nice cushion of straw over the bottom of the wagon and helped his father board the calves. As we were preparing to leave, Sarah brought out a basket of food, with extra to share. If nothing else, we will eat well on this trip. I jumped into the back of the wagon with the calves, and Eli mounted the seat in the driver's position, and off we went. We made a quick stop in Brass Castle to pick up Herbert Cooper. Herbert will be our guide and direct us to his brother's farm somewhere between Belvidere and Columbia.

It was before eleven by the time we arrived at Enos Cooper's farm. The trip was uneventful, but both Eli and I brought along our long guns, just in case. One can never be too sure of what might happen; therefore, it is best to be prepared rather than wishing you were prepared.

Enos seemed pleased with the calves, and Eli was paid well for the animals. There was talk about purchasing a pair of heifers in early June. Again, I will probably be asked to accompany Eli, but for that trip, I hope we leave Herbert back in Brass Castle. What is that saying, three is too many? Couldn't be better said if I was the first to have said it myself!

We decided after delivering the calves to take a different road home, one that passed through the town of Belvidere. We stopped in the town square to enjoy our lunch and chat with the local men from the Pequest mill who were doing the same. The news we heard was not good. A few days ago on April 19, the redcoats and some of the local minutemen shot it out in Lexington, killing eight of our own militiamen, and wounding nine. It was not a pretty scene. The redcoats continued on to Concord, where more gunfire was exchanged. When they began their retreat back to Boston, the redcoats were under constant assault from Massachusetts militiamen. Britain's army suffered from over 250 men wounded or killed. Chills ran up and down my spine as it appears we will soon be at war with Great Britain. Make no mistake, King George will retaliate, and our life will change. Pray to God that the changes will be slight and not too harsh. We finished our lunches and headed out of town for home. The conversation all the way home included many "what if we do this and what if they do that?" Truth is, only time will bring the answers to our many thoughts and fears. The only thing I can think of at this moment is thank goodness we live in New Jersey and not Massachusetts. Perhaps, just perhaps, we will escape the horrors of war. Dear God, please keep our families safe.

Eli and I arrived back at his farm a bit past two-thirty. The trip was actually easy, and spending time with my brother was wonderful. We enjoyed a cup of tea with Sarah, and then I headed back to my own farm where I knew Mariah would be awaiting my arrival to share with her how our trip went. The only trouble is this time, I had more to share than she or anyone would want to hear about.

Pieter and Albert were the first to greet me as I walked along the short path to our front porch. Although about two years apart in age, they are as close as Eli and I are. They seem to be inseparable; where one, is the other can't be far away. They told me that Mr. Van Horne had stopped by and asked if we were interested in selling him a few of the lambs. The boys said that Mr. Van Horne was thinking about starting his own herd and had an opportunity to get two lambs from a farmer south of Hall's Mills. Purchasing lambs from different lines is a good idea and will make for a stronger herd. Anyway, Van Horne will return in a few days to discuss the matter. Sounds like a promising proposition as the ewes gave us several babies this spring, and it is my desire to keep the herd at a manageable size. Mariah uses the wool for our own needs, but one can only use so much with the bulk after it has been carded, bringing us extra income. Since last year, I have sold two lambs to the local butcher and, considering that the family doesn't seem to care that much for roast lamb, selling off the young ones is probably a wise decision.

Mariah was at the window when I approached the front porch. Not wanting to take too much time discussing my day, as with it now being spring and having so many fields to ready for planting, I sat down in my favorite rocking chair anyway. Certain things a man knows in his heart is best to deal with, so I'll take the time to talk with my wife. Hmm, but perhaps leave out some of the bad things until we are alone later.

Yes, the trip was good, uneventful, and easygoing. Yes, Enos Cooper was nice (his brother not so much). Eli is well, as is Sarah and the children. The calves did well, no problems; they napped most of the way, taking in the warm sunshine. We had our lunch in the town square of Belvidere, which was delightful. And yes, the boys told me about Howard Van Horne visiting our farm today. After about a half hour of my family asking all sorts of questions, I arose from my rocking chair to head to barn and get something accomplished before this day was done. The bad part of the trip would be kept secret until the children were all tucked in for the night and Mariah and I were safely out of their earshot. Catherina followed me to the barn with all kinds of questions about the Belvidere town square and can we someday go there to eat our lunch too? I told her yes; after all, how can you disappoint a little girl with big beautiful brown eyes and a freckled face?

Later as I was repairing the plow blades, the children went about their chores. Before we knew it, the cows were milked, the animals fed and bedded down for the night. Soon most of the animals will be able to stay out in the pasture for the entire night, but I'd rather keep them in the barnyard area until at least May when we should have no need to worry about cold or freezing rain. Right now, there are several very hungry wild animals just coming out of a long winter who would like nothing more than to feast on one of our lambs or piglets. By keeping them in the barnyard area a few more weeks, I feel I am providing them with more of a fighting chance should a mountain lion, coyote, or bear come snooping around for an easy meal after dark.

We supped on some warm souse over pancakes. Tonight's pancakes were extra special, as they were made with potatoes. Eating them just reminded me that I needed to set time aside to spade the garden. Mariah's garden produced far beyond our expectations. The fruits of her labor are enjoyed daily, even in the meal she prepared for us tonight, as the potatoes Mariah used to make our pancakes came from her garden last fall. The children love helping her and get a thrill out of picking the fresh vegetables and eating them before they even make it into the house. Last year, Mariah planted some pumpkin seeds that a friend from church gave her. In the fall, the kids picked a cart full of huge pumpkins. We made pumpkin bread, pumpkin cookies, pumpkin pie, pumpkin butter, you name it, and we made it! I guess we have good soil here in this valley as we have been very lucky to have bountiful gardens. The Lord does shine down upon us!

After the children went to bed and I was sure that they were sound asleep, I finished telling Mariah about my day and the frightening news I heard during my brief stopover in Belvidere. Exactly as I thought, Mariah was speechless as just the word *war* puts fear in our hearts. Never before did a place that was days of travel from us seem so near. The problems in Massachusetts will not stay within Massachusetts. The venom of tyranny will spread like the plague and find its way into the hearts and souls of all mankind, whether a redcoat, a Tory, or a patriot. War is hell and don't ever let anyone tell you it is anything but hell here on earth! With sadness in our hearts and no words to even express how deeply we are troubled by this news, we retired for the evening and hoped that sleep would overtake our feelings of gloom with pleasant dreams.

CHAPTER 5

Eli and I were talking about planting this year's wheat crop when Howard Van Horne rode up on his horse. Mariah saw him coming and prepared another cup of tea for our guest. The three of us men sat on the front porch, and after some brief talk about things in general, we got down to the business of discussing the lambs. Howard wants to start his own flock, and after wheeling and dealing for about a half hour, Howard and I agreed that he would purchase all of my lambs and one ewe. We also agreed that when Howard yearly slaughters his lambs, he will provide me with fat which we will melt down and use in our candle-making process. I have been wanting to thin the herd and keep only what we need, and this was more than a fair deal to make it happen. Two rams and four ewes will keep us in all the wool we would ever desire at this time, plus some extra to sell after carded. Eli and I agreed to help Howard transport the sheep to his farm a few miles west of ours.

After lunch, Howard returned with his wagon and his farm-hand Sonny. Pieter and Albert helped me hitch our mule, Moses, and horse, Nellie, to the wagon just as Eli was returning after his lunch break, along with his sons Nelson and Edward. The eight of us went to work wrangling the lambs and loading both wagons; taking any little one away from its mother is not an easy task. My boys and their cousins were thrilled to ride in the back of the wagon with six of the lambs. Eli and I rode up top, and I drove the team. Howard had the ewe and three more lambs in his wagon, and Sonny rode in the back to keep the animals calm. The trip was easy, and it took no time at all to get to the Van Horne farm. The return trip was even better as I now had less sheep and more cash to put away for those unexpected rainy days. Considering the bits and pieces of information that is making their way to New Jersey, things that are taking place in the New England area are not pleasing to our ears. There will be rainy days ahead; that I am sure of.

When we returned back to our farm, Mariah and I talked about perhaps thinning our drove of pigs. The past several years, we slaughtered our three largest pigs, and both Eli and my family have had an ample supply of bacon, scrapple, souse, ham, and roasts. We decided that we will continue to slaughter the three largest and then maintain a constant drove of five pigs, selling off the extra piglets once they are weaned from their mother. The next time I go into town, to church, wherever, I will make it known that we have healthy piglets for sale. Maintaining extra animals is a drag not only on our time but also extra food that otherwise can be in reserve for all of our other livestock. The children were pleased when we shared this idea with them; after all, less pigs and sheep, less work for them too. On this farm, everyone pulls their weight.

Later in the afternoon, I hitched Moses to the plow and began turning the field on the far end of our property. This year, we will plant wheat after the rocks are picked up and carted to the surrounding hedgerows that boast of earlier collections of rocks. The winter frost causes rocks to come to the surface and makes plowing difficult. The removal of the rocks and stones is a yearly job that the children work together on. Nellie was hitched to the smaller cart and patiently stood as the rocks and stones were loaded onto the cart and then unloaded along the field's hedgerow. Just a short "get" makes Nellie move ahead a few feet and patiently await the next "get," allowing this project to be finished in a reasonable amount of time. If the weather holds out, we will plant this field with wheat tomorrow.

After supper, all four boys walked down to the Pohatcong Creek to try their luck at some fishing. They returned just as the last light of day was disappearing. Joseph caught himself a fine bass; Pieter hooked a trout; James and Albert came home empty-handed with stories of how the big ones got away just as they were pulling them in! Tomorrow, Mariah will prepare the fish for our lunch. Just as the Bible story tells us, Mariah has the ability to take the two fish and turn them into a meal that all nine of us can feast upon.

With the heat from the day warming our house more than we'd like, the children get to stay up longer on warmer evenings, so their loft bedroom has a chance to cool down a bit. If it's really hot, they also enjoy a dip in the cool brook before turning in for the night. Aside from this change in our daily routine, we try to keep to our schedule and find, by doing so, things move along smoothly. After all, the cows could care less about the weather; they just want to be milked twice a day, once in the morning and again in the late afternoon. One thing I've learned through the years is to be consistent with our milking times; unhappy cows make for cantankerous creatures.

The family sat on the front porch well after darkness arrived, enjoying the night noises and each other's company. We played a family game that we call "guess what I'm talking about." Kind of corny but fun because everyone has an equal chance to get involved. Abigail did have us guessing, or perhaps I should say trying to guess. She was actually giving us clues that ended up being the fancy rooster that her Uncle Eli recently purchased from the market in Clinton. I guess that she was amazed by the colorful feathers on the rooster as our roosters and hens have white feathers. All of her siblings praised her for doing such a good job and stumping all of us. But all good things come to an end sooner or later, and the next morning will arrive with the same amount of toil as the day before, so the children were sent off to bed at nine o'clock. The roosters could care less if we are sleeping soundly at sunrise; they will crow to their hearts content and awaken all within earshot. Sunrise will be here in no time, so Mariah and I turned in soon after the children.

CHAPTER 6

Summer is quickly fading. All of our crops have done well this season and are showing signs of the beginning of harvest. Mariah's garden has again provided us with an assortment of healthy food. The berry vines were laden with fruit, which the children picked and Mariah used for pies and jelly. The walnut and hickory trees seem to be bringing forth an unusual amount of nuts. I hope that I am wrong, but past years have taught me that when everything appears to be overproducing, we are in store for a colder winter than normal. In any case, we will do what we can to prepare for whatever Mother Nature has to offer us.

I believe that I made a good deal selling the piglets to Walter Saunders. Walter is interested in buying more pigs next year, as his brother in German Valley wants to try his hand at raising them too. Hopefully, my sows will provide another sty full of healthy piglets next season.

Mariah and I discussed our finances, and we are doing well at the moment. Our farm belongs to us, as does all the livestock. We owe no one and have a decent amount of money stashed away for unforeseen events. Now with the sale of the piglets, we can loosen our belts a bit and breathe. We believe that now is the time to treat our children to something special for all of the hard work they do to help run this farm. With that in mind, we are taking our brood to Easton to the town market. It has been several years since Mariah has visited the market herself. Since she was with child five years ago, Sarah has graciously shopped for our needs. After the birth of Abigail, now on the backside of four years old, Mariah found it easier to mind Eli and Sarah's children while they took their twice-yearly visit to Easton, then travel there herself.

Actually, it was Mariah and her persuasive ways that swayed me over to this train of thought. She reminded me that if we were back in the Philadelphia area, the children would have been long before now exposed to culture, music, more books, and a wide variety of foods, as Philadelphia is a busy port and a bustling city. The least we could do for our children is expose them to the excitement that a large town can provide. Taking them to the Easton weekly market where they can see vendors and hucksters is far beyond what they can even imagine. Just viewing the assortment of goods that are available for purchase, many of which they don't even know exists, will amaze them. Walking up one side of the main street and down the other, peering into shop windows will be just as exciting for all of us. So today, we will make our plan happen.

After the children finished their chores, we called them together and laid out our plan for the day. The excitement was more than fanciful. Each child was given a chore to help prepare for our departure within ninety minutes. Amazingly, we were in the wagon and heading out our lane in just under one hour after telling them of today's trip. This early start will allow us to enjoy a leisurely trip. We worked out a plan that I would take charge of the boys, and Mariah would take the girls. Each group would completely walk around the market area and view what was on display. On the second trip around, Mariah and I would make our necessary purchases. We would meet back at the wagon and enjoy our basket lunch, and if we had enough time, we would all walk up and down the main street, taking time to look in the store windows along the way. We would be leaving Easton before three o'clock to make sure to be home long before dusk.

We arrived in Phillipsburg and got in line for the ferry to take us across the Delaware. The amazement on the children's faces told us that we had made the right decision in coming to the market. Abigail was frightened when we boarded the ferry; actually, I believe all of the children had some concerns but did a great job of comforting each other. Once on the other side, whatever doubts they may have had faded as Nellie pulled us toward the center of town and the market. Just looking at the size of the buildings left the kids in awe. We were able to find a shady spot to leave Nellie and the wagon, and we all headed toward the moderately crowded market.

The boys and I skipped over any vendor who was selling household goods, clothing, or millinery and looked at farm implements, tack, and firearms. On our second trip around, I had us stop at a confectionery vendor where I gave the boys a half-pence to purchase some treats. By the time they were done selecting a few of these and a few of those, the sack was ready to overflow. I reminded them that it would be a nice gesture to save a few pieces of candy for their sisters. I was well aware that I would be taking some grief from Mariah for treating the boys to so much candy, but I was prepared to stand my ground, as this was the first time they were ever given the opportunity to select such treats themselves. We continued on our walk, and I was able to get much-needed brads, wads, lead shot, gunpowder, twenty pounds of salt, and five pounds of sugar for Mariah.

Mariah and the girls took a bit longer. Actually, it seemed like forever. Good grief, we were finished with our purchases, and they hadn't finished their first trip around the market. We caught up to them and said that we would see them back at the wagon. Take as long as you want, don't worry about us, we have food. But don't forget we have to leave by three o'clock at the latest.

At a bit past two o'clock, Mariah and girls showed up all smiles. Each of my daughters were carrying a few brightly colored hair ribbons that they had selected for themselves. Mariah was able to make her necessary purchases that included, among other things, pepper, baking soda, tea, and molasses. She also purchased a few items for Sarah. Since we decided that the trip up and down the main street would take more time than we had, we enjoyed a bite to eat and began our return to the farm. We promised our children that we would bring them to Easton again, and all agreed that they wanted to return to the market. The children said they really enjoyed their time and were amazed at all the merchandise and crazy people that they encountered. We arrived back at the farm about four o'clock and quickly changed into our work clothes and went about our afternoon chores. Joseph and James delivered the items that their Aunt Sarah had asked Mariah to purchase for her. It took much longer to make the delivery and return home than expected, as the boys had to relay, event by event, their day to their cousins. Their cousins have no idea, but Eli and Sarah are making plans to take their family to Easton and the market within a few weeks.

At supper, we discussed our day and how great it was to take such a trip with our family. Actually, Mariah and I really didn't get to say much, as the children did all the talking. They talked non-stop from the time the wagon left this morning until it got back to the farm this afternoon and were still talking. It appears no end in sight. The pleasure that Mariah and I got from all of this was beyond words. I must mention that when other adults are visiting our home, or we are visiting any other place, the children follow the golden rule: "children are to be seen and not heard." Mariah and I allow the children to share in our mealtime conversations. This is something that both sets of their grandparents would be seriously upset about. Our children are polite and courteous and understand how to act respectful when around other people. However, they have no idea just how lucky they are to be living here in Mansfield, and we are equally lucky to have been blessed with such wonderful gifts from God.

After supper, things returned to normal with Mariah giving the children their nightly reading lesson. As they read scripture from the Holy Book, I could hear the three younger children sitting near the front door, still babbling on quietly about all that had taken place today. Funny, it appears that they missed nothing about the trip, the trees and flowers, the fields, the houses, the ferry, the Delaware River, and the market boasting of an abundance of goods. Mariah was right in saying this trip would introduce our children to so many different and unusual everyday things that will remain with them for days to come. I can only imagine the pleasant dreams they will have tonight after settling into their beds. Tomorrow will be a busy day, as we will continue to bring in the crops and fill our lofts for the quickly approaching cold months.

As I lay awake in our bed, I pondered today's events and the ability to give our children such great pleasure. I just hope and pray that Mariah and I can continue to provide for our family, as we always have. The problems in New England appear to be getting closer to our home. The unrest in Philadelphia is disturbing. My last letter home suggested that my parents and sister consider moving here in Mansfield where it is, for the time, a much friendlier atmosphere. I already know how the next letter from my family will read—thank you for your kind offer, but no thank you. Keep enjoying your life on the frontier; we will remain in civilization for the time being.

CHAPTER 7

The call to arms has been constant. Posters have been placed in many public places asking for any available and willing males to sign up and join the cause. Eli and I stopped to pick up our mail at the Mineral Springs earlier this week and noticed a poster mounted just inside the main door. Next week, a recruitment officer will be visiting Mansfield and staying at the Mineral Springs. The battles are getting closer and closer to home. I thought, with the coming of the New Year, that 1776 might bring more peaceful times, but it seems not to be the case.

Eli and I treated ourselves to a mug of dark stout and listened in on the conversation between two younger local men. Both men seemed to be ready to step forward and enlist next week when the recruitment officer visits. It seems that one only needs to enlist for a three to six month period. At the end of that period, they can again sign on for another tour. I'm guessing that the government figures a man can be away from his farm and family for three to six months without encountering too many problems. The government does compensate the men for their service, but each man provides his own long gun and clothing; no uniforms will be issued to men other than those enlisted in the regular army. Eli, having a lame leg, is immediately disqualified. I am in great physical shape. The lingering question is how will Mariah feel about all of this? On our ride back to our farms, Eli questioned my reasons for considering signing up to go away to war. I told him that the war is here, no going away, it appears to be soon arriving at our stoop. My brother said that whatever my decision is, he will support me and my family. Should I go away for several months, he will help Mariah, Pieter, and Albert run my farm. This was a comfort to know, but in the back of my mind, I knew that Mariah would not entertain even the thought of me going to war.

The winter did prove to be colder and snowier than normal. The roof collapsed on the lean-to where we store some wagons. Thank goodness, the wagons are sturdy and took the weight of the snow. We were forced to use the sleigh often this past winter, as the snow was too deep for Nellie or Moses to pull a wagon. Even using the two of them as team put too much strain on them. The sleigh glided through the snow easily, and the family enjoyed the ride too. The snow quickly melted, and the lane is now muddy, and the main road is difficult to navigate as there are deep ruts that can bog the wagon down. Traveling on horseback solves some of the problem, but the fact that I can't transport my family without a wagon keeps them homebound. March has always been the month of indecision; as the snow melts, the roads get muddy, the winds blow. It snows some more, and we start the cycle all over again. The good news is that April is finally here, and beautiful spring weather is just around the corner.

Mariah was pleased when I returned from the Mineral Springs with a letter for her from her family. Neither of us have seen our families in almost five years. Mariah went back to her parent's home to birth Abigail; she was gone for about two and half months, and the children went with her. Unfortunately, some were too young to remember much, if anything, about our families or the Philadelphia area. I know that Mariah misses her parents and siblings. The fact that my brother and his family live on the adjoining farm gives me comfort, something that Mariah doesn't have. We both knew that choosing to live here in Sussex County would sometimes be difficult, but we are steadfast in giving our children a safe and clean place to grow up in. Letters from home help to fill the longing to have our family close. This letter tells Mariah that her father Aaron is slowing down due to age, but otherwise well. Mariah's father is a blacksmith by trade and through the years has built a reputable steady business. Not only does he shod horses but also builds and mends carriages and all sorts of wagons. Over the years, his business has provided well for his family. Mariah's brother Solomon, and Solomon's son Aaron, so named for his grandfather, work along with the elder Aaron. The business has grown, and the craftsmanship is well-known.

After their nightly reading lesson, Mariah had Elizabeth and Catherina sit near the hearth, which provide extra light, and the group darned some stockings. While they went about their chore, Mariah told stories to all of the children about growing up in Doylestown, a town just outside of Philadelphia. The children love to hear these stories, and Mariah has the ability to bring her tales to life. I don't think that I will ever tire of listening to Mariah talk about her younger days.

The children were sound asleep when I decided I would approach the idea of me signing on for a stint with the state militia. Mariah was completely dumbfounded as she did not see this coming. Looking into Mariah's eyes, I asked her "just take some time and think it through. We need to put 'us' aside and think of the future, and what will any of us have if the king rules us forever?" She just seemed to be staring into space, then whispered, "I'm not only in fear for you, but for me, for us, for our family. What would we do without you? You are our rock and our foundation. Only God knows how much we all love, adore, and praise you. I'm not sure that I can even survive without you." Trying to keep my voice to a whisper, I continued, "Mariah, this is not an easy decision for me to make. I'll be leaving you, the children, and our farm for who knows what? I just feel that I must do something to take a stand against the evil and try to make this a better home for all of us. Eli said that he would support me in whatever decision I make and be here for you and the children."

Now sobbing, Mariah hugged me, saying, "You're a good man, Isaac Deremer, and I know that you have thought this through. I also know that you believe from the bottom of your heart that this country needs you. I will support your decision, but you should know that it is with a heavy heart that I do so. God has been good to us and our family, and I know that God will bless you and keep you safe." Slightly relieved but still unsure of what direction to turn, I assured Mariah that we would put plans into place should I decide to sign up. We agreed that not a word of this was to be leaked to our children until a final decision had been made. As we were falling asleep, I knew that Mariah was holding back the tears for another time when she would be alone.

CHAPTER 8

I met Eli at his farm at one o'clock this afternoon. We rode our horses to the Mineral Springs Hotel to hear what the recruitment officer had to say about the war in general and if there were any resolutions in the near future. Sergeant Baker of the Continental Army painted quite a grim picture of what the near future holds for us. Going up against what is thought to be the best trained army in the world, the British Army, was a daunting task. Our own General George Washington was doing the best he could with our Continental Army, but many more men were needed to even think that we can win over the crown.

Baker reiterated that men who signed up today had some options for enlistment time. The sergeant said that they encouraged men to enlist for one year, but they were accepting enlistments of three or six months as well. I knew immediately that I could not, would not, commit for one year. So now what, three or six months, really a difficult choice to make? I mentally opted for three months with the possibility of reenlisting for an additional three months if circumstances allowed. Circumstances would be my health and just how far away at the end of three months I will be from my family. If the British Army is fighting in my backyard, then I want to be at my home protecting my family. Sergeant Baker will be staying at the hotel until Thursday, and those of us, and there were many, could return tomorrow and join the militia. Any and all that sign up should plan on marching to Morris Town on Thursday. Not much time to make a life-changing decision, but I made my decision last week.

During our ride home, Eli and I spoke of what might be. Eli knew last week that I would be signing up and began to lay out his plan to assist my family while I was away. He has not yet told Sarah, as he wanted to be sure that I was firm in my decision. Also, he didn't want the children to find out if something slipped out accidently. Many of our fields are planted, and most animals have given birth. Eli will help Mariah sell the lambs and piglets, and even see to delivering them, if need be. I'll be back home in plenty of time for the harvest and slaughter of the pigs. However, one of my concerns is the demand for firewood. The boys can help, but splitting the wood takes weight and strength. I guess we can tackle that task when I return. For now, we have a good supply of wood, probably enough to get through the fall and into the early winter.

I didn't follow Eli to his door, as I wasn't quite ready to discuss my intentions with anyone else until I spoke with Mariah this evening. I needed this extra time alone to try and think things through, so I slowed Nellie's pace down a bit. I have to shake the thoughts from my head and believe that my boys, with the help of their mother and uncle, can keep this place running smoothly, especially since I will be back by fall at the latest. I can't help but wonder if this place can run without me for several months.

Mariah was taking dry clothes from the fence railing, folding them and placing them into the laundry basket when Nellie and I returned to the farm. I had forgotten that today was Monday, so that meant washday. Mariah runs the household on a schedule: Monday is washday; Tuesday, she irons and mends whatever needs repairing; Wednesday, she cleans the house and loft area and then bakes; Thursday, she prepares vegetables and fruit to be saved for later use; Friday, she does catch-up, tending to anything in need of completing before the weekend; Saturday, she bakes and prepares extra food for Sunday, which is our day of rest; Sunday, we tend to our farm animals in the morning and evening, attend church and spend the rest of our time enjoying our family and each other's company.

Abigail was helping Mariah with the clean clothing. The other children were near the brook moving rocks to create a dam to enjoy when the weather gets warmer. Mariah encouraged Abigail to join her brothers and sisters so she could talk with me alone. She looked so tired and worn out from not getting much sleep, and since I shared my thoughts of signing up last week, she has been melancholy. I do feel guilty for putting her through all of this, but I also feel that I must do my part for my country, and most of all, for my children to ensure them a better future. As Mariah approached Nellie and me, she could tell by the look on my face what my decision would be. We spoke briefly about my departing in just a few days. I could see what little sparkle that was left in her eyes completely disappear. She nodded her head and started to walk back to the house. We agreed that after our evening meal, I would tell the children.

Mariah served a wonderful supper of beef, carrots, and potatoes, all cooked slowly together, along with warm biscuits. Asking the Lord to bless our food tonight seemed more heartfelt than most evenings. We truly are blessed as a family, and I pray that my going away will not change things. As we ate, the children talked about their dam project and that when the weather gets hot and muggy, they will not need to go to the creek to swim. I suggested that they continue to work on their project, as they had a good idea but would need many more stones to create their pool when the weather gets warmer.

After the dishes were cleared, Mariah served dessert, a custard pudding. We exchanged glances and decided that it was time to tell the children that I would be enlisting in the militia and going away from home for a few months. As gently as possible, I told my children I would be leaving home on Thursday and would be gone for three, maybe six months. Both Mariah and I assured them that things would be fine as Uncle Eli and Aunt Sarah were ready to help in any way needed. The questions kept coming an hour later with many *what if* questions that I could not answer. Taking time to answer those that I could helped a bit to relieve some of the fear I could see on their faces. Finally, I had all of us hold hands, and we prayed for guidance, strength, and peace.

After the children were tucked into their beds, Mariah and I began creating a plan to keep things running smoothly. We made lists for this and lists for that, trying not to forget anything of importance. She also made a list of what items that I will be taking with me on Thursday. Whatever I take, I will be carrying on my back, so I must pack only the things I will need the most. I also want to clean my long gun that I will be taking with me. I need to show Pieter how to clean and oil the long gun that my grandfather had given me years ago; I will be leaving this gun here for them should the need arise. I have taken both Pieter and Albert hunting with me many times, so they are both familiar with handling guns. I have always stressed safety first, and by allowing prey to get away was much better than taking a chance shot that could injure someone else. I know that they understand, but age brings wisdom, and my boys are just thirteen and eleven years old. They still have much to learn, and sadly by me going away, they will start learning what responsibility is on Thursday when I leave them in charge of our farm.

It was long past eleven o'clock when we retired for the evening. It is not often that we stayed up so late, but so much work went into our planning for the next few months that the time just flew by. As I lay in my bed, thoughts of the wonderful meal that Mariah had prepared for our supper and my family all seated around our table made me feel happy. I can only hope that there will be more happy times like that in our future.

CHAPTER 9

I met up with Sergeant Baker early this morning and enlisted in the militia for three months. If all goes well, I should be back home on my farm in July unless I re-up for another three months. Only time will tell whether I can be away from home and family for six long months. The sergeant reminded me that I need to report back to the Mineral Springs at seven o'clock on Thursday morning. Also, to bring my own gun, a bedroll, clothing, and a few personal items that I will be expected to carry on my back. Hands and arms must be free, with the exception of carrying my gun. We will be sworn in as a group and immediately head out for Morris Town for some basic training. He was unsure of where we will be going after our basic training. Baker was very pleased that I am able to both read and write. I was also questioned about my record-keeping skills, and he seemed pleased with my knowledge of that as well.

I started working on my to-do list that Mariah and I created last night. The boys and I finished the necessary repairs to the lean-to caused by the weight of the heavy snow. The task looked much worse than it actually was, and we got the roof back in shape in no time. After lunch, we will plow one of the back fields to ready it to plant corn. I may not have enough time to plant the corn before I leave on Thursday, so I am schooling Pieter and Albert on just how to sow the grain. I also reminded them that Uncle Eli will be available to answer any questions they may have. So much to do, so little time.

When the boys and I came in for lunch, our regular seating arrangements were changed. Catherina asked James to trade seats with her so she could sit next to me. I knew last night that she was having a difficult time with me going away. Being nine years old, she doesn't understand why people would want to harm one another. It would give me great pleasure to solve the mystery of why we can't all live in peace with each other, and I'm guessing that I am not alone in hoping for a quick end to this terrible situation. I dragged lunch out longer than usual so as a family, we could continue to discuss my leaving on Thursday.

The rest of the day went along as business as usual. Each child did his or her chores, and things ran very smoothly. After the cows were milked, I had a discussion with Pieter and Albert before we went back into the house for supper. We talked about Uncle Eli and Aunt Sarah helping in any way they can while I am away. I also told the boys if they got into some unknown dire situation not to be afraid of reaching out to Jake Beerman. I couldn't help but see the look of disbelief on their faces by my suggestion. I reminded them that Jake has been our neighbor for years, and although many believe that he is a Tory, he is still our neighbor. The boys agreed that if Jake came to us asking for help, they would immediately step up to help him out, so they guessed he would help us too. I explained that not everyone feels a need to get involved in this war; that doesn't mean that they are our enemy. Perhaps they just want to remain neutral. Let's just hope they won't need Jake or Eli or any outside help.

Supper was delicious, and conversation continued about my going away, my coming home, and that everything will be fine. After supper, we all sat on the front porch and enjoyed the evening. The children stayed up longer than usual. I guess Mariah and I are giving them as much togetherness as we can. Tomorrow is my last day here on the farm, and my head is spinning as I try to complete as much of the spring work as possible before I leave. Eli and Sarah have invited all of us over to their house for supper tomorrow. I guess a going-away meal of the sorts. I am not so sure that Mariah and I will be good company, as we both have so much on our minds right now, but perhaps we can forget some of our troubles, even if just for a few hours.

CHAPTER 10

Today was probably one of the craziest days I have lived through in some time. It seems that the news that I enlisted in the militia and will be leaving in the morning has spread quickly through the valley. Many of our friends and neighbors briefly stopped by to wish me good luck and offer their assistance while I am away. It was all a bit overwhelming to see the love and support for not just me but also my family. Not only did these people stop by our farm to wish us the best but visited many of the other homes of the men who have also enlisted. This is really a wonderful place to live.

I wrote a long letter to my parents early this morning. What encouraging things can one tell their mother when they have opted to go off to war? I tried to put my feelings on paper as to the reason why I need to fight for my country, but I may have failed miserably when trying to sway my mother to my side. After I return, Mariah, the children, and I should plan a trip to visit both of our families, even if it is for just a few days. Perhaps keeping pleasant family thoughts with me will help me get through the next few months.

The nine of us walked to Eli and Sarah's house enjoying the mild weather and looking ahead to summer. When we arrived just before five o'clock, it was chaos with their brood and ours as well. Mariah brought along two apple pies that she baked earlier in the day for our dessert. The children paired up by age and went off in their own little groups outside. This was great as it gave Eli, Sarah, Mariah, and myself time to go over a few loose ends.

Supper was ready at five-thirty, and we all enjoyed a wonderful chicken dinner with all the special trimmings that are served on the holidays. Sarah did a great job preparing this feast, and no one went away hungry. At the end of our meal, Eli brought out a special bottle of red wine that he had purchased earlier in the day from the Mineral Springs Hotel. The four of us enjoyed this special treat since wine is not only expensive but often scarce in this part of Jersey. Although the Mineral Springs Hotel is well-known for their fine stock of spirits, beers, and wines, it is still special to actually sit down and share a fine wine with my family. After enjoying our wine, we said our goodbyes as I still wanted to go over what we packed and make sure everything was ready in the morning.

I agreed to allow Eli to go to the Mineral Springs with me tomorrow morning, but no one else. I can ride Nellie, and he will bring her back to our farm after I am gone. Nellie and I have a long history as Mariah's father suggested I purchase her over seventeen years ago when the two us started to seriously enjoy each other's company. Nellie was then two years old and well-trained. She has been my sidekick since then, and I wish I could take her with me, but I will be a foot soldier. Only the higher-ups ride on horseback.

Since tomorrow will be an early up, we all went to bed before nine. The uncertainty of what the next several months holds for not only me but my family too made it difficult to fall off to sleep. I found myself praying not only for the safety of my family, but also for my decision to leave them in an attempt to make this country a better place for all of us. I truly believe that I have made the right choice, but can they continue to run the farm without me? Finally, I decided enough is enough. I can't change anything at this time, so I allowed myself to drift off to much-needed sleep.

The Journal of
Mariah Deremer

April 29, 1776–April 10, 1804

CHAPTER 11

It's been a few days since Isaac rode Nellie down the lane toward Eli's house. As Isaac promised, he did not look back once he and Nellie rode out our short path to the lane, then on to Eli's house. He said it would be too painful to watch as his loved ones faded from his sight. I tried to control my sobbing; the children didn't hold back their tears, so finally I just gave in to my emotions too. The saddest thing was to see Eli return Nellie to our barn once Isaac had marched off with the rest of the local men. Seeing Nellie's empty saddle caused chills to run up and down my spine. Eli said that there were probably thirty, maybe thirty-five, men who were sworn in at the Mineral Springs and quickly left for Morris Town in a military formation.

The children have been doing their chores, and we are trying as best we can to carry on without Isaac. Eli has stopped by once since Isaac's been gone, just to see how we are doing. I know that he is troubled that he could not have joined up himself, but with his lame leg, there would be no way he could enlist. To be honest, I am sort of glad that he couldn't go, as having him just next door gives me some comfort in knowing that he is available to help us, if need be.

The weather has been quite pleasant, and the planted fields are showing signs of green. The weeds are popping up too. The garden is doing well, but we still have many more vegetables to plant when the weather decides to stay above forty degrees all night. Even then, it is chilly, but the young plants can usually survive the coolness of the night for a brief time.

Evenings are the longest. Having Isaac's empty chair at our dinner table is a constant reminder that he is out there somewhere, not sure where, but somewhere. I've started reading my Bible with an unexpected fever after the children are tucked into bed. I'm still in

Genesis and plan on reading the entire book cover to cover and won't stop until Isaac gets back. Each night, I read a few chapters to help me pass my time and try to forget missing my husband so much. I am trying not to let my melancholy show when around the children, as they are having their own personal sadness to deal with. Catherina seems to be suffering the most and cries often for her papa. I know that it is not good to wish one's life away, but that is exactly what I am doing. I pray that the days fly by, and I am just biding my time as best I can until Isaac returns to us. I am honestly trying my best to go about my day as if nothing has changed, but everything has.

CHAPTER 12

Just as I found myself drowning in my own sorrow, Eli showed up with a letter from Isaac that he had just picked up from the mail at the Mineral Springs. My excitement was unbelievable, and my heart was almost beating out of my chest! Eli handed me the letter then gave me my privacy to read it without anyone around. The children were out and about the yard, and Eli kept them occupied so I could take my time and read what Isaac wrote. The first part of the letter was for me and not to be shared with the children, as it described some gruesome happenings that had taken place over the past month. The second part was to be shared with the children and spoke of meeting some important people and of the different places he has marched since enlisting a little over a month ago. Sadly, I cannot write back, as his unit is constantly moving, never staying in one place more than a few days.

After several minutes, I called the children into the house and shared the letter with them. I invited Eli to join us, and he eagerly accepted my offer. The children listened with a keen interest to their father's details about seeing General George Washington on his white horse when he first got to Morris Town. Isaac wrote about the beautiful homes and gardens, not only in Morris Town but also Elizabeth Town and the beauty of the ocean. He went into extra details about his brief training, the horrible food, and how he was immediately promoted to a record-keeping position. He sent along his love to each of his children and an extra hug for Catherina, which caused her to smile. Probably the first smile we have seen since Isaac left over a month ago. This pleased the children, and after some light discussion, they all went back outside to enjoy the rest of the afternoon, definitely in a happier mood.

I showed the letter to Eli so he could read about the agony of war for himself. Isaac said that there was no way anyone could prepare themselves for what he has witnessed. There were men with limbs wrapped in bloody bandages or, worse yet, missing arms and legs. Our own militiamen with ragged clothing, worn-out shoes, nasty wounds, faces with painful expression or no expression at all, just ranting and raving as if out of their minds, so much devastation. We both shared a sense of sadness not just for Isaac but all men drawn into this horrible war.

I decided after Eli left to prepare a special supper for me and my children. I had not prepared anything really special since Isaac left and thought his letter was a reason for all of us to celebrate. I made beef potpies and buttermilk biscuits, and for our dessert, a large custard pudding. As we sat around our kitchen table holding hands and thanking the Lord for our food and our letter from Isaac, the mood was cheerful. We discussed Morris Town and Elizabeth Town and what the ocean looked like and actually laughed and kidded each other. The banter was joyful, even if it would be short-lived, as it would be almost another two months before Isaac is expected to be returned home to us.

CHAPTER 13

Well, summer has arrived with a vengeance. The little pond that the children created for themselves is being used daily. Evenings we have been sitting on the front porch just hoping that the loft will cool enough so the children can get a restful night's sleep.

The children and I sheared the sheep. What a job, to say the least. I believe that every muscle in my body now aches, but we got the job done. Previous years, Pieter and Albert assisted Isaac, so they were schooled in just what to do. Everyone got into the task, and after some mass confusion, we managed to get the job done. The sheep don't look as nice as when Isaac sheared them, but their wool will grow back, and no one will take notice. Tomorrow we will wash the wool, spread it to dry, and take it to town to be carded later this week.

All four boys have been keeping up with our daily milk and egg deliveries. Being summer and the hot weather, the boys have to work extra hard to deliver the fresh milk daily. We can store just so much in our springhouse. It does take time, but the children are learning the responsibility and commitment of supplying some of the local folks with fresh milk. When the weather is cooler, they can deliver every other day, but cool storage of the milk here on the farm and also at our customer's homes is limited in the summer. We also have several other families that walk to our farm with their milk buckets for us to fill. Some of these families come twice a day, early morning and late afternoon. They have no way to keep the milk cool, so they use what they purchase as quickly as possible.

We all attended a wonderful strawberry festival at church this past Sunday after the service. The men made whipped cream which we put on top of fresh cut strawberries that several church families picked wild this past week. The whipped cream was so good because of all the cream that those of us with cows were able to skim off the top of the milk and share. When the fruit comes in season, we all seem to get our fair share. We have to because when the season is over, the fruit is gone. Thursday, the girls and I made strawberry jam. We are using some of the jam now and made extra to save and enjoy after the season is long gone. Isaac loves any kind of jam on freshly baked white bread. I feel sad knowing that the food he is eating is not prepared with my love and special care.

Isaac always enjoyed asparagus too. Our asparagus is almost done producing for this season. Asparagus is the kind of crop that you can almost watch grow. We cut twice a day as it grows so quickly, and allowing the spears to get tall and woody makes them undesirable. In the fall, we may, if weather permits, again enjoy a few more weeks of this wonderful vegetable, but we can't save it in the springhouse for more than a week, as it doesn't hold over well. I have to wonder if Isaac is getting any fresh fruit or vegetables.

Still counting the days until we will have Isaac back home with us. He has now been gone for almost two long months. When he left, he wasn't sure if he would serve for three or six months. We are all sitting on the edge of our seats awaiting his decision. Isaac is a very determined man, and he truly believes that he can and will make a difference in the future of our children by defending our country from tyranny.

Tomorrow, the children and I have been invited to Eli and Sarah's home for supper. We are all looking forward to visiting with them. We do see them each Sunday we attend church, and often during the week, but not for a sit-down meal. The girls and I will bake shortcake and sliced strawberries to take with us. We can make the whipped cream topping at Eli and Sarah's home just before serving the dessert so it will be nice and fresh. Not sure what Sarah will be preparing, but whatever she makes, it will be done to perfection.

I have included all of the children in our nightly reading lessons. I spoke with the older children, and they agreed that each one would share in helping the twins and little Abigail. Perhaps they are a bit too young to start reading, but we are trying to do things as a family, and this change includes everyone. Pieter, Albert, and Elizabeth have displayed an overabundance of patience and kindness toward their younger siblings. This brings joy to my heart and a newfound pride in them as well. Although Catherina has been a part of our little reading group for a while now, she has a bit to go before she can offer to help her younger brothers and sister, but she is there rooting for their success.

Everyone seems to want to turn in as soon as the house cools down for the evening. I guess we are all putting in 100 percent, and it is wearing us down. We are managing to get our chores done, and we now have a different prospective of just how much Isaac contributed to keep our family and this farm running like a fine-wound clock. Waiting for the return of a loved one is not only stressful, but the constant worry that goes along with Isaac being away from us has taken its toll on all of us. Just trying to keep a brave façade in front of the children leaves me completely drained of all my wits by day's end. I have discovered a new respect for Isaac that was there all along but never needed to surface, since he has gone away.

CHAPTER 14

When Pieter and Albert went out to the barnyard early this morning to milk the cows, they noticed that Nellie and Moses were not standing near the fence awaiting their morning serving of oats. They called for them, but no response, so the two went looking for them and found Nellie lying under her favorite maple tree in the back pasture with Moses standing near her. Poor Nellie lay down and died sometime during the night. The boys, in total panic, came running back into the house with the terrible news. This shook me to the core as Nellie has been Isaac's constant companion for over seventeen years. Tears began to flow as all of us went to the back pasture to see Nellie. There she lay on her side as if in a deep sleep. She looked so peaceful and appeared to have just lay down and slipped forever into eternity. Close by her side was her companion Moses. Knowing what had to be done next but not sure how to handle this horrible situation, I sent Joseph and James to get their Uncle Eli to help us bury our beloved horse. Eli soon returned with Nelson, Edward and shoves to help inter Nellie.

We decided that under the maple tree would be a good final resting place for our horse, as she really loved spending her idle time under that tree. My boys, Eli and his sons, dug a huge hole and, as careful as possible, placed Nellie into it. With uncontrollable sobbing, we recited scripture, the twenty-fourth Psalm to be exact, and prayed the Lord's Prayer as we said our final goodbyes to our beloved Nellie. Isaac, Isaac, Isaac…how will we tell Isaac when he returns home from war that his sidekick for seventeen-plus years passed away while he was gone? How will we manage to do our farm chores and fields without our sweet and loving Nellie? Nellie who just knew when to stop and when to move ahead, all without being encouraged to do so. She was a huge part of our daily life to keep this farm running. What about poor Moses who has just lost his best buddy? Will Moses be able to continue without his sidekick?

Isaac Deremer, I am angry that you went off to war and left us to fend for ourselves! We are lost in our sorrow and pray to the Lord for guidance as we go about our daily routine. Where will my strength to keep my family safe and this farm running come from? I feel that I am getting weaker with each passing day. Somewhere, somehow, I must dig deeper and find the strength to carry on without allowing myself to be buried in self-pity. Perhaps visiting some of the other women whose husbands have gone to war will bring me some peace? After all, I am not the only wife left behind to tend to all of our family affairs.

CHAPTER 15

I allowed myself some time alone. I walked to Maria Convey's house for a visit. Like me, Maria has children and a farm to look after. The two of us enjoyed a cup of tea and shared some of our unwanted experiences. Maria's children, four boys around the same age as my older sons, were also struggling but seemed to be managing much better than mine. She told me that her sons had taken over all the details of running the farm until their father returned. Their oldest son had wanted to enlist with his father, Martin, but was told no as he had to keep the farm running. Maria confessed that she too was upset with Martin's decision to go to war but respected his judgement and is trying as best she can to keep it together. I found, by just talking and sharing with Maria, I felt a bit better. We agreed to see each other again.

As the girls and I were clearing lunch from the table, James came running into the house informing us that Mr. Beerman was coming down our short path toward the house. We all went outside to greet Mr. Beerman and he, being a gentleman, duffed his hat to me out of respect. Mr. Beerman sat atop a fine chestnut-colored horse while holding the reins of a haltered mule trailing behind him. He expressed his sympathy for the loss of our horse and then offered us the use of his mule. My goodness, this act of kindness took me by complete surprise. Mr. Beerman went on to say that his sons gifted him the horse that he was riding and that he has two more fine horses back at his farm. He thought that perhaps he could loan his mule to us until Isaac returned from war. Beerman said that the mule was well-trained and very obedient. I immediately accepted his act of generosity and asked him what the mule's name was. He stated, "Mule." Believing that perhaps there was a language problem here as Mr. Beerman spoke with a heavy German accent, I asked again. Again, he stated, "Mule." Okay, so I rephrased my question, "So the mule is named Mule?" "Yes, his name is Mule, and he is six years old."

The children and I tried to hide our chuckles as we found his choice of names to be extremely practical. But beneath all of our amusement was the fact that this man, a possible Tory, came to us in our time of need and offered the use of his mule to help us run our farm. What a wonderful act of kindness! My first thought was how could I ever repay this man for such a noble deed? Jake Beerman turned over the reins to Pieter, and the boys walked the mule to pasture to introduce him to Moses. The two animals took an instant liking to each other and appeared to bond immediately. After expressing my gratefulness to Mr. Beerman again, he rode off in the direction of his farm.

During our evening meal, Pieter and Albert spoke of the conversation that their father had with them in the barn a few days before he left. It was during that conversation that their father told them that they could depend on Jake Beerman if need be. This act of kindness has really touched all of our hearts and gave us a much-needed lift. Their father was correct in saying that just because we have different beliefs, we can still come together in a time of need and help each other out. When the heart fills with love for one another, there is no room for malice.

We have decided to do our nightly reading lesson on the front porch instead of the kitchen table, as it is cooler outside. In much amazement, the new members of our reading group are learning quickly. It is a joy for all of us to share in this venture. Not only do we read from the Bible, but we also discuss what we have read and try and relate this to our daily lives. We had a very long, in-depth discussion about Jake Beerman tonight. What a true act of kindness and wonderful lesson for not just the children but me as well to try and live up to and put into practice in our daily lives. We are all getting a deeper feeling from the scripture. Perhaps it is so meaningful because we pray for the safe return of their father as well as all the men whom we know and those we don't to return safely back to their families and homes.

CHAPTER 16

Late this afternoon, Eli stopped by our farm with a letter from Isaac that he had just picked up from the Mineral Springs mail drop. Eli has faithfully stopped by the hotel three times a week, just after the stage goes through, to see if there is any word from Isaac. He also gets caught up on the news and local gossip. And men say women are the ones who thrive on gossip! Anyway, he again kept the children outside so I could have some private time to read and digest my letter.

When Isaac wrote this letter, he was still here in New Jersey, but along with his task of record-keeping, his unit will begin to build a fort along the Hudson River. Also, they have encountered only light conflict, but things are beginning to heat up. Apparently, something took place in Philadelphia on July 4 involving many influential men who got together and scripted a document they named "The Declaration of Independence." This document proclaims our right to freedom from England. I guess King George will flip over this happening.

Anyway, because of this declaration, Isaac expects more tariffs and military action to punish us for daring to break from England. Eli did tell me some days ago that a copy of this document was read aloud in the center square of Easton where it was received with the usual mixed reaction. Then, just as my head kept telling me all along it would be, but my heart denied it, Isaac said that he reenlisted for another three months. He assured me that he would return to us by the end of October, in time to complete the harvest, butcher the pigs, and chop the necessary firewood for winter. I suddenly felt lightheaded, as if all the blood in my body was slowly draining to my feet.

I tried to stand up but quickly sat back down so as not to faint. I told myself that I had to get it together for our children and face up to the fact that Isaac would not be coming home in a few weeks, but instead, it will be another three more months. I drank a cup of water and slowly collected my composure trying to put a lid on my festering anger. How could he do this to me! How could he do this to his children! What about us back home struggling to keep the farm operating without my husband and their father? This is not fair, and even worse, there is not a thing that I can do about his decision except wait it out. I closed my eyes, bowed my head, and took my troubles to the Lord. I slowly felt a bit more in control of myself and tried to think about Isaac's patriotic approach and reasoning to commit to yet another three months.

After rereading my letter, I called the children and Eli into the house to share Isaac's words with them. Isaac told the children that he was doing well. The food was not great like their Mama's, but he was being nourished and did enjoy some fresh berries they picked along the roadside during a rest stop. He is in the part of New Jersey near the Hudson River where farms are called plantations and the land is quite flat. There are fields and fields of wheat, turnips, and cabbage and even some tobacco fields. There are many gardens with several kinds of herbs that he was sure Aunt Peggy Warne would love to have drying in her herb house. The plantations seem to be worked by black slaves, men, women, and small children all laboring in the hot midday sun. Their faces are blank, and there is no sparkle in their eyes. They live in shacks. Our barns are so much nicer than their homes. Their clothing is ragged and often way to small. They seem to be friendly but very reserved as we march past their fields, fearing to look at us so as not to be chastised by the white men that stand a distance away, perhaps guarding over them. This is sad, this is wrong, this is evil, and no man should have control over another's life and well-being!

A man needs to be compensated fairly for his toil, giving him the ability to care for his family. Happiness does not necessarily mean wealth, but the basic things to support one's mere existence are not only needed but deserving to all humankind. He asked that all of us pray for these poor souls as we gather for our daily reading lesson. I continued to relay what Isaac said about building a new fort along the Hudson River, and their father, along with many more men, will be involved in the construction of this fort. Then as gentle as possible, I told them that their father would not return to us until late October. They took the news much better than I expected, believing all along that he would reenlist.

After reading the portion of the letter meant for the children, Eli spoke of slavery here in New Jersey. Yes, it does exist; no, the Deremer family does not believe in slavery and would never think of expecting anyone to work for us without being fairly compensated. Sadly, not all people have the same beliefs as our family. Albert asked his Uncle Eli if Mr. Van Horne's colored worker named Sonny was a slave. Eli had to answer Albert's question, "Yes, Sonny is a slave. Although Mr. Van Horne treats Sonny far better than most slave owners, slavery is still wrong, no matter how nicely one treats someone who is not free to come and go as they please." Gosh, what a powerful lesson to preach to innocent children—children who have never experienced such horrible actions committed by men who call themselves Christians.

After the children went back outside, Eli read the letter. We discussed Isaac's decision to reenlist for another three months. Unlike me, the decision did not come as a surprise to Eli who felt all along Isaac would commit to the cause of our freedom. Eli further stated that here in New Jersey, things appear to be calmer than in New England, so that fact may have helped sway Isaac to stay on for another enlistment. We also discussed the building of a fort along the west side of the Hudson River. The construction of this fort was authorized by General Washington himself, and it will be called Fort Constitution. Isaac believes that a second fort will be built along the east side of river to provide protection for the river from the possibility of an invasion of British ships.

Eli spoke to me with some very encouraging words about the next three months. Yes, I know that we can hang in there, and after all, we have managed to keep things running quite smoothly. Isaac has schooled the boys well in how to operate the farm. Before Eli left, I asked that he and Sarah and the children come to dinner next week. I had been saving a large smoked ham to prepare in celebration of

Isaac's return, but now that the date has been pushed back another three months, I thought it best that we use the meat. It won't be all that long before we butcher again and restock our springhouse.

Eli was pleased with the invitation and would let Sarah know as soon as he got back to his farm. My children were equally excited when I told them during our evening meal. The girls started to eagerly suggest what we can serve with the ham. I guess we will be making some applesauce and, surely, whipped potatoes. The boys suggested that if the weather continues to be sunny and hot, why not have our feast outside under the large oak tree. We all agreed that was a wonderful idea. Albert said that we could use the harvest table and benches stored in the back of the wagon shed. The excitement was contagious, and we all put forth wonderful suggestions as to how to make the meal a special time for all of us. Tomorrow after we complete our farmwork, we will begin our preparations for next week's dinner.

After the children were fast asleep and my eyes were becoming heavy, I allowed my sorrow to come to the surface of my heart. As I sobbed quietly into my pillow, I prayed for peace from my heartache. It is so difficult for me to understand why Isaac believes that he needs to fight this war. I am trying not to be selfish, but there is no other way to think about his actions. My anger is not solely directed at my husband but at the greedy King George who wants everything for himself. King George is the reason why we are at war, not Isaac who is just trying to make America a better place for me and our children. Yet, all the blame does not and cannot heal my broken heart.

CHAPTER 17

The August sun is scorching the ground. The children and I have been carrying buckets of water from the brook to the garden to keep our vegetables from drying up. Everything seems to be producing, but we could sure use some rain.

Last Sunday after church, I asked Lizzy Bryan if her daughter was well as, we have not seen her in church in the past few months. Much to my surprise, Lizzy told me that her daughter Allison Matthews is with child, and because she is six months along with a growing belly, she is now in confinement. Lizzy also said that Allison's husband, Mark, who enlisted with Isaac, is unaware of Allison's condition. Allison has had no contact with Mark since he left in the end of April. Mark is poor at both reading and writing, so no letters have been sent back home. This will be their first child as they were married last December. Oh my goodness, this is heartrending as Allison should not have to go through this alone. I am darn sure that all she really wants is to have her husband by her side to share in this joyous event. And to think that he is unaware of the pending birth of his child is downright sad.

Apparently, Mark enlisted for six months and is due back home about the same time as my Isaac in October. The baby is due sometime in early November. I asked Sarah if she was aware of Allison's condition, and she said no. We both decided to pay Allison a visit since good manners dictate that Allison stay out of the public's eye until after the baby is born. It is shameful that women must hide their protruding bellies the last several months of pregnancy, but it has been this way for as long as all of us can recall. Eli had to go into town today, so Sarah and I rode along and visited with Allison. She was not in good spirits as she has no clue where or even how her husband is and if he will be coming home in time for the birth of their first child. We did our best to ease her melancholy mood, but she certainly has a right to feel the way she does. She is being attended to by our local midwife, Margaret Warne. Folks here refer to Margaret as Aunt Peggy, and she not only sees to ladies in confinement but also tends to the sick. Allison will be in good hands with Aunt Peggy assisting her in the birth of this child. I hope and pray that Mark makes it back home to give the much-needed attention Allison will seek during the last months of her pregnancy. Sarah and I agreed to come and visit with Allison again soon. During the ride back to our farms, we discussed how sad it is for Allison to be in the dark about her husband's whereabouts. I would love to have an address where I can send a letter to Isaac. No one seems to be able to provide us eagerly waiting at home an address to send along our love and prayers. The ability to read and write makes situations like this much easier to handle, even if the letters from our loved ones cannot be answered.

CHAPTER 18

September 7, 1776, a date that I shall never forget until the day I die! The children and I were relaxing on the front porch after completing our afternoon chores. Catherina was the first to notice a group of three men walking along the lane heading toward our house. I immediately recognized two of the men as Eli and our minister, Pastor Carson. The third man was dressed in a military uniform holding the reins of his horse as he walked along with the other two men. My heart sank quickly, and my body slumped completely limp into my chair. I found myself unable to breathe or even hear my children's voices asking me what was wrong. The men approached, and Eli spoke first. Isaac was alive but had been taken a prisoner of war during a battle on August 27 in the Brooklyn, New York area.

The military man who identified himself as Sergeant Eastman now spoke that Isaac was probably being held captive on a British warship docked in the East River. My mouth opened, but no words came out. Too many thoughts were racing through my mind all at the same time. Pastor Carson spoke with the children who by now were crying hysterically and in about the same condition as I was. They wanted to know when their father would be coming home. The sergeant was unable to answer their questions as he had no idea, and so soon after Isaac's capture, they were not even sure that he was being held on a warship. All he could really tell us was that Isaac was alive at the time of his capture. He could not tell us if he was, in fact, injured or where he was at this time.

The battle was bloody with two thousand men captured, missing, killed, or wounded from both sides of the fight. My head was pounding, as well as my heart, feeling as if it was going to burst through my chest at any time. Hearing the words that Isaac was taken alive briefly gave me a bit of comfort. I immediately prayed aloud to God to spare my husband and the father of my children and to please bring him back to us. Sergeant Eastman stayed with us for another hour attempting to answer any and all of our questions as best he could. He said that he would be staying at the Mineral Springs Hotel overnight and would come back to visit us in the morning before he returned to Morris Town. He then rode off on horseback.

Sometime, I am not sure even when Sarah and their children arrived. Sarah had spent time with their children before coming to us, telling them about their Uncle Isaac and how each child could help their cousins get through this horrible situation. The children went off by themselves as a group to talk and to share their fears and address the many unanswered questions we all had. Pastor Carson went with the children, and they all sat under the oak tree for a long time where he listened to them, all the while offering his support, love, advice, and prayers. When he returned to Eli, Sarah, and me, he said that the children had found some peace sharing in this frightening ordeal. They rallied around Catherina, who seemed to be having the most difficulties and, in their own way, were helping to calm her a bit.

So many questions, no answers. What's next? When will we know anything positive about Isaac? How long will he be held captive? How can we help to free him? All I really wanted to do was to go off somewhere and just scream as loud and long as my body would allow.

I'm not sure what time I finally fell off to sleep, but my night was filled with horrible dreams that kept waking me in a state of total panic. I do know that it was well past sunrise when I finally ventured out to the kitchen. The boys were finishing up their chores, and the girls were preparing to make breakfast for all of us. Oh my goodness, all of this has caused me to stop tending to my family. The girls comforted me and said that they wanted to take care of me, that is why they allowed me to sleep in, being as quiet as possible so as not to wake me. Thank you, Lord, for such wonderful children!

A knock came on the door at about eight-thirty and as promised, it was Sergeant Eastman. The sergeant promised to keep us informed on any news about Isaac as soon as he was privy to such information. He wished us well, mounted his horse, and rode off.

The rest of the day brought visits from our neighbors and friends expressing, first, the shock and then offering to help in any way they could. It was an extremely tiring but profound day. The love that we received from everyone has warmed our hearts. I am not sure where we are headed, as we have no idea how long Isaac will be gone. The offers to help with our harvest, butchering and stocking our woodpile will surely make our lives easier to endure without Isaac. Mr. Van Horne has offered to allow Sonny to come and help us as much as we need him. I told Mr. Van Horne that I would only allow this if we can compensate Sonny in some way. We agreed that we can pay Sonny for his work by supplying Sonny and his family with some of the meat that we butcher later this fall. Also, share our vegetables and give them some of our wood. This pleased me, and if Isaac does not return to us by October, we will need Sonny's help to make it through the winter months.

Toward the end of the day, a horse and wagon came down our short path. What a pleasant surprise to see Lizzie Bryan at the reins with her daughter Allison by her side. Allison broke all manners by coming to visit us when she is very much with child. She said she didn't care because she needed to talk with me. I told Allison that when I asked Sergeant Eastman if any other men from our area were either captured, wounded, or killed during the August 27 battle, he said no, none that they are aware of. This made Allison feel a bit easier. Here it is: September and her baby is due early November, she has a right to be fretting about her husband. Allison said it was good to be out and about even if it was in poor manners; I was thrilled with her visit. She kept covered by her cape so as not to expose her large belly to my children, as if being with child is something evil! This is a strange world sometimes, as all babies are a gift from God to be cherished.

The numbness has not worn off. The reality that Isaac is a prisoner of war and what could happen to him, to us, has not sunk in. I want to believe with all of my heart that God will keep us safe and that Isaac will return to us. Now is not the time to question my faith, but that is exactly what I seem to be doing.

Tonight, we read certain passages from our Bible instead of our regular reading lesson. Pastor Carson suggested reading from the book of Psalms. As a family, we are certainly praying for a miracle to bring our Isaac back to us safe and sound. Please, dear God, bring Isaac back to us.

CHAPTER 19

Our supply of firewood is beginning to dwindle. The children and I have been canvasing the hedgerows and wooded areas carting back all fallen branches to keep a small stash of wood for emergency purposes. Now with cooler weather imminent, we need to seriously stock our wood pile. At church yesterday, I spoke with Mr. Van Horne about having his farmhand Sonny come and help get our farm ready for the long winter months ahead. This morning, Sonny arrived just after nine o'clock. The children were told to heed any and all advice that Sonny would provide. By all of us working toward the same cause, things would run smoothly, and we can slowly chip away at our long to-do list.

Sonny and the boys hitched Moses to one wagon and Mule to the other, and we all headed toward our back wooded area. Using a two-man saw, axes, and hatchets, we downed several dead trees, then began to load our wagons with perfectly cut pieces of assorted dry hardwood that burns slower and provides good heat. When the wagons returned to our woodshed, were unloaded, and ready to make a second trip, I stayed behind to prepare our lunch. I told Sonny that lunch would be ready in about an hour and to please bring himself and the children back to house. Sure enough, one hour later, they returned and washed up. The children came inside, but Sonny did not, requesting that he eat his meal under the oak tree. This puzzled the children until I told them that perhaps he didn't share the same table with the Van Horne family? Much to my surprise and without being told, the children picked up their plates and went out and sat under the oak tree and ate their meal with Sonny. My heart swelled with joy to see my children treat this man just as everyone deserved to be treated. It doesn't matter if your skin is of a different color; what matters is what is in your heart, and Sonny was gifted with a huge, kind heart. We chatted over lunch and learned that Sonny is married and has two small children, a boy and a girl.

After lunch, we made a few more trips to the wooded areas of our farm. Each time Sonny carefully chose trees that would give off the best heat. Sonny felled more trees, then we could cut and bring back to our woodshed today, telling the boys that the downed trees would be easier for them to retrieve when they had extra time. I reminded him that we would be paying him for his hard work today with firewood, some meat from our springhouse and fresh vegetables from our garden. He seemed grateful but shy.

About four o'clock, Sonny started to get ready to return to the Van Horne farm as he had his afternoon chores to complete before his day was over. I instructed him not to unload the last wagon of wood, as my boys would be accompanying him back to his home and help him unload it. Also, I sent the promised food along with them. Albert and Pieter left with Moses, the wagon full of wood and a promise from Sonny that we would see him in a few days to help us with the slaughter of the pigs.

During our evening meal, my children asked many questions about Sonny. I openly answered all questions as best I could. Albert and Pieter said that the house that Sonny and his family occupied was in good repair but smaller than our wagon shed and looked like a shack. I reminded the children of what their father said in his last letter about the horrible living conditions he witnessed near the Hudson River. Sonny's house was a shack, but at least it was protection from the weather. (Silently, I was seething as Mr. Van Horne's house is beautiful.) The question of Sonny being a slave came up too. Then questions about Sonny's wife, and was she also a slave? What about his children? Wow, my children had a difficult time accepting the cold hard fact that the entire family belongs to Howard Van Horne. Their honest, heart-wrenching comments about people who own colored people left me somewhat amazed. The children said that whenever Sonny or his family are at our house, they would be treated like we would want to be treated, with respect and kindness.

It wasn't too long after our reading lesson that we all retired for the night. I guess gathering firewood was a much more difficult task then we all expected. Isaac was always gathering and cutting wood during the spring, summer, and fall. With Isaac being captured, it put us all in a state of shock and confusion. We are leaning on each other and somehow managing to get through our days. Much thanks goes to Eli and Sarah who are relentless in their encouragement to keep us moving forward. We try not to look too far into the future, hoping and praying that Isaac will again be a part of it.

CHAPTER 20

The fall weather is quickly passing. However, I must say that the Lord took his paint brush and gave us a beautiful display of reds, oranges and rusts on our trees and bushes this year. This has been an outstanding and enjoyable season. We have a bountiful supply of walnuts and hickory nuts just waiting to be picked up, shelled, and stored for winter. I only wish we could have shared it with Isaac.

We were successful with the slaughter of our three largest pigs, thanks to the help and guidance from Sonny. He was pleased when he returned to his home with several pounds of fresh pork. After the souse and scrapple gel, we will share them as well with his family. Our lofts, root cellar, and springhouse are well-stocked for the long dreary months ahead. So much praise goes to Sonny for all of his help and commitment to assisting others.

I finished spinning my carded wool, and the girls and I were able to color the yarn with liquid strained from the very ripe berries from this past summer. After heating the ripened fruit, we strained it through cotton cloth, then placed small batches of the yarn into the warm liquid for an hour or so. The different berries gave us different colors—we have deep pink, light pink, purple, red, and blue yarn. The walnut's outer shells were also boiled, and we have several tones of brown from dark to medium tan. After the yarn dried completely, we rolled each color into balls and safely stored them under my bed.

I am teaching my girls how to knit mittens, and the beautiful colors of the yarn will make for a really fun time. I am also knitting sweaters for Pieter and Albert, as they are growing so quickly. Last year's sweaters will be stored away until James and Joseph grow into them. All of this warm and fuzzy wool made me think of Isaac and how will he keep warm. From the little information that I have been able to learn, the prison ships are plagued with dampness and so dark and chilly. The food is minimal—we probably slop the pigs better than the redcoats feed their prisoners! Oh, Isaac, please come home. We miss and love you so much. Heavenly Father, please protect, not just Isaac, but all who are involved in this wretched war.

The boys seem to have the steps to get the farm ready for winter nearly complete. Thanks to Sonny thinking ahead and dropping additional trees, the house will stay warm and comfortable. Isaac will be so proud when he learns of their willingness to keep this farm running. They even went over to see if they could give their Uncle Eli a hand with his harvest. Eli seemed to have developed a bad cold that slowed him down for several days, putting him behind with his harvest. He is listening to the advice of Aunt Peggy and faithfully drinking his cherry bark tea, which appears to be giving him much-needed relief, and he seems to be making a slow recovery. With Eli's boys and our sons working side-by-side, Eli was able to sneak some much-needed rest to recover from his illness. Thank goodness, it was just a cold, and not something life-threatening, like pneumonia.

I learned from Eli that Mark Matthews has returned home from the war safe and sound. Praise the Lord! Mark was separated from Isaac as soon as they got to Morris Town, so Eli got no new information concerning Isaac. I am pleased that Mark will be here for the birth of his first child. I am mighty sure that Allison is relieved too. The date for the delivery of their child has passed, but then babies will enter into this world when they are darn ready, so no use fretting about it. It does sadden me to think that Isaac would have completed his two enlistments by now and should have returned home to his family and farm. All we can do is hope and pray for his safe return. Life here on the farm seems to be at a standstill since he's been gone away. Yet, that is not the case, as so many wonderful things have happened in our neighbor's lives that we should be grateful for being a part of. Local men are still marching off to war, even knowing that Isaac was taken as a prisoner. I guess men believe that it can't happen to them, but no one can be so smug to believe that they can escape the horrors of war.

CHAPTER 21

We awoke this morning to the first heavy snowfall of the season. Everything was blanketed in white and looks so beautiful. Pieter and Albert decided it was time to string our heavy cords from the barn to the woodshed, to the springhouse, to the outhouse, and finally to our home in preparation for blizzard conditions that often arises during the winter months. By holding firmly onto the rope, one can be guided safely to and from any of these buildings, even in blinding, drifting snow. Becoming lost or disoriented in blizzard conditions can be life-threatening. The house can be just yards away, but blowing winds and swirling snow can easily cause one to lose their direction, especially when the lantern goes dark and one must feel their way back to our porch.

Both Isaac and Eli devised this safety measure after our first frightening encounter with Mother Nature and a storm that dumped several feet of snow on our farms. I fear for my sons venturing out in these conditions, but our animals must be cared for. They are now the men of the house, at least until their father returns to us. Milk and egg deliveries will be halted as long as conditions are dangerous. Even when things get better, the boys often ride Moses, and now Mule, to complete their expected and needed deliveries in town.

The girls and I decided to go through all of our clothing that we stowed away for the next child to grow into. Abigail is getting so tall that she is moving up into her sister's clothing. Joseph and James seem to be holding their size for the moment at least. The children asked if we could pass the clothing that no longer fits any of them on to Sonny's children. I thought that was a wonderful idea, so we left no article of clothing packed away. I was amazed at just how many things I had put aside to pass along to someone special. We discovered knit sweaters, scarves, and gloves that will fit both of Sonny's children and keep them comfortable through this winter season. In a few days, after the sun melts some of the snow, Elizabeth, Catherina, and Abigail can deliver the clothing to the Van Horne farm where they can visit with Sonny and his family.

With winter upon us, the days are short; the nights, so long and dark. We spend most of our time indoors now. The girls and I have been knitting, and they are catching on really quick. Pieter is trying his hand at some wood carving. Earlier in the fall, he watched Sonny working on a small whistle that he was carving from a piece of ash tree, and Pieter is attempting to make his own masterpiece. Albert is busy mending, polishing, and moisturizing the tact with bear grease. Taking the time to care for the leather gear will make it last for years. This is exactly what Isaac would be doing if he were here with us.

Christmas is just a few days away, and we have been baking gingerbread and cookies to take to Eli and Sarah's home on Christmas Day. I am trying to cover the sadness in my heart by baking extra special cookies. Eli took all the boys on one of our annual family hunting outings. This is something that Isaac and Eli shared every year since we moved here. As the boys got older, they too were included in the hunt. Eli had his long gun, and my boys took their great-grandfather's long gun with them too. The group went to the pond just beyond Eli's farm. Sitting quietly is one of the many requirements to be a successful bird hunter. Each one got a turn to take a shot. Once a shot is fired, whether it hits something or misses, the wait begins again. The birds all fly away in fright, but after all is calm, they return to the pond. James actually bagged a duck! All of his brothers and cousins called it the Christmas miracle as James can't hit the side of the barn with a rock. Eli bagged a goose. After removing the feathers and dressing the birds out, they were put in Eli's smokehouse to save for our Christmas dinner, and what a feast it will be! The pin feathers will be saved for stuffing in our pillows and mattresses.

I lack any holiday joy this year. I am sure we will enjoy our day with Eli, Sarah, and their children. We will all attend the Christmas Eve service at our church. On Christmas Day, we will settle down for a wonderful feast that Sarah, all of our daughters, and I will prepare.

It is difficult for me to push from my mind that Isaac chose to go away and leave his family. I am beginning to feel that he has deserted us, even though I know that is not true. The taste of bitterness is in my words and on my heart. I keep telling myself that forgiveness far outweighs the bitterness that I am feeling. Try as I may, all I really want is Isaac home, safe and sound. Really, Lord, is that too much to ask for? I hope and pray that this upcoming New Year proves to be a better year than 1776 has been to all of us.

CHAPTER 22

Oh my goodness, things are happening and so very quickly. I guess one needs to be extra careful just what they hope and pray for. We have learned that General George Washington and his Continental Army left their winter camp in Bucks County, Pennsylvania, and traveled through a severe winter storm to the Delaware River on Christmas night. Washington's army, horses, and eighteen pieces of artillery crossed the river at a place called McKonkey's Ferry, Pennsylvania, to the Jersey side, taking them from seven-thirty Christmas night until four o'clock the morning of December 26. Finally, with all troops, horses, and equipment safely on the Jersey side of the river, Washington split his army into two groups, one under his and General Greene's command, and the other under the command of General Sullivan.

Sullivan's men would take River Road from Bear Tavern to Trenton, while Washington's army would march along Pennington Road, which travels a few miles inland paralleling the Delaware River. Both armies marched toward Trenton where Hessians were lodged in Fort Trenton. The attack came as complete surprise, and the Continental Army quickly overtook the Hessians, who were apparently suffering from a bit too much Christmas cheer. Sadly, three of our men died during the battle, and six were wounded. Twenty-two Hessians lost their lives, and ninety-eight men were wounded. The American captured one thousand prisoners and seized the entire stash of guns, powder, and heavy artillery. Take that, King George!

Washington had to bring his men and all the prisoners back to their winter encampment near McKonkey's Ferry, along with much-needed food and clothing taken from the fort during the capture of the Hessians. Crossing the Delaware a second time was still a difficult task; at least, the snow and driving winds had calmed, but the ice-filled water made the trek across just as treacherous.

This, a true victory for the Continental Army, boosted the morale of the troops. Some soldiers whose enlistments were ending reenlisted with new hope that we really did have a chance to rid ourselves of that rotten King George. Others stayed on after a bonus was to be paid immediately, causing a significant number of men to agree to stay with the army for another six weeks.

Apparently, General Washington also learned that all of the British, including some Hessians, had quickly retreated north to Princeton, New Jersey. So on December 29, our army again crossed the Delaware, but this time, soldiers attempted to cross into the New Jersey countryside from eight crossing points. The snowfall from the evening of December 28 had stopped, but the weather was bitterly cold. The Delaware at several of these points had frozen over as much as two to three inches, allowing many of our men to cross over on foot. At some of the other crossings, the conditions were so dangerous that their mission to cross had been called off, and the men withdrew to a safer area to get to the other side of the river. It was New Year's Eve by the time the army and all the necessary equipment were safely on the Jersey banks of the Delaware. Washington immediately took a position across the Assunpink Creek, with Trenton occupying the other side of the creek. His army was able to beat back an assault on January 2, 1777, with a victory at Princeton the next day. This sure caused the British army to flee all the way back to Morris Town. Good ridden, redcoats!

Here in Mansfield Woodhouse, we couldn't be more pleased. In church, we praised the Lord for all the wonderful things that have happened in the past few weeks. At home, we pray for all of our troops and their continued safety. All of these battles are really quite close to home. Closer than any of us care to even think about. Then there is Isaac, my dear husband, father of my children, oh, Isaac, please be safe. With such cold weather, we pray that somehow you can find some peace and a bit of comfort. I feel so guilty that we are here warm and safe in this wonderful home that you built for us. We have food, we have shelter, we have each other, but all we want is you, my dear Isaac. Please, Lord, just make this war go away and let us live in peace forever.

CHAPTER 23

The weekend started out being cold and blustery, but beautiful sunshine gave way to the dismal winter weather. Looking ahead, we have only forty days until the first day of spring. Hopefully, the Lord will see fit to bless us with lots of sunshine and help melt all this snow.

Today in church, Mark and Allison Matthews had their son Abraham baptized. What a beautiful, healthy child! To celebrate this joyous occasion, after church, we all shared a wonderful cake that Allison's mother, Lizzy, baked, along with some punch. It has been a few weeks since we were able to make it to church. With what seemed like constant bad weather, we are finally enjoying other people's company. It seems that we have been snowed in most of this winter season. The deep snow made it difficult for Moses and Mule to tread through. Although we were surprised immediately after one especially heavy storm to have a knock on our door. To our joy, it was Sonny checking on us! He did come into our home but refused a hot cup of tea. He said that he just wanted to check on us and make sure that everyone was well. He gave Pieter a few tips on his carving project and talked about this upcoming planting season. His wife and children are well, and he thanked us for the clothing that the girls delivered to his children a few months back. We sent him home with some scrapple and souse; all the while, he protested, saying that he did not stop by for a handout. Well, certainly we were aware of that, but just the same, we insisted that he accept our offerings.

While at church this morning after the baptism, Eli discussed with the boys what needs to be done to prep our farm for the spring. All the fields are blanketed with snow, so it is much too early to think about planting. However, it is not too early to begin mucking the barn and stables. Although we try to keep these areas mucked, manure piles up quite quickly outside the buildings. The process of clearing this away before the ground becomes muddy and bogs the wagon down, needs to begin at the first signs of a thaw. Also, the manure will fertilize the fields and eventually be mixed in with the soil.

CHAPTER 24

The animals are birthing, and spring is surely all around us. It is wonderful to be able to walk about without the weight of mud bogging down our footwear. The daily visits of our neighbors coming to purchase our milk and eggs is a true pleasure. Exchanging light banter and hearing about some of the good things that have been happening in our neighbor's lives is uplifting.

With spring finally here, all of the neighbors will be attending a barn-raising at John and Ellen Castner's farm. Early in the winter, their barn caught fire when a lantern exploded after it was dropped on the barn floor. The fire spread quickly, but they were able to save all of the livestock and some of the farming equipment. However, the barn burned completely to the ground, and they lost all of the hay. Several men have been helping to put up some of the framework, but more manpower is needed to complete the project. So on Wednesday, weather permitting, all families that are available to pitch in and give a hand will show up at their farm, just a mile past our Mansfield Woodhouse church. The women will bring food, and all capable males will be involved in the construction. It will be a time of hard work but also a way for our community to come together to show our support for one another. With all the expected workers, the exterior of the barn should be near completion when we leave for home in the late afternoon. The feeling of being a part of the community and helping a neighbor is very uplifting.

The girls and I are busy planning what and how much food we should make and bring with us to the barn raising. Also, during the lull, the women will do some quilting. Each family will work on their own quilt instead of sharing in the creation of one blanket. We have been collecting and cutting squares from any and all usable fabrics we find around our home. Sometimes a part of a dress or shirt may be worn out, but the rest of the item can be transformed into something new. The more colors, the prettier the quilt! Old Mrs. Davis gave us several pieces of fabric that she no longer needs or wants. She gave up quilting a few years ago when her eyesight started to fail her. Once the milky film starts to travel across the eyes, there is not much that can be done to improve one's vision. Hopefully, blindness will not take away her ability to care for herself—a chilling thought, but a fact of life.

Eli brought me a letter from back home that he picked up from the mail drop earlier today. Mama is feeling her age, and Papa is slowly accepting the fact that slowing down is now a way of life for him as well. The tension in Philadelphia has spread to Doylestown too. Mama said that she is afraid to speak freely while in public. The king's henchmen are everywhere. Families openly boast that they are Tories and throw their support to the king of England. The cost of common everyday items are starting to be out of reach for so many people. Mama said that families are planning on spading every piece of soil, even flowerbeds, to plant food in place of anything that can't be consumed. Not a wild berry or walnut escapes the eye of the needy. So frightening to think that this is happening to us. I do pray that Papa, Mama, and the rest of our family will come stay with us, even for a short time, until all of this terrible fighting stops. I know that my hope and desire will fall upon deaf ears. I am also beginning to believe that there is no end in sight for this horrible war.

CHAPTER 25

We attended a strawberry festival at the Castner farm in appreciation for the help with the barn-raising earlier in the spring. I guess that love is in the air, as it was announced that John and Ellen Castner's daughter Ruth will betroth Harold Taylor in September. Ruth and Harold make such an adorable couple, and their abundant smiles tell the world just how in love they are. It's been almost eighteen years since my parents announced that Isaac had asked for my hand in marriage. So much has happened since then. I wouldn't change a thing! No that is not true, I would rid the earth of war if I only could!

Sarah and I also learned that Allison Matthews is again with child. This little one is expected to arrive early next year. She is not the only woman expecting a little bundle of joy; Helena Hoppock and Susanna Carter are due to deliver in the first part of the New Year as well. I guess Aunt Peggy will be busy helping with the safe delivery of these wee ones. After moving to our valley, she has delivered so many babies that we women just feel a bit more at ease with her assisting in the birthing of our community's children.

Since the weather has been so beautiful, many of our farmers are ahead of schedule with their planting and can turn their attention to the necessary upkeep of their farms. The gristmill has started grinding the winter wheat, and the tannery is busy preparing pelts from the late-spring trapping season. From what I have heard, the beavers have been especially bothersome on Scott's Mountain. They have downed many trees, dammed a few streams, and caused flooding to good farm land. Trapping these creatures has become a full-time endeavor for Mr. Lomerson and his sons. The pelts will bring a very generous price when they are shipped back to Philadelphia.

Beaver skin hats seem to be the fashion of day, at least in the city; here a raccoon skin hat seems to fill the purpose perfectly fine.

Two nights ago, during the new moon, we had all of our windows open as there was a pleasant gentle breeze blowing through our house. As I lay awake, I could hear the high-pitched yelping of a pack of coyotes somewhere in the not-so-far distance. It appeared that the coyotes were hunting, as I could also hear the bleating of sheep. Next, the crack of a rifle, and then silence. The lack of any sound whatsoever was eerie. The children heard it as well and came downstairs. As a group, the boys were determined to go outside and investigate. I was going to stop them but decided that they were the men of house, and I should allow them to do their job. Each of the boys took a lit lantern with them. Pieter carried Isaac's grandfather's loaded long gun. When they came back inside, they said that all of our livestock seem fine, and no animal showed signs of being stressed. In the morning, when the locals came for their daily milk and eggs, I learned that coyotes took down one of Mr. Van Horne's ewes. Mr. Van Horne was able to scare them off with the firing of his long gun.

I have now gone through all the firsts since Isaac left to serve his country. As a family, we have celebrated all of our birthdays, holidays, and my wedding anniversary without my husband by my side. It has been a year, one month, three weeks, and four days since Isaac rode Nellie out our short path onto the lane. All I have to do is close my eyes to relive his departure as if it were yesterday. It has been a year of nightmares, heartache, and fear for my entire family. I heard from Eli that Washington's Army and the British Army are working on what is called a prisoner swap. This is where both sides trade men who have been taken prisoner of war. From what Eli has told me, most swaps are regular army and men with rank, not volunteers. Although Isaac is a volunteer, this has given me something to hold on to. Maybe, just maybe, Isaac will be one of the lucky few who are traded and sent back to their families. I can only hope and pray that this is so.

CHAPTER 26

It is with deep sadness that I pen this entry. Christopher, the son of James and Carol Smith of Hall's Mills, lost his life on Monday when he fell from his horse. Christopher was racing the horse along with two other boys to the swimming hole when the horse took a fright, reared up, and threw the boy off. Dr. Donaldson from Turkey Hill was called in to attend the thirteen-year-old but could offer no medical assistances as the head injuries were so severe that the boy did not regain consciousness and passed away just hours later.

Today, both my family and Eli and Sarah's family attended the burial in the Mansfield Woodhouse Cemetery. As I told my children, Christopher was just being a boy, doing what boys do, having fun and looking forward to a dip in the swimming hole to cool off. One never knows when their time has come to meet the almighty Father. Best that we live our lives as faithful and useful as possible. Love one another and thank the Lord for each day that he has blessed us with. Silently, but with feelings of guilt, I thanked the Lord that it was not one of my children. I know that my thoughts are not Christian, but my maternal feelings are keeping me from thinking properly. I just don't know what I would do if faced with this horrible tragedy, with or without my husband by my side. God blesses us with children; they are precious gifts from God, and I guess that he calls them back home when they are needed up in heaven.

The garden is thriving this year. Lately, we have had the right amount of rainfall at all the right times. The garden has produced so well that we have sold some of our extra produce to the folks who come to purchase our milk and eggs. This is very exciting to the children, as it proves that hard work is worth the effort. The boys also delivered a generous bunch of sugar beets to Mr. Beerman's farm.

While in town earlier this month, the boys heard Mr. Beerman tell Miss McCullough from McCullough's General Storehouse that his beet crop was a failure this year. Just to show some gratitude, we thought it would be a nice gesture, since we have plenty, to share with his family. After all, he lent us Mule and continues to state that we can keep him until Isaac returns, gets back on his feet, and can purchase a plow animal of his choosing.

The pig and sheep herds have again been weaned to an amount that we can easily manage. For some unknown reason, we did not get the number of piglets that we expected. Just the same, the sale of the extra animals help to keep this farm running. Our shearing of the sheep proved easier this year than last. I guess one learns from mistakes made in the past, as the entire process moved along much smoother.

Eli brought us a letter from my parents in Doylestown. He said that he too got a letter from back home. Both my parents and Eli and Isaac's parents are doing well but are complaining about the lack of certain imported things, such as tea. We are also feeling the squeeze of these tariffs from King George. In place of black tea, we are often brewing fresh mint tea that we pick from along the side of our brook. The minty taste is refreshing and enjoyed both hot and cold. Yes, it has taken a bit to get used to the change, but change can be good. We still enjoy a pot of black tea on occasion, and we serve it to any guests who may pop in, but something different can often be fun too. When the cold weather nears, we will harvest as much mint as possible to save for winter. We will hang the herb upside down by its stem to dry in our root cellar. The mint will store well during the colder months and be available whenever needed.

Sarah managed to get her hands on a loom from a distant relative back in the Philadelphia area. The small loom arrived on the stagecoach from Easton to Mineral Springs Hotel late last week. It was in great shape considering it rode atop the coach during its entire trip to the Mineral Springs, surviving the bumpy pothole-filled dirt roads. Eli had to fashion a few new wooden pegs that were missing so he could put the contraption together for us. So very exciting for all of us, and we have all tried our hand at weaving, but it is a slow, tedious process. Together, Sarah, our daughters, and I are weaving a very colorful blanket. We take turns adding row upon row of our spun woolen yarn to the blanket. Once finished, the blanket should last for years. I guess once we become accustomed to working the loom, things will progress quicker. But for now, we are experiencing hours of frustration and sore hands and fingers. Taking turns helps, and each of us is eager to sit a spell and try out the loom. The fact that both Sarah and I have had no formal lessons on what to do with such a devise means that we are flying by the seat of bloomers, but we will not allow our mistakes to discourage us. Sarah sent a letter back to her Philadelphia relative asking dozens of questions. An answer to her letter could take weeks, so we agreed to approach Mr. Greene, our local tailor for some much-needed tips. If we can make this loom work for us, I will not sell as much of our carded wool as in years past. It is fun thing to do and something for all of us females to enjoy. All weaving needs to be done during the daylight hours using the bright sunshine to keep our work area well lit. Candlelight doesn't illuminate our work area well enough, making it difficult to even distinguish thread colors and patterns.

CHAPTER 27

The children and I were finishing our afternoon chores when the sky started to darken. I told the boys to round up the animals and bring them into the paddock and barn. I had a bad feeling about the color of the sky and the pending rain. The winds picked up quickly, and I ordered everyone up to the house. We laid the chairs on our porch over on their sides and got into the house just as we were hit with heavy rain pounding against the house on a sideways slant. We got all the shutters battened, and I scooped a few of the larger embers from our firebox and placed them into the hanging kettle, putting the lid ajar on the top of the pot. Rain was falling into the chimney and down into the firebox, smothering out what heat that was left from our noonday meal.

Later, the hot embers will be used to help start a new fire to cook our evening meal. If we don't save a few embers in the kettle, we will have to go to Eli's home and ask for a few of their embers to restart our fire. The dying fire was causing an unwanted smoky atmosphere within our home, so we cracked one of the shutters just enough to draw the unwanted smoke out of the house. The sound of the thunder and lightning overhead was deafening. We huddled together in the darkness around our kitchen table attempting to make small talk. Although we had a lit candle on our table, it offered little comfort. With each loud bang and flash of lightning that found its way through the cracks in our shuttered windows, we felt less and less secure.

After what seemed like hours, but was actually perhaps twenty minutes, the storm passed, and we could see light coming through the shuttered windows. Storms that usually build quickly often move away equally as fast. We opened the front door of our home, and there before us was a magnificent rainbow arching above us. The colors were so vivid and beautiful against the blue cloudless sky. This pleasant scene made us feel as if what had just taken place was not a terrifying storm but just perhaps a bad dream. We stepped out onto our porch to take in this wonder. As we basked in its beauty, Elizabeth screamed and pointed to the east in the direction of Eli and Sarah's farm. Thick black smoke was rising from one of the buildings, not the barn but one of the outbuildings.

Lightning must have struck the building, catching it on fire. All of us stood frozen from fear, but within seconds, we were somehow able to begin running as quickly as possible toward Eli's farm. As we neared the farm, we could see that it was the corncrib that was on fire, completely engulfed in flames. My family quickly joined Eli's family and the Bryan family who live on the farm just beyond Eli's in forming a bucket brigade, transferring buckets of water from the brook to the fire and then back to the brook to be filled again. It was apparent that the corncrib was a total loss, but we were dousing the flames to keep them from catching another building on fire. Within forty-five minutes, the flames were out, and our bucket brigade stopped. Being late September, the corncrib was almost void of ears of corn, making the fire a bit easier to extinguish.

We regrouped near the house when we noticed Nelson approaching us in a daze, staggering and in pain from apparently catching his britches on fire. Shock and fear gripped all of us. Eli ordered the boys to run and find Aunt Peggy as quickly as possible. They obeyed and ran toward the west along the lane that would intersect with the Aunt Peggy's road. Eli and Elwood Bryan carefully assisted Nelson back to the porch of the house and removed the badly burned britches and tried to make him comfortable. What can one say or do when looking at Nelson's blistered and blackened leg? My girls and his sisters stood back and just stared in disbelief. Thoughts of "will he be all right? Will he lose his leg? Is he going to die?"—just so many horrible thoughts going through all of our minds at this time that no one spoke.

Nelson's screams of pain and agony echoed not only off the walls of the house but also within our hearts. All of us just standing there helpless and unable to do anything for the poor child to ease his discomfort. Aunt Peggy arrived on horseback with her black medical bag within fifteen minutes of discovering Nelson's injuries. The boys arrived back at Eli's farm about ten minutes later, exhausted from their task of summoning the local doctor. Aunt Peggy first gave Nelson a mixture to drink made from twigs and bark of the willow tree to help to ease his pain then went about cleaning and dressing the burns. When done, Nelson's leg was completely wrapped in soft white bandages. The extent of Nelson's injuries will not become apparent for several days, but for now, he was to stay well-hydrated, continue to take his pain medicine, and keep off his leg until Aunt Peggy returned in the morning.

Word spread quickly about the fire, and before the sun started to set, several of the local men stopped by to offer any help that Eli might need. Eli's response was the same: "Please pray for my son and his quick recover." Some of the men said that they would return in the morning to help with the milking and feeding of Eli's animals. The idea to lessen the burden of tending to his farm will allow Eli and Sarah to both assist Nelson in any way they can.

Just before dark, we arrived back at our farm. After checking on our livestock, we went inside our house. No one seemed to want a big supper, so we had some bread and jelly for our evening meal. The uncertainty of Nelson's condition left us all feeling uneasy. It was James who said that the beauty of the rainbow was quickly lost because of the fire. Albert quickly jumped in saying that it could have been so much worse had the lightning struck the barn or even their house. That was a chilling thought as this accident could very well have happened on any farm here in our valley.

The embers that I had earlier removed from the firebox had fared well in the kettle, and we used them to restart our fire, adding some dry wood from our woodshed. We will need the hot coals in the morning to prepare our breakfast and start our day with a cup of nice hot mint tea. One less thing to do in the morning to get our day moving along.

We again found ourselves seeking relief from the book of Psalms. Why do terrible things happen to nice people? After sharing our inner thoughts, we ended our group reading session tonight with a special prayer for Nelson. What more can one do as Nelson's recovery is now in the able hands of our Lord?

As I lay in my bed going over the day's events, I couldn't help but think of Isaac and if the storm passed over where he is being held prisoner. Are they sheltered from the storm? Was it as frightening in his area as it was in ours? Then thoughts of Nelson and all the painful days that lay ahead of him. All so very sad and frightful. I said one final prayer for Nelson's full recovery then drifted off into a well-deserved state of sleep.

Chapter 28

Nelson seems to be recovering from his burns and getting stronger by the day. Youth was on his side as he seemed to come through the entire ordeal with few problems. His leg is a bit stiff, but Aunt Peggy thinks that it will eventually return to full mobility, just give it some time. The corncrib has been rebuilt in the same spot as the one that burned. Eli and his other children have started filling the crib with dried ears of corn to use as feed for their livestock through this upcoming winter. Luckily, the fire was late summer, and not much of last year's corn remained in the crib to be lost to the blaze.

The feel of fall is in the air. Crops are turning brown and awaiting their turn to be harvested. My boys are figuring things out for themselves and taking the steps, as best they can, to begin preparing the farm for yet another long winter. Over this past year, I have enjoyed watching all of our children grow not only physically but also spiritually. They have formed a special bond with each other that no one dare think of penetrating. Since Isaac marched off to war, we have become a very close-knit family. We have all leaned on one another from time to time. This is when I miss Isaac the most. Here I go again, me on one of my pity trips when only God knows what Isaac is going through. At least I have a roof over my head, food on my table, my children by my side, and my church to fall back upon. What does Isaac have? A cold, damp rat-infested ship in the middle of the East River! Oh Lord, please make this end soon, not just for our family but for all families torn apart by war.

It seems like a new baby was not in God's plans for William and Helena Hoppock. The little one arrived much too soon and died shortly after his birth. There is not much anyone can do for babies not ready to enter this world. So sad for everyone in the Hoppock family, especially Helena who did everything right to bring this wee one to full term. We all attended the graveside service in the Mansfield Woodhouse Cemetery earlier this week. Isaac and I were so fortunate that all of our children were born healthy, even the unexpected joy of our identical twin boys! Joseph and James now make a game of people not knowing which one they are talking to. There are days that they fool me as well. The little devils think it is funny and actually enjoy tricking people. This is all in good spirited fun, so I allow them to play this harmless ruse.

Sarah, the girls, and I have greatly improved our weaving skills. We are creating a blanket that actually has taken on the proper shape and close weave of a warm and inviting coverlet. It has taken us many hours to reach this step in the process, but we are determined to use our fine wool and make a blanket for each member of our families. I have to say that it is very rewarding to watch as our yarn turns into a not only a wonderful, but also colorful, creation. We can only make one blanket at a time, but we share in the process, and this helps move the work along much quicker.

In two days, we will all be paying a visit to the Harte farm. Last week, Lewis Harte injured his right arm, and it is now in a sling. Most of his fall harvest and fieldwork has been completed, but the neighborhood is going to his homestead to help shell his corn and prepare it for the gristmill. Helping someone in need is what we are all about. I don't think that any of us could have gotten this far without the help of our family, friends, neighbors, and church. Old Mr. Bryan will be there with his fiddle keeping us entertained as we go about our work. We might even get a few brave couples that do a do-si-do or two. Square-dancing is so much fun; just wish Isaac was here to dance with me. To dance with another would be so unfair to Isaac that I would never consider the thought of it. The girls and I baked several little honey cakes to take along and share. There will be plenty of other baked goodies made by the other women for all of us to share also. It will be fun and something for both Eli and my family to look forward to. Once the corn has been shelled, Martin Convey has offered to help Lewis get it to the gristmill for grinding. One more thing checked off Lewis's never-ending to-do list.

CHAPTER 29

Sonny again came to our rescue. This year, the firewood cutting, slaughter and processing the pigs went along so much easier. I think that Sonny is beginning to feel more at ease being around all of us. However, he still would not come into the house to eat his meals, so the children ate outside with him. My children adore this man with the huge heart and kind demeanor. I so wish that he and his family could come and live with us, where they could be free to do as they wish. Sonny could work for us, and we would pay him for his toil. This is all just a dream, as Sonny and his family belong to Howard Van Horne, and even the thought of buying their freedom is so far out of our reach that we are wasting time just thinking this way. I guess giving him and his family food, wood, and clothing is about all we are legally allowed to do. The thought of slavery just turns my stomach! Howard Van Horne, you are a rotten, evil old man. Someday you will rot in hell for your sins of taking freedom away from another human being.

Eli stopped by this afternoon with news that a prisoner swap is about to take place. A sergeant from the Continental Army was again staying at the Mineral Springs Hotel attempting to recruit more men to join the cause. Eli spoke with him in great length about Isaac being captured and held on a prison ship in the East River since August 27, 1776. According to this sergeant, the swap is supposed to include prisoners from those ships, as the men being held there are existing in deplorable conditions. A sudden spark of life jumped from deep within my body to my lips. An instant prayer, praising my Lord and savior for just the fact of bringing the prison ships to the attention of the army gave me newfound joy. Could it be? Will Isaac be one of the lucky men released and allowed to return home to us?

Finally, I was able to calm myself enough to ask Eli when he thought the release might happen. The sergeant believed that it would happen very soon before the snow flies. The children heard my excited voice and gathered around to see what all the joy was about. Eli spoke for me as I was far too excited to think for myself. The children were told that this might happen, and that it was reasonable to believe that their father could be one of the prisoners traded for a British soldier. According to the sergeant, letters were being written to the families of those men soon to be released, informing them of when this trade will happen and when to expect their loved one's arrival back to their homes and families.

After Eli left for his home, the children and I just sat around the table overjoyed but cautious at the same time. Could this really be true? Are our prayers being answered? Will Isaac soon come walking through our door, and we will be a complete family again? We all decided that we deserved to take a leap of faith and believe that God had answered our prayers and that Isaac will be coming home soon. With that said, we decided to make a list of things that we all wanted to do before Isaac walked through our door. With this newfound energy, the things that we placed on the list soon filled the slate. Preparing for his arrival is foremost in our minds. Special meals of favorite foods and desserts; a nice plump bed with lots of coverlets and pillows; stacks of firewood close to the door; what to and what not to ask him about his time away from us—just so many things to consider, and all so very exciting. We will start working on completing the list first thing in the morning. Tonight, we will read from our Bible and praise the Lord and be optimistic that this will really happen.

After the children were safe and secure in their beds, I found myself in deep thought. Will Isaac be the same man who went away to fight for our country, or a stranger to all of us when he returns back to his farm? In all likelihood, he will be suffering from the horrors of war. How can anyone see people physically and mentally damaged by war and not suffer themselves? Just the mere fact that he was forced to spend all that time on a prison ship will lay heavy upon his heart and mind. But who can I discuss my fears with? Who will understand my concerns and offer some kind advice? I know of a man who lives just on the other side of our mountain who fought in the French and Indian War back in the late 1750s into the 1760s. George Brown, known as the Captain, is often seen in town, so perhaps I can ask Eli to go and speak with him. I cannot as a woman be so bold as to strike up a conversation with a strange man, let alone inside a saloon, so maybe Eli will do it for me? But then, Isaac and Eli always refer to the Captain as an old knock-kneed sac of hot air. They claim he has his own seat in the saloon of the Mineral Springs Hotel. Any new face that ventures into the Mineral Springs Hotel falls prey to the Captain who will go on and on about his war stories. Yes, he did fight in the French and Indian War and was a member of the Jersey Blues, obtaining the rank of captain. Most of his fighting was in faraway places, including upstate New York and Montreal, Canada.

Here in New Jersey, the Indian raids were happening less and less along our side of the Delaware. All we really got out of all of this was more increases in our taxes to help pay for the war. We can thank old King George for all of this, just as he is responsible for this horrible War for Independence we are now involved in. Should I ask Eli to speak with the Captain, or should I not ask Eli? This back-and-forth "yes, ask him, no don't ask him" was causing me additional stress that I did not need at this time. I picked up my Bible and read the story of Ruth, one of my favorite stories. I could feel myself beginning to relax and finally blew out my candle and drifted off to sleep.

CHAPTER 30

It has been almost three weeks since Eli relayed the news of a pending prisoner release from the sergeant at the Mineral Springs. After sleeping on my idea of asking Eli to speak with the Captain, I decided that I would not put any additional pressure on him. I know that Eli does not care for the man and that he would be uncomfortable seeking answers to my personal questions. I also know that if I did ask, Eli would have begrudgingly honored my request. There will be many more requests placed upon Eli when his brother returns home from war. Those requests will be eagerly accepted by Eli and fulfilled willingly.

We attended the Harvest Festival at church this past week. As Pieter directed Moses and our wagon toward the Mansfield Woodhouse Church, we passed along the side of the church cemetery. Suddenly, as if on key, everyone became silent. There near the inside of the stonewall, close to the entrance into the cemetery, were two newly dug graves. These empty graves were filled with layers of straw and branches, then topped off with more limbs and branches to keep them from caving in. The content of the holes was piled close by and covered over with additional straw and branches forming a protective cover.

I had forgotten that with winter soon approaching, it was the custom to prepare for the inevitable death of perhaps a family member, friend, or neighbor. Cold weather causes the ground to freeze solid, and digging a grave is no easy task. Preparing a few burial sites allows for a proper resting place for those poor souls that have gone on to meet their maker during the winter months. Even so, it was an eerie sight and caused unnerving feelings. Attempting to ease the fear of my children, I began to recite the Lord's Prayer aloud; everyone immediately joined in. Thinking back to that moment, it was strange to pray over empty graves, but one never knows if they will be the one to pass on, spending eternity in one of those prepared resting places. Silently I prayed that my family would remain safe and healthy, outsmarting the grim reaper.

Eli and Sarah are doing all they can to keep our hopes up that someday soon we will receive our letter from the army telling us of Isaac's release and when to expect him back home with us. Eli continues to visit the Mineral Springs three times a week just after the stages passes through. My mother used to tell me and my siblings that a watched pot never boils, meaning keep yourself occupied, and time will pass quicker. We have been busy and have completed all the things on our lists in preparation for Isaac's arrival. The boys have the barns and outbuilding clean and orderly. The amount of firewood that they have filled the woodshed with should carry us well into next spring. The girls and I have cleaned our home from top to bottom and then bottom to top. The waiting to hear anything about Isaac has caused all of us to become anxious, feeling as if a powder keg is ready to blow at any minute. As we sit down to take our meals, we discuss our feelings and openly talk about our fears and anxiety all the while praying for Isaac's safe return. This waiting game is growing old very quickly.

CHAPTER 31

We had a light dusting of snow last night. Not much, but just enough to cover the ground with a thin coating of the white stuff. It appears that the cold weather has settled in for the duration of the winter season. Our animals all have nice thick coats to help them endure the cold. When the weather becomes bitter, they will no longer spend as much time out in the paddock or barnyard. The boys turn the animals out for a few hours each day if the sun is shining brightly upon us to give them a chance to move about. Winter is not my favorite season, as most of it is spent inside the house trying to keep warm. Bundling up just to make a trip to the outhouse is not my idea of a good time.

Pieter and Albert were returning to the house after completing their afternoon chores when they noticed a horse and rider quickly approaching our farm. They immediately recognized the rider as their Uncle Eli. Both boys burst through the front door of the house excitedly announcing that Uncle Eli was coming. It took only seconds for all of us to step out on the front porch to greet him. As he dismounted his horse, he was waving a letter in his left hand. Could this be? Is this the letter from the army telling us that Isaac was a free man? Eli handed me the letter, and without hesitation, I tore it open and read it aloud. It was our long-awaited letter, and it confirmed that Isaac had been traded for a British soldier a few days ago. Isaac was being tended to by an army doctor, and they expected him to be ready for honorable discharge from the United States Army on or about November 21.

Suddenly, I felt light-headed and thought that I would faint. The boys brought me back into the house and seated me at the table. Tears of joy streamed down all of our faces, including Eli's who throughout this entire ordeal remained a strong driving force. I handed the letter to Eli to finish reading as at this time I was completely overwhelmed with so many joyous feelings that I felt incapable of digesting the important details that followed. The letter continued to read that we could expect Isaac to arrive back at our farm about November 23. He would return by wagon from Elizabeth Town to our home.

Oh my goodness, today is November 20; Isaac could be heading home within days! As Eli was readying to leave for home, I told him it would be fine to spread the joyous news amongst the neighborhood. He said that he would be more than pleased to share the wonderful news with anyone he may encounter in the next few days. After he left and I arose from the table, I felt as if I had wings on feet and I was gliding through the house. Dare I outwardly show my joy, or should I wait until my husband is here safely home with his family?

The rest of the day was spent tending to any detail left undone. I decided that a nice pot of chicken soup with lots of carrots and dumplings would be a welcome treat for anyone. I will make more than enough to share with Eli and his family when they come to call. The boys said that they would prepare a chicken for me after they had completed their chores in the morning. The girls will help make the dumplings. I wanted all of the children involved in the preparation of welcoming their father back home.

Later in the evening, after our reading lesson, we spent time reminiscing about the months Isaac has been away. Yes, it has been difficult, but I believe that we are going to have many more difficult days ahead once he returns home. We cannot be so complacent to believe that he will be unscathed by all that has taken place. After all, we have suffered as well, not nearly like him, but we each have our own nightmares in need of banishing from our memory. With his return, we will probably be able to put those nightmares to rest, but for Isaac, it will be a lifetime before he can, if ever, find peace of mind. We need our faith now more than ever. It is God who will see us through this painful yet joyful reunion that is about to take place. It is God who will keep us together and help us find a way to work through all of our heartaches.

CHAPTER 32

Praying, pacing, fretting, praying, pacing, and fretting, over and over again for the past two days—that seemed to be all that we were capable of, aside from our daily chores to keep the farm running. Finally, just after noon on November 23, Catherina saw a large wagon being pulled by four horses traveling along our lane toward our farm. The excitement was so jubilant but somber as well, if that is even possible. As the wagon came closer, I could see that it was Conestoga wagon handsomely painted with a bright white linen cover. Two soldiers were atop in the driving position handling the four huge draft horses. It had been years since I observed anything like this since we left Doylestown and built a new life here near the frontier. My family and I have often seen this type of wagon, as this is built for heavy-duty work and a common sight here on the edge of the frontier, but not one so grand.

The wagon turned onto the short path toward our home and came to a stop in our front yard. I did not see Isaac, and fear started to take over my joy. Another soldier came toward the front of the wagon and peered out at all of us, giving us a wave and smile. I felt a bit of relief, but where was Isaac? The two soldiers who were handling the team climbed down from the wagon and greeted us. We were told that Isaac was resting on a cot in the back of the wagon and would be helped down from the rear. By this time, we were joined by Eli who just arrived on horseback; he had also observed the magnificent wagon headed toward our home and came to assist, if needed. I was frozen in place, not sure what to think or do. Where was Isaac? Why hadn't he at least waved to us as the wagon pulled onto the short path that leads to our house? Was I overreacting or just being practical? At this moment we had come so close to having our Isaac back, yet I felt so far removed from what was taking place.

The two soldiers went to the back of the wagon with Eli in tow. A ladder-like set of steps was placed behind the wagon to assist Isaac in climbing out and down to the ground. Oh my goodness, this man cannot be my husband: this is an old man, bent over and far too skinny to be my Isaac! Panic and fear were quickly taking over my emotions. Dear God, please help me get through this! Dare I even hug this poor downtrodden man? Then I saw it; the smile that went from ear to ear. It was our Isaac, and he was alive and grateful to be back home with his family! I rushed to his side to take one of his arms and help him to porch. Eli took the other arm, and we gently guided him to the porch steps. Tears were running down our faces, joyful tears, tears of relief, and smiles on our faces.

The children at first were just as frightened and unsure as I, but now gathered around him, all talking at once. We got Isaac safely into the house and in his seat at the end of the table. Eli asked the soldiers if we could offer them some hot soup, a cup of tea, or just a cup of water. They politely refused, saying that they had to begin their return trip to Elizabeth Town, as more men like Isaac needed to get back to their families too. We graciously thanked them and then bid them goodbye. Our shy Catherina stepped forward and gave each soldier a hug and tearfully thanked them for bringing her papa back home. Then, just as quickly as they arrived, they were gone.

Now what do I do? How can I act as if nothing has happened when it is so obvious that the man sitting at our table has just been to hell and back? I prepared everyone a nice cup of hot tea, and we sat around our table. Slowly, the tension began to disappear as conversation about how were we doing and how the children had grown made us feel as if we were a family again. After serving the tea, I ladled bowls of chicken soup to feast upon as we continued to make easy talk around the table. Isaac was pleased with the soup and seemed to really enjoy it but ate very little. He said the army doctor told him it would be awhile before his appetite returned. For months, he had been given the bare minimum required for one to exist while on the prison ship. We decided that perhaps by eating several small meals a day, it would help him get his strength and appetite back sooner. Eli stayed for a few hours, then left, promising to return in the morning. Now we were alone as a family, and I knew full well that sooner or later, he would be asking about his beloved horse Nellie. Please, dear God, not now.

After a short time passed, the children went outside to tend to their afternoon chores. Isaac and I would be alone for at least forty-five minutes, perhaps an hour. Now was the time to gently as possible break the news that Nellie had passed while he was away. Searching for words, somehow I managed to tell Isaac about the boys finding Nellie's lifeless body under her favorite tree. I told him that I was sorry but felt that he needed to know. Also, I told him about Jake Beerman loaning us the use of his mule until Isaac was back and able to select another horse or mule himself. I could see the pain in his eyes, but he said that he fully understood my need in telling him about Nellie before the news came to him as a complete surprise. I told him that the boys managed to run the farm, taking responsibility seriously and did a great job.

We shared a good laugh when I relayed my story about the shearing of the sheep and how terrible they looked after we completed the job. I also shared with him about Mr. Van Horne's helper Sonny saving the day by helping us prepare our farm for the cold months these past two falls. I believe that all of this conversation helped to get Isaac back in spirit to his farm. I also believe that he has many things that he will share with me when he is ready, and I will not pressure him until he is truly ready. There will also be things that he will never share, just kept inside his heart, never to be released. Then Isaac asked if I would mind if he took a nap in our bed. He said that he was exhausted and needed to just close his eye for a short time. I helped him into our bedroom and assisted him into bed. Once in our bed, the smile that came across his face was heartwarming. I could tell that he was enjoying the comfort of his own bed. After a few more minutes of chitchat, Isaac drifted off to sleep.

The children returned from their chores, and we tiptoed about the house so as not to awaken Isaac. They were a bit concerned for their father, but I explained that lots of rest would be one of the most important things to help him heal quicker. We took turns just checking on him and found him to be in a deep sleep.

We had our daily Bible reading and joyfully lifted our prayers up to the Lord for returning Isaac back home. We prayed for all of the men awaiting release, and their families too. We retired for the evening at about seven o'clock. Isaac was still sleeping comfortably, and I did not disturb him. I left a shaded candle burning in the center of the kitchen table just in case Isaac awoke and at first didn't recognize his surroundings. For the first time in over a year and a half, my husband was sleeping by my side. Tears began to run down my cheeks. Tears of happiness that Isaac had finally come back home to us. But mixed in with the happiness were tears of concern and fear that my husband would not be the same man who rode his horse out our lane on April 29, 1776, and off to war.

I still find it difficult to understand his need to fight for his country to make this a better place for his children. There seems no end in sight for a peaceful resolution to this horrible war. Both King George's army and the Continental Army seem to crisscross New Jersey in pursuit of one another more often lately, and the battles continue. Please, dear God, just make it stop—end the killing of one another, and let us live the rest of our lives in peace and brotherhood.

CHAPTER 33

It has been six weeks since Isaac's return to us. Christmas has come and gone and as we begin to rebuild our lives in 1778, let it be a much kinder year for all.

Isaac is slowly getting his strength back. The rash called scurvy that covered his body caused by the lack of good food and vegetables when he was held captive has all but disappeared. Aunt Peggy has visited with us several times just checking on Isaac's progress. She provided Isaac with a mixture of healing herbs to stir into hot water and drink daily. She also provided her miracle pain reliever—a liquid mixture of willow tree bark and twigs, which has helped with the severe back pain caused by pleurisy. Aunt Peggy said the constant cough was caused by the dampness in the prison ship and is responsible for the pleurisy. It will take some time, but with lots of rest, water, and good food, it will eventually go away. She also told him to stay out of the barns and cold weather. This is proving to be a bit more difficult than I expected, as he is antsy and wants to jump right back in and do his share of the work.

The boys are wonderful and are fighting him tooth and nail, giving him no excuse to think he has to help them. They keep telling him to rest until spring, which will be here before we know it. Begrudgingly, he is listening. Pieter and Albert are also continuing to step up and tend to the fire during these dreadfully cold nights. They take turns trading places every other night. Whoever is in charge of keeping the fireplace well-stocked with logs so we have sufficient heat throughout the night drinks several cups of water just before going to bed. About halfway through the night, they will awaken to the call of nature, and after tending to this call, they put more wood on the fire. In the morning, the house is a bit chilly as the fire is again dying down, but within a half hour of placing more wood on the fire, we are comfy cozy once more. I offered to take a turn, but the boys politely dismissed my suggestion. Their father's request to help was met with a flat-out no.

Isaac has enjoyed the visits from many of our neighbors and church friends. These visits are what is keeping him sane and able to stay in the house where he belongs until he is healed. However, our favorite and most reliable visitor is Eli. Eli comes by each day, if just for a few minutes, to check on all of us. Sarah and children have visited as well, bringing some of her special apple-filled cookies to share. They say that laughter is the best medicine, and we all seem to be doing our share of laughing, and it does make the soul feel lighter.

The snowfall has been constant with anywhere, from a dusting to a few inches every day. It seems like it has been winter forever, but we are not even halfway through January. Should we go anywhere, it will be by sleigh, as the wheels of the wagon will only bog down any attempt to travel through the three feet of snow that is now covering the ground. Once we do make it out our path and onto the lane, travel gets a bit better as the snow on the busier roads has become packed down. The boys are trying to keep up with their milk and egg deliveries but must be especially careful not to travel too fast and cause the sleigh to tip over on its side.

We all know that boys will be boys, and they tend to seek the thrill of quickly gliding through the snow without much thought of being dumped into a snowbank. So far, I have gotten no complaints of cracked eggs being delivered to our customers, so they are being cautious, at least until their deliveries are completed. What happens after that is anyone's guess. No sense in questioning any of them, as they will stick together like glue with the details of their trips into town being quite mundane. I must say that the smiles on their faces tell a much different story, and I am sure that they are being mischievous. As long as Moses, Mule, and the sleigh are fine and the boys return with no broken bones, let them have some fun!

I am unable to keep my house running on a schedule, as I do the laundry when the weather allows me. During the winter, I do the wash indoors with water being carried from the brook into the house to be heated over the fire. Filling the wash and rinse tubs is a real chore, and I need to be careful about getting too much water on the floorboards. After, I lug the wet laundry outside, placing it over the paddock rails in hopes that the sun will stay out long enough to dry it. Most of the time, I bring the clothing back into the house frozen stiff as a board. In warmer weather, I do the laundry outside, heating the water over an open fire near the brook making the task so much easier. Bath time, that is a whole different story. Dragging the huge tub into the house near the blazing fire, setting up blanket screens for privacy around the tub, getting the water from the brook, bringing it into the house, and then heating it takes a lot of time.

Then ever so often, we need to empty the tub and begin the process all over again. Sometimes, we melt buckets of snow we retrieve just off the front porch, but a full bucket of snow hardy equals a quarter of the bucket of water when melted. This is why we sponge bathe most of the time, taking a bath just once a month. If we are experiencing a snowstorm or freezing rain, we hold off our bathes until we get better weather, whenever that may be. In the warmer weather, we often bathe in the brook.

CHAPTER 34

We have survived yet another winter. The March winds are helping to dry up the muddy roads. We can still experience snow and freezing rain for yet another six weeks, but we feel hopeful and ready for balmy weather.

Isaac is slowly recovering but is still not his old self. Aunt Peggy stopped by this past Friday and suggested that perhaps Isaac should take a few hot bath treatments from the Mineral Springs. The Mineral Springs Hotel and Baths are well-known, and this is why we have a stagecoach stopping at the hotel traveling from Easton to Elizabeth Town on Mondays, Wednesdays, and Fridays. On Tuesdays and Thursdays, there is a stage that comes through from Elizabeth Town and continues on to Easton. From Easton, there are many different stagecoach routes carrying people to places like Philadelphia, Hazelton, and several other cities throughout the colonies. Many people visit the Mineral Springs to seek comfort from the hot mineral baths or showers the hotel provides. Local folks visit also and gather the mineral water to take home to drink throughout the week. Much to my surprise, Isaac agreed to try a few treatments. Eli will take him by wagon as Isaac is still too weak to walk or travel on the back of one of Eli's horses. Eli has already made the necessary arrangements for three mineral bath treatments beginning midweek.

Yesterday, we were all able to attend church. It was wonderful to be outside in the fresh air. It was a bit chilly, but we wrapped up in blankets to and from church. This is the first that Isaac has left the farm since his return in November. The trip was tiring for him, but he really enjoyed the company of our friends and the ability to worship God in our church. We also witnessed the baptisms of two new members of our church community. The Carter families' little girl Christine and the Matthews families' daughter who was born in early February named Ruth. Both babies were alert and seemed not to be bothered by the "pass the baby" routine they were forced to endure. After all, who doesn't like holding an infant? Children grow so quickly, and having the opportunity to hug a little one is such a joy. It made me think how quickly our children have grown. Pieter is now almost sixteen.

I shudder at the thought that he will soon be seeking a partner to share the rest of his life with. I truly hope that he finds someone who brings him the happiness that Isaac and I have found. After our church family enjoyed some cake and punch in celebration of the baptisms of these two little ones, we left for home. Eli, Sarah, and their family left the same time. Eli said that he would come by on Wednesday about noon to accompany Isaac to the Mineral Springs Hotel for his treatment. The rest of the day was spent just enjoying our family. We again played "guess what I'm talking about." We even sat on the porch in the sunlight for a short time, taking in the changes to the earth that spring brings. The skunk cabbage is beginning to pop up near the brook, a sure sign that warmer weather is just around the corner.

CHAPTER 35

Eli arrived at our farm just past noon with his smaller wagon. I was a bit concerned when Isaac took his seat next to Eli on the top of the wagon. I was hoping that perhaps Isaac would stretch out in the back of the wagon, but it wasn't so. Being married for all these years to this man has taught me to keep some of my suggestions to myself, as from a man's point of view, my suggestions are considered nagging. So as difficult as it was, I kept my thoughts to myself. Eli said that he would drop Isaac off at the hotel and run some errands in town. He asked if we needed anything from Sarah McCullough's store, to which I replied no thank you. Then they were off to the Mineral Springs and a hot mineral bath for Isaac to relax in.

The wagon returned about three o'clock, and the men climbed down and came into house. Both men accepted a cup of tea, and Eli visited for a short time, allowing me to catch up on family news. About thirty minutes later, Eli got up from his seat and was ready to head back to his farm, telling Isaac that he would return on Friday to take him for his second treatment.

After Eli left, Isaac began to tell me just how wonderful his hot mineral bath was. The hot water actually relieved some of his pain, and for the moment, he was feeling better than he had in months. Isaac said that his male attendant was named Amos and couldn't have been more helpful. Amos arrived at the Mineral Springs Hotel late last fall with his wife, Jasmine, and daughter Ruby. They are living in one of the small cottages across the road from the hotel. Another older woman who also resides in yet another cottage minds Rudy and two other small children while their mothers work as female attendants at the hotel.

Amos said that he is from Carteret, where his family still operates a general store in the black section of town. The couple became very concerned when the British Army took control of Fort Lee and feared that they would soon take control of their town as well. They made the tough decision to leave their family behind and move out into the countryside where for the moment things appear to be calmer. Someday Amos wants to start a business of his own, but that is still a dream that is a long way off. The rest of the evening, Isaac appeared to be in a much better mood. The restlessness that he had been experiencing since his return home in November disappeared. His spirit seemed to have been lifted, and he acted like the husband and father we knew before he went off to war. I thanked the Lord for this wonderful change in his personality and prayed that it would last.

CHAPTER 36

Eli and Isaac returned from the Mineral Springs about three o'clock this afternoon. This was Isaac's last treatment, and he said that he is starting to feel like the old Isaac. We discussed the possibility that he continue to take the mineral baths for a few more weeks, even if he takes two treatments a week instead of three. Much to our surprise, Isaac agreed as long as he could take himself to his scheduled mineral baths. After much coaxing from both Isaac and Eli, I agreed as long as he went by wagon, as I felt it was too soon for him to travel on horseback alone.

The two men also discussed looking for a new horse for Isaac. The thought that perhaps Jake Beerman would consider selling us Mule was considered. Mule and Moses have become good companions, and we thought it would be to our benefit if they were allowed to remain together. Isaac will then take his time to find another horse that he feels comfortable with. Even though Isaac was away from the farm all of those months, the boys were able to turn a profit by selling the lambs, piglets, wool, and grains. Taking some of this money to purchase a new horse for Isaac will not only give him a lift in spirit but help ease his pain of losing Nellie. The men discussed several local breeders that were worth checking out. But early next week, Isaac will visit with Jake and see if he agrees to allow us to purchase his mule. If not, we will be looking for both a work animal and a riding horse.

After Eli left, I spoke with Isaac about purchasing a horse for each of our older boys. Both boys have worked hard to keep this farm running while their father was away. Also, so very soon, sooner than I wish, Pieter will be wooing a young lady and in need of getting to and from her home. Albert, well, I hope he takes a few more years to figure out the attraction between lads and lasses. Much to my surprise, Isaac said that he would give it considerable thought. The two additional horses need not be as grand as the one I hope Isaac selects for himself but will provide our boys with some freedom to get around the valley easily. When Joseph and James become of age, we can do the same for them, but thankfully, we have some time before needing to attend to that detail!

With the weather slowly warming, it will be only a matter of time before Isaac returns to his daily schedule and wants to prepare the fields for planting. He seems to be doing so much better, and continuing with the mineral baths will help get him back to where he was before he left to go off to war. The boys are lecturing their father on the need to take it easy and not jump in with both feet. Isaac is actually heeding their advice and has visited the barn during the afternoon milking and feeding without lifting a finger. I am sure this is eating away at him as he is the type of man who wants to constantly be doing something, but for the time being, he is watching and not doing. Last evening, Pieter, Albert, and Isaac went over what crops to plant and which fields to plant them in. Isaac is allowing the boys to continue to make many of the decision for this year's planting. He also seems pleased with their choices and open to new ideas from both boys on how to make planting easier and more efficient. Hearing this conversation between a father and his sons warms my heart.

CHAPTER 37

Today is April 29, 1778, two years to the day when Isaac rode Nellie out our lane and went off to war. In the past two years, we have all grown not only in age but also in our faith. So much has happened in this world that it is difficult to keep up with all of the changes. Some of the changes are good, but most seem to be caused by King George and are not in the best interest of the colonies. I still find it difficult to understand why Isaac felt the need to leave his family and go to war. Since he returned home to us in November, his health has steadily improved. He has gone back to working his farm with the help of his sons.

I believe that he has found a new appreciation for all things big and small. He has not shared much of what he went through, especially while on the prison ship. Perhaps he has shared with his brother Eli, but not with me. I often notice that he is deep in thought and very quiet. Sometimes he just stares off into space, noticing none of his surroundings. I cannot begin to even imagine the horrors that not just Isaac, but all soldiers experienced while away. The only thing that Isaac tells everyone is that war is hell, and all other options need to be explored before embarking on such a dreadful journey. I also know that war has changed Isaac's heart and mind forever.

Late this afternoon, Eli stopped by with some wonderful news; he received a letter from Nelson and Sophia Deremer, Isaac and Eli's parents, informing us that they are coming to visit. Isaac and I have not seen his parents since I went back home to birth Abigail eight years ago. Eli and Sarah have not been in their company for almost seven years. This will be the first time that Nelson and Sophia visit what they call the frontier. They have traveled to Trenton but never any farther north in New Jersey. This is really exciting news for all of us. They will be arriving from Doylestown to Easton next Tuesday and stay over for the night at the Hotel Easton.

In the morning, they will travel on the Easton to Elizabeth Town stage that stops at the Mineral Springs. They plan on visiting until the following Thursday when they will take the stage from the Mineral Springs back to Easton, again stay overnight and then travel back to Doylestown on Friday. They plan on staying with Eli and Sarah, as they have an extra bedroom. When Isaac and I built our home, we designed it with a great room and one-bedroom downstairs and a full loft upstairs. Eli and Sarah planned their home with a great room and two bedrooms downstairs and a full loft upstairs. Had his parents planned on staying with us, we would have had to sleep in the loft, and the boys would have slept in the hay loft in the barn during their stay. This arrangement would have pleased our boys but been rather inconvenient for Isaac as he is still in need of a good night's rest. By staying at Eli's home, no one is uprooted from their bed during their visit. The children are over the moon with the news that their grandparents are coming for a visit.

Sarah and I got together to plan meals and ideas to keep Grandpa and Grandma Deremer entertained. Aside from sharing our evening meals, they will attend church with us on Sunday morning. The Harte family has a hoedown planned for next Thursday that the entire community has been invited to. Lewis Harte said that he wants to thank all the families who stepped up last year and helped in any way to shell his corn and get it to the mill when he injured his arm. The dance starts at six o'clock and will last into the darkness. It seems like the entire valley has been invited, so it should be fun for all. The girls and I plan on making and bringing potato pancakes with souse. Sarah and her daughters will bring mincemeat rounds with brown gravy.

We are sure that Grandma Deremer will have a special recipe that she will want to make and bring along also. All the food is spread out on long tables to be shared by everyone. The variety is astounding, and a little of this and a little of that fills our plates quickly. There will be several kinds of dessert to enjoy after our meal as well. The beverage is almost always provided by the family hosting the event. Mr. Harte said that there will be tea, milk, apple cider, and water for all. Each family brings their own plates, cups, forks, knives, and spoons. Sometimes a place to wash our dishes is provided, but many times, we return home with dirty dishes and wash them up before going to bed for the night. This will be fun for all, and I can dance with my husband to my heart's content!

Isaac visited with Jake Beerman a few days ago and expressed our sincere appreciation for loaning us Mule when we were in need. Isaac then asked if Jake would consider selling Mule to us, as the animal seems to have become a companion for Moses. Jake agreed, stating that he really didn't need another work animal. The men settled on a price, and Isaac bought Mule on the spot. Before leaving, Isaac admired Mr. Beerman's horses and questioned where one could purchase such fine animals. Jake shared the breeder's name along with a good recommendation for the owner of the farm, which was located in German Valley. Later when the children found out that Mule now belonged to us, they were ecstatic and happy that Moses would have a friend forever.

Chapter 38

It has been an unbelievable three weeks. Isaac's parents left for home last Thursday. Their visit with us was wonderful. Both families shared the evening meals together, changing houses to host the meal each evening. Grandpa and Grandma arrived with a large trunk of very special things. Sarah and I each got beautiful beige-colored shawls with fringe trim. Eli and Isaac were each gifted an awl and heavy-duty needles to help them when they need to repair anything leather, even our shoes. Each child from both families got a book. The children were so overjoyed that their excitement stayed with them for the entire visit of their grandparents.

To have their own book was something that was never even thought about, let alone really happen. Some of book titles were *Robinson Crusoe, Gulliver's Travels, Aesop's Fables, Tales of Mother Goose,* and *Catherine the Great.* It was nearly impossible to get the children's noses out of their books! This also presented a bit of head-butting when it came time for our nightly reading lessons, as they wanted to read their new books and not the Bible. They also tried to bring their books to the table at mealtime. We put a quick squash to that idea. Since they each have a book and will probably trade with each other, we set thirty minutes as our nightly reading lesson. This was more of a fact that we need to read our Bible and pray together than depriving them of the newly acquired vices of city life. Underneath, both Isaac and I are overjoyed seeing them so excited and interested in reading. We will probably read a few of their books as well.

We enjoyed the hoedown at the Lewis Harte farm. Elwood and William Bryan, Joshua Roy and Lester Brown fiddled the night away. The food was wonderful, and if one went hungry, it was their own fault. Even Grandpa and Grandma said that they hadn't had that much fun dancing since they were young and just started to enjoying each other's company. It was truly a good time for all. Isaac and I must have danced more than any other couple. The next day, Albert came to Isaac and asked to talk with him alone. The two went for a short walk, and Albert asked his father if he noticed Pieter getting sweet on Lilia Beerman. Isaac said yes and that it wasn't anything that Albert should be worried about. After all, Lilia cannot be responsible for her grandfather's association with the British, and no one knows for sure if Jake is in fact a Tory. Isaac then reassured Albert that Pieter and Lilia enjoyed a few dances and some conversation, which is what lads do when they begin to notice lasses.

Later, Isaac told me about his conversation with Albert, and we both thought that perhaps Albert was jealous of his brother talking and dancing with a young lady instead of standing around with him. I knew it would only be a matter of time before Pieter took a liking to the young ladies. I hope and pray that he chooses wisely when becoming serious with any young lady. We have raised our children to be respectful, God-fearing and grateful people, so I hope these traits stay with them through life's easy and challenging times.

CHAPTER 39

Again, the seasons have slipped by far too quickly. The war rages on with no end in sight. The British moved out of Philadelphia shortly after Isaac's parents returned to their home in Doylestown. After their departure, General Washington appointed Benedict Arnold military governor of the city of Philadelphia. The new headquarters for the British appears to now be in New York. The move was met with a severe battle in the Monmouth area, and the Continental Army showed the redcoats just what we are made of!

A crazy story has made its way to here in Mansfield Woodhouse that a woman named Molly Pitcher manned a cannon and joined in the fight against the British during the Battle of Monmouth Court House. First, this woman brought water to the weary cannoneers, but when her husband was wounded, she took over his position and continued the fight by loading powder and cannonballs into the cannon and firing it herself! Oh my goodness, what a brave woman, as I do not believe I could have stepped forward and fired a cannon even at my enemy. I can only imagine that perhaps there are more heroic stories like this one yet to make its way to northern New Jersey.

Sadly, our troops will again be in need of food and proper clothing. Isaac and Eli discussed the possibility of delivering a wagon of food to our soldiers if they camp for the winter near us. Keeping this in mind, we have saved up any and all extra food to share if we are given the opportunity. The men will keep an ear tuned as to where General Washington will set up his winter encampment, and hopefully, we can do our part and at least provide a meager meal for some of the brave men fighting for our freedom. This season, we planted an extra acre of potatoes, turnips, beets, cabbage, and carrots with the intent of delivering the food to our army. Isaac also had a conversation with the boys about selling only half of this year's piglets and lambs. He suggested that we raise the remainder until late fall when we can butcher them and include some fresh meat for the troops as well. Everyone agreed, and Eli will provide a few heifers from his herd also. The Oxford mines are working full force turning out cannonballs for our troops. But with winter just around the corner, the mines are soon to become idle until we again have milder weather. More and more families here in Sussex County are joining the cause for freedom and doing whatever we can to support our troops.

Isaac, Eli, Pieter, and Albert visited the horse farm suggested by Jake Beerman in German Valley a few weeks back. Isaac fell in love with a very well-mannered mare whom he named Dara, after an old family friend. Dara is four years old and of good breeding stock and seems to be very gentle. After much wheeling and dealing between Isaac, Eli and the breeder, a deal was made for two older mares that were used for breeding purposes only. The two mares were nearing their end of usefulness, so the farmer allowed them to be purchased for farm use only and not to be bred. Both horses had limited training and had to be saddle broken; Isaac and Eli felt that this was something that Sonny, Mr. Van Horne's farmhand, could assist them in doing. Both boys were pleased, excited, and proud about taking on the responsibility of owning their own horse.

Training of the horses started soon after their arrival on our farm with good progress. The boys are now able to saddle up and run errands on horseback. In fact, it seems like we are coming up short on errands for them to run! We have even created a few unnecessary trips into the village just so they can enjoy riding their horses and showing off their newfound freedom to the village folks. However, Isaac has laid down the law that there will be no riding alone after dark, stressing safety in numbers. Traveling alone along dark roads is not safe for the rider or the horse. Recently, highwaymen robbed a man on horseback near Quarrytown. They took the horse and all of his possession that he carried with him. The man managed to walk back to his home with a nasty bump on his head and empty pockets. As of yet, the horse has not been found and is probably miles away, never to be seen again.

Sarah, the girls, and I have completed our sixth blanket. With each blanket, the process becomes easier, and the blankets lovelier. Each family now has three completed blankets to enjoy for all our toil! We are also busy quilting and find that this is a project that we can take with us when visiting friends. Lizzy Bryan just finished a star quilt; pieces of fabric are stitched together to form a star design, then several stars are joined together to make the blanket top. Later, the top is matched with a bottom piece and then filled with stuffing, and everything is then sewed together. Her designs are absolutely beautiful, and her skill amazes me. She is also a very talented dressmaker, and that skill has many women seeking her out to make a once-in-a-lifetime dress for a special occasion.

This past Sunday, we had a pleasant surprise when we attended services at the Mansfield Woodhouse Church. Amos, Jasmine, and Ruby came to worship with us. Isaac had invited Amos several times to come and join us in worshiping God. Everyone seemed to welcome the family with open arms. I believe it was a bit uncomfortable for Amos, as men and women are seated across from each other, not side-by-side. In fact, our church has two doors on the front; the one on the left is for men to enter the sanctuary, the one on the right is for women and children to enter the sanctuary as well.

Male children up to the age of nine years stay with their mother or female guardian along the north side of the church. After they turn ten, they sit with the men of the congregation along the south side of the church. I often find this arrangement strange, as a husband and wife cannot sit beside each other. I am not sure of just who created such a custom, but I'm guessing that when the younger couples sit together, the closeness could cause a distraction, and then they do not pay attention to the message being delivered by the pastor.

Anyway, Amos and his family are just lovely people and a joy to be around. One couldn't help but notice that Ruby is a beautiful child; her clothing gives away the secret that she is not from this area, as the fabric is of fine quality. Her parents are equally attractive, well-dressed, speak eloquently, and seem to make a nice couple. I recall Isaac saying that someday Amos wants to start his own business. I am not sure what type of trade he has in mind, but he appears to carry himself as that of a successful businessman. I do hope that they will continue to worship with us and find their niche here in Mansfield. Moving from the city to such a remote place as this valley takes a lot of adjustment—which I can tell you for sure!

CHAPTER 40

So far, this January 1779 is proving to be dreadfully cold. Late this past December, Isaac sent a letter to the Continental Army in Morris Town asking where the troops would be camping for winter. Isaac explained that the people of Mansfield Woodhouse had extra food that was planted for the purpose of sharing with the men, and the food needed to be delivered. A reply was returned quickly, and arrangements were put in place. Ten soldiers from the Continental Army arrived with four Conestoga wagons just before the snow started falling. Isaac, Eli, and many of our local men loaded three of the Conestoga wagons with vegetables, apples, venison, elk, beef, lamb, pork, blankets, and warm outer clothing. The fourth wagon was loaded with hay and oats for the military animals.

The caravan left Mansfield Woodhouse very early on January 10, but not until the soldiers, horses, wagons, and cargo were blessed by Pastor Carson. The army delivered the supplies to General Washington's winter encampment at Valley Forge, Pennsylvania. Three wagons of food are just a mere drop in a bucket, but every little bit will help and show our troops that we do really care. The entire valley jumped in and made this endeavor a real success. The men spent many hours hunting on Scotts Mountain to provide the venison and elk. The women were busy knitting hats, scarves, mittens, and socks for the men. We were even able to have a shoe collection where a few dozen worn but still useful pairs of men's shoes were also donated for the cause. Everyone agreed that we would plant extra food in the spring, and if this rotten war is raging on next winter, we will provide more wagons of food and supplies for our troops.

I heard gossip that Isaac and Eli picked up at the Mineral Springs Hotel that Benedict Arnold is living it up in Philadelphia.

Actually living very extravagantly by anyone's terms. He has become infatuated with a young lady named Peggy Shippen. Unfortunately, Miss Shippen is the daughter of Judge Shippen, who has family members that are die-hard Loyalist. This family is in total support of the Crown and British Army. The Shippen family is related to the owners of the Oxford Iron Mines located just miles from Mansfield Woodhouse. The Oxford Mines manufacture cannonballs for the Continental Army, so I'm guessing this branch of the family are not Loyalists? One has to wonder just why such a great war hero of the Continental Army would allow himself to get sweet on a young lady from a powerful family of Tories. Gosh, General Arnold fought against the British in many battles, almost dying from his injuries during the Battle of Saratoga in New York state. No sense in wondering, just stay far away from our valley!

The Indians recently relocated a large portion of their village about a mile upstream along the Pohatcong Creek. The constant demand for firewood caused them to travel farther away from their village, so they have now moved closer to a steady supply of wood. With this move, they are now nearer to our little village, and the Lenape have constructed several of their cone-shaped wigwams and longhouses. Some folks are unhappy about them setting up camp about a mile and a half from us, but for the most part, the Lenape tribe keeps to themselves. Strange, as these people were here long before us but are treated poorly by many of our citizens. Our family has always tried to treat them with kindness and gladly shares when we have an overabundance of fruit and vegetables.

The Indians are very careful so as not to infringe upon our farms and are looking to just live in solitude, keeping to themselves. They plant their fields of corn, squash, and beans and kill the deer and elk only when they are in need of meat. Aunt Peggy often visits with them to share herbal treatments and ways they both tend to their sick. In fact, it was the Lenape that constructed what they call a sweat lodge that they use for cleansing and curing their ailments. Red-hot stones are gathered and placed in a small hut; water is poured over these stones causing steam to form and surround the person, in turn making them sweat. It is believed that the sickness or evil spirit is sweated out of the body after sitting in the hut. Then the person is either doused with cold water or plunged into a nearby stream to close the pores. They then wrap themselves in a blanket and stay near the fire to dry and rest. I can surely understand how this could make a person feel better because after taking the mineral bath treatments at the Mineral Springs Hotel, Isaac felt so much better and experienced less pain.

I must say that I am not fond of the Lenape custom for remembering those who have passed away, but they probably snub their noses at some of our traditions as well. I have heard that when one of their people die, old or young, the name dies with them. The Indians do not say that person's name ever again because it would bring sadness to the family. I cannot tell you how often I speak of my Grandma Kelly, my mother's mother. Each time I think of her, the memories bring a smile to my face. I do not want to ever forget those special times that Grandma and I shared, not ever! I look forward to the day when I can make special memories with any grandchildren that God may bless us with.

CHAPTER 41

It seems like with a blink of the eye, we are enjoying spring weather. The winter was terribly cold and snowy, but it is now a thing of the past. Isaac and the boys have several of the fields planted and even turned the sod over in my garden. The girls and I spent several days planting our vegetables, but we still have a few more things to plant. We must patiently wait another month until the threat of a frost is gone. Keeping his promise, Isaac again plowed more ground to plant extra food for our soldiers. This year, they extended the area to perhaps an acre and a half. Again, we planted potatoes, carrots, turnips, beets, and cabbage. Several families have also planted extra to share with our army. Should this wretched war end before the harvest, we will travel to the Easton market and sell our extra vegetables. The children find this proposition to be very exciting; I pray that this is what happens to our "army garden" because that would mean that the war is over.

More gossip about Benedict Arnold, but gossip that I am not pleased to learn. He apparently betrothed Peggy Shippen earlier this month around the second week of April. This displeases me and causes me great concern. Just how can a war hero marry a Tory and live happily ever after? I guess in all reality, it can happen, but I'm not quite ready to accept a happy ending to what I believe is a nightmare in the making. Besides, Arnold could have been her father, as he is thirty-eight and she is just eighteen years of age. I sure hope that the Lord blessed this marriage, as they will need all the divine help that they can get.

Pieter wanted to attend a sing-along wagon ride hosted by the Hixson family that lives close to Changewater. The Hixson family attends our church and are lovely people who have three teenagers:

two daughters and a son. Somehow, Pieter convinced Albert to attend with him, as Isaac would have disapproved of traveling that distance on horseback alone. Well, it appears that both boys had a wonderful time and met some new friends in the process. Albert said that there were thirteen of them in all, and they had a really good time. Lilia Beermen attended, as well as a young lady named Amy Dickenson, whom Albert took a liking to. The sing-along wagon ride started at four o'clock and ended at seven o'clock with everyone enjoying a basket supper as they sang and toured the countryside. Jason Hixson, the couple's son, accompanied the singers with his fiddle playing. Even more amazing is just how Pieter and Albert got Joseph and James to do their evening chores so they could attend. Isaac stepped in to assist the twins as they lack the experience that their older brothers have in milking the cows. So now it begins, our sons are discovering what life is like off the farm! They, however, need to understand that life is not all fun and games. They will be expected to continue doing their share of the workload until they decided to stake out on their own. Hopefully, from a mother's point of view not any time soon.

The girls and I made almost fifteen dozen candles earlier this week. It took the entire morning to complete this task, but we were down to our last dozen candles, and it is unwise to allow our stock to dwindle to the last few. It was nice enough to do our work outdoors and enjoy the spring weather, making it less of a chore and more of a fun activity. Also, with such beautiful weather and a gentle breeze, we were sure that the firming process would easily happen. Isaac got the tallow from Howard Van Horne a few weeks back when Van Horne butchered some of his sheep. We built a nice fire and melted our tallow in our smaller cauldron until it was nice and smooth. Using long sturdy sticks that were much longer than the size of the firepit, we draped several twenty-six-inch pieces of wicking evenly over the center of each of our sticks.

With Elizabeth on one end and Catherina on the other end of the stick, they gently dipped the wick into the hot tallow, pulling it back up and allowing it to drip and slightly cool. This dipping in and pulling the stick back up process was repeated several times until we created nicely tapered candles twelve inches long and about one inch around at the bottom. The stick with the newly made candles was carefully moved to a rack that Isaac made for me many years ago, where they were allowed to hang and slowly cool down to become nice and firm. Using the additional sticks, we repeated the steps until all of the tallow was gone. After waiting several hours for this firming process to happen, we carefully cut the portion of the wick draped over our sticks, giving us two nice candles each time we cut the wick. These candles will be given another ten more days to fully set. The longer we allow the candle to set, the slower they will burn, giving us the light we need during the dark hours. It is very important to keep our lit candles away from drafts, which causes them to burn much too quickly. Often, to avoid this problem, we will place a glass shade over the entire candle, thereby preventing any possible draft access to our lit candle.

We use the fat or tallow from sheep, as it is not too smelly when the candle is alight. Bee's wax is preferred but costly and often scarce in our area. Many years ago, we tried using lard, the fat from a pig— goodness gracious, it stunk to high heaven when lit! We learned early not to try that again. If sheep fat is in short supply, we can also use fat from cows as our second choice, but never ever will we use lard again for anything but baking. Later, in the fall when Van Horne butchers sheep again, we will get more mutton tallow and hopefully make enough candles to get us through the long dark months when daylight is minimal. We store the candles in a punched metal container with a lid, in our root cellar. This container keeps rodents away from the candles and during the warmer months keeps them firm. During the summer, our use of candlelight is far less than in the winter months, when it seems as if darkness goes on forever.

Eli, Sarah, and their children shared a meal with us today. We decided to have our chicken and dumpling meal at noon instead of in the evening. The weather was beautiful, so the children enjoyed themselves wandering about outside. The four of us sat on the porch after our meal enjoying cool mint tea. Sarah and I discussed just how much we miss our families back in Doylestown. It was wonderful seeing Nelson and Sophia Deremer, but I have not seen my parents in eight years; it has been seven years since Sarah has visited her parents. Letters from home are so welcomed, but they don't fill the empty spot in our heart. The four of us discussed how we could make a trip to Doylestown possible in the near future. The men came up with the idea that in the fall after the harvest, one family could travel to Doylestown for a brief stay, return home, and the other family would make the trip. This way whoever is left at home will tend to the business of both farms for that brief amount of time.

The excitement that Sarah and I shared was contagious! Was this even possible or just a dream? I so want to see my parents and soon, as they are aging, and only God knows when he will call them home. I suggested that after the crops are planted and the animals have given birth could also be a good time to take such a trip. The weather would prove to be more favorable than later in the fall. Traveling by stage with nine of us would be difficult, as most stages carry six, eight passengers at the most. The only reasonable way to travel would be using Moses, Mule, and our best wagon. We could plan on a stopover at an inn near the halfway point which is Kintnersville, Pennsylvania, so as not to travel during the darkness. The animals would be fed and put out to pasture for the night getting much-needed rest. After a bite to eat in the morning, we would set off for the second half of our journey, arriving in Doylestown late afternoon, perhaps early evening at the latest.

The conversation continued on and on with lots of wonderful input from the four of us. All possibilities were taken seriously, and time slipped by quickly. We all decided that my suggestion that earlier in the year was better and would work for both families. So now we have a time frame, and both Eli and Sarah insisted that Isaac and I travel first. They will tend to our farm and animals while we are away. It will take us two days of travel each way, and we will visit our families for three days. Not a lot of time to see and enjoy everyone, but we agreed that this would be a trial. Perhaps next year, if both families again agree to look after each other's farms, we can do it for a few more days. Before we even realized it, it was time to get doing our afternoon chores. We all hugged and agreed to meet at Eli and Sarah's house in the morning after our early farmwork was completed.

We supped on soup, bread, and butter. Isaac decided that he would tell the children of our plan, and they were so excited that the announcement was pure joy for all of us. We all discussed what had to be done before we could even think of a trip like this. We made lists of things that had to be taken care of. Actually, there wasn't a whole lot of things that needed to be completed before leaving our farm in the care of Eli and his sons.

Isaac selected a date, May 3, just a few weeks away, as our departing date. If the weather is fair, we will leave at sunrise, and by sunset we should be safely in Kintnersville; arrive in Doylestown late May 4; visit through May 7; leave for home at sunrise on May 8, staying over again in Kintersville and arrive back home the evening of the ninth. Before I could go to bed, I had to pen a letter to our parents telling them of our plans. Isaac will mail them for me after our visit with Eli and Sarah tomorrow. After I turned in, I lay awake going over all the details of the trip again and again. I thanked my Lord for making this happen. I know that Isaac was excited too but just didn't openly express his joy. This trip is so important to me as I sincerely miss my family. I'm not sure of just how much my older children remember from their last trip to Doylestown when I went back home to birth Abigail. I do know that they will remember this trip for many years to come.

CHAPTER 42

It has been an amazing fast-paced few weeks, but we managed to get everything in order, and we are making our way to the Delaware River! We were only a short distance from our home when we started singing our praises to the Lord. I am not sure that our joyful voices pleased everyone at such an early hour but, then again, rise and shine and enjoy this wonderful morning!

Moses and Mule were not very happy when we boarded the ferry to take us across the Delaware. Isaac and the boys gathered around them, gently stroking them, hoping to give them some comfort. However, they survived the bumpy ride across the water and seemed pleased to have their feet back on solid ground. Isaac, Pieter, and Albert took turns driving the team, making sure that the pace wasn't too quick for our two mules. Mules are very strong and could pull us along all day without a lot of discomfort, but we were in no great rush and wanted to travel along about four miles per hour. Our destination for the night was Kintersville, which is around twenty-five miles from our home. After a few rest breaks and stopping to enjoy our basket lunch, Isaac figured it would take us about nine hours before reaching our overnight stop. All our travel will be in daylight, as night travel is far too difficult, and the road and bridges are in poor condition. If we traveled during a full moon, we may have considered staying on the road a bit longer, as the moon would have provided us with light to see the road ahead. Not even the stage-coaches take chances of traveling on dark roads.

As the town of Kintersville came into view, all of us felt a bit relieved as this part of our journey was now behind us, and by this time we had become weary travelers. We still had a few hours of daylight but decided not to continue, as neither Isaac nor I was sure of how far and what accommodations the next town could provide. The boys requested to campout in the wagon for the night as the weather was warm and pleasant. Isaac thought their request was a good idea and helped them create comfortable places to stretch out and relax. After Isaac got a room for the girls and both of us, the wagon was moved closer to the hotel's stable for the night. Moses and Mule were unhitched and put out to pasture after being provided with a generous amount of oats, alfalfa, and water. We all sat down together inside the main dining room of the small but cozy hotel and dined on beef stew and biscuits. We called it a day at about seven o'clock, and the five us sharing the room went to sleep quickly. We cannot speak for our sons as we believe that they probably gabbed through the night, as they were sound asleep when Isaac went out just after sunrise to awaken them to come inside for breakfast.

After Moses and Mule enjoyed their morning meal, they were again hitched to our wagon. We left the hotel about seven o'clock to begin the final leg of our journey to Doylestown. All of us found the speeding stagecoaches to be hair-raising. They traveled much too quickly over the poor roads and didn't seem to care about sharing the road with other travelers they encountered. We quickly learned that we needed to get out of their way as fast as possible. We were also left in a cloud of dust that stung our eyes and caused some of us to cough. Both Isaac and I have traveled by stagecoach when we were younger. This was the main means of getting to the city of Philadelphia, which is about twenty miles from Doylestown. I guess because travel was just a short distance, the stage did not need to race along and get to its next destination on a time schedule? But then again, I was years younger than today, and reckless speed may not have bothered me at that time in my life—however, it sure does now!

As we plodded along, the scenery was becoming more and more familiar to both Isaac and myself. Again, we made several rest stops and enjoyed a basket lunch. It was late afternoon as we slowly made our way up a gentle grade. Isaac and I gave each other a quick glance as we knew that once we made the top of the grade, Doylestown would be in our view. At the top, Isaac had Albert halt the mules and told the children that they were looking down upon our hometown, and within an hour, we would be at Pop-pop and Grammy Plumley's house. My excitement caused me to become childish as I thought of my parents and family.

Isaac brought Moses and Mule to a stop in front of my parent's house just as the front door of the home burst open. By this time, I had moved to the front seat of the wagon and was climbing down as my mother was coming toward us with open arms. My mother's hug, a hug so tight and warm, caused me to have tears of joy, never wanting it to end. Then my father was next to embrace me and whispered how happy he was that I had a safe journey back home. The children and Isaac did not escape the hugs and seemed more than pleased to jump in and take part in this joyful reunion. Mama said that supper would be on the table in about a half hour, giving us time to settle in. As we gathered around the Plumley table, we held hands and thanked the Lord for getting us safely here, for family and for the food that was being provided. The pork and sauerkraut was perfectly prepared, the whipped potatoes were lump free, and the apple sauce had a tad bit of cinnamon in it. Everything just as I remembered from when I was a child. We talked, laughed, and shared tales from the past staying up past nine o'clock. Tomorrow was going to be a busy day for all of us, as my brother, sisters, and their families would be joining us for a huge welcome home celebration. I guess it was about ten o'clock when we dimmed the lantern and fell off to sleep. I believe that I fell asleep with a smile on my face.

Papa and Mama took us for a walking tour of Doylestown after our breakfast. We visited Papa's carriage and blacksmith shop, which the children found to be very interesting. My brother Solomon and his son Aaron showed my children a custom-built fancy carriage made for two passengers that was near completion. Living near the frontier, we would have no need for such a fancy luxury, so we found it to be delicate and not so useful; but just the same, a fine display of craftsmanship. As we continued on our walk, the children were amazed to see all the little shops and their goods nicely displayed in the shop windows. Joseph asked about the things up on top of the poles that so often lined the street.

Pop-pop explained that they were lanterns that burned whale oil and were lit at night so one could see as they walked the streets after dark. All of the children just stared at him in awe, never imagining lit streets. Pop-pop continued to explain that as dusk was nearing, men known as lamplighters pulled a cart with jugs of oil, a ladder, a lit lantern, and long wicks made of twisted reeds. They would use the ladder to climb up to lantern, fill it with oil if needed, and then light the oil using the already-lit reed. When the full moon provided light, the lamplighters would light every third lantern so as not to waste the precious whale oil. Then as daybreak was occurring, the lamplighters were back on the street extinguishing the lamps, only to return to the streets again at dusk.

As we continued our stroll, we came to the office and print-shop of the *Doylestown Gazette*. This was the local newspaper that was published Monday, Wednesday, and Friday. No one published a Sunday paper, as Sunday was a day of rest and time for worship and family. James took a real interest in the printshop and asked if he could go in for a visit. Isaac said yes and accompanied him into the shop. The rest of us continued on with our stroll as Isaac and James would catch up later. The owner and publisher of the newspaper, Mr. Stevens, welcomed Isaac and James. Isaac encouraged James to do the speaking as he was the one truly interested in the whole process of printing, not just a local newspaper, but the printing press in general. Mr. Stevens explained what had to take place to print a page and how the stencil letters were placed in the form and then spread with ink. He even allowed James to lower the press, thereby creating one page at a time.

Sometime during this process, Lucas Freeman, Mr. Stevens's reporter, came into the printshop. Mr. Stevens explained who and what Lucas did for the newspaper, and James was now taken in hook, line and sinker. The two men were so kind and willing to explain just how Lucas went out on the town to get a good lead and how he took his notes and created news stories for the paper. By the time the two were finished talking, James was given the title of James Deremer, Junior Frontier Reporter. Once a month, James was to send a short story back to Mr. Stevens, who in turn would publish the story if he liked the article. Mr. Stevens gave James paper, pen, and ink to record his story and instructed James to return the story postage due, mailing it from Mansfield Woodhouse to Doylestown. If Mr. Stevens liked James's story, James would be paid a half pence for each four stories published.

The next morning at six o'clock, James was to return to the *Doylestown Gazette* office and spend the entire day with Mr. Stevens and Lucas Freeman. James was excited beyond belief by this wonderful opportunity being presented to him. He thanked both men profusely over and over again as he and his father were leaving the newspaper office. The two had spent well over three hours at the newspaper office, so they decided to walk straight back to Pop-pop and Grammy's house. James talked the entire way back about possible stories he could write about Mansfield Woodhouse and the frontier.

The family enjoyed a late lunch that included my brother and sisters and their families. Having everyone together under the same roof was a real treat. My sisters brought baskets of food to be added to what Mama had prepared for our luncheon. There was so much food, we could have fed the army! The house was quite crowded, but no one seemed to mind, as the adults ate in the dining room, and the children and their cousins ate their meal on the back porch. The conversation was wonderful, and we were able to do lots of catching up. When my sister heard that Isaac and I would be attending a play the next evening with his parents, his sister Julia and Julia's husband, they decided to dress me for the affair. They said they would return to Mama's house around five o'clock tomorrow evening to help me dress and fix my hair for our evening out. This was so exciting, as my sister's clothing is tailor-made and not plain cotton dresses. I agreed and actually found myself looking forward to a bit of pampering.

The luncheon dragged on into supper with plenty of food for all. After we ate, we all took a walk a few blocks away to a town park. It was past the supper hour, and a group of men were setting up to play their musical instruments in the gazebo in the center of the park. Once the music began, the children were enthralled. The music that they made was very uplifting, and many people sang along; some folks even danced to a waltz. Time slipped by quickly, and before any of us realized it, it was seven-thirty. My brother's and sisters' families left for their homes, as they had to get up and attend to business in the morning. The children wanted to stay for just one more song, and we gave in.

What a glorious day that the Lord had provided! Everyone was in their beds just a bit before ten o'clock and probably sleeping soundly within minutes of laying their heads upon their pillows. Again, my dreams were sweet, and my heart was filled with happiness.

We awoke to our second full day of our visit with my family. Isaac left James in the care of Mr. Stevens and Lucas. Grammy packed him a wonderful lunch to get him through his day. James barely touched his breakfast as he was just too excited to think about food. Pop-pop said that he would gladly return to the newspaper office at four-thirty and walk back home with James.

My sisters arrived as promised at five o'clock to pamper and dress me for dinner and a play that Isaac and I attended with his parents that evening. I selected a dress that was a pretty light blue with lace trim that belonged to my sister Vivian. The dress fit perfect and appeared to be made just for me. My sister Lydia loosely braided my hair and added some of Mama's beautiful lily of the valley sprigs from her flower garden and a light blue ribbon. When I came downstairs, my children were in total awe as they had never seen me dressed so elegantly. Isaac's look told me that all was well and that we were both taken back to the days when we were young lovers and the world belonged to only us. The surrey arrived at six-thirty sharp with Isaac's parents. Again, the children were amazed by the site of the surrey carriage as it would not be practical where we live.

Dinner was wonderful. It had been years since we dined on oysters and seared beef tips. The play was written by a local man and was about a young man struggling between going off to war or staying home with his family. Goodness, the plot hit home and could have been written by Isaac or myself. The star actor barely escaped the British and returned home to his family safe and sound. I believe that both of us would have preferred to attend a play with a different plot, but we made it through to the final act and sort of enjoyed it; to say the least, it was extremely patriotic. Nelson and Sophia delivered us back to my parent's home before ten-thirty. They did not dally but left for their home; as the horse had to be stabled, the wagon put away and Nelson had a meeting at his surveyor's office in the morning.

The next morning after breakfast, Isaac took the boys to visit his father at the Deremer Land Surveyors office, which is located on the southern end of town. Isaac wanted the boys to see how their grandfather operated his business. Nelson was sorely disappointed when Isaac and I decided to make our home in Mansfield Woodhouse, as Isaac had been training to become a surveyor himself and would have probably taken over his father's business. Actually, this trip back to our hometown made me question many things. Are we really happy in Mansfield? Have we deprived our family of the joys that city life has to offer? Will I even be satisfied with my life when we return back home on Sunday? So much to ponder and not a single answer to my many questions.

The girls and I went with Mama to visit some of her friends whose children I grew up with. Each home that we visited was nicely furnished with the best of accessories. Lace and linen on all tables and oil lamps to provide light, unlike our candles and crude oversized wooden kitchen table. All was beautiful, but was this the life I really wanted? Both my parents and Isaac parents provided their families with a very comfortable lifestyle. We chose to give up the social status and make our own way. I feel safe and secure living away from the hustle and bustle of the city. Yes, we do without many things, but we also gain much more—peace and quiet; wonderful, loving neighbors; and beauty all around us. I secretly began wondering if my children were regretting the county life. We will find out when we return to our modest log home.

About midafternoon, all of my family that could break away and visit Mama's house returned. We enjoyed cake and punch as we talked the afternoon away. As it neared the supper hour, we said our goodbyes and promised that we would not stay away so long, perhaps even return next year. This gave me something to look forward to until we meet again.

After our evening meal, we gathered our clothing and personal items and packed our bags in preparation for our early morning departure. We spent the rest of the evening sitting on the front porch just enjoying each other's company and watching people passing by. We all retired by nine o'clock.

We were all up at sunrise and rearing to go. After a wonderful hearty breakfast prepared by Mama, we headed out the door, but not without a full basket of goodies to enjoy on our trip back home. Isaac had Moses and Mule hitched to the wagon; all our bags loaded, and I was still goodbying. I think the girls and I waved our arms off until we could no longer see Pop-pop and Grammy. I tried to disguise the tears that were running down my cheeks, but I just couldn't overcome my moments of sadness. I am sure Isaac felt a tug at his heart too but knew how to hide it. It had been a wonderful few days, and now we had to return to our real life in Mansfield Woodhouse.

Our return trip was identical to the trek that we took to arrive in Doylestown. We stopped over in Kitnersville for the evening and again were on the road to home about seven o'clock the next morning. After the ferry brought us back to New Jersey, a sense of urgency crept into our bodies. All we wanted now was our own home and beds. We arrived back at our farm just after six. Isaac sent the twins to Eli and Sarah's home to let them know that we were safely home and come over for a visit if they wanted. Twenty minutes later, Eli, Sarah, and their family were sitting on our porch listening intently to details about our wonderful trip. Isaac and I brought back a basket of extra special goodies for Eli and his family in appreciation for tending to our farm while we were away. They were excited and looking forward to their own adventure to Doylestown in less than two weeks. It was past eight when we said our goodbyes and began preparing for the morning. Tomorrow, it will be back to our regular lives and well-honed routines. We had wonderful memories to cherish from this trip back to our roots. James now has a job as a junior newspaper reporter that will keep him occupied for several hours a month. The girls picked up a few ideas to include in their embroidery samplers, and all of the boys learned about blacksmithing and surveying.

As we were falling asleep in our own bed, I thanked Isaac again for making this trip possible. He said that it was a team effort, and we all worked to make it happen. Isaac was also pleased that we traveled to Doylestown to visit but also said that he was happy to be back on our farm. I am not so sure that I feel the same about our farm as I did before our trip back home. Only time will tell, but then again, I take my wedding vows very seriously, and the part "until death do us part" means that wherever Isaac is, I shall be, now and forever. I prayed one final prayer praising all the wonderful things that had taken place over the past week and allowed myself to close my eyes to welcome sleep.

CHAPTER 43

Eli, Sarah, and their children had a wonderful trip to Doylestown a few weeks after our return. Isaac and the boys tended to Eli's farm, just as they tended to ours when we visited back home. It seems that this arrangement benefited all, and we are talking about perhaps doing it again next year.

Upon Eli and Sarah's return, we had more than an earful to tell them about a group of Loyalists led by James Moody who, on May 27, made a raid on our jail in Newton. The group freed eight men, all Loyalists, after they broke the door, found the keys to the cells, and released all the prisoners except those who were jailed for civil crimes. The group fled into the darkness. The nerve of these renegades!

James has taken his newspaper reporter job very seriously. He submitted his first story about living near the frontier and how rough life is far away from the city limits. Isaac and I proofed his story several times before the three of us deemed it worthy of submitting. It was quite a surprise for all of us when James received a copy of the edition of the *Doylestown Gazette* with his story on page two in the mail a few weeks after submitting his script. Mr. Stevens was apparently pleased with his junior reporter's work. A letter included with the newspaper said that he really enjoyed James's story and to keep up the good work. James's head is in the clouds despite both Isaac and I telling him to practice some modesty and stay grounded. He is working on his next story about the Lenape Indians.

Pieter has taken quite a liking to Lilia Beerman spending much of his spare time with her. Lilia appears to be a very nice young lady and, unlike her grandfather Jake, leans toward the colonies freeing themselves from England. She is seventeen, the same age as Pieter, and her beliefs can and most likely will change within these next few years of her becoming of age. When around Lilia, we do not fear speaking our mind about nasty King George. Will this be Pieter's lifelong partner? Only time will tell.

CHAPTER 44

The harvest has been bountiful this year. Isaac is preparing a letter to send to the army questioning if they have any idea where General George Washington will camp with his troops for the winter. Unfortunately, the war rages on with little hope that anything will be resolved within the near future.

The weather is turning chilly, and most trees have dropped their leaves as well as their generous crop of nuts. The girls harvested heaps of walnuts and hickory nuts and have them spread out drying in the barn. In about a week, we will shell the nuts and harvest their meat to be enjoyed over the next year. Hickory nut cake is a favorite with this family, a bit difficult to shell but truly a treat.

Sarah, the girls, and I have now finished yet another woven blanket. It just seems that finding time to work on the loom is getting more difficult. We have James writing his short stories for the *Gazette*, Pieter wooing Lilia Beerman, Albert getting heavy into trapping and our farm duties. Now with darkness closing in earlier each day, we can't seem to set aside the time needed to work the loom. At least, we have all gotten to experience how to make the contraption work and produced some wonderful blankets in the process. The girls have learned how to take the carded wool, dye it, and then spin it into yarn. This in itself is a real accomplishment that will be useful as they eventually set up their own homes.

Eli and Isaac delivered a generously loaded wagon of split firewood to the Mansfield Woodhouse Church. Each family that are members that can cut down trees take turns providing the necessary wood to heat the building. Depending on just how cold this winter season will be will determine if our turn will come around again. Let's hope not, as we deserve a mild winter for a change this year!

Eli and Isaac also made a special trip over to the Thatcher cabin along the Pohatcong Creek. Jon and Hilda Thatcher have lived in the valley for years. Jon worked side jobs for several of the local farmers, but age seems to be catching up with him. This past summer, he took ill from some kind of nasty bugbite. Aunt Peggy has been treating him to no avail. When the boys were delivering eggs and milk to their cabin recently they noticed that their woodpile was low. After telling this tidbit to Isaac, Isaac decided it would be neighborly to bring them the much-needed firewood to help them through the winter season. Eli immediately jumped on board with idea.

When the brothers delivered the wood, the Thatchers were in tears and ever so grateful. Eli questioned the couple and found out that they were also low on food but would never beg from neighbors. A second trip was made to the Thatcher home with scrapple, bacon, beef, carrots, potatoes, turnips, cabbage, cornmeal, and apples. Jon and Hilda were told that Isaac and Eli would return around Christmas to see how they were doing. Thank the Lord that the men discovered the needs of these people. It's our mission in life to tend to those less fortunate, and sharing some of our food is not only the right thing to do but the Christian thing to do.

CHAPTER 45

So much for a mild winter! The snow has been falling and falling and falling. The Continental Army is camping in Jockey Hollow, just outside of Morris Town, this winter season. December 15, the army arrived here in Mansfield Woodhouse with twenty huge wagons that the community filled to the top with fresh vegetables, sacks of corn-meal, flour, fresh meat, poultry, and apples. The ladies of the area worked hard since last year's donation, knitting socks, scarves, hats, gloves, and warm blankets. Two of the large wagons were loaded with feed for the animals too. The participation was wonderful, and again, Pastor Carson blessed the soldiers, horses, and wagons before they returned to Jockey Hollow. The soldiers told us that the snow seemed even deeper at their camp than what we have here in Mansfield. Twenty wagons were a huge endeavor on our part, and one can only pray that we are not alone in our concern and generosity for our fighting men.

Christmas will be here in a few days. Isaac, Eli, and the boys went out on their annual bird hunt. Nelson bagged a wild turkey, and a good sized one too! The feast will be at our home this year, and we will be preparing a turkey, a pheasant, and two ducks as our main course, along with lots of vegetables. The girls and I have been baking cookies and fancy breads to serve for dessert. Isaac asked that we please bake some extra cookies for the Thatcher family, which he will deliver to them on Christmas Eve. Yesterday, Abigail and Joseph churned a fresh batch of butter. Abigail wanted to do it all by her-self, but the churning process can be tiring so Joseph was there to take over and give her a break when needed. I believe they may have attempted to make too much butter at one time by pouring all of the skimmed cream in, instead of part. They managed to complete the process, but both were complaining. We all enjoyed a cup of butter-milk with our evening meal.

Both of our parents sent us a letter wishing us a Merry Christmas and blessings for the season. These letters, as well as all the letters since we arrived back home, tell us just how much they miss us and wish that we would consider moving back to Doylestown. I feel their pity, but I also know that even the thought of returning to live in Doylestown is not an option. Both Eli and Isaac are very happy here in Mansfield and have no plans to return to city life. I have had several months to ponder the idea of returning to what I left behind. I quickly dismissed these thoughts, as my place is by my husband's side, wherever that may be. Visits back home and letters in the mail will have to fill the empty spot in my heart for my family. Life would be easier if we were in Doylestown, but we long ago chose to settle down far from the rush of urban life. Life is good here, and we certainly have plenty of room to spread our wings. I thank the Lord for that.

CHAPTER 46

It is now the middle of February, and finally it appears that we are getting a reprieve from the unbelievable constant snowfall. The sun has been out for the past few days, and the temperature has gone a few degrees above freezing, so we are seeing some snowmelt. This is such a welcome treat for everyone here in New Jersey. Will it last? Probably not, but we take whatever we can get and enjoy it while it lasts.

Isaac and I did not exactly see eye-to-eye last night when our sons came to us for permission to help work Mr. Lommerson's lime-kiln. With the break in the weather, Mr. Lommerson has started the fire in his kiln and added the limestone. The fire has to be fed around-the-clock, as it takes several days to reduce the stone into lime powder. Lommerson is in the habit of recruiting young men and teenagers to take care of the fire because they need to camp out around-the-clock near the kiln in often crummy weather.

Nelson and Edward were approached earlier this week and asked if they would like to tend the fire and be paid for their services. They were also told that they could bring along their cousins to help, and they will also be paid. This is not an easy or safe task as the boys remain near the kiln for several days until the fire is finally allowed to burn out after the rock turns into powder. Quicklime, as it is called, can be very volatile and can burst into flame if not careful. Several years ago, Ezra Bryan's brother, Theodore, was hauling a cartload of lime from the Lommerson kiln to his fields when a bump in the road caused a mini-explosion killing his mule and near fatally injuring Theodore. Theodore suffered burned flesh, causing painful scaring that plagued him the rest of his life.

Now my husband thinks it would be a wonderful experience for our sons and nephews to operate the limekiln during this short break in the weather. I strongly opposed and voiced my opinion several times during the discussion. I also lost my fight, and the boys and their cousins will begin their constant watch until the stone has been reduced to powder, most likely within five days. This process is done during the winter months, as in the spring the lime is spread on fields to neutralize the acid soils and help crop production. Normally, it is not spread on a field yearly; sometimes a dose lasts three years, with ten years the maximum amount of time. So I am preparing baskets of food and drink for my sons as well as some for their cousins. I am sure that Sarah is doing the same thing, and I am darn sure that she is not pleased with the outcome of this adventure either!

Isaac will deliver our wagon with a cover over it to offer some protection from the weather, setting the open back of the wagon about twenty feet from the mouth of the kiln. The wagon will keep the boys off the cold ground and perhaps provide a bit of shelter from the cold and any wind that may kick up. Pieter will be in charge of a long gun with instructions—for emergency protection only. In other words, no horsing around, as having possession of a gun is serious business. Both Eli and Isaac have total confidence in the boys and believe that this is a wonderful way for them to think for themselves and participate in teamwork. I pray to the Lord that they are correct in their reasoning. Isaac also advised me not to create a beaten path between our farm and the limekiln; just let the boys alone to do their job. Sure, a mother wants to have her sons spend days in front of limekiln and not be able to pamper them. Really, at least just a little, flat-out no! Drat!

Isaac said that he would do the milking and tend to the animals, the chores the boys usually do. The girls stepped in and said that they would help their father. Elizabeth and Catherina have helped with the milking before, but it was a learning experience for Abigail. Isaac kept a close eye on her around the cows for fear of one kicking and hurting her. It is never a good idea to stand directly behind any hooved animal, as they are all known to kick. Cows are not as jumpy as horses, but even a calm mule can put out a good one-two;

when dealing with sheep, pay close attention to the horns as they like to headbutt. I learned this after being butted across the barnyard, spending days recovering from a bruised rear end. The best advice is keep your eyes and ears open and be on the lookout for a cranky animal. Isaac seemed to really enjoy his time with his daughters, and the morning and afternoon chores were completed in about the same amount of time it takes their brothers.

Mealtime was strange, with only five of us at the table for dinner. I couldn't help but take notice that the general conversation was toned down, and the subjects touched on were kinder in nature. The house was so quiet and peaceful. Boys will be boys, and the constant teasing and tormenting of their sisters was not missed. But I am sure that we will welcome them back home with open arms.

CHAPTER 47

April showers brings May flowers! Our spring housecleaning is nearly complete. It is so wonderful to be able to open the door and get fresh air into the house. I guess the winter of 1779 into 1780 has been one for the record-keepers. The drifts of snow will probably still be here in June as they are so deep.

The boys all made out fine tending to the Lommerson Limekiln, just as Isaac predicted. They spent a total of six days tending to the kiln, and Mr. Lommerson was quite generous paying each of the boys. He may be thinking ahead to next year and hoping that they will again tend the fire to keep the kiln operating. They all said that they had a wonderful time, a bit challenging and exhausting, but worth the time and effort.

Scuttlebutt has it that Benedict and Peggy Shippen Arnold have a son who was born sometime last month. For goodness sake, he could be the child's grandfather! Yes, I know several men who have lost their wives and remarried younger women, but this couple just annoys me to no end! Perhaps the fact that she is a Tory and he a patriot is the cause for my distress. But truthfully, I should just mind my own business and not allow this couple to upset me. Really trying, but not working!

As in the past few years, we again are planting our army garden. Oh, dear God, why can't this terrible war end? Isaac received a wonderful thank-you letter from General George Washington himself, thanking the wonderful people of Mansfield Woodhouse for generously sharing our food with his army. Isaac passed the letter around town after reading it during church last month. It is currently tacked upon the community message board at the Mineral Springs Hotel. From the sound of things, more people have decided to plant extra vegetables to harvest and share with our military. The thought of our community coming together is such a feeling of pride.

James, our junior frontier reporter, received his half pence as compensation for the four stories that he submitted and were printed in the *Doylestown Gazette*. He is currently writing an article on Aunt Peggy and her herbal cures. I must say that the boy is sure dedicated to his writing and spends all his spare time working on perfecting his skills.

Earlier this week, Harold and Ruth Taylor became the proud parents of identical twin boys! What a blessing, and grandparents John and Ellen Castner couldn't be more pleased. The Taylors also have a daughter who is about two years old. We rarely see this family, as they are farming the old Robinson place on the east side of Beattystown. Perhaps they will have the boys christened in our church, just as they did their daughter.

Jon and Hilda Thatcher survived the winter. Eli and Isaac made it a habit to check on them each time they were in the area. Jon said that he is improving and expects to be back working in a few weeks. The couple are forever grateful that our families provided for them during their difficult time. Jon expects both men to allow him to repay the favor by doing odds jobs around our farms. I know that Eli needs to move his privy this spring, so I'm guessing he will allow Jon to help. Eli and his sons are already creating a huge pile of stones for the new privy as well as extra to fill in the current pit once the outhouse has been moved to the new location.

Moving an outhouse is hard work. First, one must dig a deep hole, at least five to six feet deep and three feet square, then line the pit walls with the stones. Next, the outhouse has to be carefully placed over the pit and leveled. The old privy pit, which is filled with waste, has to be carefully filled in with stones, a project that can take several days because an improperly filled privy pit can cause a sinkhole. During the filling process, a coating of lime is applied daily over the pit to keep the odor down and help control the flies. After the pit is filled with as much stone as possible, dirt is added, again taking several days to allow the dirt to slowly settle and fill the pit.

Filthy work but a necessary job. The size of one's family depends on how often a privy has to be moved. The more people that use it, the more often it has to be relocated. Most privy locations last five years. If one has a small family, it can last ten years.

CHAPTER 48

Isaac returned home from checking for mail at the Mineral Springs with a smirk upon his face. My first thought was, now what does he know that I don't? After teasing me with suggestions that I really don't want to know, he spilled the beans. Well, for goodness sake, Isaac learned that Benedict and Peggy Shippen Arnold and their young son are staying at the Shippen Manor in Oxford! The Shippen Manor is but seven or eight miles from our home. Apparently, the family is taking a bit of a break before continuing on to Arnold's next military appointment at West Point, located along the Hudson River in New York state. Boy, could I feel my blood begin to boil! Just what we need: a rich, privileged Tory and her patriot husband in the area! I don't mind him as much as I dislike her. Isaac said that the couple and their child would only be staying in Oxford for a few days, as Arnold needs to report to West Point in early August when he will take command of the fort. I guess she can't cause too much harm in the few days they will be staying with her uncle and his family.

Last week, the men of our community met at the Mineral Springs Hotel with our local county representative for an update on recent Sussex County and state legislation matters. Our elected representative, Elroy Schmidt from Phillipsburg, travels twice monthly to our county seat in Newton. Mr. Schmidt often holds meetings throughout his district to brief the men on things such as road maintenance and current happenings in our area. Schmidt is up for reelection soon, so I guess he is buying drinks for all area men in hopes that they will keep him in office. Isaac and Eli said that they see nothing wrong with reelecting this man, as he is so much better than the official who lost to Elroy last year. Too bad, women can't have a say in all of this and be able to cast a vote. I would love to address many issues concerning

Mansfield as we seldom see our own militia in this area. Isaac feels we are lucky that the battles are still fought away from our homes, and the militia go only where they are needed. I guess he makes sense, but for peace of mind, it would be nice to know that they are actually close to the Mansfield Woodhouse area protecting us.

We also learned that a new building will soon be constructed across the Pohatcong Creek from Elwood Bryan's farm. An application for a license to become a tavern stand, meaning that they will sell liquor, limited food, but no lodging, has been forwarded to our county seat. The location is in town, just off the main road from Easton. The Mineral Springs Hotel caters to many well-to-do strangers, either here to enjoy the mineral springs or just passing through. The area folks often feel uncomfortable mixing with them, so it will be interesting to see how much local business this new establishment will take away from the Mineral Springs Hotel. Henry Creveling owns the land and is providing the necessary funding to build the structure. Word has it that Henry's son-in-law, Jacob Echman, will be the barkeeper. We have seen quite a bit of growth in this area since moving here from Doylestown. But with that said, we have a long, long way to go before this place we call home can even slightly be compared to what we left behind. Perhaps that is a good thing?

We took another trip to the Easton town market a few days ago. Our sons had money that was burning holes in the pockets of their britches. When they got paid by Mr. Lommerson for tending the limekiln, Isaac sat them down and discussed the importance of saving some of their hard-earned money for a rainy day. The boys agreed to save a generous portion of their pay; the rest they could use to treat themselves for a job well done. James has been making money with his junior reporter's job, and Albert has been quite successful with his sale of pelts, so they had their sit-down chat weeks earlier and appear to be heeding Isaac's advice.

So with money to spend, it was the boys who took all the time in the world to explore what was being offered by the many vendors at the market. Isaac accompanied them in hopes of guiding the boys to make wise choices and not throw their money into the wind. The girls and I had a wonderful time and visited almost all of the vendors, skipping the farm equipment, tack and firearms displays. We treated ourselves to some beautiful cloth remnants that we will work into a patchwork quilt we plan on creating. It was a wonderful family day, and I got the opportunity to stock up on some of the items that we cannot purchase from our local store. We arrived back home in plenty of time to do our afternoon chores. After traveling to Doylestown and back, going to Easton was an easy trip.

Our nightly Bible studies continue with a smaller group. A few weeks ago, Pieter and Albert had a discussion with Isaac and me and asked to be excused from our nightly readings. We told the boys that we would consider their request. After much pondering and thinking back in time to when our Bible studies stopped, we had to admit that by age fifteen, we were both excused from the nightly readings. I discussed all of this with Sarah before making our decision, as I did not want to cause any problems as Nelson is also fifteen years of age. Isaac, however, told both Pieter and Albert that he expects them to attend church every Sunday until they are no longer living under our roof. The boys eagerly agreed and said that they never considered not attending church but just felt that they had outgrown our Bible studies. With Pieter now seventeen and Albert fifteen, I have to ask myself just where the time has gone. I believe that we have provided our boys with a solid foundation, and they will continue to grow in their faith, just in a different way.

CHAPTER 49

What a rat, scoundrel, despicable human being! My heart aches from hearing the news that Major General Benedict Arnold tried to sell us out to the British. The tidbits of news reaching Mansfield Woodhouse relay an act of treason committed by this poor excuse of a man! General Washington was to meet with Arnold at West Point for an inspection and visit with his dear friend on September 24. After his arrival to West Point, Washington learned of a plot hatched by Arnold to deliver our fort to the British, when British Major John André was earlier found with papers exposing the plot to capture West Point in his boot. Arnold learned of the capture of André just hours before Washington and his men arrived at the fort. Benedict escaped downriver to where a British ship was anchored, which then took him to New York Harbor.

Washington found the fort to be in "a most critical condition." It was Arnold's plan to turn General Washington over to the British as a prisoner of war. He also offered up the over three thousand troops stationed within the fort and surrounding area, for either death or prisoners of war also! Benedict left West Point in such a rush, he left his child and wife behind! Even though I dislike Peggy Shippen, to leave her and their child behind is wicked! So now, all of my concerns as to why a war hero would permit himself to get involved with a Tory woman has come full circle. Infatuated by beauty, Arnold allowed himself to be taken into the spider's web of deception! What can one say except God, please bestow your blessings upon America and all the people who are steadfast in the cause for our freedom from England! We are also hearing that André was hanged by the neck until he died for being a British spy.

Fall is here, and the beauty of the season is being proudly displayed on the trees we call swamp maples. Brilliant reds and oranges cloak the hills and valleys, with each tree seeming to try outdoing the others. This is my favorite season, and I so wish it could last forever. I have been enjoying a daily afternoon walk with Isaac. Our walks are twenty to thirty minutes but truly medicine for anyone who might be melancholy. The autumn sunshine is so much nicer than the summer sun as it warms the soul and doesn't bake the skin. Enjoying its warmth is a true gift from God, so uplifting and refreshing to one's spirit.

It was during one of these fall afternoon walks that Isaac and I discussed giving a percentage of the milk and egg sales to our four sons. Up to now, all the money was added into the family tin and used for necessary household and personal items, such as tea, brown sugar, shoes, fabric, and so on. The boys have worked very hard on keeping our customers satisfied, venturing out to make their deliveries in all kinds of weather. Pieter, now being seventeen years old and very interested in Lilia Beerman, needs to make an effort to put money aside for his, and perhaps their, future. Albert could follow in his brother's footsteps too as he seems to have taken a liking to Anna Smith.

Friendships are wonderful and could someday blossom into something more special—who can say for sure, but one cannot live on love alone, and saving for one's future is a great idea for all. The profit from the egg and milk sales is a boost to our family income, but everyone does their share to keep this farm running. We are doing quite well with the sale of our piglets and lambs in the spring, so it was decided that the family tin would keep one quarter of the sales, and the boys would equally split the difference. Then we took a real leap of faith and decided that the sales generated from the folks coming to our farm for their milk and eggs would be somehow shared with the girls. This was really a difficult decision as usually a young lady is cared for by her parents and then kept by her spouse. It is believed that females do not need money or an income, so we are entering into uncharted waters with any radical decision we make.

We decided that Isaac would search our farm for large cedar or walnut trees and harvest the wood for a special chest he will make for each of our daughters. When we visit the town markets, we can purchase linen cloth, threads, and quilting materials that I will help the girls create necessary items to fill their "hope chest" with. If and when the girls become brides, they will have a chest full of necessary items to begin their new life. I so remember my grandmother sitting with me by the fire creating my first cross-stitch sampler. I was so proud of my finished work of art, and it still hangs proudly in our home today.

We also decided to set aside some money for each daughter that will be used for special material to make a dress for her wedding day. Each daughter will have the opportunity to pick her own fabric and color. Some vendors at the Easton weekly market carry beautiful calicos and plaids, as well as solid fabrics in a variety of colors and a selection of lace and ribbon trimmings. These items are quite costly, but a wedding is a very special occasion, and a bride wants to shine in her special dress.

We attended a fall festival at our church earlier this week. It appears that the planting season was favorable for the pumpkin and squash crops. Elwood Bryan took the prize for the biggest pumpkin; it measured forty-six and a half inches around! The Mineral Springs Hotel purchased the pumpkin from Elwood, and I'd love to know just how many pies they get from that big boy! The weather was pleasant, so all the festivities were held outside. There were games for the children, pie-eating contests, apple-bobbing, something for everyone who wanted to get up and join in the fun. Mrs. Carson, wife of our pastor, took a prize for her elderberry jelly, Helena Hoppock for her strawberry jam, and finally Carol Smith for her rhubarb pie. There was plenty of fresh baked bread to spread the jellies on and samples of so many different kinds of pies to taste. Each one of us present, young or old, got to cast our vote for the winning jelly, jam, and pie. I think most of us went home with a bit of a bellyache from overeating! How could one resist such enticing creations?

CHAPTER 50

Isaac received a letter addressed to the wonderful people of Mansfield Woodhouse that some of General Washington's army will again have a winter encampment in the Morris Town area. On December 17, our army arrived with twenty huge wagons. It is such a privilege and honor to be able to help our fighting men by supplying them with food. We again outdid ourselves as the wagons were packed tightly with our vegetables, fruit, and grain and fresh meats. Just as we've previously done, the last two wagons were loaded with feed for the animals. The soldiers that drove the wagons and their escorts took some time and shared some of our tea and fresh-baked treats with us. I guess the weather is holding out, and the little amount of snow that has already fallen isn't presenting any travel problems. We even had a brief blessing of the soldiers, wagons, and horses along with our prayers for safe travel and hopes to end this horrible war. When the caravan pulled out, everyone seemed to be in good spirits and started discussing ideas for our next "army gardens." This community is just amazing!

We learned from the soldiers that our General Washington and his wife, Martha, spent some time in Hackettstown in early November. The couple visited the home of Martha Wilson, widow of Lieutenant Robert Wilson, who lives along the main road through Hackettstown. It appears that Mrs. Wilson entertained a party of perhaps thirty people, including the Washingtons. When word spread of her distinguished guests, a crowd formed in the street by the house to catch a glimpse of our commander-in-chief. General Washington appeared outside of Mrs. Wilson's home to inspect a fine horse owned by one of the invited guests. The people in the street were ecstatic to be able to have the honor to just see our general. I can only imagine their excitement as I would have loved to have been a part of this group as well. I have traveled to Beattystown, but not the extra five miles into Hackettstown.

Christmas and New Year are quickly approaching. One has to wonder just how time manages to pass by so quickly. We thank the Lord for our good health and that of our children. Without good health, one has nothing. Money can cause evil in this world with greedy people wanting the riches of others who have toiled long and hard to make it in this world. We all entered into this world empty-handed, and we will all leave this earth empty-handed. Money is surely a necessary evil, but God gives us all what we really need to survive: his steadfast love.

CHAPTER 51

1781 appears to be starting in a bad way. We hear that on January 1, despite Mansfield Woodlouse's effort to provide food to the soldiers encamped near Morris Town, food was scarce, and men were not only going hungry but also lacked proper clothing. So on New Year's Day, about 1,300 of the Pennsylvania troops mutinied. Several officers were killed or wounded. The mutineers set out on a march toward Philadelphia where they intended to demand that Congress take steps to relieve their situation. General Wayne and two of his officers followed the mutineers, who never did make it to Philadelphia. The group reached Princeton on January 3, then Pennsylvania Governor Joseph Reed arrived the next day. The governor, the general, and the mutineers negotiated several days until January 8 when both sides seemed to be able to reach a settlement; the men returned to their winter encampment.

As if that was not enough disturbing news, on January 20, two hundred to three hundred soldiers who were encamped in Pompton decided that a second mutiny was necessary. This group was headed to Trenton to make their demands known. Their march took them through Chatham, where another encampment was holed up. General Washington ordered General Howe to march to Pompton from West Point to quell the uprising with five hundred troops on January 22. When the mutineers reached Chatham on January 24, none of those troops wanted to join the march and convinced the soldiers to return to Pompton.

General Howe and his troops arrived at Pompton on the twenty-seventh. In order to keep control within the Continental Army, Howe treated the mutineers with firmness. Three of the leaders of the mutiny were singled out by the mutineers themselves to be executed on the spot by a firing squad made up of other mutineers! Twelve other mutineers were to be the executioners. The first two men were quickly extinguished of their life; the third man in a state of total shock was pardoned, and his life spared. The scene caused dreadful shock and quickly ended any future thoughts of mutiny. Isaac commented that the success of any army depends on proper discipline and subordination, without both, it would be every man for himself. Oh, dear God, please have mercy upon the souls of the dead and allow peace to find its way into the hearts of those left standing.

Eli and Isaac were discussing the possibility of purchasing additional farm land to the south of our property. The land is hilly on both our side and the backside of the mountain, but it also contains several flat acres that have been planted for years. Edward Parker, who owns the property, plans on relocating to Amwell Township just outside of Flemington. The entire farm consists of approximately seventy-five acres with perhaps sixty being suitable to be planted. The hilly areas are good for grazing livestock and very favorable for the planting of fruit trees, not much more. The house and farm buildings are on the other side of the mountain, along the road that eventually leads to Mineral Springs. Eli asked for a few more days to commit to the purchase; Isaac is already deciding on what to plant in the fields!

We had a nice discussion after Eli left for his home. What if we purchase the property and have our older sons overseeing the running of the farm? Pieter will be eighteen in a few months and has proven himself capable since he helped manage our farm when Isaac went to war. Albert will soon be sixteen and, although not really fond of farming, could perhaps start an orchard and sell his harvests at the markets. The hilly area would need to be cleared, and timber could also be sold to offset the cost of the farm. So much to consider with limited time to make a decision, as Eli and Isaac have been given first choice for the purchase. A few more men are interested in property as well.

The deal will depend upon the attitude of both our sons. Isaac will surely assist in getting the farm up and running after that the boys will have to commit to making it at least pay for itself. There is a bit of a shadow of doubt in our minds, as Isaac had the wonderful opportunity to follow in his father's footsteps and eventually take over the surveyor's business Nelson owns in Doylestown. This was not Isaac's goal in life, and his decision seriously disappointed his father when we moved here to Mansfield Woodhouse to create our own future. Will our sons accept Isaac's offer, or will they go off in search of their own adventure and excitement?

CHAPTER 52

Eli rode into our lane with vengeance, white as a ghost, and appeared to be totally distressed. He had just picked up the mail from the Mineral Springs, and both he and Isaac each received a letter from their sister Julia. Julia wrote that Sophia, their mother, took sick with scarlet fever and asked her brothers to please come to Doylestown as quickly as possible. I felt myself begin to tremble from the top of my head all the way to my toes. The brothers had a quick conversation and decided to travel to Doylestown on horseback, leaving within the hour. It was now about one o'clock in the afternoon, and the sun was brightly shining, giving the men several more hours of daylight.

On horseback, they could travel faster than by wagon, so they figured they could reach Doylestown well before midmorning tomorrow. Eli went back to his farm and said he would return as quickly as possible. Isaac and I frantically gathered together the necessary clothing, snacks, and his long gun and ammunition and filled his saddlebags. As promised, Eli returned in about a half hour. The two brothers were off to Doylestown and hopefully learn some good news about Sophia. One cannot pray enough, asking for God to grant his healing powers upon Sophia.

After much haggling, Isaac and Edward Parker struck up a deal that both men felt comfortable with, and we now own another farm. Eli bowed out of the deal, as his sons are now sixteen and twelve, and he believed it would be just too much of an endeavor for him to handle more acreage at this time. The purchase of this seven-five-acre farm, including the house, barn, outbuildings, and some old farming equipment, set us back $200. Isaac really didn't want to spend more than $125 or $150, but with the sale of the timber to offset the initial purchased price, he felt he could live with deal. Pieter and Albert were very pleased with the possibilities of becoming their own boss. It was on the north side of the hill of our new farm where I found the two working when I walked up to tell them about Grandma Sophia and that their father and uncle were already on their way to Doylestown. The pair said that they would finish the job at hand and head back to our house. By the time they arrived, the other children had gathered at our kitchen table, and we began to work out a plan to keep the farm running while their father was away.

Here we are again, gathered around our table, drawing from each other's strength to carry on. We held hands, and I led us in a prayer, then we all recited the Lord's Prayer. I asked that Pieter and Albert go to assist Nelson after our milking was done. Joseph, James, and I would step in and take over whatever else needed to be done, so Pieter and Albert could help their cousin in any way they could. Nelson had never been left in charge of their farm, and I felt that he could use some help. The girls would continue doing their regular chores. I said that I would hold supper until Pieter and Albert returned so we could all eat together. Everyone agreed and tried to keep ourselves busy, so as not to dwell on the events that were taking place. Just the words *scarlet fever* caused one to quiver in fear, and now it has found its way into our family. No one asked any questions about the possible outcome for Grandma, as it was already known that recovery from this illness can be grim. Adding Grandma's age to the situation increased the possibility of a less-than-sunny ending.

The milking, feeding, and bedding down of all of our animals moved along smoothly. Pieter and Albert did assist Nelson with the milking. Ruth, Nelson's older sister, also stepped in to help in any way she could. Sarah too created a plan to keep things running as smoothly as possible, as their family was just as melancholy with learning of the sad news about Grandma as we were.

We all sat down to supper at six o'clock, not bad for all the finagling to get our chores completed. Our mealtime grace was more about helping Grandma than thanking the Lord for the wonderful food he had provided. We discussed the fact that we were unsure when we could expect Isaac to return home. With this in mind, we would continue to run the farm using the plan we worked out earlier, as it seemed to have worked well for all of us. I assured my family that their father would write to us as soon as he had some news, good or bad. In my heart, I felt an ache and just hoped and prayed that all would turn out well for Sophia. Sophia's illness was now in the hands of the Lord.

We all retired at about eight o'clock, even though the darkness of night had not yet settled over our valley. I believe that we were all suffering from the stress of the news about Grandma Sophia. All of us also wished that we could have accompanied Isaac and Eli to Doylestown to hug and kiss Grandma and perhaps to tell her we loved her just one more time.

CHAPTER 53

It has been seven days since Isaac and Eli left for Doylestown. Pieter, Albert, and Nelson have faithfully checked for mail at the Mineral Springs. Today they returned home with a letter from Isaac. Everyone gathered around the table, and I read the letter aloud. It was with profound sadness that Isaac had to tell us that Sophia entered the gates of heaven the afternoon of their arrival. Isaac said that they arrived in Doylestown about nine o'clock that morning, and Sophia was grateful that she had her sons by her side. As the day moved on, she became delirious, slipping in and out of consciousness. Her fever was relentless, and by seven o'clock, she became unresponsive and peacefully breathed her last breath with her husband and children surrounding her bed. The funeral took place the next morning and was just immediate family members so as not to pass the scarlet fever on to others.

Grandma was laid to rest in the town's burying grounds, buried in the same plot as her parents were laid to rest many years earlier. We all sat speechless, unable to move with tears streaming down our cheeks. Through a sobbing voice, Elizabeth said that she was grateful that we were able to visit Doylestown a few years ago and will always remember Grandma Sophia for her love of books. Then each child began to open up and relay one special thing about Grandma. We got our Bible out and turned to Psalms 24, seeking relief from our sorrow. I then quoted a couple verses from Ecclesiastes 3:1–2, "To everything there is a season, and a time to every purpose under heaven, a time to be born and a time to die, a time to plant and a time to uproot."

We prayed. We prayed for Isaac and Eli and Julia and Grandpa Nelson. We prayed for Grandma Sophia and thanked God for allowing her to be such a special part of our lives. We prayed for our family as well as Aunt Sarah and their cousins. Slowly, we started to feel a bit better, but we all knew we would be carrying an empty spot in our heart for Grandma Sophia. I passed along a few words of wisdom to my children, that the gift of remembrance is just one of God's special gifts to help mend a broken heart. Grandma Sophia will forever be a part of each of us as we carry her in a special place within our hearts.

Isaac's letter did not tell us when he and Eli planned on returning back to their farms. I was not even sure if the family was yet allowed to mingle with other people. Perhaps they had to remain quarantined for several days to make certain that they were free of the illness. I am sure that another letter is coming our way with more information, so we will have to just wait and see.

We sort of got our emotions together and as a family walked to Sarah's house. Tears were now flowing freely as we all joined in prayer. Sarah made tea and shared her apple cookies with us as we reminisced about our recent visit to Doylestown and Grandma Sophia's visit with us earlier. Sharing in our grief helped give us a bit of relief. After a few hours, we returned to our farm and went about our afternoon chores. Life does go on even in times of sorrow, as the cows need milking and animals need to be fed. Time waits for no one.

CHAPTER 54

Isaac and Eli were gone for about three weeks. When they returned, both said that they were grateful for being back home on their farms. The brothers stayed with their father in an attempt to help him begin to adjust to a way of life without his wife of almost forty-five years. Julia's son Michael has been helping Grandpa Nelson with the surveying business as an apprentice. Nelson said that Michael is smart as a whip and catching on quickly. This was a relief to everyone as the day will come when Nelson can no longer manage his business alone. Having Michael by his side will also be company to grief-stricken Nelson.

With the help of Isaac, the boys planted corn, hay, and alfalfa in several of the fields on our new farm. They want to sell the crops to those who do not plant but have perhaps a few horses, cows, and chickens to feed. However, Isaac advised that this new business should cater to only people residing on the south side of mountain. Jeremiah Smith has provided feed to the locals on the north side of the mountain and our valley for years, and it would be unfair to interfere with his business. They seemed to understand and said that they will only place their advertisements in the Hall's Mills area and beyond.

The mixture of many varieties of hardwood trees have been logged and brought down both sides of the hill. Eventually, the logs will be made into boards. This will be difficult, as everything will be done by two-man saws, framed pit saws, handsaws, and axes. The boys have started to plant apple saplings in the newly cleared area. When we get several days of rain that will soak the ground, Moses and Mule will help to pull the stumps. A mountain top spring will provide the necessary water required for these trees to make it through the hot summer months. However, remembering to carry buckets of water to the trees will be a daunting task. So far, Pieter and Albert have been very attentive to the needs of these trees.

While Isaac and the boys were working about the new farm, they had a visitor stop by to chat. General Daniel Morgan from nearby New Hampton was on his way back to a division of the Continental Army in the south and thought he recognized Isaac. The two men talked for about an hour sharing concerns about this terrible war. General Morgan truly believes that we will win this war against King George. They discussed the peace committee that Congress recently formed to consider negotiations with the British. Morgan said that among the members of the committee are Thomas Jefferson, Benjamin Franklin, and John Adams. These are all power-ful and honorable men who are representing the colonies. I sincerely hope that General Morgan is correct in his beliefs, as a resolution toward peace is foremost in all of our hearts.

CHAPTER 55

As summers go, this one had a wonderful growing season with our fields and gardens abundantly producing. It is very sad that Mr. Warne's gristmill caught fire and burned quickly to the ground. Fine dust within the building caused by the milling of the grain and a spark, probably caused by friction, are attributed to the start of the fire. Once the spark meets the dust, a small explosion occurs, creating a fireball within the mill, engulfing the interior of the building. A bucket brigade was formed using the water from the Millbrook to no avail. All who were aware of the fire came to help, and they doused the surrounding ground with lots of water as dried sheaf and grain husks were scattered about and could have caused an even greater fire. Benjamin Warne said that he would rebuild as soon as possible. In the meantime, local farmers will have their grain processed at the mill in Pleasant Valley. Luckily, this mill is just a short distance to the east of our farm.

Isaac started the hope chests for our daughters. He selected three cedar trees from different locations on our farm and sawed them down. He brought them back to the barn and created rough boards from the trunks. These boards will be left in the barn to "season" and have been weighed down to keep them flat and to also allow them to dry slowly over the winter. In the spring, he will plane the boards to make them smooth and begin to build the chests. This will be quite a project and probably will not be finished until late next fall. The inside of the chests will have to be made smooth by sanding. Isaac is not sure how he will finish the outside of the chests; perhaps, he will make each one a bit different, as each of our daughters are different from one another. Knowing the attention that Isaac gives to details, there is no doubt that the chests will be beautiful.

Eli and Isaac stopped by the Mineral Springs to check for mail and decided to enjoy a mug of dark stout. The captain was there, as usual, and yakking it up. They learned that in late September, Washington's Continental Army and French forces under General Rochambeau lay siege to the British in Yorktown, Virginia. The battles raged on until October 19, when Lord Cornwallis surrendered the British forces. Cornwallis was hoping for British enforcements to come to his aid, but it never happened. Something called the Articles of Capitulation were signed by Cornwallis and our Generals George Washington and Jean-Baptiste Rochambeau, and Admiral Francois de Grasse. The British and German soldiers laid down their arms. According to the captain, the war is over. Could this be true? Did the captain imbibe in a bit too many nips of rum? Despite Eli and Isaac calling him an old knock-kneed sac of hot air, they both hung on to every word he said. Why has it taken almost two weeks since this surrender occurred to reach our ears here in Mansfield Woodhouse? I was breathless when I heard this news and so wanted to believe it too.

As our family gathered around the table for our evening meal, the grace that Isaac prayed not only gave thanks to the Lord for our food but also for seeing us safely through this long terrible war. The children questioned what it would mean to America with King George gone. Isaac wasn't sure how to answer their questions as our new government was still being created but assured them that all would be well. In time, each state would elect our own representatives to govern us, and each county would have local men such as Elroy Schmidt. One thing was for certain, tariffs would stop, but the flow of such things as tea and brown sugar might also. As a new country, we may find ourselves in a struggle for ways to obtain goods that are imported. Only time will tell, but one thing is for sure, life in America will be better without greedy King George.

As we all retired for the night, I found joy in my heart. A joy that hadn't been there since the start of this war in April 1774. God has looked down on America and bestowed upon us our right to freedom. What joy and comfort to no longer worry about redcoats stealing food and livestock, beating our citizens and burning our buildings. Sweet dreams tonight, but I shall never forget all of those who sacrificed to make this happen. May God bless their souls.

CHAPTER 56

As Mansfield Woodhouse begins yet another year, let 1782 be one of posterity, hope, and health for all. Our volunteers have returned back to their homes and farms, and life is attempting to pick up where it left off for these men and their families. It seems that Loyalists began fleeing America, heading north to the Canadian provinces. Some have even boarded ships that sailed back to British colonies in the Caribbean and across the Atlantic Ocean to England. There is still much turmoil, as our government has no money, and those who fought are demanding to be paid.

We have been busy sprucing up our new farm. Pieter has proclaimed his unwavering love for Lilia, and her father has given him permission to marry his daughter. The wedding will take place in May at the Beerman farm. The newlyweds will take up housekeeping in the two-room cabin on the farm, just over the hill from our home. Lilia and her mother, Grace, are busy sewing curtains for the windows. The men are working outside the cabin, in between snowflakes, making sure the roof and outbuildings are up to snuff. Fredrick Beerman, Lilia's father, has taken a great interest in the barn area as he plans on gifting the couple two cows and a mule to help them begin building their farm. When spring arrives, Isaac promised Pieter some lambs, piglets, and also a few hens and a rooster. It doesn't seem to be much of a start, but their animals should quickly grow into good-size herds within a few years.

It is too early to tell if the saplings made it through their first winter. Albert has done his best to protect the young branches from heavy snow and ice. Isaac advised not to remove all of the snow from around the trees, as the wildlife graze on the buds and twigs when the winter limits their search for food. It is reasonable to believe that some of the saplings will not make it through their first winter. One just hopes that most of the trees will take root and thrive.

Mr. Lommerson has again approached the boys to tend to his kiln. I feel much more comfortable with them accepting the work than last year. Pieter said that he would help this year, but if asked again for the next year, he will be unable to help as he will be a married man with responsibilities to tend to at his own home and farm. The weather needs to break before the thought of heating up the kiln, so perhaps this will take place in a few weeks. The girls are excited at the chance to work with their father taking over their brother's chores while they are away. I guess all is good, for the moment anyway.

Work on Benjamin Warne's mill has come to a complete stop due the winter weather. This new mill will be constructed of stone gathered from the surrounding area fields. What little work that has been completed on the walls makes me think that it will not only be a sturdy mill but also a beautiful structure.

CHAPTER 57

The wedding was just beautiful. The bride looked lovely in her dress of lavender calico and tiny daisy-like wild purple flowers in her hair. Pieter looked as handsome as ever in his white shirt and dark britches. Pastor Carson preformed the ceremony, which took place under a large flowering crab apple tree. I am guessing that perhaps there were fifty people witnessing the joining of hands of these two wonderful young people. After the service, we enjoyed white cake with butter-cream frosting, wild strawberries, and punch. The ceremony took place at ten o'clock, and after enjoying everyone's company, the party broke up about one o'clock. It was such a lovely sunny day, and what a wonderful day to begin a life together.

It will be a bit strange not having Pieter under our roof, but at least he is just over the hill and not far away. We most likely will see him several times a week, as he will be here often sharing in the work-load to help keep this farm running. Isaac and Pieter agreed to work together on the plantings, harvesting of crops, and butchering of the pigs. By working together, Pieter will be compensated with feed for his animals and pork for his table. Eventually, Pieter will have more than enough work to keep him busy on his own farm, and as the other children go out on their own, we may need to consider hiring some outside help. But that is hopefully a long way down the road.

Our first lunchtime meal seemed strange without our son. Pieter's chair will often remain empty, as he has moved on to a new life. However, Isaac did make me feel a bit better by saying that our son has turned into a fine young man, and we have gained a daughter in the process. Perhaps in a year or two, we will find ourselves in the new role of grandparents. Now that will be a true joy, as a baby is a wonderful gift from God.

CHAPTER 58

Letters from back home tell of the worldwide epidemic of influenza now arriving in Philadelphia. I quickly wrote back to my family and encouraged them to come and visit with us until the spread of this illness has been contained. Of course, I already knew their response that Doylestown so far has escaped the illness, and in a few months, the cold weather may help to kill the spread of the sickness. I am not sure that the cold weather will slow the spread of this terrible illness, but perhaps if they stay housebound everyone will be safe. One can only pray that Doylestown is far enough away to escape affliction.

Pieter and Lilia were our Sunday noon dinner guests. We all attended church then came back to our house for a stew made of beef, carrots, and potatoes all slowly cooked together. For our dessert, we enjoyed an apple pie. After our meal, Pieter made the announcement that he and Lilia were expecting a child due sometime in March. Oh my goodness, this was wonderful news, and everyone was so excited. The girls realized that they were going to be aunts in seven months and, even before this child was born, were offering their services to help care for the little one any way they could. The boys, well, boys will be boys, they thought the announcement was great, but it ended there.

Isaac and I are over the moon and couldn't be more pleased. Lilia said that she has already talked with Aunt Peggy, and everything seems just as it should be. Having a child in the late winter or early spring will be easier on Lilia, as there is not much one can do when the weather is dreadfully hot and the mother-to-be is terribly uncomfortable. Also, manners dictate that the mother stays out of the public's eye once her belly begins to show, and people tend to stay indoors during the winter months when she will be in confinement. Lilia will be welcomed anytime at our home and Sarah's, as well as her parents and siblings, but that is about it. She will need to stay away from church too until she delivers the little one. Why is a woman with child shameful in the public's eyes?

CHAPTER 59

Lilia appears to be doing well. She has gained some weight, and her tummy is now showing, and she still may have another month before she stays in confinement. Pieter appears to be a nervous wreck constantly worrying about Lilia. He doesn't even want her to walk to her mother's house for fear of her hurting herself by falling or some freak accident. Both Isaac and I have tried to calm him, but I guess he is suffering from a case of first baby jitters. As Lilia said, Aunt Peggy told her to continue to do all she can until her discomfort slowly makes some tasks too difficult to complete. Lila will surely know when that time comes.

Isaac brought me a letter from my sister Vivian. I seldom get letters from my sisters, as our mother usually relays all the news from Doylestown when she writes, so I was very stressed opening it. Isaac and I both sat down at our kitchen table, and I opened the letter and began reading it aloud. The letter said that Papa was suffering from a bad case of influenza and has been in bed for the last week. Mama has been tending to Papa and is now showing signs that she too has caught the illness. Vivian wanted to ask if it was possible for me to come to Doylestown to help out. She and my other sister Lydia have been tending to both our parents for the past week, bringing soups and all sorts of food to their house hoping that they would eat. Papa has eaten very little and is now almost refusing to eat at all. Mama has been eating soup but now feels sick all the time and doesn't really want to eat. In tears, I asked Isaac what I should do. We were both at a loss for words as the influenza is highly contagious, and the condition of my parents described by my sister wasn't rosy. They are both in their late sixties and, although have enjoyed good health, one just never knows if and when our Lord and Savior will call them home.

After composing himself, Isaac suggested that he take me to Easton before dark, stay over with me in a hotel, and then I catch the stage to Philadelphia at sunrise tomorrow. I will be in Doylestown before six o'clock tomorrow evening. When I am ready to come back home, I will send a note to Isaac, and he will meet me at the stage when it arrives in the evening in Easton; we will again stay overnight and return to our farm early the next day. Isaac said that all would be fine on the farm. The girls are old enough to prepare meals for all of them, and Sarah is nearby to assist if need be. I guess this was the plan; after all, what else can I do? I need to help my sisters in any way possible and pray that I not fall sick to the influenza myself. I started gathering my things that I needed and packed my bag. Isaac went out to find the children and tell them of our plan. Albert would be in charge of things until Isaac returned tomorrow. The concern on the children's faces said it all: no need to tell them that everything was going to be fine, as I tried that with Grandma Sophia, and that didn't work. We had a bite to eat, and Isaac and I were on the road by three o'clock. Traveling after dark is too dangerous, so we needed to be in Easton by sundown.

After Isaac got us a room in the Hotel Easton and unhitched the wagon and stabled Dara, we enjoyed a simple supper in the dining room of the hotel. Both of us were completely exhausted and were in bed sleeping by seven o'clock.

We had breakfast in the hotel at five o'clock and met the stage out in the front of the place at six. It was still dark, so we waited until the day was dawning, and off we went. I waved goodbye to Isaac and lost myself in my own misery. The stage started out with four passengers, including me, but along the way, we stopped and left passengers and sometimes picked up a passenger or two. I arrived in Doylestown at five-thirty, and it was getting dark. I gladly walked the few blocks to my parents' house as being crammed into the stage, with only a few short breaks made me stiff and sore. Lydia answered my knock at the door and instantly began hugging me and shedding tears. She and my sister Vivian had now reached total exhaustion. Mama was running a fever but wouldn't leave Papa's side and get the rest that she needed to even think of beating this illness.

Lydia said that our brother Solomon stopped by twice a day, in the morning and around suppertime on his way from work to his home. Solomon would run any errands or pick up whatever we might need from downtown. The local doctor, Doctor Clark, stopped by every morning to check on both Papa and Mama, but other than that, there was little that he could do. Goodness, things were not looking good.

Lydia and I climbed the stairs to our parent's bedroom where we found Papa in bed asleep but laboring to breathe, and Mama in a chair next to the bed with her head resting against Papa's arm. Mama appeared to be sleeping, so we quietly left the room. I told Lydia to go home, and I would sit with our parents through the night.

I brought another chair into the bedroom and tried to make myself comfortable. It was well past midnight when Papa stirred and woke Mama up. It was quite a surprise when Mama noticed that it was me and not one of my other sisters. She seemed to be overjoyed with me being there. Papa awoke from the commotion and gave me one of his loving smiles. After sharing hugs and kisses, I told them both that I would be staying for a while and that Mama should be in bed resting, as I would see to whatever had to be done. She agreed and joined Papa. After helping Mama get ready and into bed, I went across the hall to my old room and lay across the bed. Both Papa and Mama looked completely exhausted and drawn out. I prayed for a miracle and God's healing power to help my parents. The next thing I knew, the sun was coming through my window, and it was morning.

I checked on my parents who were now ridden with fever and having difficulty breathing. Lydia said the doctor would be by in the morning, and I just prayed that he would come sooner than later. Solomon was surprised when I opened the door to his knock. I expressed my concerns to him that I thought both of our parents' conditions were failing since I arrived last night. He told me that he and our sisters had had this conversation a few days ago, and according to the doctor, there was nothing that could be done to stop the illness. We both went upstairs to check on our parents. Solomon tried to awaken first Papa, then Mama, to no avail. They were burning with fever, and the cool cloths that I had placed on their fore-heads quickly turned warm.

The knock on the front door was the doctor's and not a minute too soon. He checked Papa first and then Mama and, with a grim look on his face, said that he felt they were reaching the end of the ill-ness. There was nothing that he could do to relieve the struggle they were having just to breathe, and both appeared to be unresponsive to his touch. Solomon and I just stood there dumbfounded. Doctor Clark expressed his sympathies in the inevitable loss of our parents. After the doctor left, Solomon and I placed our hands on our parents and prayed to God to either intercede with a miracle or bring them to the gates of heaven peacefully. Lydia and Vivian arrived about ten o'clock, and we took turns tending to Papa and Mama, attempting to keep them comfortable in any way possible.

Doctor Clark returned about six o'clock. The sun had gone down, and our vigil continued. The doctor decided to stay with us for a bite to eat. Lydia had prepared corn chowder, and we all supped around the dining room table. The doctor spoke of all the years that he had been attending to our parents. Of hearing of the births of each of their grandchildren and just how proud the two of them were. He also looked at me and said my parents often referred to me as the maverick of the family for living so close to the frontier. About an hour later after checking on our parents and finding no change in their condition, Doctor Clark left for the night.

Solomon took the first few hours of sitting near the bed, while my two sisters and I napped in our old rooms. It was sometime after one o'clock when Solomon noticed Mama was especially still and checked on her. Mama appeared to be shallowly breathing, so he awoke us to come and sit with him. As the four of us sat there, we questioned if this was even possible, as Mama seemed to only have had a touch of the influenza, but we quickly dismissed this idea as we now believed that she was probably extremely ill but hid her condi-tion from us so she could tend to her husband of almost fifty years. Mama stopped breathing just as the day was dawning. Papa stirred, and within the hour, he took his last breath. Perhaps Mama waited for Papa so that they could enter the gates of heaven together? For years and years, they looked after each other, and now they entered eternity together. The disbelief and pain were overwhelming. Thank goodness for Solomon's take-charge demeanor, as he helped us muddle through the next few hours. Doctor Clark returned and officially declared our parents deceased and notified the undertaker. He also highly suggested that we stay away from the public for five days, and at that point, as long as we showed no signs of influenza, we were free to go about our daily lives.

My sisters and I prepared our parents for their funeral, bathing them and dressing them in their Sunday best. It was a daunting task, but it had to be done. The undertaker and three assistants arrived within a few hours with two wooden coffins. It was all so sudden, but the doctor said the burial needed to be done as soon as possible to prevent any additional spreading of the illness. The gravediggers had already dug the two graves and were waiting for the undertaker to arrive so they could finish the burial. By early afternoon, my parents had been laid to rest in their final resting place, next to my mother's family, in the Presbyterian Church yard. Their pastor, Pastor Davidson, gave a short eulogy and read the twenty-fourth Psalm, and we prayed. Only our immediate family attended the service due to fear of being the next victim of this epidemic. We all went back to Papa and Mama's house and cried and cried and cried.

After a nap, I penned a short letter to Isaac telling him of our loss. My sorrow was so raw that I couldn't even find the words to put it on paper. I told him that I would be unable to leave Doylestown for at least another five days as the doctor suggested we all stay away from the public, and if we experience any signs of the influenza—fever, nausea, muscle ache, breathing problems—to come and get him immediately. He also reassured us that just because we have been exposed to influenza doesn't mean that we will necessarily come down with the sickness. We all appear to be healthy, and age is on our side. This sickness seems to claim the young, the old, and the fragile.

The next few days, the four of us tended to the business of settling the estate and making decisions as to what to do with my parents' home and belongings. Solomon had taken over ownership of the blacksmith and carriage business three years ago, so he was the rightful owner. Aaron, Solomon's son, might be interested in buying the house as he and Lucy Cartwright plan to wed soon, as her father has given his approval to this marriage. Solomon said his son is a real saver and would most likely have the funds to purchase the property. We all agreed and hoped this is so, as our parents would be pleased to have their grandson and new wife move into this home and make it their own. I carefully selected a few of Mama's dishes and wrapped them in napkins to protect them during my trip home. I also picked out several pieces of jewelry as a keepsake for each of our daughters. For the boys and Isaac, I carefully selected some of Papa's flintlock handguns from his vast collection—these I will carry with me and not place on top of the stagecoach during my trip home. Limited room to bring items back to Mansfield made it impossible to safely pack Mama's special dishes. My sisters said that they would save things for me, and when Isaac and I come to visit, I can take them then.

I sent another letter to Isaac asking that he meet at the Easton Hotel on Wednesday. This actually allowed me three more days to make sure that I was influenza-free. In no way would I want to be responsible for bringing this epidemic to the Mansfield Woodhouse area. The night before I left, I made a quick visit to see Grandpa Nelson. I have continued to send letters to him telling about what is happening in our lives and the baby that is expected to arrive in March. He has not answered my letters, but I am sure he is still suffering from his loss of Sophia over a year ago.

Solomon accompanied me to the stagecoach stop, and we said our goodbyes. I tried to encourage him to come and visit us in Mansfield, but he just gave me a smile. The stage arrived in Doylestown about six forty-five, and we were off and running. We followed the same route back to Easton, so often stopping to either pick up or drop off someone. We arrived in Easton in near darkness which I found to be scary. The stagecoach had lamps that were lit, but I feel it is unsafe to travel after dark. Isaac was out in front of the hotel to greet me. It was such a joy to be with my husband again after the horrible experience I had just gone through. We enjoyed a late supper in the dining room of the hotel and got caught up on the things that had happened since I took the stage to Doylestown. The children are fine, and the girls did an excellent job making meals for the family. Lilia is feeling well, and Pieter seems to be calming down a bit. We retired after nine, and I fell immediately to sleep with my husband by my side.

Goodness, we actually slept in and never left Easton until after nine o'clock. We were back in our home before noon and so happy to be there. I silently was dreading the questions that the children would be asking me about Pop-pop and Grammy Plumley. I knew that their questions were out of love and something that I had to talk with them about so they too could find some kind of closure from their deaths. As we ate our lunch, I answered their questions, and we all shared in yet another crying session. I gave to our daughters the pieces of Grammy's jewelry that I had selected for them, and they seemed pleased. I allowed Isaac to make the decision as to when to give the boys the guns that I had brought home from Pop-pop's collection. Isaac felt that Joseph and James needed more practice concerning the proper handling of firearms, so unless he was with them, they were not to touch the guns. Pieter and Albert were given their guns and warned that handguns could be even more dangerous than long guns. All firearms must be handled with care and always assume that they are loaded. One cannot take back the shot once it has been fired, no matter how much wishing and hoping you do.

As I was falling asleep in my own bed, I found myself realizing the reality of the past week and half. I had lost both of my parents within an hour of one another. We were rushed into the burial to prevent the possibility of infecting more people with this deadly epidemic. How could a woman who is now forty years old, with a husband and children, feel so alone and empty? Now, all of my letters I write back home will not go back home but be addressed to one of my sisters. In the matter of a few weeks, my life had changed completely. I pray that the Lord will help see me through my time of sorrow. I also prayed for my family's safety and that of our unborn grandchild. Life is so short; cherish each day as if it were your last.

CHAPTER 60

Lilia had been in labor for over two days with little progress in sight. Aunt Peggy had come and gone, checking on her several times. Lilia's mother, Grace, stayed by her side making her as comfortable as possible. Pieter asked that I too stay, but I decided it would be best if I just visited several times during the daylight hours. Lilia is in good hands with her mother and Aunt Peggy, so unless one of them asked for my help, I would not get in their way.

The weather was balmy for the middle of March, so Aunt Peggy asked Pieter and Grace to help Lilia take several short walks about the yard of their home. Her suggestion really got things moving along, and after almost fifty hours of labor, and not without a struggle, Jacob Aaron Deremer entered into this world. The infant was quite feisty, very alert, and had a wonderful set of lungs. Lilia was totally exhausted and in need of rest from her lengthy ordeal. When Grace placed the baby in Pieter's arms, my son suddenly had an expression of amazement and love on his face, the likes of which I had never seen before. When I got to hold Jacob, my heart swelled with pride at the thought that this little bundle of joy was our first grandchild, so precious and truly a gift from God. Albert was working around the barn when Pieter shared our joy and asked his brother to pass along the good news to Papa, Aunt Sarah, Lilia's father, and grandfather, Jake. Soon the house was overflowing with not only love but also well-wishers.

With Lilia resting and baby Jacob being pampered, I went back to my home and picked up where I had left off three days ago. The girls asked to stay and visit with Pieter and their new nephew for a bit longer. They arrived back home in time to do their afternoon chores with smiles on their faces. I think all of us were on cloud nine and looking forward to our next visit with Jacob and his family. Perhaps 1783 will be a wonderful year after all!

Isaac brought me a letter from my brother Solomon. We both sat at our kitchen table as I read the letter aloud. Solomon presented our father's will for probate after an inventory of both of their possessions had been conducted. Aaron and his future wife, Lucy, purchased our parent's home and will live there after their marriage in June. They also selected some of the furniture, cookware, and dishes. My sisters, Solomon, and I agreed that much of the contents of the house would be gifted to the grandchildren as mementos of their grandparents. Within a few weeks, the estate should be settled, and Solomon advised that I will probably have to return to Doylestown for my share of the estate. We are entering into planting season, and the animals will be birthing, so the timing is not good for farmers, but as Isaac said, I will need to sign papers to legally sell the house and pay off any remaining debts. He also said that we will deal with it when it happens, no sense in needlessly worrying. Sometimes I feel that needlessly worrying is part of my middle name.

CHAPTER 61

I returned to Doylestown in June just in time for Aaron and Lucy's wedding. Much to my surprise and joy, Isaac accompanied me. This time, we took the stage from Mineral Springs Hotel on Thursday and left Easton at sunrise the next day. We arrived in Doylestown before six o'clock that evening. It was very sad to return home without my parents being there to greet me. I did my best to keep a happy face during this trip. We stayed with my sister Vivian, and she and her family were excellent hosts.

Saturday, my sisters and brother and I finished settling our parent's estate. Much to my surprise, my share of the estate totaled a bit over $2,700! Never in my imagination did I consider our parents to be of wealth. Aaron's wedding was held late afternoon on Saturday and quite lovely; his bride seemed to be very nice. Sunday after attending our old church, we enjoyed our noon meal at Isaac's sister Julia's house. Isaac's father, Nelson, was there for the meal too. Although Nelson is physically well, he has a sadness about him that hasn't lifted since the death of his wife, Sophia. Julia visits her father several times a week, and they all enjoy a family meal together each Sunday. Monday, we visited with more family and old friends. Just past sunrise on Tuesday, we left Doylestown for home, arriving back in Easton at sunset. We again stayed at the Hotel Easton and left early Wednesday for Mansfield Woodhouse. We were safely at home well before noon on Wednesday and happy to be back to our farm. Albert and the girls did a wonderful job keeping the farm going while we were gone.

It is great news that the construction of Benjamin Warne's mill is moving along nicely. The building is huge and being made of stone; it appears to be a fortress. Will it be ready to grind the grain this fall? We may have to take our harvest to the mill in Pleasant Valley this fall season.

Henry Creveling's tavern stand has quite the business. Jacob Echman seems to be doing a great job managing the place. The Mineral Springs Hotel has lost some of its business as the tavern stand is much more laid back then the hotel saloon. Isaac and Eli stopped in a few times for a mug of dark stout and enjoyed the company. They heard that the captain hung on to his seat at the hotel and has only stopped by to spy on the locals. Isaac said everyone about town knows the captain's stories and pays him no mind; this is why he is still at the hotel snaring the newcomers to listen to his war tales.

We have also been getting bits and pieces of a preliminary peace treaty with the British that is taking place in Paris. Sometime this past April, John Adams, Benjamin Franklin, and men I am not so familiar with, John Jay and Henry Laurens, traveled to Paris to negotiate this treaty. Goodness, just get it over with!

CHAPTER 62

The harvest is over, and our lofts, springhouse, and root cellars are filled. Pieter and Albert have done well for themselves selling hay and oats to several men in the Hall's Mills area. As promised, they made no attempt to infringe on any of the customers taken care of by Jeremiah Smith. Especially since Albert has taken quite a liking to Anna, his daughter.

Isaac heard that last week, General Washington officially gave a farewell address to the army and formally discharged his soldiers. His resignation as commander in chief will take place soon, if it has not already been done. I guess we can safely say this rotten war has ended, with or without a signed treaty. Praise the Lord, and may we all strive to live peacefully together.

Jacob is almost nine months old already. What an adorable baby, not just because he is our grandson, but he is also chubby cute! Lilia is back to her old self and tending to their home and family. When the weather is nice, they enjoy sharing in our noonday meal each Sunday they attend church.

Jason Hixson seems to have adoring eyes for our Elizabeth. I caught the two of them several times exchanging long glances during church lately. After the service, they shared in a bit of conversation before we left for home. Gosh, my children are growing too quickly.

Isaac did a wonderful job with the hope chests that he built for each of the girls. Each chest is the same size but has a special craving that Isaac created. Elizabeth's chest has trailing roses carved into the front, Catherina's chest has tiger lilies, and Abigail's has sprigs of lily of the valley. The girls were thrilled to receive the chests as a gift from their father, and his workmanship is impeccable. We have started making towels, dishclothes, and tea towels for their chests. Each has worked diligently on their samplers and are almost completed. They have learned so many different types of stitches, and the samplers display their creativity. Once this project has been completed, we will begin lessons on tatting. Tatting is actually lace making and can be used to trim off the collar of a dress or blouse, doily or even the bottom of a tea towel.

Jasmine and Ruby paid us a visit earlier this week. A few weeks ago while at church, Jasmine said that she was looking forward to a trip back to her home in Carteret, since she felt safe that the war was over. Well, she and Ruby took the Elizabeth Town stage last week and went to visit her family. They said they had a wonderful visit, and it was really difficult to return to Mansfield Woodhouse. I told her that I could relate to her dilemma, as I experienced the same thing when we went back to visit our parents in Doylestown. Being used to civilization and then returning to the country is difficult. Jasmine knew how much I like rice and to be able to make a nice rice pudding, so she brought me five pounds of rice. What a wonderful, thoughtful gift! The two stayed to visit and enjoyed a cup of tea. I wondered to myself if Amos, Jasmine, and Ruby would return to Carteret and his families general store now that the war is over. It would be sad to see them go, but I know that their family has a well-established business, and there are many more opportunities for Amos in the city than here in the country.

The war caused many people and their families to become uprooted, and now they face the challenge of whether to return to the places they left behind due to war or stay and continue rebuilding their new lives, wherever that may be. For some, returning is not an option, as their homes, even towns, are in shambles from cannonballs or burned to the ground. As Isaac often says, war is hell.

CHAPTER 63

It appears that the snowfall doesn't slow the affection between a lad and lass. Albert asked to borrow the sleigh so he could take Anna Smith for a moonlight ride. The couple, along with friends Laura Harte, and Will Weller, took a ride to Hampton and back a few evenings ago. They stopped by our home, and I made the shivering group some hot cocoa with gingerbread. It was fun to watch the four of them laugh and enjoy their time together. When they left to go back to the Smith farm, they invited Elizabeth to join them. I was quite surprised that they would invite a younger sister to join in their fun. Elizabeth is still raving about the fun she had and hopes that she is asked again to share in another adventure.

The girls and I attended a quilting bee at Susanna Carter's home. Sarah and her girls were invited as well. We were making a quilt for a wedding gift for Aunt Peggy's daughter, Charity. Susanna thought it would be a nice gesture if all of the area women contributed to the quilt, as Aunt Peggy has in some way touched all of our lives. What fun, we stitched and chatted the afternoon away. Lizzie Bryan agreed to put the finishing touches on our work. While at the quilting bee, I couldn't help but notice the spectacles that Agnes Kinney was wearing. When I commented on her not having to remove her spectacles to see afar, she said that they were new, and she could see both near and far with the same pair of eyewear! She continued to say that they were called double-spectacles and had recently been invented by Benjamin Franklin of Philadelphia. Oh my, how wonderful to not have to change spectacles to see properly. What will they think of next?

The occasional newspaper that makes its way to Mansfield Woodhouse from Easton relays details of the Treaty of Paris, the document officially ending the war. Finally, it was officially ratified, and England has set us free. Thomas Jefferson, John Adams, and Benjamin Franklin are in Paris attempting to now negotiate commercial trade agreements with foreign countries so we can trade some of our natural resources for things like spices, cocoa, and tea. If we are able to trade freely with other countries, we will no longer need to depend on any one area to supply us with our needs.

James has been doing quite well with his short stories from the frontier for the *Doylestown Gazette*. He recently questioned Isaac about traveling to Easton to visit the *Easton Daily Paper*. Isaac said it was a great idea to explore new possibilities, but due to the unpredictable weather, a trip to Easton would have to wait a few more months. Isaac also suggested that James take the time and put together some of the articles that have been published to show to the editor of the *Easton Daily Paper*.

CHAPTER 64

Jason Hixson approached Isaac at church this past week and asked for his permission to visit Elizabeth. Albert was standing near and overheard the conversation and joined in, saying when opportunity presents itself again, perhaps he, Jason, Elizabeth, and Anna could enjoy a sleigh ride. Isaac felt a bit relieved by Albert's suggestion and agreed as long as the four of them participated. We have plenty of snow on the ground, so all we need to do is wait for a well-lit evening. As difficult as it is, Isaac needs to loosen the reigns on Elizabeth and give her some freedom, as she is now a young lady of eighteen years.

Levi Dickenson of Beattystown called an impromptu meeting of all the men who were at church. Levi was asking for suggestions on how to assist Harold Taylor and his family, who lost everything on Saturday due to a terrible house fire. Harold, Ruth, and their children managed to get out of the house uninjured, but the fire spread quickly due to gusting winds. The family has moved in with Ruth's parents, John and Ellen Castner, until they find a new place to live. Harold will have to travel every day back to the farm to tend to the animals. The Taylors have been renting the farm from Mr. Robinson for the past few years. Since the farm does not belong to the couple, Levi was looking for ways to get them back on their feet. Such a terrible thing to lose everything you own, but thankfully, God stepped in to save them and their children. Mr. Robinson was said to have suffered from extreme stress watching the fire and had to be taken back to his home to try and calm himself down. Several suggestions were raised, but Levi wants to speak with Mr. Robinson and find out if he plans on rebuilding the house. The message that we are here to help will be passed along at that time.

Now to pen some pleasing news, Eli and Sarah's daughter, Ruth, will betroth Gerald Smith, son of Jeremiah and Rebecca Smith. Gerald is also the brother of Anna, whom Albert is sweet on. Eli made the announcement in church—it was quite a busy Sunday morning, that's for sure. The wedding will take place in late spring at Eli and Sarah's farm. Ruth and Gerald make such a handsome couple, and everyone wished them well. Sarah couldn't have been more pleased with Ruth's choice and the fact that their daughter will remain close here in the valley. Goodness, two of our young ladies marrying in the spring of '84!

The twins, and their cousins, Nelson and Edward, went ice fishing earlier today with great success. The boys said they had quite a time finding a place to cut the hole because the cold temperatures has allowed the ice to freeze thick. Once they found their perfect spot, it took them awhile to chisel the large hole through the ice. Despite the misery of the day, they managed to catch a mixture of bass and perch, eleven in all. James and Joseph brought home five, and the other six went with Nelson and Edward. I decided to make them for our evening meal. After filleting the fish, they were coated with cornmeal and baked until they were nice and flakey. It was a real treat for this time of year, and we all ate our fill.

CHAPTER 65

John and Ellen Castner invited the entire valley to a corn roast at their farm. This was a way of saying thank you to everyone that in some way, big or small, showed their support in helping Harold, Ruth, and their children after their home was destroyed by fire. It seemed like everyone attended, even if just for an hour or two. Susanna Hoppock got the women together over the past few months, and we created one large quilt and three smaller ones for the children. I can tell you that these quilts were made out of love for Ruth and her family. Elwood and William Bryan fiddled, and many of us danced.

It was at this corn roast that I learned of an amazing happening. In France this past January, a huge balloon was built by two brothers named Joseph-Michael and Jacques-Etienne Montgolfier. They constructed this balloon out of silk and lined it with paper. They filled the balloon with a new gas they had discovered that was lighter than air when heated by an onboard controlled fire. Magically, the balloon gently climbed from the earth and floated in the air carrying seven passengers to the height of three thousand feet for over thirty minutes, safely landing and boasting about the adventure. Flying in the sky like a bird amazes me. What is this world coming to? Several of the menfolk said they would take a ride; most of the women said no way.

Yet another summer is coming to an end. Early in June, we had quite a bout with cicadas. The noise they created was deafening and most annoying. Our crops fared well, and aside from the shells that they deposited practically everywhere when shedding their outer covering, they were gone within two weeks. Sonny said that the insects actually died after laying their eggs. The eggs will stay buried in the ground for an unbelievable seventeen years, and then the life cycle begins anew. So I ask myself, just what is their purpose other than to completely annoy us with their high-pitch sounds? I never remembered these most useless bugs from my childhood, although Sonny assured me they were there. The hawks sure got their fill of both live and dead cicadas, so perhaps they are here as a food for the birds? I doubt it, but I have no other reasonable explanation, but I need not worry about them for another seventeen years.

CHAPTER 66

Another year, another chance to begin anew, may it be filled with peace and love for all. Early spring, we can expect a new little one to arrive as Ruth and Gerald are expecting their first child in April. Sarah and Eli are over the moon with joy and eagerly awaiting this little bundle of joy.

We also hear that Benedict and Peggy Arnold are thriving in England, where they were more or less encouraged to move. After the horrible attempt to steal our West Point, Peggy and her son moved back to her parent's home in Philadelphia. Arnold joined the British Army and was given the rank brigadier general. This man was truly a hero at the battles at Fort Ticonderoga and Saratoga, to name a few, but he jumped sides and actually fought against the same men he once fought alongside! The Arnolds, for safety concerns for their growing family and themselves, had to leave America and now reside in England.

The year 1785 may see yet another marriage within our family. Albert and Anna seem to be totally committed to their relationship. It would not surprise Isaac and me if the two decide to become husband and wife. Albert has been building quite a nest egg with the profits from his fur trapping. He has also recently discussed with his father the remaking of the carriage house that is part of the farm we purchased from Edward Parker. The carriage house sits a short distance from Pieter and Lilia's home. It is a sturdy structure and has a second floor and also has a rock-lined cellar. It would need a fireplace, chimney, well, and privy; but that is certainly doable. Albert even drew up a sketch of what the inside of the carriage house could look like.

The snow-covered roadways have allowed for several evening sleigh rides for Albert, Anna, Elizabeth, and Jason. Isaac is still having a difficult time in letting go of his firstborn daughter, Elizabeth. One can only imagine what lays ahead for Abigail when she finds someone that tickles her fancy. Given the fact that Abigail is the baby of the family and Isaac's last daughter, the ability to let her "go" will be very tough.

I received a nice newsy letter from my sister Lydia. Solomon's son Arron and wife, Lucy, are also expecting a child due sometime in the early summer. The couple have put their own creative touches on Papa and Mama's house, and Lydia said it looks very nice. It still makes me sad when I think of my parents and just how quickly they became ill and passed on. I am forever grateful that I was able to give them each a hug and tell them that I loved them one more time. Sometimes, life just seems unfair, but I also truly believe that God is in control, and He has a reason for all things, big and small.

CHAPTER 67

The entire valley suffered from a severe thunderstorm that caused our crops to lay over and become matted down. We hoped for a few days of gentle breezes to dry out the hay, wheat, and barley crops to help get it off the ground, even just a bit, but it wasn't to be. We lost much of the hay to mold; what could be salvaged was measly. After much hard work, we managed to get a portion of the wheat and barley to the mill, but it is going to be a very lean winter season, to say the least. The corn fared well, and we will have food for our animals, but we will have to ration the hay. I guess we dare not complain, as it has been many years since we suffered from crop failure such as this due to violent storms. The apples endured the storm and are not quite ready to be picked.

Work on the carriage house is almost complete. Stone for the fireplaces was collected from our hedgerows and created beautiful hearths. Two fireplaces needed to be constructed as Albert's home has a second floor, not a loft, so each floor has its own heat source. This will be double the amount of wood needed for cold weather, but it was necessary to have heat in the upper part of the house. Water was found on the first try, so the well is just off the front door of the home and a real convenience. Anna, her sisters, and her mother, Rachel, have been working to polish and shine the inside of the house in preparation for Anna and Albert's late-October wedding. It is such a pleasure to watch the giddy groom and bride-to-be; it brings back so many happy memories.

Elizabeth and Jason seem to get along nicely. Jason visits every Sunday after church and shares our noonday meal with us. Isaac is becoming accustomed to having Jason around, and Jason has no problem jumping in to help, such as assisting with the remaking of the carriage house. So will Elizabeth be our next bride? My mother's intuition tells me probably yes! Catherina has yet to show interest in the lads, but she does have many friends, but no one special.

It is strange not to have our daily Bible reading lessons. Abigail is now fourteen and often sits with me while I read from my Bible, but our studies have ended. We still enjoy discussing the Bible stories as we go about our daily chores, but we no longer have reading lessons. It does make me sad, but the purpose was to teach our children to read and write, as well as learn the scripture, and we have certainly accomplished what we set out to do.

James visited the office of the *Easton Daily News* and was able to convince the editor to allow him to write a column about the Mansfield Woodhouse area every few weeks. His column will include local news, both good and sad, as well as happenings and current events from our area. He will be compensated for anything that he writes that is printed.

On the urging of Julia, Isaac and Eli traveled to Doylestown to visit with their father, Nelson. Nelson is now showing the signs of old age, as he is extremely forgetful and having trouble moving about. The brothers left on horseback mid-May and stayed in Doylestown for three days, visiting with relatives and friends. Albert took charge of our farm, and Nelson stepped up and handled the affairs of Eli's farm. Things went rather well, and I am so happy that the brothers got to visit with their father and enjoy his company. One just never knows when the good Lord will call any of us back home.

CHAPTER 68

Albert and Anna's wedding was lovely. They married in our church, and the bride's parents served everyone who was lucky enough to be invited, cake and punch. They quickly settled into their "new" home and appear to be doing well. We see Albert every day as he is still helping Isaac with the animals and in the spring will help plant the crops. Eventually, Albert hopes that the fruit trees will thrive and become his means of making a living. He stills traps, but since priorities have changed, not as often as before his marriage.

In church last Sunday, Jason and his father, Bert, talked quite a while with Amos about the demand for work as a cooper. Jason has been working as an apprentice with a cooper in the Hackettstown area and has almost completed his training. The three spoke of the need for wooden kegs, buckets, tubs, and barrels in the city area. Since the war has thankfully ended, the need for powder kegs has all but fizzled out. Since Amos is from Carteret, Bert thought, perhaps Amos could suggest a way to market items that Jason plans to make. Amos suggested that Jason go to Easton and visit a few of the breweries and distilleries in hopes of supplying them with some of the barrels used in the sale of beer and whiskey.

The fall harvest went well, and the slaughter of the pigs brought yet another season to an end. It just seems as if the years are passing by faster with each year. Sonny stopped by to offer to help with the slaughter, and Isaac gratefully accepted his offer. Sonny knows by now that any work he does with or for us, he will be fairly compensated. Things that used to be simple tasks are now beginning to become more difficult to do with each passing year. Are we really getting that old, and just when did all of this aging begin? Even Sonny's children are no longer little tots but teenagers themselves!

All of our sons took part in annual "bird hunting" adventure, along with Isaac, Eli, and Eli's sons. Gerald was invited to join them as well. Their day out was well worth the effort as the group came back with two geese and two ducks. Sarah and Eli are hosting the Christmas meal this year, and it will be quite a feast. It will be even more special with the birth of their first grandchild, Sid, this past April. The girls and I have been baking cookies and both ginger and pumpkin breads to take to Sarah's on Christmas. That is, if the family doesn't eat all of the pumpkin bread before Christmas Day!

CHAPTER 69

The bugbite that Jon Thatcher has been suffering with the past several months has claimed his life. Aunt Peggy was never quite sure what type of bug actually bit Jon. There for a while, Jon appeared to be getting his strength back and even helped Eli move his privy. This past fall, Jon started getting weaker and weaker until he was bedridden. He passed away three days ago, and today we all attended his funeral. The couple had no children to help them, so Isaac and Eli made sure they had ample firewood, and the community helped with food too.

Hilda has a brother Lester who lives in Monmouth who came here to Mansfield Woodhouse to attend to things as Jon's condition worsened. Lester and his sons are cleaning out the Thatcher home and moving Hilda back to Monmouth to live with them. Immediately following the funeral, I saw Bert and Jason Hixson talking with Lester for what seemed like a very long time. Well, according to Elizabeth, Bert has put in an offer to buy the Thatcher property. The plan is that Jason will live there and start his cooper business. The property is about eight acres, has a cabin, wagon shed, and a good-size barn. The barn has plenty of room for Jason to operate his business inside and still have room for storage of his inventory.

The weather has been mild since the beginning of March. Actually, the winter could be considered mild as well. We experienced moderate snowfall and no major winter storms, so I guess we can expect an early spring. The fields are still too wet to plant, but the March winds will do their trick and dry things up quickly.

Isaac brought me a letter from my sister Lydia this past week. All is well with my family in Doylestown. They too had a mild winter and an easy time keeping the walkways cleared. As with each letter from back home, my sister wanted to know when we will be visiting again. I am uncomfortable with Isaac and me traveling to Doylestown with both Albert and Pieter no longer living at home. The farm's chores are too much for the girls to handle, and James and Joseph aren't really into farming. Unless we take the whole family to visit, I don't see me traveling to Doylestown anytime soon. One can only hope that we can make the trip sometime in 1786 before yet another year ends.

CHAPTER 70

The corn was better than knee-high by the 4th of July, so this growing season has lots of promise. Even our garden is doing great. The rain is just at the right times so I haven't had to carry water from the brook to keep my plants happy.

Bert Hixson was able to purchase the Thatcher place, and Jason is busy establishing his business. The cabin was in need of minor repairs but was built nice and sturdy. With a place to live and the start of a new business, Jason asked Isaac for his daughter's hand in marriage. Despite the fact that we both saw this coming, Isaac still appeared to be shocked at the request. He did say yes, but deep within his heart, he wanted to say no. Seriously, what more could a father want for his daughter? Jason is a very nice young man, has his own home, and is starting a business. I like the fact that Elizabeth will be about a half mile away, and we will see her often. The wedding is planned for late September.

James, Joseph, Nelson, and Edward traveled to Phillipsburg to watch the passing of a steamboat on its way to Belvidere. The boat has been making its way up the Delaware River from Trenton for the past few days. It does not travel during darkness. Being steam-powered, it doesn't depend on the wind to push it along. This appears to be the latest mode of travel. From what we hear, there are a few of these boats navigating the Mississippi River carrying people and goods from one town to another. The boys said that it is a forty-five-foot vessel that puts out lots of black smoke. There are oars on both sides of the ship that are run by the steam, that in turn pushes the boat through the water quite rapidly. Quite a strange site to see without men operating the oars. They all agreed that it was quite a spectacle and worth the trip to see it.

The entire valley was invited to another hoedown at Lewis Harte's farm. The festivities started a bit later due to the heat, but boy was it fun. The Bryan brothers, Joshua Roy and Lester Brown, again provided the music. What a wonderful time to visit with our friends we seldom see. Each family brought a dessert, and Lewis provided the drinks. Since it was a beautiful full moon, everyone stayed until well past ten o'clock. It was a joy watching both the young and old get up and dance. Albert and Anna danced a few dances, even though she is expecting their first child sometime in February. Isaac and I must have been up dancing more than any other couple. We just had lots of fun!

CHAPTER 71

Elizabeth made a beautiful bride wearing her special dress that was made just for her by Lizzy Bryan. In late July, we made a trip to the Easton market, and Elizabeth selected a pretty green calico fabric, fancy-looking pearl buttons, and off-white lace trim. Lizzy designed a beautiful drop-waist dress that fit Elizabeth perfectly. Elizabeth pulled her hair up into a bun and added some tiny white flowers. She looked stunning. The wedding took place here on our farm, and we had almost forty people attend. Even though Amos and Jasmine were guests, I just don't know what I would have done without their help. Amos took charge of serving the drinks, and Jasmine and Lilia cut and served the cake. I got to enjoy my day and visit with our friends and family. As a wedding gift, Bert and Emma Hixson gifted the Thatcher homestead to the newlyweds. What a wonderful thing to do! They are now starting their marriage debt free, a dream so many wish they had.

Anna will soon be confined to her home and visit with only family as her pregnancy moves along. Such a stupid thing to have to stay hidden while carrying a child. Aunt Peggy believes Anna should not expect this little one until the end of February, perhaps even early March. But as a mother who has been through this six times, babies come when they are good and ready. All the calculating only gets you is a maybe delivery date, and all the wishing is just a reason to stress about something that is out of our control and in God's hands. Praying, now that can help ease the anxiety. One can never pray enough.

Sonny paid us a visit a few days ago. He and his family are doing well. However, according to Sonny, Howard Van Horne is not well. Within the last months, Howard has slowed his pace and rarely comes out of his house. Isaac believes Howard to be in his early sixties, and as we all know, no one lives forever. Abigail asked Sonny what will happen to him and his family if Mr. Van Horne should die. Sonny reminded Abigail that he belongs to the Van Horne family, and his future will be up to Mrs. Van Horne and her children. Thoughts started to race through my mind. What if Sonny and his family are given their freedom? What will Sonny do? Where will the family live? Then I snapped back to reality feeling terribly guilty as Howard needs to pass on before any of this should even be thought about.

My entire family joined us for our evening meal. It was wonderful having everyone squeeze around our kitchen table, holding hands and thanking the Lord for all the good that he has brought us. Catherina, Abigail, and I prepared a feast for our meal. Isaac and Eli were very lucky and brought down an elk earlier this week. Tonight, we shared one of the large roasts from this huge animal, along with vegetables from our root cellar. It was such a joy to be able to share in our children's lives. I missed this the most when we moved from Doylestown to here in Mansfield Woodhouse. Now I get to live it through my children.

CHAPTER 72

Tears stain my paper and cloud my eyes making it difficult to write. Anna carried her child into the third week of February, going into labor about noon on Tuesday. She struggled in pain finally delivering the baby early Friday morning. The baby was born with the cord tightly wrapped around her neck. Aunt Peggy did all that she could, but the child apparently had the cord around her neck long before her birth, and she could offer no help. Why God? Why take a perfect little girl with ten fingers and ten toes, lots of golden hair, and chubby cheeks?

My heart broke as I held her in my arms, such a perfect little gift from God but one not meant to keep. Anna did everything to perfection and now is in such despair we are unable to comfort her. Albert is in a daze and, at this time, unable to help Anna. Now one of those graves that is dug in the late fall and filled with branches and straw, just in case, will be the final resting place for our little angel Ester. My heart aches for Anna, Albert, baby Ester, and my entire family. I pray that God eases our pain and helps our family get through this terrible time.

This afternoon, baby Ester will be laid to rest in our church cemetery. The sun came out a while ago, not sure why, as everything seems to be in shades of gray. Isaac carved a special lid for the tiny wooden coffin that will entomb our precious little angel. He worked the entire night through to have it completed before this afternoon's burial. He carved a baby bunny surrounded by daisies. He is distraught, and this is his way of dealing with his pain. Each of us seem to be searching for the magic that will take the pain away. Prayer helps, but I guess it will take time for all of us, especially Albert and Anna to find some relief. I cannot imagine their pain and feelings of guilt, despite the fact that it is was in no way their fault. As Pastor Carson told us earlier, "Don't try to seek an answer as to why God called little Ester home because there is no answer." There is never a life without sadness, and I guess the grief we feel is a sign that we truly care and that love has no bounds.

Albert said Anna is unable to attend the funeral. Helena Hoppock stopped by their home to offer condolences and some kindness to Anna. She offered to stay with Anna while Albert attended the service. Albert was grateful for her offer and not having to worry about Anna at home alone while Ester is laid to rest. So much sadness and confusion. Please, Lord, help us get through this, amen.

CHAPTER 73

The summer sun has been blasting down upon us! The earth has become scorched, and we desperately need rain. All our crops are holding their own, but if we don't get rain within a few days, we can plan on an early harvest. I can't remember a summer where all we did was carry buckets of water from the brook to the garden. The girls and I have been watering our plants every day for the past several weeks. Our vegetables are producing but only because of our relentless watering. When the rain does arrive, please, dear Lord, make it a gentle rain that lasts a few days, soaking the parched ground.

Elizabeth came to visit and have a cup of tea with me a few days ago. She shared with me that she and Jason are expecting a baby sometime in early April. I questioned her as to why she wasn't excited about this joyous news, as I surely found it to be wonderful. She said that she is but was afraid to show it because of Albert and Anna. Oh my goodness, her concern for her brother and his wife caused an ache in my heart. I explained that Anna will feel a bit of sadness but will understand and want to share in her happiness. I also shared that I believed Anna may be again with child as she has been very piqued and queasy the last few weeks. Elizabeth said that she and Jason planned on announcing the news this coming Sunday when everyone comes back to our home after church for Sunday dinner. I promised to keep her secret to myself and that she not say anything about Anna, as I could be wrong about her condition. Having been there six times, it would surprise me if there is no upcoming announcement from Albert and Anna on Sunday as well.

We were invited to supper at Eli and Sarah's home tonight. As we walked along the lane to their farm, I realized how our family was getting smaller. A few years ago, there would have been nine of us;

now we are a family of six. The same goes for Eli's family, as Ruth and Nelson have now gone on to start families of their own. Sophia will wed George Oberly, son of Oscar and Verna, from Still Valley, in early December. It pleases me to see that all of our children have done well with their choice of a mate and appear to be making it on their own. I truly believe that we have the Lord to thank for all the goodness he has blessed us with.

CHAPTER 74

Isaac hitched the smaller cart to Moses, as James and Joseph now ride their horses to church. So with just Catherina, Abigail, Isaac, and myself, there is no need for the larger wagon. We met the rest of our family at church. Pastor Carson preached a wonderful sermon and managed to finish in just a bit over an hour. When he becomes long-winded, the little ones begin to squirm; the mothers become anxious, and time seems to stand still. Stressful for everyone who has to deal with cranky little ones.

All of our children and their families came back to the farm for our Sunday meal. When I first got up this morning, I put a pork roast along with sauerkraut into the kettle over the fire to slow cook while we were at church. All I needed to do was finish cooking the potatoes, whip them, and put the apple sauce and bread and butter on the table. The girls helped set the table and get the containers of mint tea from the springhouse. We all sat down at about one-thirty, held hands, and gave thanks to the Lord for all the goodness that he has provided.

It was during dessert that Elizabeth said she had some good news to share, that she and Jason were expecting a child in early April. I kept my eyes on Anna to see her reaction and was pleased to see a smile on her face. After Elizabeth finished, Anna spoke up and said that she and Albert also had some good news to share, that they too were expecting a little one due around April as well. Everyone was overjoyed with the wonderful news. It looks like 1788 is going to bring at least two new babies into our family. I did notice a sadness on Lilia's face, as Jacob is now four years old, and he is still an only child. We are surely thankful for Jacob, but we would be pleased to see him have a brother or sister, or both. By the look on Lilia's face, it won't be happening before April of next year.

I overheard the children talking amongst themselves about the convention that has been taking place in Philadelphia since May. This convention is hashing out liberties and laws for our new nation. The group of representatives from each of the thirteen colonies have agreed on terms of just how this country will run our government, naming their document the Constitution of the United States. The document is now being passed along to each colony for their review and approval. Who would have ever thought of any of this prior to greedy King George squeezing us so tightly and imposing tariffs and taxes on things necessary to survive. Praise the Lord that the war is over, and may we all lay our weapons down in peace and solidarity.

After everyone had left for home and the chores were done, Isaac and I relaxed in our rockers on the front porch. I asked Isaac what he thought Sonny's future would hold if and when Mr. Van Horne passes on. Isaac appeared to be a bit shocked by my question but gave it considerable thought. After he suggested several possibilities, I asked him if we could buy Sonny and his family's freedom. I had my inheritance from my parents, and we could use some of that money to free the family and perhaps build a small home for them here on the farm. I continued to say that James and Joseph appear not to be interested in staying on the farm, and Isaac will soon need help with the daily chores and upkeep of the farm.

Isaac sat quietly for several minutes pondering the idea. When he began to speak, he said that he had no idea how much a human being is worth to a slave owner, let alone the entire family. He wasn't even sure who he could ask such a horrible question of. The city newspapers run ads all the time to buy and sell slaves, so he was guessing that would be the place to start. Considering that all of Howard's children have left the Mansfield Woodhouse area, the farm will probably be up for sale. As far as building a proper home for Sonny and his family, that was definitely doable. Isaac stressed one thing and that was that Sonny would be paid for his work, he would no longer be a slave, and although we paid for his freedom, we would not own him, his wife, or their children. I was overjoyed that Isaac and I were in agreement with Sonny and his family's future. We decided that this was our secret, and not a word to anyone until we put together a solid plan and the time arrives when we can act upon it.

As I was falling asleep, I thought of all the wonderful things that were taking place within our family. God has been good to us, and we need to share with those who have so much less than us. As I fell off to sleep, I remember thinking that the Lord is truly great.

CHAPTER 75

The snow held off until after Sophia and George's wedding on December 4. The wedding was held in Eli and Sarah's home. Our family, George's family, and of course, Sophia's family witnessed the brief ceremony led by Pastor Carson. Sophia looked beautiful in her scarlet-colored dress. Sarah did a wonderful job of arranging her great room to entertain thirty-two people. The newlyweds will be living in Still Valley on George's parent's farm. Not too terribly far away, perhaps six miles from her family.

Eli and Isaac, along with the boys and sons-in-law enjoyed their annual bird hunt. Returning from their day of hunting, Jason shot a six-point buck. The animal was taken to Eli's farm, which was the closer of the two, and processed there. Jason was excited to be able to add meat to our smokehouse. After the group butchered the buck, a portion was shared with Eli, who immediately placed his meat into his smokehouse. The deal is, and always was, anything, and everything is shared equally when hunting as a group. After the rest of the meat is smoked in our smokehouse, Jason will share the venison with all of us.

Scuttlebutt tells of information about a new family that will be moving into the area named Case. This family is having a store front built with living space above the business on the west end of the village. The family is from Elizabeth Town, where they operated a general store for many years. The stock will be a much wider variety of necessary household and farming items. There was an advertisement posted inside the tavern stand seeking a clerk to assist in running the store. Joseph took a real interest and visited with Amos for thoughts on what to include in his letter. Joseph asked Amos why he wasn't applying for the position, and he said that he wasn't quite financially ready to leave his job at the Mineral Springs, as it would also cost him his housing. At this time, having a roof over his family's head was the most important thing.

Christmas dinner was at our home this year. The girls and I decided to make it a covered-dish type of meal. For the first time ever, I asked each family group to bring a favorite dish to share so I had less to do. It worked really well, and the variety was refreshing. Sarah said that she would do the same next year, as we are getting older and all the preparation to make this feast happen is getting more and more difficult with each passing year. Plus, it freed up some extra time to just enjoy our family; after all, being together and sharing our love for one another is a big part of what Christmas is all about to our family.

CHAPTER 76

Easter was March 25 this year and couldn't have been much earlier. I am fond of Easter being celebrated in April, as blooming flowers and trees make me think of the earth reawakening and the start of a new beginning. Hopefully, 1788 will be a joyous year for all.

We certainly experienced a very hectic but joyous few weeks with the arrival of two new gifts from God. Anna delivered a baby girl on March 29, and all went well, and both mother and child are doing fine. Albert and Anna named their little one Anna-May. Elizabeth delivered her daughter on April 6, and both mother and baby are also doing fine. Jason and Elizabeth named their child Faith. Oh my goodness, both babies are absolutely adorable and perfect in every way. But then, I'm their grandmother, so I will never see anything but perfect. Thank you, God, for such wonderful gifts!

The winter snow is all but a memory, and the March winds have done a great job drying up the muddy roads and wet fields. Isaac has been able to plow the higher fields and ready them for planting. Pieter and Albert have been helping with this huge task. The fruit trees on the hillside have rooted well and appear to be burdened with blossoms. The lambs are ready to be sold, but Isaac has not heard a word from Howard Van Horne, as he always requested first pick. Isaac mentioned that perhaps he will ride over to the Van Horne farm and ask to speak with Howard. He doesn't want to sell the lambs out from under Howard's nose but does need to know if in fact Howard is even interested in adding more sheep to his herd. Oscar Oberly expressed an interest in possibly purchasing some lambs during Sophia and George's wedding. If there are extra lambs, Jason requested two to help keep the grass and weeds under control around their house and barn. Sheep are not fussy eaters and surely keep everything trimmed but must be watched so they don't do too good of a job and rip the grass out by its roots.

Construction is moving along on the future home of the Case General Store. Mr. Case is extremely interested in Joseph as a full-time clerk when the store opens. He has also selected a young man named Jeffrey Thomas from Good Springs as a part-time clerk. Joseph is very excited and can't wait to begin his career as a clerk. The store should be completed by late summer. Mr. Case is staying at the Mineral Springs Hotel and visits the construction site daily. He is also schmoozing it up with the local folks in hopes of getting some of their business once his store opens.

The *Easton Daily News* seems to be pleased with James's work. It is James's desire to get a weekly column, and although the editor has not yet agreed to this arrangement, he is being sent out to cover area events of interest for the paper. James has been spending more time in Easton than here on the farm. Isaac suggested that perhaps now is the time to find somewhere to board close to his place of work. Boarding from a family is far less expensive than taking a room at one of the local hotels. I'm not sure that James is ready to take that step. He expressed concern of coming back home if he boards elsewhere. I told him his bed would always be here, and we will always welcome him with open arms. Moving out on one's own is so different than marrying. When couples marry, two people begin a new life together. I believe that James may fear being alone and isn't quite ready to leave the safety of our home.

A few weekends ago, James, Joseph, and Edward went eeling at the Pleasant Valley mill pond. We have heard people rave about having to beat off the eels with a stick, so the boys tried their luck. They were very successful and returned home with a huge basket full of eels. Isaac and Eli helped the boys skin the eels and string the skins up to dry. Eel skin is very strong and, once dried, is very useful around the farm to bundle things when short on cord. Sarah and I prepared the eels the next day after church, and the meal was shared by both families; what a special treat enjoyed by all.

CHAPTER 77

Joseph started his job as a clerk at the Case General Store and absolutely loves the work. He works Monday through Friday, 7:00 a.m. to 6:00 p.m., and a half day on Saturday. No business is open on Sunday, as Sunday is our day to offer our praises to the Lord. Jeffrey Thomas works part-time and travels with Mr. Case back to Elizabeth Town to keep the store's inventory well-stocked. Isaac and I visited the store shortly after it opened, and both agreed that Mr. Case has quite an inventory of both household and farming implements. He also stocks gunpowder, wads and lead balls, an array of brads, saws, bear grease for treating leather, limited sewing needs, candles, beeswax, wicks, and so much more. He does stock some staples, such as brown sugar, flour, vinegar, molasses, salt, and pepper but not as much as Sarah's McCullough's store.

Mr. Case said that it was not his intention to put Miss McCullough out of business, but to make easier access to many necessary items needed for farming and life here in the country. Both Mr. Case and his wife, Liz appear to be lovely people. They also have a daughter Emily who seems to have caught Joseph's eye. Emily is a beautiful young lady about the same age as our Joseph. All three members of the Case family have started to attend the Mansfield Woodhouse Presbyterian Church.

Albert and Annie invited Catherina to their home for a small dinner group three weeks ago. Also invited to this get-together was Anna's cousin Robert Gardner from Harmony. It appears that Anna was playing matchmaker, as Robert and Catherina are both a bit shy. It also appears that this matchmaking may have worked, as the two have been in each other's company several times since they were introduced to one another. Robert's family operates the Gardner

Stables in Harmony where they breed, train, and sell horses. They are also blacksmiths and on the side, build and repair all types of wagons.

Earlier in the summer, Isaac paid a visit to the Van Horne farm to question Howard about his intent to purchase lambs this year. Isaac was taken aback when he spoke with Howard, as the man is now nothing but a skeleton. Mrs. Van Horne said that Howard has not felt well for over a year and seems to be slowly slipping away. Isaac never asked Howard about purchasing lambs, as the answer was quite apparent that the man could no longer tend his farm. If it wasn't for Sonny, the entire place would be slowly turning into shambles. Isaac told Howard that he heard he was not feeling tip-top and just stopped by to say hello and hoped that he would feel better soon. The couple's youngest daughter was visiting from out of town and helping her mother look after Howard. Isaac stayed about thirty minutes and, when leaving, offered his help in any way needed. Golly, we are glad that Sonny tipped us off that Howard was not well, as it would have been a complete shock to Isaac accidentally finding out about Howard's condition.

CHAPTER 78

On their return trip from the gristmill, Isaac and Eli picked up the mail and were going to enjoy a mug of dark stout at the Mineral Springs. However, both men received a letter from their sister Julia, and as they surmised, the contents were sad. Julia penned that their father Nelson had passed away in his sleep on Saturday, the same day the letters were written. The funeral service was scheduled from Nelson's home on Monday morning.

Today was Wednesday, so Nelson's funeral had already taken place. Julia requested both brothers come to Doylestown, especially Isaac, as he was appointed executor of the will. Isaac and Eli headed back to their homes and since it was still early afternoon decided to leave for Doylestown today. They would travel on horseback as long as daylight allowed them, finishing their journey tomorrow, arriving in Doylestown long before sunset tomorrow. The big question was just how long would they be away? How long does it take to read a will and settle an estate? Nelson's grandson Michael purchased the surveying business several months past, but the house and any outstanding debts needed to be tended to. Isaac doubted Nelson had any debts, but he may have extended credit to friends. Eli told Isaac that he would see him in about an hour and headed to his home. Isaac found me tending to my garden and shared the sad news with me. We went into the house and quickly prepared for Isaac's departure within the hour. A profound sadness settled over us as we didn't have a chance to say goodbye to Nelson.

Yes, the sons had visited and sent letters home often, but not being able to say goodbye left an empty spot in Isaac's heart. Had we still resided in Doylestown, we would have attended the funeral services. Isaac prayed that his father would forgive him for not being by his side in his time of need. With all of our sons out on their own, milking the cows and tending to the animals will now fall upon me, Catherina, and Abigail.

After Isaac and Eli rode off, I visited with Pieter and Albert to share the sad news. As expected, the boys stepped up and said that they would see to the animals being tended to until their father returned. They also said that they would check with Edward to see if he needed help keeping up with the farm chores until Eli returned home. There was a sadness about us, but not the same sadness we experienced with Sophia. I guess we prayed for Grandma Sophia to get well, and now we were praying that Grandpa Nelson finds peace in eternity.

CHAPTER 79

Isaac and Eli were gone for close to a month. They hung in there to settle Nelson's estate so they would not have to travel back to attend to loose ends. Julia's son Michael expressed a desire to purchase the house, and the three siblings agreed on a price, so that detail was solved quickly. The contents of the house were shared with the family and offered to my sisters, brother, and their families as well. Julia agreed to store some of their father's special things that the brothers wanted to keep, to be gathered up on another trip to Doylestown.

Riding on horseback limited what could be brought back home. When all was settled, each sibling got a whopping $4,800! I cannot believe that the two traveled back to Mansfield with that much cash on them. Thank goodness, I was unaware of this as I would have fretted from the time they left Doylestown until they arrived safely home. The good Lord was on their side, that is for sure! It was decided to keep the amount a secret from everyone but Sarah and I. We did the same thing with my inheritance from Papa and Mama as the outside world does not need to know our personal business. Money can cause people to do evil things. Jealously feeds greed and is also responsible for many wrongdoings.

Isaac was back home less than a week when we received word that Howard Van Horne had gone home to meet the Lord. Although it was expected, the news was still a bit of a surprise. We attended the funeral today at the McKinney Cemetery along with probably most of the valley. Howard was well-known and a respected businessman. After the service, Howard's sons Kenneth and Samuel approached Isaac and invited him to visit the farm tomorrow midmorning. The young men said that their father had great respect for Isaac's honesty and integrity, and they wanted to discuss some business with him.

This conversation came as quite a pleasant surprise, and Isaac agreed to meet with them tomorrow. This evening, we discussed possible reasons why the sons invited Isaac to their farm. We also discussed our plan to buy Sonny and his family's freedom. Isaac did a bit of research and believes that $1,000 would be a generous offer, hoping to get the family to agree on $750. We prayed together that the Van Hornes would agree to free this fine family.

Falling asleep was difficult as I kept thinking about Sonny and his family. What if the children decide to move their mother to Bergan County with them and take Sonny too? What if he is included in the deal to sell the farm? I guess we could afford to buy the farm, but what would we do with it? We certainly do not need another farm to run, as getting our everyday chores finished on our farm is becoming more and more difficult each year. I have complete trust in Isaac and know that he will do the right thing, so I decided to allow sleep to overtake me.

CHAPTER 80

Isaac was a bit nervous as he rode Dara out our short path and headed toward the Van Horne farm, not knowing quite what to expect. He met with Kenneth and Samuel Van Horne, as requested, and all of his concerns quickly vanished when the family offered Isaac an incentive for assisting in selling the farm; in exchange for him overseeing the sale of personal property, livestock, and the farm, they offered him Sonny and his family. Talk about being dumbfounded, Isaac said that he was speechless!

The family said that they were not fond of their father using slave labor when he could have afforded a hired hand. They continued to say that I had treated Sonny with kindness when he came to help out while Isaac was away at war. The family really liked Sonny, his wife, and children and wanted to be assured that they will be treated kindly, and they truly believe that we will treat them fairly. The sale of the farm and personal property will be a huge undertaking, but Isaac shook hands on the deal instantly. The family will keep the fine steed Howard rode himself and two mules and wagons to haul the items they are taking from the house.

Isaac would have first pick of everything else and arrange for an auction to sell the farm. After the handshake, the two sons handed Isaac a signed document transferring ownership of Sonny and his family to him. The three of them then went out to the barn area where they found Sonny hard at work and delivered the news of the sale to him. Isaac said Sonny began to weep as he feared that he and his family would be sold separately and that they would never see one another again. I cried when Isaac relayed this to me: how awful that a human being has to be frightened that his family could be taken from him. Isaac said it happens often, and the slave owners that do such a thing should spend eternity in hell. Hell is not good enough!

Sonny will stay put on the farm for the time being, continuing to care for the animals until they are sold. After the farm has been sold, Sonny and his family will come and live on our farm where they will be paid for their toil. The Van Horne family expects to leave the area with their mother within the week. What is left in the house will be Isaac's responsibility to try and sell or, if all else fails, give away. All of the business discussed is to remain confidential for the time being. The family does not want nosy people sneaking around their property causing trouble. All I could say was praise the Lord! Now we need to step up our game and build a proper home for Sonny and his family. Isaac has a ton of work ahead of him to get the animals and farm sold. God is great!

CHAPTER 81

The Van Horne daughters and their mother left the area and headed back to their own lives in Bergan County by stage. Kenneth and Samael packed two wagons with special things from the house, hitched the mules to the wagons, and they too headed back to their homes, with Howard's fine steed in tow. Howard did not have any cows but raised and sold pigs, goats, and sheep. He also owned two more horses, several different types of wagons and a fancy carriage. Isaac prepared signs and delivered them to all the businesses, hotels, and tavern stands within a reasonable distance from the farm, listing what was for sale. He contacted Melvin Cooper, who was known for auctions and the farm, equipment, livestock, the house, and eighty-two acres were advertised for auction November 3. This only gave Isaac less than a month to get things in order as all of the items needed to be inspected, cleaned, and displayed for the sale.

Meanwhile, back at home, temporary housing for Sonny and his family was taking shape. All of our sons and sons-in-law jumped in to help. Renovations were being done to the large tool and wagon shed that sits along the brook below the main house. The place is not beautiful but secure, waterproofed, and protected from the cold winter chill. Sonny and Tulia found it to be wonderful as it was more than twice the size of the home they live in on the Van Horne farm. The family also got to pick out furniture and housewares that was left over from clearing out the Van Horne home. Tulia was timid, but Isaac encouraged her to take what she wanted as what was left had to be disposed of before the new owners moved in. The look of happiness on Tulia's face warmed Isaac's heart. Isaac also promised a special cabin would be built just for them come next spring on a spot of their choosing.

Isaac hasn't had the time to sit with Sonny and Tulia to tell them that they are no longer slaves and that we do not own them, as they are now free. After things settle down and the Van Horne farm deal is completed, we can get this straightened out. Right now, I can't even have a reasonable conversation with Isaac as he is totally stressed. He knew that overseeing the sale of the Van Horne estate would be a daunting task, and now he is living it.

CHAPTER 82

The weather held out for the auction on November 3, and it was well-attended. The livestock and farm equipment sold quickly. The farm itself didn't bring the price that the family had hoped for. A man named Herbert Jenkins, from Flemington, offered the final bid and is now the new owner. Jenkins said that his son Adam will be managing the farm, and they plan on breeding and selling Jersey cattle. The Jersey produce excellent milk and can also be used as draught animals. It will be interesting to see how many farmers line up to buy his cows. Out here, we use oxen or mules to pull our carts and heavy loads.

A few days after the auction, Kenneth and Samuel returned to Mansfield Woodhouse to collect the profit from the sale. They didn't appear to be upset about the estate selling for less than they had hoped. In fact, they were grateful that it was over. I know that Isaac was more than pleased that he had completed his part of the bargain. Isaac was actually surprised when the Van Hornes insisted that he take $25 for all the work and time he put into the sale.

Sonny, Tulia, Kit, and Toby seem to be happy in their new temporary home. Isaac had the sit-down discussion with Sonny and Tulia a few weeks ago. The couple was concerned when Isaac said that they were now free people, but they were welcome to stay with us here on the farm. This area is all that the children know, and it has been home to Sonny and Tulia ever since Howard purchased them at a slave auction on the Philadelphia docks. Isaac assured them that they can stay with us as long as they wish and that Sonny and Toby will be paid for their work. If Tulia and Kit help with the garden, laundry, housework, whatever, they too will be paid. They appeared to be confused, but as Isaac said, they will get used to their new life and surely enjoy it more.

The Christmas season is quickly passing, and we can only hope that the cold weather moves on as well. The start of a new year is a fresh start for all of us. Isaac and I will both turn forty-seven next year, quite a scary thought as to how we got from 1742 to 1789 so quickly. As these last few days of December come to a close and yet another year is upon us, I thank the Lord for all that has taken place. It has been for the most part a year of fulfillment as well as ponderous. The fact that Howard Van Horne had to die to allow Sonny and his family the freedom that all humans deserves haunts me. I wonder if Howard entered the gates of heaven or is spending eternity in hell. I can only hope that he was granted forgiveness.

CHAPTER 83

The fields are planted and appear to be growing nicely. The farm is in good repair, and our lambs and piglets have been sold and delivered to the prospective buyers. We are well ahead of our schedule, thanks to Sonny and Toby. The two of them freed up time for Pieter and Albert to tend to the orchard and Pieter's fields. In between all of this spring work, a cabin is being built for Sonny and his family, along a gentle slope next to a bubbling spring. Once the home is finished, the men will build a small springhouse similar to the one Isaac built for us. Tulia has the beginnings of a nice garden and is still telling us that this life is like a wonderful dream. Isaac reminds her that this is what their life should have been all along, and they deserve every bit of the good fortune coming their way. Amen and thank the Lord that things worked out the way they did. Both Isaac and I couldn't be more pleased to share our farm with Sonny and his family.

Things for our country seem to be moving along as well. The first Congress met in Federal Hall, New York City, this past March. The Electoral College announced that George Washington was elected unanimously as our first president of the United States. John Adams was elected vice president. President Washington was inaugurated on April 30 in New York City. We did not have a direct presidential election, but both men were chosen by representatives from each states. The population of the state will depend on how many electoral votes that state will have. Quite confusing, to say the least, but it seems to get the job done. We couldn't be more pleased with both of these men. Now let's get down to business and somehow get our soldiers paid for their service.

Our family continues to grow with the news of four more littles ones due late this year and early 1790. Anna and Elizabeth are both with child in our family. Ruth and Sophia will each give Eli and Sarah two more grandchildren, one late this year and the other early January. Sadly, we have not heard any baby news from Pieter and Lilia. Jacob visits with us often when Pieter stops by to assist Isaac. Jacob is such a pleasure to be around and wants to be my little helper. God, thank you for the gift of grandchildren!

Catherina and Robert have become very serious in their relationship. A proposal of marriage seems to be in the air. Hopefully, Isaac will have an easier time letting her move on into a new life than he did with Elizabeth.

Joseph really enjoys his work at the Case General Store. The store seems to be doing well, and Joseph says he has little time to take a break, even to enjoy his lunch. We're not so sure that he isn't attempting to impress Mr. Case to win him over, as Joseph is sweet on his daughter Emily. To see the two talk after church each Sunday leads us to believe that their relationship could evolve into more than friends.

James has taken a room in a boarding house in the city of Easton. As long as the weather is good, he comes home late Saturday, attends Sunday church service, and comes back home for our family dinner. He leaves to go back to Easton late Sunday afternoon. He absolutely loves his work with the newspaper.

Then there is our baby Abigail, even now that she is fifteen. She seems content mixing with her cousins Bella and Laura. They make a wonderful trio, and so far, none of the three are overly interested in the lads. I am sure that this will change and very quickly.

CHAPTER 84

Jason is ending the year with a handshake and a promise to provide whiskey kegs to the Kempton Distillery in Easton. He took the advice that Amos suggested and traveled to Easton paying a visit to the largest distillery. He has been working long hours, but the company likes his product, so he just may have to take on a hired man. It is wonderful to see someone begin a business, putting their heart and soul into it, and watch as things take shape and the business begins to grow.

Ruth and Gerald are the proud parents of a son they named Luke. Little Luke was born December 20 and is in good health. Eli and Sarah couldn't be more pleased. We are still awaiting the other three arrivals, and if they don't arrive soon, they will be New Year babies. Anna, Elizabeth, and Sophia are all doing well, so we have to remain calm as I am sure they too want all of this to be over.

Sonny, Tulia, and their children are very pleased with their new home. Tulia invited Catherina, Abigail, and me over of a cup of tea—something she said she had never done. It was a joy visiting with her and Kit, and the scones were marvelous! Tulia said that she can't thank Isaac and me for all that we have done for them. We thank the Lord that all of this was able to come about.

The farm is ready for winter and whatever it may bring our way. The butchering of pigs went well, and Isaac again had our four largest pigs slaughtered. With all the work that Sonny does to help with keeping this farm running, he received a generous share of the meat as well.

Adam Jenkins seems to be working hard to keep the old Van Horne place running. He now has a herd of perhaps twenty Jerseys. They are beautiful animals, but then so are our Holsteins. All of them produce the same product, milk, but I'm guessing Jersey may have richer cream?

Joseph got the nerve to ask Mr. Case if he could take his daughter Emily for a moonlit sleigh ride. He assured him that Catherina and Robert would also be coming along for the adventure. After coaxing from his wife, Mr. Case said yes, and Joseph is over the moon. Somehow, Bella and Laura got Edward to agree to take their sleigh out too, along with Abigail. The group had a wonderful time visiting with Lucy and Rosa Hixson in Changewater. As Sarah said to me later, the empty nest is quickly approaching.

CHAPTER 85

This spring should be one for the record books. It seems as if every-thing bloomed on cue, and the earth is alive with beauty. We are also alive with beauty as the births of the three littles ones has brought joy into all of our lives. Sophia gave birth to a son that the couple named Raymond, on January 3. George is pleased as punch with the birth of a boy and is already making plans for working the farm together. Elizabeth birthed next and gave us a beautiful granddaughter they named Grace, on January 15. Finally, on February 3, Anna presented us with a grandson that they named Ellis. All of the babies and their mamas are doing fine, and we can now breathe a sigh of relief that things went well for everyone.

Today, as we travel to church, we will celebrate the christening of Raymond, Grace, and Ellis. Both Sarah and I baked special cakes to enjoy after the church service. We will also serve punch along with the cake. Ruth and Gerald had little Luke baptized a few weeks ago. It seems as if every week brings a new little one into the family of God.

After church, our family came back to the farm for our Sunday family dinner. Abigail whispered to me as we were putting the final touches on our meal to look at her father, and Robert engaged in a very serious conversation near the paddock. Both of us traded smiles, and I whispered back that *mum* was the word. After our meal was finished and we were enjoying dessert, Isaac said that he had an announcement to make. He told us that he had given his blessings to Robert to marry Catherina. The joy was contagious! The couple plans to marry in September and will live in Harmony on Robert's family farm. I fought off a tinge of sadness as Catherina would not be living in the neighborhood, but Robert is expected to be a part of his family business.

After our family left, Isaac and I sat briefly in our rocking chairs on the front porch and enjoyed the beautiful weather. We talked about Catherina's wedding in September and how it will be just the two of us, Joseph and Abigail. It won't be long before Abigail finds her soul mate, and Joseph seems to be well on his way preparing a life with Emily; soon, our work as parents will have come full-circle. With Sonny and Toby running the farm, we can visit back home more often. Perhaps take in some city plays and enjoy fancy food and drink. Time seemed to have passed by so quickly since we married in 1762. This world is also constantly changing, and I'm not so sure we are keeping up with the fast pace. But at least we have each other and God to praise for all of our good fortune.

CHAPTER 86

We are enjoying one of the perks of James working for the *Easton Daily News* when he comes home on Saturdays bringing the past week's newspapers with him. Eventually as our area grows, the paper may be delivered to the Mineral Springs mail drop, but I really don't see that happening for a few more years. Saturday evenings, Isaac and I read each addition cover to cover. We have gleamed so much information concerning current events and area happenings that we would have otherwise learned of weeks, if not months, later. In this past week's papers, we learned that Benjamin Franklin passed away in Philadelphia on April 17. Franklin was eighty-four years old! My goodness, what a long productive life for one of our country's true patriots.

Isaac, Catherina, Abigail, and I visited the Easton weekly market in search of special material for Catherina's wedding dress. This was the first time Isaac walked the market alone in years. He shopped for all of our necessary items and some for Sarah, finishing up well before Catherina had made her decision. We were in and out of Easton in less than three hours, which is also a new record for all of us. Later, Catherina and I visited with Lizzy Bryan to discuss what type of dress Catherina wanted Lizzy to create for her.

When Eli and Isaac stopped at the Mineral Springs earlier this week to check for mail, they were told that the captain hadn't come by in several days. Apparently, he was suffering from some type of lung affiliation and too weak to travel far from his home. The two men decided that they would pay him a visit the end of the week when they travel to Hall's Mills on business. Despite the fact that the captain tends to stretch the truth when telling his war stories, he did serve his country and has often done good things for many folks here in the valley.

Elizabeth and Jason appear to be doing well. Jason has taken on a full-time employee named Roger Deacon, from Stewartsville. The two seem to work well together and are keeping up with the orders from the Kempton Distillery. Jason also keeps the Case General Store and Sarah McCullough's store supplied with buckets and washtubs.

All of our children appear to be doing well, and we thank the Lord for his mighty hand in all of this good fortune.

CHAPTER 87

The middle of September was the perfect time to host Catherina's wedding. The dress that Lizzy Bryan created for her was stunning. Catherina chose a lavender cotton with tiny white dots throughout the fabric. Lizzy trimmed the dress with dainty white lace and tiny white buttons. Catherina pulled her hair back off her face and allowed it to cascade down her back. She placed tiny white daisies in her hair, and she looked absolutely beautiful! The wonderful weather allowed us to hold the ceremony outside under the oak tree. We had an exceptionally large group of people invited to witness their becoming husband and wife, as the Gardner family is quite large. Tulia and Kit baked the wedding cakes, and they were delicious. The day was joyful, and by late afternoon, the couple left for their new home, a four-room cabin on the Gardner farm in Harmony.

We have been so busy lately, and I need to catch up on the happenings. On July 10, the US House of Representatives voted 32-29 to approve creating an area they named the District of Columbia. The land was taken from portions of Maryland and Virginia. On July 16, the group declared this area to be called Washington DC. Our capital will eventually be constructed in this place, and all the laws and business of our newly created government will take place in this yet-to-be city.

Early August, the results of the first US census was announced. The population of the United States of America for the year ending 1789, is 3,939,214 people. This figure sadly includes 697,624 slaves.

Pastor Carson is talking about stepping down as our pastor and making way for a younger man to minister to us. The demands of tending to the needs of the congregation is becoming more than Pastor Carson can handle. He will stay in the Mansfield Woodhouse area and assist if called upon but wishes to be relieved of the demands of tending to his flock full-time. Hall's Mills has been visited by a man named Bishop Francis Asbury. He has been an invited guest of Colonel William McCullough and his family. This man is of the rather new Methodist-Episcopal faith. Folks that have traveled to Hall's Mills say he preaches a glorious sermon. Perhaps someday, Isaac and I will travel to Hall's Mills and listen to one of his sermons ourselves.

CHAPTER 88

December tricked all of us with quite mild weather. I guess it was just a prank, as January seemed to be the coldest that we can remember. The snow started to fall after the New Year, and each day we expect to see at least flurries. I am guessing that we have a generous two feet of snow on the ground, and we still have another week to go before February turns into March.

Everyone was able to make it to church yesterday and back to the farm for lunch. The grandchildren are growing up so quickly. They are now becoming my little helpers. After our meal, Catherina and Robert made an announcement that they are expecting a little one to arrive sometime late August. Everyone was excited and happy for the couple. Catherina feels fine and is thrilled at the thought of becoming a mama. I have to wonder if there will be more announcements before 1790 is history.

Joseph and Emily seem to be spending all of their spare time together. Every other Sunday, they have dinner at our house with the rest of the family. The next Sunday, they dine with the Case family. This seems to please both families, as we have made our Sunday noon meal a family tradition. Emily seems to enjoy her time with us, as she is an only child. Sometimes it becomes a bit noisy for her, but she is slowly getting used to all of our shenanigans.

James brought a stack of newspaper to pour over. He hasn't been able to visit weekly with the constant snowfall, but when he does make it, we sure enjoy his company. In this stack of papers, we learned that in late November, President George and Martha Washington moved to a temporary location in Philadelphia where they will reside until the building of Washington DC is completed; they are residing at 524 Market Street. The actual business of the country will be conducted in downtown Philadelphia. Who can say how long it will take to construct the capital building and a new residence for our president and his family. It seems that whenever government is involved, time moves slowly.

Isaac and Eli have visited with the captain a few times. He appears to be suffering from consumption, and a rather severe case as well. I fret about the men visiting as this can be contagious, and I surely wouldn't want to pass any illness along to our little ones, and especially Catherina with her being with child. The men claim that the captain comes outside to greet them, and they go to the barn where it is open with lots of fresh air. Not all people exposed to such an illness will find themselves infected if they are healthy themselves. I pray that the captain can find some relief from his discomfort and that Dr. Donaldson can in some way cure him.

Next week, we will be saying goodbye to Pastor Carson, as his request for retirement has been accepted. We will meet our new pastor, Pastor William Kent, at that time. Pastor Kent is married with two little ones. It will be a huge adjustment for our church, but sometimes change is good.

CHAPTER 89

My heart has been torn from my chest. The pain that I am feeling just won't ease, even briefly. My tears won't stop coming, and I can't even get myself out of bed each morning without Isaac and Abigail's help. It has been two weeks since our beloved child, Catherina, went home to meet with the Lord. I keep asking God *why?* Why did you take our beautiful healthy daughter from us? Why now when she was with child? I know that God can hear me, but he hasn't given me an answer, a reason as to *why her?*

We were all together at church the Sunday before, and Robert and Catherina came back to the house for our family meal. Catherina was happy and thrilled that her tummy was showing. Her sisters pampered her, and she so enjoyed their attention. Then on Wednesday, Robert's brother Zeke rode into our lane and begged us to come to the Gardner farm in Harmony as quickly as possible. Isaac, Abigail, and I immediately set out for Harmony. Somehow, Zeke with the help of Sonny managed to contact the rest of our family and tell them to come too. Last week, Catherina stepped on a board near the barn that was covered by weeds and punctured her foot with an old rusty nail. She seemed fine on Sunday but took sick Tuesday and by Wednesday was confined to her bed. The doctor was called, and he said that she appeared to be suffering from lockjaw. She could barely move her head from side to side and was unable to speak when we arrived at her bedside. Thank goodness, she recognized us and knew that we were there for her. The infection traveled through her body and slowly took over, causing her untimely death late Thursday evening, with our family and Robert surrounding her bed.

Pieter, Albert, and Jason stepped in and helped arrange for Catherina's burial in the Mansfield Woodhouse Cemetery. Robert was thankful for all of their help, as he found himself unable to even think. The funeral was held that Saturday, and Pastor Kent preformed the graveside service. Somehow, Isaac found the strength to make it through those terrible days. He kept saying that she was his little girl with big beautiful brown eyes and a freckled face. The sorrow is unbearable. We not only lost our beautiful Catherina but our unborn grandchild as well.

Why God, why aren't you answering my questions? I need answers; no, I demand answers! I am so angry at you for taking my child. This is not fair and, if nothing else, please give me some comfort to ease my pain.

Abigail and Elizabeth instructed me to sit down at my kitchen table as they read to me from my Bible. I was angry and really didn't want to listen, but slowly, very slowly, I started to regain a bit of composure. They read many of the passages that I read to them when their grandparents and baby Ester went home to meet their maker. It will take much more time to allow my anger to dissipate, but reading the word of God has relieved a bit of my pain. I pray that God will forgive me for lashing out at him, but I just can't help myself. Please bring some sunshine back into our lives.

CHAPTER 90

Catherina would have been a mother by now. We should be holding a new grandchild. None of this was meant to be. Instead, I am still searching. Searching for answers as to why God chose to rip our Catherina from us? Life seems so unfair at this moment, and I can't seem to find a way to justify why it had to be our child. Pastor Kent has visited with me several times and talking with him has helped a bit. I still find it difficult to read from my Bible, but I am seriously trying. In the scheme of things, Isaac and I should have passed on before our child, which is the way it should have been. I would have gladly given my life in exchange for our daughter's, but that was not in God's plan.

The captain, whose real name was George Brown, passed away a few days ago and was buried with military honors in the cemetery at Hall's Mills. I did not go, but Isaac and Eli paid their respects and said that the funeral was well-attended. I guess the saloon at the Mineral Springs Hotel will never be the same without the old knock-kneed sac of hot air. May he rest in peace.

James told me that he met a young lady from the Phillipsburg area named Ellen Dodsworth. Her father is a tailor and has his own business near the Delaware River. The two have enjoyed several walks and a lunch at the Hotel Sussex. He asked if he could bring her to one of our Sunday dinners. I, of course, immediately said yes. I am thrilled, and Isaac was pleased with the news as well.

Abigail, Bella, and Laura attended a hayride at the Dickerson home earlier this week and enjoyed their afternoon. Edward took the girls to Beattystown and picked them up after the hayride was over. Abigail said that she met a handsome young man named Kenneth

Cole, and they seemed to get along really well. She invited Kenneth to our church some Sunday.

Joseph and Emily seem to be happy as a couple. Last week, Mr. Case allowed her to attend a barn dance with Joseph near Hope. The couple, along with Cole Robertson and Roberta West, had a great time.

Sonny and Toby have more than stepped up to attend to our farm since we are all suffering from the death of Catherina. Tulia and Kit have visited with me often, and I have allowed them to help me with my housework. Actually, they are doing most of the work as I am finding it difficult to concentrate and do the task at hand. Tulia has been so supportive and kind-hearted, just like her husband, Sonny. I have feelings of guilt, as I know that Tulia has suffered greatly, being ripped from her family years ago to be sold to yet another slave owner. Sonny and Tulia have each other, their children, and no other family. Tulia is not even sure where she or Sonny once called home. She said that she tries to remember her mother's face, but the memory seems to be fading. That conversation brought tears to my eyes as why do good people endure needless pain? Mankind can sometimes be heartless.

CHAPTER 91

Today is April 7, 1791. It has been one year since our beautiful Catherina entered the gates of heaven. It has been a year of pure hell. I still search for an answer as to why God had to take our precious daughter. My faith seems to slowly be returning, but I must say that I look forward to the day when Catherina and I will meet again.

Robert visited with us a few days ago. He wanted to tell us that he is trying to move on with his life and has met a young lady from the Harmony area. He will never forget Catherina, and her death lays heavy upon his heart. He also said that he doesn't want to spend the rest of his life alone and was asking for our blessings to allow him to have a deeper relationship with the young lady named Jane. We gave Robert our blessings, believing that Catherina would never have wanted him to mourn until the day he passes on to the next life. It was so special and thoughtful of Robert coming to us and having this heart-to-heart talk. We prayed that things would go his way and that his home will be filled with love, laughter, and the gift of children.

Abigail and Kenneth seem to be a couple. He comes from a very nice family that has a well-established orchard in the Beattystown area. A large portion of their harvest is taken to the Hudson River area and sold. Kenneth has given many good tips to Albert about his orchard and has helped prune the trees as well. All the children seem to like Kenneth. Abigail seems to have stars in her eyes when anyone mentions his name.

Joseph got up the courage to ask Mr. Case for Emily's hand in marriage. Mr. Case was a bit gruff with coming back with an answer, but his wife stepped in and encouraged him to accept Joseph's proposal. Their wedding is planned for August, and we are now on the lookout for a place for the couple to call their home. They are looking at a small cabin on the Warne property that is available to rent. This would be perfect as it is just down the road from the store.

CHAPTER 92

Joseph and Emily's wedding was beautiful, but the weather was dreadfully hot. Mr. Case asked if we could hold the wedding on our farm as he has little space to entertain several people in his yard. We happily agreed, and the ceremony took place under the big old oak tree. Emily looked just lovely in her dress of light blue muslin, trimmed off with ribbon, made by a seamstress from Elizabeth Town. The Case family went over and above with the wedding cakes and treats, but then inviting the entire community to attend was also a bit much. They also had fiddlers attend, and there was dancing after the ceremony. Thank goodness for Elizabeth, Abigail, Jasmine, Tulia, and Kit for being our servers. Amos, Sonny, and James did a great job keeping the punch cups filled. It was a very busy but wonderful day for all of us. The couple was able to rent the cabin on the Warne farm, so they will be close at hand.

Toby seems to be sweet on a young gal who lives in one of the cabins owned by the Mineral Springs. This young lady, along with other family members, are employed as attendants by the hotel. She seems to be very nice and on occasion attends services at our church along with Ruby.

Goodness, these children are growing up right in front of our eyes. Ruby is now quite the young lady, almost sixteen years of age, and still as beautiful as the first day we laid eyes upon her. Amos keeps a very close watch on her now that he manages the general store in Hall's Mills. Ruby and Jasmine both work alongside Amos, and the business is said to be thriving. We still see them each nice Sunday when we worship together. Amos often speaks of Bishop Asbury and wants us to someday come to one the Methodist-Episcopal services held at the McCullough's barn. Bishop Asbury travels, actually he is called a circuit rider, going from town to town. He visits Hall's Mills whenever he is in the area, staying at the McCullough's home. Isaac is very interested in hearing what this man has to say about the Holy Book, so we will definitely look forward to hearing one of his sermons in the near future.

CHAPTER 93

1792 will bring forth new life! Our family is expecting the birth of three more grandchildren: Anna is expecting a little one to arrive about mid-April, Elizabeth is expecting her third child in late May, and finally, Joseph and Emily are expecting their first child the beginning of June. In Eli and Sarah's family, Ruth is due to give birth within a few weeks, and Sophia appears to be not too far behind. Goodness, babies, babies everywhere!

Benjamin and Liz Case are jumping for joy over the news that they will become grandparents. Joseph has been promoted to the position of general store manager, whatever that means. With the promotion, he got a raise in his pay. Mr. Case, or Benjamin as he has requested that we call him, is seeking another part-time worker to help Joseph in the store. I guess the business has been steadily growing. Isaac and I both agree that the inventory is amazing, so we can understand the need for more help.

Kenneth asked Isaac for Abigail's hand in marriage. I was within earshot when the request was made. I prayed that Isaac would be able to allow Abigail to be cared for by another man. As her father, he just doesn't want to let her go, especially since the loss of our dear Catherina. But he quickly gave his approval, and the wedding is set for late June. Surely, all of our ladies will have delivered their little ones by then.

This leaves our James as the lone wolf. He seems to be very interested in Ellen but not ready to commit. Perhaps it is because of his crazy workload, but the editor seems to like his work. But one has to ask just how long Ellen is willing to wait for her knight in shining armor?

In Eli and Sarah's family, Laura has become sweet on Paul Jenkins, son of Adam and Evelyn Jenkins, who operate the old Van Horne farm. Isaac sees Paul in town on occasion, but not to converse with. Their farm seems to be successful and have a generous herd of Jersey cows.

Isaac, Eli, and several other area men met at the Mineral Springs recently to hear our county representative Elroy Schmidt discuss current events happening in our Sussex County area. According to Elroy, Sussex County is experiencing a population growth. We should expect some of the amenities only found in the larger towns to be available in the Mansfield Woodhouse area soon. I seriously believe that this man is dreaming as it will be a long time, possibly years, before this area will experience tremendous growth.

CHAPTER 94

Sophia actually delivered her baby girl ahead of her expected arrival date. She and George named the child Amy. Ruth went past her supposed delivery date and gave birth to a little girl that she and Gerald named Susan. Both little ones were christened the end of February. Albert and Anna are the proud parents of another little girl whom they named Charity. Elizabeth birthed a son on May 25 whom she and Jason named Charles. Finally, Emily presented Joseph with a son on June 2 that the couple named Benjamin in honor of her father. All mothers and babies are doing well.

Abigail made a beautiful bride in her yellow dress with white lace and buttons. She pulled her hair back into a bun and added some pretty yellow buttercups and ribbon to her dark hair. The day was beautiful, and we again had Tulia and Kit bake our wedding cakes. The Cole family brought along a variety of fresh berries to share with all of the guests. They also brought along a generous amount of their homemade applejack. Boy, did that get the party hopping. The couple will take up housekeeping on the Cole farm. Abigail will be a bit further from us than our other children, but she has promised to continue attending our church and being a part of our weekly family meals, weather permitting.

Our three newest grandchildren were baptized by Pastor Kent in the middle of July. Charity and Charles slept through the entire event. Benjamin fussed a bit but then fell off to sleep as well. Tulia and Kit made the cake and came along to help serve it with the punch.

Toby and his girlfriend Lea have been attending church regularly. We often enjoy Lea and her family's company, but now we enjoy having Toby as well. As a couple, they must be getting quite serious, or how could a young lady convert a nonchurchgoer into attending? This is joyful news for our church family.

CHAPTER 95

The farm is ready for winter. Isaac, Sonny, and Toby cut an amazing amount of firewood to be shared among us. Tulia and Kit helped me make thirty-four dozen candles that we will also share. Our supply of candles should keep us until next spring as it is now only Isaac and me most of the time. James has been arriving on Sunday morning at church, returning to the farm for our family meal and then heading back to Easton well before dark, so we no longer need candlelight for the loft area. Our grandson Jacob does occasionally come for an overnight stay, and we sleep in the children's beds in the loft. He loves me to tell him bedtime stories. Grandchildren are truly gifts from God.

When James visited on a Sunday a few weeks ago, he gifted Isaac and me a book called *Old Farmer's Almanac* written by Robert Thomas. The book is filled with lots of tips and useful farm and household information. It also has the phases of the moon and predicted weather forecasts. It is a really fun book to read and very thoughtful of James to give this to us.

The newspapers that he brings us are also enjoyed. On October 12, there was a special celebration held in New York City honoring Christopher Columbus who arrived in the New World three hundred years ago! Then on October 13, the cornerstone of the White House was laid in Washington DC. It will be quite a while before our president can call it home. Finally, On December 3, George Washington was reelected to a second term as our president.

Locally, here in the Mansfield Woodhouse area, two new homes are being built in our village. The Housel family from Spruce Run is having a two-room cabin constructed and plans on moving in late spring. Mr. Housel hopes to operate a saddle and tack shop from a building behind his home. Abram Fritts from Oxford is having a one-and-half story cabin and a barn constructed for him and his wife, Nellie. Mr. Fritts is a blacksmith by trade and hopes to start a business in his new barn. Perhaps Elroy Schmidt was correct in saying that our area is quickly growing.

CHAPTER 96

A new year and a new adventure! According to the January 12, 1793 *Easton Daily Paper*, a hot-air balloon lifted off from the prison yard at the Walnut Street Jail in Philadelphia at 10:00 a.m. on January 9 with a pilot named Jean Pierre Blanchard. Blanchard is a Frenchmen and speaks very little English. Tickets were sold to get up close and near the balloon to witness this event. The cost was $5 for the best seat and $2 for a back seat. President George Washington, John Adams, Thomas Jefferson, James Madison, and James Monroe attended and were the official witnesses to this historic event. President Washington penned a letter for Blanchard to give to the property owner when he landed, beseeching them to oppose no hindrance or molestation to the balloon or Mr. Blanchard upon landing.

Forty-six minutes later, the balloon landed in the Clement Oak area of Deptford, New Jersey. The farmer in his field watching this strange event came toward the balloon with a pitchfork in hand. The letter was useless as the first people that made their way to the massive thing that came out of the sky were unable to read. Blanchard spoke the name George Washington, and the people understood and helped him fold up his balloon. They placed it on a wagon and helped him get back to Philadelphia, about fifteen miles away. Before he left, Blanchard was able to secure signatures or marks on a paper proving that he landed in Deptford. Upon arrival back to Philadelphia, the crowd was awaiting his return, and some claimed that the city had shut down to be witness to such an event. Well, we are certainly happy that all went well for everyone involved, including the poor unsuspecting landowner who was frightened to near death at the sight of such a thing!

Our paper dated March 5, 1793, told us about the second inauguration of President George Washington in Philadelphia on March 3. It appears that there was quite a bit of pomp and circumstance, along with much partying after the swearing in actually took place. My sister Lydia's letter, written the day after she attended the event, stated that the crowd was tremendous, and the streets were packed with carriages. It was wonderful to witness but near impossible to return home to Doylestown.

Isaac and I attended a sermon given by Bishop Asbury this past Saturday in Hall's Mills. Goodness, the service was well attended, and we completely enjoyed the message that was preached. Elisha and Mary Thatcher from Good Springs sat with us and couldn't have agreed more. It has been quite some time since I have felt so refreshed from hearing the word. Bishop Asbury is an excellent speaker, and the hour-and-a-half slipped by quickly. We both look forward to the bishop's return, and we will encourage Eli and Sarah to join us. We enjoyed a cup of tea with Amos and Jasmine before heading home. I was still feeling the Holy Spirit within me the entire past week! Is this God's way of giving us some relief from the sorrow we still are suffering with? I truly want to believe that it is so.

Chapter 97

Oh Lord, have mercy on us! Isaac brought me a letter from my sister Vivian. Vivian said that since July, the city of Philadelphia has suffered from an outbreak of yellow fever. No one seems to know the exact cause, but there are two possible culprits: the first is the ships that are docking almost daily bringing refugees from the Caribbean escaping a slave revolution. It is believed that they were infected before arriving here in America. The second is the poor sanitary conditions, including open sewers with human waste and dead rotting animals that are infested with all types of bugs due to the extreme hot weather and lack of rain. Gosh, I know little about yellow fever except it is deadly and often called sailor's fever because it is found in the tropics.

Vivian said that those inflicted suffer with a high fever and chills, then, as if by magic, they go into remission for several days only to have their skin turn yellow and go into a stupor. They throw up black vomit and waste away as there is no known cure. At first, it was a few deaths a day, now in September, more than a hundred people a day are dying from this terrible death. The illness has not found its way to Doylestown and pray to God that it doesn't. It has been so bad in Philadelphia that Congress has moved to nearby Germantown. Anyone who can get out has left the city for refuge in the country. Vivian said that our family is associating with a tight circle of people and are staying away from busy areas. Golly, what can one say or even think when hearing of such horrible news? Now is the time for the power of prayer. Dear God, please see the folks of Philadelphia through these horrible times, amen.

Eli and Edward recently had a man-to-man conversation about Edward's future intentions. Since Nelson married Hilda Baylor and removed himself to Phillipsburg to assist her father in his brewery business, Eli has been unsure of what to expect of Edward. Well, Edward said that he wanted to stay on the farm and truly enjoyed the work. The two decided that it was time to bring on a hired hand. Donald Perkins of the Mineral Springs area is now working full-time for Eli. This move has relieved Eli of a considerable amount of work. So today, Eli, Sarah, Isaac, and I traveled to the Clinton town market. It was a real treat for me as I have not journeyed past Spruce Run. The four of us took our good old time and even dined in the Clinton House Hotel for our noonday meal. Sarah shopped for a special wedding gift to give to Laura and Paul, who will marry in a few weeks. We arrived back at our farms just before five o'clock to find that all the afternoon chores had been completed. What a joyful and wonderful day. The four of us look forward to more of this!

As Isaac and I sat in our rocking chairs on our front porch, we reminisced about years ago when Eli, Sarah, and the two of us did fun things together. Raising a family and running a farm has a way of changing one's priorities. It appears that we have come full circle and can now revert back to some of those fun times. God has been good to all of us, even with the loss of our dear Catherina, her unborn child and baby Ester. The pain of our loss is still with us and will be forever, but who are we to question God's plan?

CHAPTER 98

Laura and Paul's wedding took place on one of the most beautiful days that fall has given us. Eli and Sarah did a wonderful job of hosting the special day. Tulia and Kit baked the wedding cakes, and they were delicious. The Jenkins family seems to be very nice and were friendly to everyone. The newlyweds will live on the Jenkins's farm, just a short distance to the west of our farms.

My sister sent me another letter informing me that whatever was causing the yellow fever seems to be subsiding. Things are slowly returning to normal in Philadelphia, and Congress has returned to get back to conducting the country's business. The question of how and why all this came about seems to remain unanswered.

Isaac and I have been attending church services in Hall's Mills as often as we can. We feel that we can truly relate to Bishop Asbury's sermons and return home refreshed and feeling alive spiritually. Elisha Thatcher is so filled with the Holy Spirit that he is considering erecting a small church along the hillside on his farm and will welcome all to worship with him. His intent is to make worship easier for all the folks on this side of the mountain. Quite an endeavor, to say the least.

All of our children and grandchildren seem to be doing well. We look forward to our Sunday family dinners, and those who can, do attend. James often brings Ellen along, and they appear to be crazy for each other, but for some reason, James has not popped the question. I would love to meddle, but Isaac told me to keep my thoughts to myself. Time is ticking by, and I don't want to see James lose his chance at true love. What's a mother to do? In Isaac's own words, "Please keep your lips closed tightly." Good grief, men just don't get it!

Isaac and I attended a fall festival last Saturday afternoon at the Castner's farm. The invitation was open to all families in the area. I met Abram and Nellie Fritts who recently built a home in town. Abram seems to be doing well with his new blacksmith business. Amos, Jasmine, and Ruby attended also. Amos said that business has been so good that he was able to take on a fulltime clerk. The festival also brought out several young families, and just seeing how quickly the littles are growing brings joy to my heart. There were so many things for families to do, but I think the bobbing for apples was the most popular. Lizzie Bryan won the cakewalk. Our son-in-law Jason won the log splitting competition, but Toby came in a very close second. Donald Perkins beat all the men by a long shot in the corn-husking competition. The men played horse shoes, and women chitchatted. Time slipped by, and before any of us realized it, it was time to leave for home.

CHAPTER 99

The first month of 1794 has slipped by quickly. February is just two days away. I guess time went by so fast due to the lack of severe winter weather. For the most part, this month has seen cold but not well below-freezing temperatures. We've had only a dusting of snow, and the roads are solid for travel, so we were able to venture out often.

Sonny, Toby, and Isaac engaged in a serious conversation early last week. Toby and Lea want to marry within a few months. Toby asked if Isaac would consider renting the tool and wagon shed for the couple to live in. This is the building that was converted into temporary housing for Sonny and his family when they first came to our farm. Isaac said he saw no problem with allowing the couple to take up housekeeping on the farm but wanted to discuss it with me first. The thought to discuss it with me first warmed my heart, as in most families, the men make all the decisions. My opinion matters to Isaac, and for that, I am forever grateful. We discussed the arrangement, and I said yes but thought they were deserving of a nicer place to live. We agreed to allow Toby and Lea to live in the shed with the understanding that a new cabin would be built for them within the next year. As far as paying us rent, the rent would be part of Toby's pay in exchange for working for us. Toby and Sonny are vital to the daily operation of this farm; for this, we thank the Lord.

Eli and Isaac stopped by the Mineral Springs Hotel to check for mail yesterday and treated themselves to a mug of stout. They said that business seems to be picking up. The last few times they went inside the saloon, the place was nearly empty of patrons. I guess the yellow fever scare in Philadelphia caused many people to stop traveling. Perhaps this was a good thing, as no one in this area that I am aware of came down with the yellow fever. This is truly good news.

Jake Beerman is in poor health. Lilia expressed her concern for his recovery when we enjoyed a cup of tea earlier today. Lilia said that her grandfather is seventy-five years of age and claims he is just plain worn out. Goodness, most people are pleased to reach the ripe old age of sixty-five, so Jake is surely considered an old geezer. He has worked hard his entire life, and the kindness that he showed me and my children when Nellie died will never be forgotten. I prayed with Lilia and searched my heart for words of comfort to help ease her pain. Life seems to toss us into many unwanted situations, but we must learn to take our troubles to the Lord.

Later, Sarah walked over for a short visit and enjoyed a cup of tea with me. She wanted to share the news that she and Eli will be grandparents again. Laura and Paul are expecting their first child sometime in August. The two of us discussed how it just seemed like yesterday that we were rocking our babies to sleep, and now these same babies are rocking their own littles ones.

CHAPTER 100

Well, I guess we should have expected some type of retribution for the mild January. On May 17, the entire southern New England area suffered a heavy frost. This affected all kinds of crops, and it just might have caused crop failure for the hay, barley, and wheat in that area. I can't recall experiencing heavy frost so late in the spring. It is not usual to have lite frost that causes minimal crop damage. Even chilly morning temperatures into the middle of June, but not heavy frost. Thank goodness, our area escaped this mean buffoonery from Mother Nature.

Toby and Lea were married the end of May. Pastor Kent performed the ceremony on the lawn of the Mineral Springs Hotel. Lea fixed up the shed nicely, and the two have settled in, enjoying married life. Isaac and I certainly wish them a lifetime of love, joy, and a house blessed with healthy children.

Yesterday, Jake Beerman was laid to rest beside his wife, Gertie, in the McKinney Cemetery. The threat of bad weather held off until after the burial, and then the skies opened giving this area some much-needed rain. Many people came to say their good-byes to Jake, as he was quite well-known. Jake was known for always helping his neighbors in their time of need. He will be missed.

Aunt Peggy has slowed her work as a midwife. She will now only tend to the women here in the valley. Being called out all hours of the day in all types of weather has become too much for her. Thankfully, she will continue to tend to the sick in our neighborhood as well as confinement cases. She has trained another woman from the Hall's Mills area that will take over the midwife work on that side of the mountain.

CHAPTER 101

Bella has taken a liking to a young man from the Spruce Run area named Roy Burd. Sarah really likes Roy, but when asked, Eli says that Roy is so-so. Fathers not wanting to part with their daughters can drive a mother crazy!

Our Christmas celebration will be held at our home this year. The annual bird hunt was rather successful, and we will enjoy roast goose as well as duck. We invited Tulia and her family to come and join us, but they politely declined. We will be adding another guest to our family tradition: Laura and Paul are the proud parents of a little girl they named Sylvia. Sylvia was born the first week of September and christened a month later by Pastor Kent.

It has been another successful year for Jason's business. The McKinney family has now started a small distillery just west of the Warne mill. William McKinney ordered two-dozen small kegs with the promise of more in the upcoming year. Being local, delivery was an easy chore.

Elisha Thatcher showed Isaac his proposed plans for the church that he wants to build on his property. The church will be constructed of stone and will include an adjoining cemetery. Elisha hopes to begin his work as soon as the frost is out of the ground. Being December, he has at least four months before he can start building. Elisha is also seeking circuit riders that will take turns delivering the Lord's message. I have mixed emotions about this, as we have been members of the Mansfield Woodhouse Presbyterian Church since we moved here from Doylestown. I have to admit that I completely enjoy the sermons preached by the Methodist-Episcopal circuit riders, but feelings of guilt are creeping up my spine.

My children are pleased with the idea of this new church and have full intentions of becoming faithful parishioners. I told Isaac that no matter what, I want to be laid to rest near our beautiful daughter Catherina and granddaughter Ester. He agreed, but I have some doubt that we will be welcomed to enjoy eternal rest in the church cemetery if we change religions. As Thatcher's plans become reality, I will have a heart-to-heart talk with Pastor Kent. For now, tight lips and much prayer will hopefully ease my stress.

CHAPTER 102

1795 is starting to look quite promising. James asked for Ellen's hand in marriage, and Mr. Dodsworth gave his consent. The couple will marry in April in Phillipsburg, this brings me much joy, as a mother only wants the best for her children. I know that James can care for himself, but sharing a home with a loving wife is one of life's special gifts; the second, being the amazing gift of children. We are all overjoyed by the announcement and wish them the very best.

The winter for us was what I would call normal. We have experienced days below freezing, snow and sleet, but that is what winter is about. But according to the March 17 edition of the *Easton Daily*, England suffered from the coldest temperatures ever recorded for the month of January. England has kept records on daily temperatures and weather conditions since 1659. Wow, I just find that to be an amazing feat!

Work has started on the church that Elisha Thatcher is having constructed on the southern slope of his Good Springs property. Although slow going because of the unpredictable spring weather, progress is being made. We can actually see the Thatcher property from Albert's orchard, and it is quite interesting to see the church rising from the ground, reaching for the heavens. Elisha hopes to have the building ready for worship by late summer or early fall. One thing is for sure, this project is not without heaps of scuttlebutt.

Work is to begin on a new cabin for Toby and Lea. The cabin will be near Sonny and Tulia's cabin so they can share the springhouse. Albert drew a nice sketch with ideas that he gleamed from the couple. The cabin will have a great room and two smaller rooms on the main floor with a loft above the two smaller rooms. One main fireplace will heat the home and be used for cooking as well. There will be both a back and front door and a nice-size front porch to enjoy at the end of the day.

Isaac discussed the preening of the flock of sheep. Since Mr. Van Horne's passing, the sale of lambs has slowed. In fact, Isaac has controlled the mixing of the rams with ewes to keep the births to a minimum. We still want a small flock for their fleece, so thinning the herd to one ram and two ewes maybe the way to go. Let us hope that the ram doesn't take sick and leave us with no lambs. Farming seems to always be a gamble—a fifty-fifty chance that things will go as we hope. But then, who are we kidding as it is God's plan, not ours, that determines when the sun rises and sets each day. Let us be grateful for each and every day that he gives us here on earth.

CHAPTER 103

Ellen and James were married in the Phillipsburg Presbyterian Church. It was a lovely service and attended by many friends of the family. John and Helen Dodsworth hosted a reception for the couple in a small dining area within the Hotel Sussex. I'm guessing that perhaps fifty people attended this party. When Isaac and I married, our families also hosted a reception for us in the same manner. Out here near the frontier, people are far less formal. It was a lovely few hours, and the Dodsworth family seems to be very nice people. The couple will reside in Phillipsburg. Returning home from the wedding, I realized that James will no longer come home to sleep. Just as the other children, his bed will remain empty. Although this is what a parent wants for her child, when it happens, a bit of sadness finds its way into the heart. Are these tears streaming down my face tears of joy or sadness? Perhaps both.

The cabin is finished, and Toby and Lea are making it their home. I seriously thought that the couple would make an announcement as Lea appears to be a bit piqued lately, but no good news was shared. I guess I'm getting rusty as I am usually spot-on about these matters.

Work on the church is also moving along. Much of the stonewalls are completed, and it stands tall and proud along the hillside. Elisha said that Pastor George Banghart has agreed to hold a service one Sunday a month in this new house of worship. Thatcher has three, perhaps four, other pastors he is attempting to secure to preach once the building is completed. Hall's Mills is creating plans for a new church in their village as well. I'm guessing these same preachers will conduct services in that church too. As of now, all the Methodist-Episcopal services are being held in a large barn on the

William McCullough property. This is where Isaac and I go when we want to hear Bishop Asbury preach. These services are well attended, and I can certainly understand why they need a house of worship that can accommodate all who wish to hear the word of God.

Recently, on a pleasant spring day, Sarah, Tulia, Kit, and I walked the pastures and hedgerows and removed the nightshade, pulling it out by its roots. This is a yearly chore; however, we seem to have its growth under control. As we walked, we chatted and enjoyed each other's company, making the task pass quickly. We placed all the weeds we pulled into a burlap sack and brought it back to the barn area where Isaac will later burn it in the firepit. We do not want our livestock to ingest any of this nasty weed, as it can cause them death, or with our cows, even contaminate the milk without us detecting the danger. We certainly do not want to pass along milk that can sicken and, even worse, cause death to anyone. After we finished our fields, we walked to Sarah's farm and cleared her fields of the nasty weed as well. What fun, and boy, can we gals talk!

CHAPTER 104

The summer has been uneventful for the most part. Just when we begin to fret about dry conditions, the Lord sends rain our way. We may experience an early harvest, as crops seem to be a bit ahead of other years. Our corn was not knee-high by the 4th of July but was hip-high. I guess the ability to get our crops planted in early spring contributed to this long, productive growing season. For this, we praise the Lord!

Elisha Thatcher's church now has a roof. The workers are placing the windows and doors as I write. It won't be long before all are invited to come and hear God's word. I approached Pastor Kent and discussed our attending some of Bishop Asbury's services in Hall's Mills and how they truly moved us. I was a bit taken aback when the pastor said that we must search our hearts and souls, digging deep within and seek what is best for us. Wow, I'm not sure that it's all that easy to leave behind a church we have been a part of since coming here in 1762. Sarah agrees with me, and she is experiencing anguish as well. Eli and Isaac are ready to move on to a new church, pastor, and congregation as if this is just an everyday occurrence. The children don't seem to be bothered by pulling up stakes and moving on, so is it just me and Sarah? Are we being a bit ridiculous in having a difficult time with change? Our babies were baptized in this church; some were married in this church, and sadly, some were buried from this same house of worship. I searched my Bible for some hint that I am doing the right thing, but I'm not finding relief. Please, Lord, hear my pray for guidance and offer me the much-needed strength to handle this transition in my faith.

Our Sunday family meals continue with everyone enjoying visiting with each other for those few precious hours. This past Sunday, the grandchildren helped me make the biscuits. We now have a coating of flour about the kitchen area, but it was so well worth the bit of mess, and I can still hear the laughter and joy from our beautiful little ones. After dessert was served, Abigail said that she and Kenneth had an announcement: they are expecting a little one sometime in March. This was better than wonderful, as I know how desperately Abigail has wanted to become a mother. Elizabeth suggested that we all hold hands and say a prayer for Abigail, Kenneth, and the long-awaited little one. What a moving gesture, and I saw more than one teardrop being wiped from several faces. I also caught an interesting glance between James and Emily. Could they be the next to make an announcement?

Later, when all of our afternoon chores were completed, we sat on the front porch enjoying the quiet. We talked about the wonderful news of Abigail being with child and how good things do come to people who wait. We talked about the sadness within our hearts with the death of Catherina and her unborn child. Thoughts about baby Ester are still painful after all of this time. How does one let go of sadness and allow themselves to move on? Perhaps, the memories are meant to ease the sadness and think of only the wonderful life we shared with Catherina. But we were not able to make joyful memories with baby Ester or Catherina's unborn child. What is there to hold on to except the pain and sadness? At least, we were able to cuddle baby Ester's tiny body and see her innocence and beauty. I guess we will have to wait until we make our journey to heaven to learn more about our unborn grandchild? Until then, we must trust in God and his mighty plan for all of us, all the while trying not to allow our hidden misery to surface.

CHAPTER 105

The cold weather is settling in quickly. Isaac, Sonny, and Toby have the farm ready for the winter. Our lofts, root cellars, smokehouse, and springhouse are well-stock for the pending winter months. We are all looking forward to a bit of a break from our chores. Tulia's and my garden provided us with a generous amount of fresh vegetables, so I guess the rainfall we did receive was plentiful. The root crops seem to have thrived this year, as Tulia, Kit, and I filled baskets of potatoes, onions, turnips, beets, and carrots. The harvest was so bountiful that I was able to set aside some of my crop for Joseph and James, who do not have the room for large gardens. Eli and Isaac are even enjoying a few days of hunting on Scott's Mountain. Venison would be a nice addition to our springhouse after it has been smoked and provide us with many wonderful family meals.

As we prepare for yet another year passing us by, we find ourselves slowing down. Having Sonny and Tulia helping us with our daily chores is such a joy as everyday things seem to be burdensome. By the end of each day, our bodies ache, and the cold weather seems to find its way into our joints. But with the arrival of 1796, there will be the joy of not only Abigail's expected little one sometime in March, but also the news that Joseph and Emily are expecting a little one to arrive in April. Finally, James and Ellen are expecting a child sometime in May. All the mothers-to-be appear to be doing well, and Isaac and I couldn't be happier for them. This joy is medicine for our crankiness and uplifting to our souls. I do have a nagging concern, and that is about Lea. Lea appears to be downtrodden and lacking energy lately. Months back, I thought that perhaps she was with child, but Tulia has said nothing about Lea, not even a hint as to why she appears ill. I pray that she feels better, but she too has a heavy workload as she is still an attendant at the Mineral Springs Hotel. Now that the cold weather is here, business at the hotel should slow down, so hopefully, Lea can get some extra rest.

Last week, our entire family attended church at the Thatcher Methodist-Episcopal Church. The church is beautiful and quite roomy as well. Again, there are two doors on the front, one for the men and one for the women and children. The pews are benches without backs and arranged in rows on either side of the church. In the middle of the long aisle is a stove that provides heat when needed. It was cold this past Sunday, so the warm stove was greatly appreciated. The men sit on the north side of the church, and the women and children on the south side. Several steps above our seating area is a small platform that the preacher stands on while delivering his sermon. Above this platform is a beautiful large glass-paned window. There are also windows along both sides of the church.

As promised, the first sermon was preached by Pastor George Banghart, and it was quite powerful. The service was well attended, and many local people seem to be pleased to have easy access to a house of worship. Next summer, Bishop Asbury has promised to visit and formally dedicate this church, and that will be a service we all look forward to attending. I thought that I would have feelings of guilt attending a different church, but to my amazement, I felt as if I had always been a Methodist. From the little that I have gleamed so far, the differences between Presbyterian and Methodist aren't as vast as I had imagined. Yes, they are different, but not powerfully different. I feel more at ease listening to the preaching of God's message, so perhaps I have found my way back home? Isaac is pleased with the sermons as well, and I believe that we may become study worshipers along with our children and many local folks.

Elizabeth and Jason asked permission to host our family Christmas meal at their home this year. Sarah and I were taken back by the request but after a bit of conversation decided that it was time to pass the torch and gave our blessings to the couple. Everyone who attends will still bring their special covered dish for all to enjoy, and Sarah and I will help Elizabeth, at least for this year, get things moving along. Actually, I felt as if a yoke had been lifted off of my shoulders and found myself joyfully singing as I baked my ginger-bread cakes and molasses cookies. Apparently, my jovial mood was contagious, as Isaac seemed in better spirits too. Being together as a family is wonderful; all the work involved to make it happen is just plain exhausting.

CHAPTER 106

The Christmas holidays went by far too quickly. Elizabeth and Jason did a wonderful job of hosting our family get-together. Sarah and I offered our assistance, but Elizabeth created a to-do list for her siblings and cousins; and goodness, things moved along without a hitch. Everyone teased Abigail about her large belly and the fact that she was either carrying twins or would birth a child with extra knees and elbows. I had to just sit back and smile as I too lived through this sort of teasing when I carried our twin boys, James and Joseph.

It does appear that Abigail is overly with child, so she may deliver two little ones instead of one baby. In less than three months, we shall see who was correct: a boy, a girl, two boys, two girls, or a boy and a girl. The excitement was quite fanciful, to say the least, and Abigail didn't seem to mind all of the attention. Our other two mothers-to-be joined in the fun too. Joyfully, all our expectant ladies are doing well and eagerly awaiting their deliveries. They were discussing the fact that their newborns will be the first to be christened at the Thatcher Methodist-Episcopal Church—truly food for thought.

Edward hitched their horse to the sleigh and gave Sarah and me a ride to Lizzy Bryan's house earlier this week. Several of the area women got together to do a bit of quilting and a lot of chitchatting. It was nice to get out and visit with our friends, and as always, the dessert was a welcome treat. The conversation of the afternoon was Thatcher Methodist-Episcopal Church. Everyone seemed to have an opinion and were not afraid to voice them. Sarah and I felt a bit uncomfortable being questioned by some of the ladies who are faithful to the Mansfield Woodhouse Presbyterian Church. These women believe that the two of us abandoned our faith and jumped on board some crazy newfounded religion. Within seconds, we realized we were outnumbered and kept a false smile on our faces and tight lips. We were never so pleased to see Edward return to take us back home. The nerve of those old biddies and spinsters! Later, while sharing how my afternoon went to Isaac, he just smiled and said that I should have expected some discord. Discord, I feel it is outright war! Phooey on attending the next quilting bee, I'll stay home and knit!

Isaac brought me a letter from my sister Vivian, and it was very newsy. Lydia and Solomon are doing well, as is the entire family. Recently, Vivian ran into Isaac's sister Julia in downtown Doylestown, and her family is also well. Two new businesses have been quite successful, a millinery shop and a German bakery. Since our last visit, there have also been several new homes built just a few blocks from where we were raised. A fancy café opened late fall in the Doylestown Hotel, and the food is excellent. This news makes me feel pangs of sadness as I dearly miss my parents, family, and the city. I feel guilty even writing such a thing, but life close to the frontier has been difficult at times. We do without the nice tablecloths, china, special foods, and fancy clothing that I was raised with to exist in the middle of nowhere. I dearly love and cherish my husband, but at times, I become melancholy, perhaps feeling sorry for myself. A trip back home would be heaven-sent.

CHAPTER 107

I am pleased to write that we have babies—lots and lots of babies! Abigail gave birth to identical twin girls on March 14. Kenneth is still on cloud nine! The girls were named Clara and Claudia; Mama and babies are all doing well. Emily birthed a feisty little boy on April 17 that they named Morgan. Morgan's big brother, Benjamin, is so excited to have someone to play with. Finally, Ellen delivered a girl on May 5 they named Naomi. The joy on James's face the first time he held Naomi was absolutely precious.

The joy in Isaac and my heart is overflowing, and we thank the Lord for the gift of these beautiful, healthy children. On June 30, all four babies were christened by Pastor Banghart at our new church. Goodness, I had forgotten the extra mothering needed to keep twins content, if that is even possible. Abigail has her hands full, and that is a fact. Kenneth's mother helps Abigail every day as she lives on the homestead too. All the babies fared well during their christenings, and everyone was invited back to Elizabeth and Jason's home for cake and punch. Kenneth's family thankfully left the applejack at home.

July 4 was the twentieth anniversary of the signing of the Declaration of Independence, 1776–1796. Boston honored this date with a huge celebration. A gentleman named John Lathrop of Boston penned the following words: "It is now acknowledged as a fact in political geography that Liberty descended from Heaven, on the 4th of July, 1776. We are assembled on this day, the twentieth anniversary of her advent, to sympathize in those pleasures which none but freeman can enjoy, to exchange these mutual congratulations, which none, but freemen can express." I am so proud of our new country, and God has surely blessed all of us with our freedom from England. Let all of us never forget the hardships, heartaches, and tremendous loss of life, both American and English, who paid the ultimate price, thereby allowing the birth of our new nation.

As promised, Bishop Asbury paid a visit to Thatcher Methodist-Episcopal Church on August 9 to dedicate our church, and he preached a glorious sermon. The church was packed with people, standing-room only. It was so pleasing to the heart to see folks travel from near and far for this very special day. Bishop Asbury had been in Hall's Mills earlier in the day to lay the cornerstone for their new meeting house. We also learned that what we believed may have been scuttlebutt was actually steps to have the name of Hall's Mills changed to Asbury. Most, if not all, of the community is for this change in name, and it will be in honor of Bishop Francis Asbury. Our county representative Elroy Schmidt is helping the village make their wish for a name-change happen. Apparently, it is not as easy as some would like to believe, as the village name has been recorded in the Sussex County records, but Elroy said it can and will happen. Wow, this could take some getting used to, but I like the name change.

CHAPTER 108

The autumn weather is beautiful. The harvest is in full-swing, and it appears that we may have a two-week lull in getting our grains to the mill. Sonny assured Isaac that he and Toby could complete the harvest, and now would be a good time to take that trip to Doylestown that Isaac had mentioned several times this past season. After much soul-searching, we decided to travel back home, this time by stage.

I penned a letter to each of my sisters telling them of our expected arrival and asking if they can accommodate us for a few days, or should we make arrangements to stay at the Doylestown Hotel? I'm not even sure that the ink had dried on my letter to them when I received their letter stating that in no way would we be staying at the hotel. The first few days we will stay with Vivian and her family; the last part of our stay, we will be guests of Lydia and her family. I can feel the excitement begin to build from my toes traveling to the top of my head. Our travel plans will be the same as earlier trips, leaving Mansfield on a Thursday, staying over in Easton, and arriving in Doylestown late Friday.

Isaac completed a few farm chores that he has been dragging his feet to get done. I did the same in the house and made arrangements to have Tulia make use of any vegetables that are ready for harvest while we are gone. We had our usual Sunday family day, attended church, and all who could came back to the farm for a slow-cooked dinner of stew and biscuits. We spent a lot time reminiscing about the last time as a family we traveled to Doylestown. How James caught the reporter bug, Uncle Solomon showed us his fancy carriages, and Grandpa Nelson explained to us his surveying business. They all wished that they were joining us, but family obligations need to be attended to first. As each family was leaving, we got lots of hugs, kisses, and wishes for a safe and wonderful trip back home. Going back home is wonderful; leaving my family behind in Mansfield Woodhouse, even for just a week, is bittersweet.

CHAPTER 109

Eli and Sarah took us to the Mineral Springs Hotel before noon on Thursday. The weather was pleasing, and Isaac and I were the only passengers on the Elizabeth Town to Easton stage. I hoped that perhaps the lack of travelers would encourage the driver to take it slower; after all, what's the rush? We made a stop in Stewartsville and Phillipsburg and then on to Easton in what I call record-breaking time! Good golly, where's the fire? I was so pleased to pull up in front of the Hotel Easton that I loudly praised the Lord for our safe arrival!

After a hardy breakfast, we boarded the stage to Doylestown before dawn and waited for the first crack of daylight to begin our days trek. Two other passengers boarded with us, and talk ranged from politics to the economy to speedy horses. For me, it was quite boring; for Isaac, he was in his element. After two rest stops, we arrived in Doylestown at about five-thirty. Vivian was awaiting our arrival, and it was wonderful to see her smiling face. After lots of hugs and kisses, we walked back to Vivian's house. The evening was beautiful, and stretching our legs after our long trip felt good. As we walked and chatted, I noticed lots that had been vacant on my prior visits were now boasting of new homes.

Vivian said that I will be aghast when we take a walk downtown tomorrow; so many new shops and places of business. I felt a tug at my heart as my hometown was quickly changing, and it just didn't have the same little town quaintness about it. When we arrived at Vivian's home, we were met by my sister Lydia and brother Solomon. What a joy to see them, and again there was a lot of hugging and kissing. Vivian had her dining room table set to perfection with beautiful china and stemmed glassware atop a lace tablecloth. In the center of the table was a lovely vase of freshly cut mums and candelabrums on both ends of the table. This is how Mama used to set her table when special people visited. I could feel tears beginning to cloud my eyes—I could think of nothing but my parents and how much I missed them. Isaac noticed my moment of despair and placed his arm around me to help comfort my pain and brought me back to reality.

Our evening meal was baked ham, whipped potatoes, vegetables, and fresh pineapple. I couldn't remember the last time I ate fresh pineapple. For our dessert, Vivian baked a peach cobbler topped with whipped cream. What a way to start our visit! We sat around reminiscing about our earlier days in Doylestown. Since Isaac was also from Doylestown, he was able to be a part of our conversation. Before we knew it, it was ten o'clock. Everyone said their goodbyes, and we retired for the night before eleven o'clock.

After our Saturday morning breakfast, we all took a stroll to Solomon's carriage shop. We had a short conversation with our nephew Aaron, and not wanting to keep Solomon and Aaron from their work, we continued on our way after about fifteen minutes. The shop seemed to look the same as when my father ran the business. We continued on our way and walked past our old home. The sadness returned, but I managed to put on a happy face and took notice that other than more flowers, the house appeared to look as it did when Papa and Mama lived there. I guess I am being silly to hope that things remained the same as my last visit. Time holds still for no one, and we best keep in step or be left behind.

We had our lunch in small café near the busy section of Doylestown. Vivian was correct in saying that there were many new shops. A few years ago, I would have wanted to meander in and out of each shop, taking the time to look at all the fancy wares, but I no longer have a desire for unnecessary things that would serve no purpose back in Mansfield Woodhouse. Isaac paid a visit to the *Doylestown Gazette* to say hello to Mr. Stevens. He shared how well James is doing and that we owe it all to Mr. Stevens for giving James the chance. Mr. Stevens said that it is not often that he gets the feeling that someone would be a successful news reporter, but he immediately had that feeling about James.

We are truly pleased that he gave James the opportunity and James persevered. In the evening, my sisters pampered me and dressed me for the theater. My sisters, their husbands, my brother, his wife, Isaac, and I dined at the Delaware House along South Main Street. It was quite a fancy restaurant, and I am glad I wore one of my sister's dresses. The food was excellent, and Isaac and I both enjoyed the crab cakes. After our meal, we attended a play written by a local playwright and director called Amelia Finds Happiness. Goodness, it was fast-moving; the music was wonderful, and we all enjoyed the twisting, turning plot. What a fun evening with my family!

Sunday, we all attended church. After church, Isaac and I visited with his sister Julia and her family. It was joy to see her family all doing well. After our noonday meal, we strolled past the Deremer Land Surveyors office. Julia's son Michael worked along with his grandfather Nelson and seems to have learned the trade as the business is thriving. With all the new building in the area, I can surely understand Michael's success, and we both wished him well. We continued on with our stroll and walked past the Deremer homestead where Michael now resides. A few updates have been done to the outside of the house, but other than that, it looked the same as when the children were still living there.

We visited both cemeteries where our parents were laid to rest to place flowers on their graves. Does one ever get over the loss of their parents? How I wish for just one more of mother's hugs and my father's kiss on my cheek. How I hope that I was just as good a parent to my children as my parents were to me. If I could have just one more chance to say I love you and thank you for being there for me. Now I say these words over the grave of the two people who really, truly knew me and loved me and was always there for me. Gosh, the ache in my heart is still there after all this time. I wonder, will it ever go away? We continued on our walk, finally returning to Vivian's home where we packed our things and moved to Lydia's house for the next few days.

Monday, and where has the time gone? Last night, Isaac went to bed, and Lydia and I sat and talked until almost midnight. We never stopped talking, just like when we were teenagers and shared in everything. Lydia asked if we would like to visit Philadelphia, as it is twenty miles from Doylestown. I decided that I no longer found the hustle and bustle of city life exciting. I now seem to enjoy serenity and consistency in my life. Today we hitched the horse to the carriage and went on a picnic just outside of Doylestown. We enjoyed our picnic on the banks of Cooks Run. Isaac and Lydia's husband, Brad, fished the afternoon away. Both men hooked some nice-sized bass that Lydia later prepared for our supper.

Papa and Mama used to picnic here with us on lazy Sunday afternoons. It seems the only thing that changed was the trees that now provided even more wonderful, dense shade. After our fish fry, we were joined by Lydia, Solomon, and their spouses on the front porch of Vivian's home. Isaac attempted to convince my siblings to come and visit with us. He told them that they would like the change of scenery and laid-back pace. Isaac suggested that they come as far as Easton, and we could take a day trip to the Mansfield Woodhouse area. I felt a spark of hope that Isaac may have hit upon a solution to get my family to come and visit. We shall wait and see.

All of our siblings were at the stage stop before dawn on Tuesday. It was a bittersweet goodbye to what has been a wonderful whirlwind visit. We boarded our stage and off we went, full speed ahead, toward Easton. I was so frightened by the quick pace that I held Isaac's hand so tightly, I cut off circulation in both his and my hand. We arrived safely in Easton just after sunset. I praise the Lord for our safe arrival. We enjoyed our evening meal in the hotel dining room, and I even partook of a glass of wine that seemed to calm my nerves. We were soundly sleeping about nine o'clock.

The Easton to Elizabeth Town stage departed Easton, and we were among the five passengers aboard and the only ones not to take the stage through to its final destination. Eli and Sarah were waiting for us when the stage pulled into the Mineral Springs. It was great to be back home, and the trip was absolutely wonderful. I must say that it will be a long time before I am ready to embark on such a journey. There is truly no place like home.

Lilia met us at our home and invited the four us to come and have lunch with their family. We put our bags in the house and off we went, this time walking, to Pieter's house just over the hill. Lilia had prepared a delicious meal of beef with potatoes and vegetables. Albert and his family joined as well. What a welcome-home surprise! Jacob is now thirteen and has become a most pleasing grandson. Albert's children still allow me to give them heaps of hugs and kisses. What a wonderful way to end a great vacation.

This evening, as Isaac and I sat in our rocking chairs on the front porch, we spoke of how the Lord has really been good to us. Yes, we have suffered with the loss of loved ones, but knowing that the Lord is by our side has made our grief a bit easier to handle. The Lord has provided us with all that we have needed to survive and a wonderful family. Our marriage of thirty-four-plus years has for the most part been blessed. I just don't know how I could have gotten this far without my Isaac by my side. Tomorrow, I will write thank-you letters to Julia, Vivian, Lydia, and Solomon. Tonight we will just enjoy the solitude and each other.

CHAPTER 110

Fall slipped into winter, and here we are in yet another year. The holidays were filled with God, family, and love. Elizabeth and Jason again hosted our Christmas day meal. It started snowing a few days after Christmas, and it seems like we have had snow every day since. New Years Day 1797 brought us a generous foot of additional snow on that day alone! Gosh, we must have over three and half feet of snow on the ground, and it's just the middle of January. We have managed to get to church as the trip is about a mile, but we would have never made it without our sleigh.

Last week during full moon, Isaac asked me to go for an evening sleigh ride. We stopped and picked up Eli and Sarah, who at first thought we were out of our minds. Within a few a seconds, they got their outdoor clothing and blanket, and off we went. The four of us acted like giddy youngsters; it was so much fun and something none of us had done in years. We even enjoyed hot cocoa when we got back to Eli and Sarah's home. We decided that with the next well-lit evening, Eli and Sarah will pick us up, and we will again revert back to our earlier selves and laugh the evening away. The looks that we got from our children when we told them about our sleigh ride during our Sunday family day was priceless. One thing is for sure, the four of us are not ready to lay down our hoe and call it quits!

Tulia stopped by earlier this week, and we enjoyed a cup of tea. She is really concerned for Lea, as all she does is sleep. Lea awakens in the morning and prepares Toby's breakfast then goes back to bed. She gets out of bed when Toby comes in for lunch, but immediately after lunch, she lies down again, saying that she has back pain and is dreadfully tired. During the evening, after supper, she does manage to spend time with Toby but retires early. I suggested that she talk with Aunt Peggy as she may have some kind of medicine that will help Lea feel better. I didn't say anything to Tulia that I believed Lea was ill just after she and Toby married. Besides, Tulia certainly didn't need my unsolicited opinion.

Sarah and I were again invited to Lizzie Bryan's house to enjoy a quilting bee. We were back and forth as to whether to go or stay home. Isaac questioned why we would want to miss the event as we both enjoyed quilting. Yes, we do enjoy quilting, but being verbally attacked for worshipping elsewhere is just unfair. Isaac said that if the ladies start to cause us concern, nip it in the bud and tell them they are out of line, and the two of you will not discuss your personal relationship with the Lord. In his words, "that ought to quiet them." Well, we attended and actually enjoyed ourselves. The troublemakers were unable to make it. Oh, what a crying shame! We wondered if they stayed away because they knew Sarah and I would be attending. If that was the case, we were pleased as punch that they stayed home. Besides, the shoofly pie was excellent, so without them attending, we got a second slice!

Isaac and Jacob stopped in to visit Amos at his store while in Asbury today delivering a load of hay. Amos told them that a man named Gilbert Kelsey came into the store and was asking all sorts of questions about the Asbury area. It appears that Kelsey is considering starting up a bakery in one of the vacant buildings close to the Musconetcong River. Is Asbury that large that it can support such a business? The families around here bake their own bread and sweets. I can see him making a living if he planned on opening a bakery in the Phillipsburg area, but not in Asbury. This makes me think back to what our county representative Elroy Schmidt said a few years ago about our area growing in population, and soon we can expect amenities only found in the urban areas. Perhaps I will need to be corrected, but I still believe our sparse population cannot support such a venture.

CHAPTER 111

James has been bringing us copies of the *Easton Daily* when he and his family are able to attend church and our Sunday family dinners. This past winter has been crazy, but when I actually think about it, it is just as winter should be—unpredictable. On March 4, John Adams was inaugurated as the second president of the United States of America! Thomas Jefferson was also sworn in our vice president. Let freedom ring loud and long!

Aunt Peggy asked Dr. Holmes from Asbury to look in on Lea, as she is still not well. Tulia said that the doctor seems to think that Lea may be suffering from something called Bright's disease. Aunt Peggy explained that Lea is having problems with her kidneys, and there is really not much one can do to help her. Perhaps bed rest, lots of water, and time will relieve some of her problems, but other than that, there is no known cure. Toby is beside himself and rightly so. They planned a life together with a future that included children. Mr. Bowman from the Mineral Springs Hotel wants Lea to try a few of the hot baths. Since Lea has been a dependable employee of the hotel working as an attendant, Mr. Bowman expects no money for the treatments. We do hope and pray that she can find relief from the mineral baths. Isaac has offered the use of our wagons and mules to safely get her to and from her appointments. The mineral baths helped Isaac, so we pray they will help Lea too.

CHAPTER 112

It seemed like all summer, there was some type of secret mission unfolding in front of my eyes. I questioned Isaac several times, and he said it appeared that the girls seemed to be doing a bit more whispering during our Sunday family day. When I attempted to join in the girls' chat circle, the tone reverted back to normal, and the talk was about children, gardening, or sewing. I started to believe that I was becoming a victim of softening of the brain; after all, we are now fifty-five years old, and the mind seems to be the first to quit on us. After that thought, I prayed to push the fear away and deal with what could be the slow but sure demise of my very being.

Eli and Sarah invited Isaac and me to go with them to the Easton market. It was an especially nice September day, and with Sonny and Toby helping with the farmwork, we quickly agreed to join them. I wondered why we embarked on this journey midmorning as usually we set out immediately after the farmwork was completed. Isaac kidded Eli when he arrived in his fancy wagon, but Eli brushed it off, saying the ride would be easier. So off we went for a day at the market. The two men were talking about Theodore Oberly wanting Eli to look over a young bull that Oberly was offering for sale. Eli and Theodore have been doing business for years. When we got to Stewartsville, we veered left and headed toward the Oberly farm, so Eli could take a quick look at the bull.

When we arrived, Eli guided the wagon around the side of Oberly's barn. There in front of us stood my brother, sisters, Isaac's sister Julia, and their spouses with smiles on their faces! I let out a loud scream of joy and caused all around us to jump in fright. Eli jumped down from the wagon to help me to the ground before I made a fool of myself, tumbling onto the dirt lane. Isaac came around the wagon and joined us in the biggest hug session created by humankind! Our families had come to visit us, and the surprise was heart-stopping! The surprise only got better when we were escorted to the picnic grove on the other side of Oberly's Pond. There we met with all of our children and grandchildren. It was a surprise get-together for Isaac and my fifty-fifth birthday. Aha, this must have been the secret mission the girls were plotting! Tears wouldn't stop. I just couldn't help myself.

Here we were amongst our family; goodness, we had both our children and Eli's children and grandchildren and then our siblings! Oh my gosh, I still have shivers of joy going up and down my spine as I write this! We enjoyed a lunch of fried chicken, spiced cabbage, biscuits, and punch; after, we had birthday cake and watermelon. What a wonderful gift, and the joy of seeing everyone together was a bit overwhelming. I believe that I thanked the Lord one hundred times for shining down upon the day and for all of us being together. At about two o'clock, the party was breaking up as our children had to go back and tend to their afternoon chores. We lingered longer and were told that our siblings would be coming to visit us tomorrow. Oh my, I was not prepared for any visitors. Abigail whispered to me that they had that covered too; while we were enjoying our day out, Tulia and Kit were tidying up our home. My girls thought of everything!

My siblings and their spouses were staying at the Mineral Springs Hotel; Julia and her husband, Thomas, were staying with Eli and Sarah. They arrived yesterday on the Easton to Elizabeth Town stage and were actually dinner guests of Elizabeth and Jason last evening. The dinner was also attended by most of our other children. Eli and Sarah and several of their children also were able to attend. We were completely dumbfounded, and to think, this all took place right under our noses. One thing can be said: some people can sure keep a secret around here! It appears that everyone knew except Isaac and me. What a joy to be together.

The next day, Thursday, everyone came to our farm for a good hardy country breakfast of scrapple, souse, bacon, eggs, potato pancakes, apple sauce, biscuits, and jelly. I can't thank Tulia and Kit enough for all of their help. They got to my house the same time the men were starting the morning chores. We all worked liked busy bees and had everything ready for our guests when they arrived about eight o'clock. Tulia wouldn't stay, so I made sure that her family shared the wonderful food too. The twelve of us ate, chatted, ate some more, and continued our conversation on just about everything under the sun. In the evening, we shared a meal at Eli and Sarah's house. Sarah prepared a wonderful chicken dinner; I brought along two apple pies and a peach cobbler that were still warm from the oven for our dessert. We all enjoyed special wine that the men selected from the Mineral Springs Hotel.

Friday morning, we met in the dining room of the Mineral Springs Hotel and enjoyed being served breakfast. At about ten o'clock, we managed to all squeeze into a carriage that Eli borrowed from Elwood Bryan, and off we went toward Easton. Our family will stay over at the Hotel Easton and will take the Easton to Philadelphia stage early tomorrow. Arrangements were made for an extra stage on standby just in case there were additional folks also planning on traveling this line tomorrow morning.

We said our goodbyes at about three o'clock as we wanted to be back in Mansfield before dark. Eli, Sarah, Isaac, and I were still in our glory when we arrived back home. Our family actually came to visit—something they said would never happen. Solomon said he liked the Mansfield Woodhouse area, but our sisters made no mention either way. At least, they made an attempt, and after all, a visit to Mr. Case's store cannot be compared to a general store in Doylestown.

Eli and Sarah sat with us on our front porch talking about the wonderful few days we shared with our family. Sarah said that it was Elizabeth and Abigail's idea, and she and Eli immediately jumped in to help. I am still amazed that our family actually made this trip. Eli and Isaac were so proud to show our family what they were able to create with bare hands: perseverance and faith in God. Thank you, Lord, for absolutely everything!

CHAPTER 113

Pieter and Albert stopped at Creveling's tavern stand on their return from town for a mug of stout. They then stopped by to visit me and Isaac and relayed some gossip they had just heard. Scuttlebutt has it that a man named Jasper Harding is considering starting a saw mill just south of town where the creek bends and drops a bit, causing a mini waterfall.

For several years, the Indians encamped near this location but have since moved four miles upstream. The property has an ample supply of standing trees that Mr. Harding plans to use for his business. Construction on a home and the mill are expected to begin in the spring. Isaac and the boys discussed the remainder of the seasoned trees be brought down from the hillside where the orchard now stands. The trees have been kept off the ground to allow the free flow of air to delay rot. Perhaps some of these logs could be floated down the creek during a freshet to the new saw mill and be processed into planks and boards. This saw mill will be well received and is long overdue, as our area seems to be growing steadily over the past few years.

The cold weather is settling in quickly. Isaac, Sonny, and Toby have the farm ready for winter. The crops seemed to have produced well this past season. Old age took Sally, our favorite cow, this past summer. Sally was such a sweet, kind animal who would follow us as we walked the pastures. She did make it to the ripe old age of twelve, and nothing lives forever, but we miss her. Isaac said that our two remaining cows will provide more than enough milk for the two of us, Sonny and Toby's families. We are now only selling milk and eggs to those folks who walk to the farm. Since the children have left home, we no longer make deliveries to the townsfolks. Jacob Smith has taken over the few customers we catered to, and this has kept everyone pleased.

As we wrap up another year, I have especially warm memories about these past twelve months. Isaac and I turning fifty-five doesn't exactly give me joy, but we have traveled this road together and for that I thank the Lord. The greatest gift of 1797 was the gift of family and us being together. I cannot remember a time when we were all together since perhaps Eli and Sarah's wedding, over thirty years past. I pray 1798 will give us more of these fun and special times with our siblings and families.

CHAPTER 114

Progress on the Jasper Harding homestead and saw mill is moving along nicely. The winter was quite mild, and due to this, spring arrived with little fanfare. Pieter and Albert brought us a wonderful bucket of maple syrup earlier this month. The two had mentioned that the tapping would most likely happen earlier this year due to the rather mild winter. After they collected their buckets and the sap was cooked down, they ended up with almost seven buckets of maple syrup. This brought back the memory of me standing beside the huge cauldron, suspended over the blazing firepit, with my wooden paddle, stirring the boiling sap until I felt as if my arms were going to fall off. Finally, after what seemed like forever, the sap turned into a nice dense syrup. Dreaming of the sweet taste of the maple syrup kept me going. I am sure that Lilia and Anna were the ones with the stirring paddles, and they too prayed that the sap would quickly thicken into syrup, just as I once did.

Amos and Jasmine attended church this past Sunday. I asked where Ruby was, as she always attends church with her parents. Jasmine told me that Ruby was in Carteret living with her grandparents. Ruby decided that she wanted to learn more about dressmaking, and since there are no shops here in Mansfield Woodhouse, she will remain in Carteret until next year. Ruby showed a real interest in sewing, and Amos believed that she would benefit from being an apprentice in a dress shop. Isaac and I congratulated the couple on their daughter's brave move. Silently I thought that Ruby will not be returning to reside in Asbury as the draw of city life to a young lady is very enticing. Just the same, I pray that she has success in her desire to improve her seamstress skills.

Also, this past Sunday during our family meal, Joseph and Emily made an announcement that they are expecting a little one sometime in mid-November. What joyous news, and we are all happy for them and their two sons. It would be nice if this time it's a girl, but we will be happy for the delivery of a healthy baby, no matter what. Joseph said that Mr. Case was discussing helping the couple buy a place of their own, one that has growing room. Both want to stay close to the store and are not interested in owning a farm, just a modest house with room for a horse and perhaps a cow and a few chickens.

Jacob seems to have taken a real interest in Hannah Convey, granddaughter of Martin and Maria Convey. Jacob is now fifteen and quite the handsome young man, if I must say so myself! Hannah is a lovely young lady, and it is so nice to watch the two of them engage in conversation after church. They have known each other for years, but I guess their friendship is becoming a bit more serious. Lilia was quite concerned that the two were becoming much too friendly. I said to Lilia that the two of them appear to be sweet on each other, and if their relationship is meant to be, it will be. I am sure that she is concerned for her son, but one cannot keep the apron strings tied to a child forever. Children grow up and eventually move on to begin a life of their own. This is all in God's plan, and all is good.

All of the prayers that were lifted up for Lea over the past months seemed to have helped. Dr. Holmes was amazed at her recovery and is allowing her to return to work a few days a week. Tulia believes that it was the mineral baths that helped Lea recover. I think it was the abundance of prayers. Having faith will see you through even the worst situations. Toby is so grateful for his wife's recovery and seems like a new man himself. God is great!

The weather has been so nice that Tulia and I churned our butter out on the front porch. Once the two of us get talking, time passes by quickly, making it less of a chore. Since it is just Isaac and me, the larger portion gets divided between Tulia and Lea's family. We also share the buttermilk. The loss of Sally still lays heavy upon our hearts. Isaac was right when he said we no longer need three cows, as last week I had some milk that soured. I dislike wasting anything, but no one wants sour milk. Tulia told me about a recipe for sour milk biscuits. She said that she would try to remember the ingredients as it had been years since she made it. This would be a wonderful way to use something that otherwise will be added to the pig's slop.

Tulia also told me that Kit has become very romantically involved with a young man named Abel. Tulia is very concerned, as Abel lives on the Coleman farm just past Stewartsville. Abel is a slave! Tulia has tried to make Kit understand just how lucky she and her family are living here on our farm. If Kit marries Abel, she will be considered property of the Coleman family. Should Mr. Coleman decide to sell or trade Abel, Kit may not be part of the deal. Any children created from their marriage will also be property of Mr. Coleman. In fact, Kit and any children could be sold or traded to different owners or even sent to another state. All of Tulia's advice seems to fall upon deaf ears as Kit is head over heels in love with Abel. Furthermore, whispers through the grapevine tell of Mr. Coleman not treating his slaves well. In all fairness, if there is ever fairness in holding a person against their will, Mr. Van Horne provided shelter, clothing, and food for Sonny and his family. This in no way makes it right, and slavery needs to be abolished from this earth forever! Does Kit really want this for herself and possible future children? All I could do was give Tulia a long hug, and we prayed together.

Isaac and I sat on our porch late this afternoon sharing in how our day went. I mentioned Kit and her fondness for Abel. Isaac said that Sonny also spoke about his great concern for Kit should she marry Abel. Although we can't save the world, Isaac said he would pen a letter to Perry Coleman and ask if he would consider selling Abel to us. If the cost is reasonable and a deal can be made, perhaps Abel can come and live on our farm. We know nothing about this young man, so when Isaac sees Sheriff Winters, he will ask him if he knows of any reason to steer clear of Abel.

CHAPTER 115

Emily is now in confinement but doing well. She is expected to deliver the little one in about two months. I will be very surprised if she makes it that far. This past Sunday, our family decided to cast ballots for either a boy or girl. After tallying up the ballots, it appears everyone is rooting for a girl. Emily is carrying much differently than she did with the two boys, and she admits that she also feels different too, so we shall just have to wait and see.

James brought us our newspapers, and to our surprise, we found an advertisement for Kelsey's Bakery in Phillipsburg. Well, well, I guess Asbury wasn't the place to start a bakery after all, Gilbert Kelsey. Just the same, we wish him luck. And that appears to be the good news. The bad news was a bank robbery on September 2. The Bank of Pennsylvania located in Philadelphia was robbed of $162,821! I can't even imagine that much money, and what in the world would one do with so much money? The paper stated that it was the first bank robbery here in the colonies. Goodness, I hope that it is the last!

Isaac was ready to give up on Perry Coleman as the letter he penned weeks ago went unanswered. Well, lo and behold, Mr. Coleman and his son Paul appeared on our step. He said that he had to wait for Paul to return from the Monmouth area to read Isaac's letter. Apparently, Perry Coleman cannot read or write. Mr. Coleman asked Isaac to explain why he wanted to purchase one of his male slaves, Abel. The trio sat on the front porch and talked for close to an hour. Try as I may, and goodness I tried, I could not listen in on their discussion. When I heard the two visitors leaving, I quickly rushed to the porch. Apparently, Mr. Coleman was readying to sell Abel to a gentlemen farmer from the Valley Forge area. Isaac reluctantly offered $500 to purchase the young man. Coleman said he would think about it, as it was a bit more than the gentlemen farmer had offered and would let Isaac know in a few days. Isaac questioned as to why Perry chose to sell this particular slave? Coleman answered that the young man had a mind of his own, and although he appeared to be smart, Coleman did not need or want a slave that could think for himself. We both decided to keep the purpose of Perry Coleman's visit a secret, at least for the next few days.

CHAPTER 116

The renovated shed that housed both Sonny and Toby's families is now the home of Abel. Perry Coleman agreed to sell Abel to Isaac for $500. Upon Abel's arrival, Isaac, Sonny, and Toby sat Abel down and had a man-to-man talk with him. Abel is expected to pull his weight, and Isaac also expects Abel to compensate us for the cost of his freedom. Isaac and Sonny agreed that this arrangement shows Abel that good fortune does not come without a cost. Kit is pleased as punch that she can freely love this man and not worry about him, her, or any future family being ripped from each other. Tulia and Sonny said that they will be forever grateful for us taking the bold step to secure Abel's freedom. It will be only a matter of time before this couple affirm their love for one another in the eyes of the Lord.

Joseph and Emily are the proud parents of a beautiful little girl! This little bundle of joy was born on October 27, and she is named Lucy. Lucy is absolutely adorable, and her two big brothers couldn't love her more, even if they do complain about her crying. Babies will be babies, and we thank the Lord for her good lungs.

The men got the farm ready for winter, but after learning of terrible snowstorms in New England, November 17 through 21, they put up the cords earlier than usual. Prayers were lifted up in church for the hundreds of folks who are said to have died due to this blizzard. Perhaps New England was caught off guard and not prepared for this event? But then, New England usually gets snow well before we do here in New Jersey. So sad, but it was an eye-opener to step up our winter preparations and get our tasks completed in a timely manner.

Jasper Harding and his family have settled into their new home. The saw mill construction is well on its way to completion, but not quite ready to operate. The Harding family consists of Jasper, his wife Veronica, their three sons and daughter. Jasper visited with Jason looking for work, and he is now helping to deliver whiskey kegs to distilleries in the Phillipsburg and Easton area.

We got Christmas greetings from both of our families in Doylestown. Everyone seems to be in fair health and a happy mood. According to Julia, more houses are popping up all around town, keeping Michael and his surveying company busy. Solomon is considering slowly phasing himself out of the blacksmith and carriage business. I guess that Aaron has proven himself as being quite talented as return customers are requesting to talk with him instead of Solomon! Building a name for one's self will surely keep this business going. Papa put his entire life into this venture, and I am so pleased to see that my brother and nephew keep up the tradition of honesty and hard work. A free ride in no way, shape, or form exists and is only the daydream of the ne'er-do-well.

CHAPTER 117

The New Year began with a boom, or perhaps I should say, a thunder snow. It started to snow early on December 31 and continued throughout the day. Just past midnight, or January 1, 1799, a clap of thunder shook our house and jarred us out of bed. When Isaac opened the front door, the blowing snow gave us quite a chill. Then again, another boom, and yet another. We questioned if this could really be a winter thunderstorm, as it had been decades since we experienced this weather condition. I heated some milk and made us hot cocoa, and we sat at the table waiting for the storm to pass. It was perhaps thirty minutes before we no longer heard thunder and things became eerily quiet as the snow was still falling at a heavy pace. After about an hour, we returned to bed and were able to enjoy sweet dreams until the morning. Sonny said he and his family had never lived through anything like thunder, lightning, and snow together and added that it would make him happy if he never experienced again.

Abel has proven himself to be quite talented and willing to step up and join in any farm chores. With Sonny, Toby, and Abel doing the daily chores, Isaac doesn't even have to go to the barn. When the weather breaks and the fields need planting, Isaac will join in and again work his farm.

Isaac had a private meeting with Sonny last week, and the two discussed the future of our farm. Isaac assured Sonny, he and his family would always be welcome and a part of our family and this farm. However, Isaac said that eventually this farm will be unable to provide for all of us unless we find a way to increase our profits. In a few months, Abel and Kit will marry, and hopefully Sonny and Tulia will be blessed with grandchildren. Lea is improving, so she and Toby may also be blessed with children too. So Isaac questioned Sonny if he could think of a special crop or fruit that we could plant, some type of service we could offer or perhaps even become beekeepers? Isaac feels that we need to find a niche to safely carry us into the quickly approaching next century. Sonny said that he would give the conversation serious thought and hopefully have some ideas to share with Isaac.

CHAPTER 118

Abel and Kit were married the middle of April, and the spring weather was so nice that the festivities were held outside in Sonny and Tulia's yard. Besides Isaac and me, the family entertained perhaps fifteen close friends. Abel, like Sonny and Tulia, does not know where his family is now. He arrived at Perry Coleman's farm when he was just a young boy, possibly coming from somewhere in South Carolina. He said that his father was a large, strong man, and his mother died soon after giving birth to his brother. Immediately after his mother was buried, he found himself a part of a group of mixed-aged males, two of which were his older brothers, all shackled and chained together, walking hours on end each day until they arrived in Philadelphia where he became the property of Perry Coleman. Coleman did not buy Abel's two older brothers. Abel also has a younger sister, and he is clueless of her whereabouts. Isaac assured Abel that those days were forever behind him and ahead lay a bright future, free from slavery.

Herbert Cooper fell prey to highwaymen. They took everything but his shirt and britches after hitting him on the top of his head with an oak limb. Herbert was returning to Brass Castle after a town meeting at the Washington House. Actually, the meeting ended before dusk, but Cooper stayed to chat with a few of the men he seldom saw. The distance to his home was perhaps a mile. Sheriff Winters was notified, and the two robbers were found in a dive in Phillipsburg. Herbert's horse was tied up to the hitching post out in front of the saloon, along with the thief's horses. Cooper is very lucky in two ways: the first, he is alive; and the second, that he got his horse back. These two hoodlums will be away for a while as they serve some jail time. It is never a good idea to travel in the darkness alone. Sometimes safety in numbers doesn't even help, but at least the arrests have sent a strong message to all bums!

Sonny stopped over for a chat. He shared some of his thoughts about expanding the farm. Since this valley has wonderful soil and root crops do extremely well, Sonny thought that perhaps potatoes, turnips, rutabaga, carrots, and beets could turn a profit if taken to a town market. He also questioned the wholesale of the produce to the Cole family, Abigail's in-laws. The family seem to travel often to the area of the Hudson River to sell their applejack, and root crops prove to be the best to travel a distance to market. There are markets that are closer, but Sonny felt the nearer to the big city, the higher the cost for quality produce. This caused Isaac to pause as we were able to produce a large amount of root crops on about an acre and a half of land when we were helping to supply our troops with fresh food. Isaac liked the idea, and the startup investment was next to nothing so the two men got down to the planning of how much ground to till and what to plant. Being the end of April, crops needed to be in the ground within a few weeks. They decided to begin with the plot prepared for the army and reach out to the Cole family to see if they would be interested in purchasing our vegetables to resell. If all goes well, next year, more ground can be prepared and planted.

CHAPTER 119

August in New Jersey is showing her true self—hot, humid, and sticky. The amount of rain the valley has received since the start of summer has been the bare minimum to keep the crops from wilting. Although the root crops seemed not to mind the wretched weather. Tulia has kept all the men supplied with gallons of Switchel to keep them working in the heat of the day. She calls this beverage haymaker's drink and claims the recipe was brought to America when slaves arrived here from the Caribbean. She mixes molasses, apple cider vinegar, water, and fresh ginger together, and the men folk love it. I am not so fond of this drink, but I do not spend hours in the hot sun. I would rather see the men labor early morning and late afternoon, but men will be men, and no sense in me asking them to sit for a spell. I guess that would be considered nagging!

I was tending to our wash when Eli rode down on our short path rather quickly. Isaac saw him coming and walked from the paddock over to me to greet Eli. Eli said that he just picked up the mail from the Mineral Springs, and there was a letter for Sarah from her niece Gayle informing us that her mother, Sarah's sister, Margaret (we call her Maggie) took sick a few weeks ago, and the doctor wasn't sure what the illness was. Gayle asked that Sarah please come and give Maggie some much-needed encouragement to help her through this illness. Maggie has become bedridden and is in a lot of pain. Her brain is functioning, and she is aware of her surrounding but slowly giving up. Eli asked that Isaac take him and Sarah to Easton this afternoon so they can board the stage to Doylestown at sunrise tomorrow. Isaac immediately said yes and that he would be at Eli's home in about an hour. I stepped up and said that I was coming along too.

Toby met Isaac in the barn and said that he would hitch the horse to our best wagon and bring her up to the house. Isaac noticed Sonny coming back to his home for his noonday meal and told him we would be gone for the afternoon but should be home before sunset. Tulia told Isaac that she would bring in my laundry before dark and make sure that Albert and Pieter were aware of us making this trip. Isaac and I got ourselves together and picked up Eli and Sarah and were off to Easton at about two o'clock. Before leaving Eli's farm, I told Edward to stop over and share meals with us if he so desired. He said that we would surely see him.

The trip to Easton was uneventful, and we left Eli and Sarah in the front of the Hotel Easton where they would be staying for the night and meet the stage in the early-morning hours. Sarah said that she would send us a letter after she learned more about her sister's health. Eli thought that they would return to Mansfield Woodhouse by stage so Isaac wouldn't have to come and pick them up. We all hugged and prayed a short prayer for their safe arrival in Doylestown and Maggie's recovery. We were back to our farm by sunset, and as promised, my laundry was neatly folded and inside our front door. Afternoon chores had been completed, and the animals were bedded down for the night. We sat on the front porch enjoying the evening and agreed that the best thing for us was to have Eli and Sarah next door. Exhausted, we retired well before nine o'clock; both of us looked forward to a good night's sleep.

CHAPTER 120

Sadly, Maggie passed away a few weeks after Eli and Sarah traveled to Doylestown. Eli came home alone after a week to attend to his farm. Sarah wanted to stay with her family, and Eli agreed that she should be with her sister. The doctors never did discover just what ailed Maggie, and she passed away the first week of September. When Eli received the sad news through the mail, he left on horseback immediately, riding well into the night, arriving in Doylestown just in time for the burial.

Eli visited Solomon and Aaron's blacksmith and carriage shop and purchased a used carriage and harnesses so he and Sarah could return home together. The trip back home took two full days but they arrived safely. Sarah is so melancholy but also thankful that she was with her sister in her final days. I quoted a verse from the book of Job reminding Sarah "that the Lord giveth and the Lord taketh away." Our walk on this earth is but temporary, but what awaits us in heaven continues through eternity.

Earlier this summer, when the Cole family traveled to Weehawken with a wagon loaded with applejack, Kenneth passed along Isaac's name and address to a merchant that deals in fresh fruit and vegetables. Isaac received a nice letter from Simon and Son, dealers of fresh fruit and vegetables. The letter stated Earl Simon was interested in purchasing root crops directly from Isaac and would pay top dollar to have them delivered to his business in Weehawken. After several back-and-forth letters between the two, Isaac agreed to deliver a wagon load of produce. The first week of October, Isaac and Jacob traveled along with Kenneth Cole and a helper, who delivered a wagon of applejack near the Simon and Son store.

The wagons left early morning, traveled until darkness; the men bedded down with the wagons and cargo and finished their journey on the second day. I was not pleased with the travel plans, but at least, Isaac and Jacob were in the company of another wagon. Isaac asked Sonny to accompany him, but Sonny has yet to travel far from the farm out of fear of being captured and sold into slavery once again. (I truly can't blame him and pray that this never happens. The evil of some men for the sake of money.) Mr. Simon was very generous and paid Isaac well for the fresh produce. Isaac promised that next year, more acreage would be planted and perhaps we can deliver double the amount of produce next season. Earl said that he would also be interested in apples and pears from Albert's orchard. When Albert learned of this offer, he was more than pleased. I guess all the hard work to keep his orchard producing nice fruit will pay off. When Sonny learned of the value of the produce, he was pleased as well. His idea to increase the profits of this farm was a wonderful proposition.

Chapter 121

Christmas day has passed. It was again filled with love and family. I should be joyful, but I have sadness in my heart. So much has happened that should lift my spirits, but my heart feels burdened. Eli is not well. His quick trip to Doylestown on horseback to be with Sarah has taken a huge toll on his health. He finds it difficult to stand for any extended amount of time. This year, he did not join in the annual bird hunt fearing that he would slow down the rest of the party. All of the men said that they wanted him to join them no matter what, but he could not be persuaded. Isaac considered canceling the event, but I said that I believed it would make Eli feel even worse. I know that Isaac is really troubled by his brother's pain and discomfort, but sadly, he does not share his feelings with me.

On December 16, James came down our path on horseback and alone. This scared the liver out of me! He brought us the news that our beloved commander in chief, George Washington, had died on December 14 from some type of throat infection at his Mount Vernon home. A feeling of numbness spread through our bodies leaving poor Isaac speechless.

Maggie's death still causes Sarah much grief. As young girls, we all played together in Doylestown, and now Maggie has gone home to meet our maker. One has to ask who will be next, as we are all approaching the age where our time is now dwindling.

I am truly pleased with the wonderful root crop and the profit made from this great venture. I cannot thank the Lord enough for the bountiful harvest. Isaac feels more at ease that future crops will support and keep this farm running.

Tulia stopped by the other day for a cup of tea and shared the news that Kit and Abel are expecting a little one to arrive sometime in late winter. This is truly joyful news, and Tulia and Sonny are so pleased that they will become grandparents. We prayed for the well-being of both Kit and her unborn child. We also asked the Lord to bless Lea and Toby with the child that they are so eagerly awaiting.

So as the New Year and next century approaches, I have prepared myself as best I can. I will burn the bayberry candle that the grandchildren gave Isaac and me for Christmas, on December 31. Legend tells us to burn the candle to the socket, not allowing it to extinguish, as it will bring an abundance of blessings to our home. I have also made preparations for our New Year's Day meal of pork and sauerkraut to bring us more goodwill. Underneath all of these attempts to make 1800 a year of hope and prosperity, I pray for our family, friends, and those not as lucky as we are, to find peace, love, and faith in our Lord. Here's to a new century and future that only God knows what he has in store for each of us, amen.

CHAPTER 122

On February 2, Jacob and Ellis ventured out into the hillside orchard and set up camp to await the groundhog, hoping that he would not see his shadow. The orchard seems to have an abundance of ground-hog holes, so the boys figured one would pop his head out and fore-cast what the weather will be until spring arrives. If the groundhog sees his shadow, it will be frightened by it and will scoot back down into his burrow, informing us that we are in store for another six weeks of winter weather. If the groundhog does not see his shadow when he leaves his burrow, mild weather is on its way. Well, the two cousins sat on the hillside in freezing conditions for several hours, and not one groundhog even bothered to make an appearance. Aside from the boys near freezing to death, I wonder what old Mr. or Mrs. Groundhog were doing—hibernating, of course! Perhaps flipping a coin would bring better results? A bit warmer at any rate.

We have our first baby of the century, and it's a boy! Abel and Kit are the proud parents of a precious son they named Elisha. Elisha entered into this world on March 2 and is doing well. Tulia and Sonny are still walking on water over the birth of their first grand-child. We pray for a life of good fortune for little Elisha.

During one of our recent Sunday family days, the boys were discussing some scuttlebutt about a fancy road that may travel from Morris Town to the Delaware River in Phillipsburg. A nice smooth road would be wonderful, but the boys said that there will be toll-gates along the route; people will have to pay to use the road! Isaac said that no meetings have been called about this alleged new road-way. He believes that citizens would need to be informed of such a venture, as it most likely would run right through the village. Apparently, fancy roads where one has to pay a fee to travel upon is all the craze, so it will probably be just a matter of time, and we will have this unwanted pain-in-the-neck modern form of travel. I don't see this making life easier for us local folks, as I believe making people pay to use a road is pure nonsense!

Sonny has been laying the plans for a much larger plot to raise our root crops this year. He believes that with the help of Toby and Abel, we can easily manage two, perhaps three, acres of land. Isaac wasn't quite sure, as going from a bit over an acre to three is a big jump and a definite leap of faith. He, however, agreed to let Sonny handle the entire project, from tilling the soil right through to the harvest of the vegetables. One thing is for sure, Sonny, Toby, and Abel are sure pulling their weight to keep this place moving forward. We now need to pray for a good growing season. Work on turning the soil will begin within a few weeks. Goodness, it seems as if one season is just running into the next—time is passing by so quickly, like the speed of a mighty steed!

CHAPTER 123

There was quite a ruckus last night coming from the old Van Horne homestead. A little past three, we were awakened by the crack of a rifle. It was our August full moon, and apparently, the valley had a visit from a mountain lion. Adam Jenkin's Jersey cows took a fright and trampled down the rail fencing and ran amok. Toby and Abel went to help the Jenkins family round up their livestock. The bright moonlight allowed us to see cows on the road near Thatcher Church and a bit farther down the valley close to Jason and Elizabeth's home. It took the men the rest of the night, but all of the livestock was found, and the rail fence mended. Toby said there was talk about forming a hunting party to go after the big cat. I guess it is safe to say where there is one, there is surely more.

The *Easton Daily* reported that the US capital has moved out of Philadelphia and relocated to Washington DC, this past June. President Adams is residing in a hotel near the building site of the Executive Mansion, which is not expected to be completed until late October. Progress is being made, and I am so proud of our new nation.

Writing about Philadelphia, the paper also posted the results of the August 4, 1800 US federal census. Philadelphia is our largest city with a population of 41,000! The total population of the mighty United States of America is 5,308,483 of which 893,602 are slaves. Golly gee when our grandparents came here in the 1600s, this was mostly wilderness inhabited by Indians. For the most part, the white folk have run the natives out of this area to who knows where. Some things just don't seem to make sense.

Our root crops seem to be thriving. Sonny, Toby, and Abel planted the full three acres with all the same vegetables as they planted last year, plus one new type, parsnips. The three men are truly excited about the progress the plants are making, even with the fact that we have had more rain than usual. Isaac believes that Earl Simon will be more than pleased with this year's harvest.

Joseph, Emily, and their three children appear to be quite content with the addition that was added to their home. They moved into the old Wilson property several houses to the east of the Case Store. The house was only two rooms, and Benjamin, Emily's father, offered to pay for a large addition to the house. Goodness, the inside of the place looks like a castle—now all they have to do is fill the empty rooms with furniture! Lots of room, lots of wood to keep the place warm in the colder months.

CHAPTER 124

Our President John Adams and his family are now residing in the Executive Mansion as of November 1. The newspaper even gave the very impressive address as 1600 Pennsylvania Avenue! Now all of the nation's business will be conducted from the District of Columbia. Kind of has a nice ring to it, and the mansion is huge with many rooms to attend to the business of our growing country.

This year, Isaac did not travel to Weehawken to deliver our produce. Albert, Jacob, and Abel traveled with Kenneth Cole and his helper just as last year. The root crops that were delivered to Simon and Son pleased Earl Simon, and he looks forward to continuing this arrangement for many seasons to come. Earl said that he would gladly purchase as much produce as we can grow, as he has expanded his area to include vendors in several other towns along the Hudson River. The apples arrived in Weehawken in excellent condition, but the pears did not fare well. Perhaps the pears will be sold locally as travel over the rough roadway caused noticeable bruising to the fruit. Earl Simon did purchase them but at a drastically reduced price. However, everyone returned home safe and sound and very pleased with the season's profits. Abel was quite excited about making this trip as he has traveled no farther than the Coleman farm, and now our farm, since he was purchased from the slave market years ago. It also appears that Jacob and Abel have become close friends. Jacob is seventeen, and we believe that Abel is nineteen or twenty years of age. They enjoy working side-by-side and fishing together when they find the time.

The Harvest Festival was held on the farm of Elwood Bryan. Everyone near and far was invited to join in the celebration. Much to our joy, Eli and Sarah were able to attend. We had corn-husking and log-splitting competitions. Many bobbed for apples, and we all sampled the pies, jelly, and jams and voted for the winners. This was truly a family day with fiddlers playing almost nonstop music to dance to. The attendance was even larger than last year with lots of great conversation and food. I believe that the beautiful weather brought so many folks out to enjoy the autumn afternoon. This is always the one festival where we meet people that we seldom see throughout the year but truly enjoy. The Bryan family really outdid themselves, and both young and old were grateful to be a part of such a fun time.

Eli is still not himself. His lame leg gives him constant pain, so Isaac suggested that Eli enjoy a few hot bath treatments from the Mineral Springs Hotel. Begrudgingly, Eli agreed to three treatments that will begin on Monday. Isaac has confidence that Eli will begin to feel relief after just one treatment. Pray to God that he is right and poor Eli can find something to help feel him better.

CHAPTER 125

1801 arrived without fanfare but delivered our valley with heaps of snow. During the long months of being confined to our home, Isaac and I discussed the possibility of building a proper home for Abel, Kit, and Elisha. The renovated shed was never meant to be a permanent residence. Isaac said that he will not be a part of the building process but will gladly do small tasks. This third cabin will be erected in the same area as the homes of Sonny and Toby. This venture will take all of our available sons, grandsons, and Sonny's family to complete. Working together, Isaac believes that the family will be moved in before the fall. When the weather breaks, construction can begin after the regular daily farmwork has been completed.

Sonny stops by every day to check on Isaac and me. He brings us fresh milk and stays and chats with us for a bit. This has been a difficult winter for both Isaac and me. We have skipped attending church because of bad weather. We now find that any tiny excuse seems fine and can keep us homebound. We need to get off our bottoms and get out to church. Sometimes it just seems to be a chore to put on our warm clothing, get the horse and wagon hitched, and go anywhere. Our children are not pleased with us and have no problem letting us know when they come for our Sunday family dinners. Being chilled to the bone when we go out of doors is not only a bother but also painful in our knees, hands, actually anything that is supposed to move when we move doesn't always work that way, and often I find myself being stopped in my tracks.

We haven't seen much of James, Ellen, and Naomi as travel has been difficult for them as well. They made it to our home this past Sunday and brought us our newspapers. We have a new president, President Thomas Jefferson, who was inaugurated on March 4.

Jefferson is the first president to be inaugurated in our new nation's capital, Washington DC. Our vice president is Aaron Burr. Gosh, three presidents already in this newly formed nation—where has the time gone?

Pieter brought us a letter from the Mineral Springs mail drop from my sister Vivian. Vivian said that everyone seems well, and life is good in Doylestown. Solomon has officially retired from the blacksmith and carriage business. Aaron has purchased the business and now has two full-time workers, as business is good. Vivian said that the town is expanding out toward Philadelphia, and the Deremer surveyors are often seen working just about everywhere in town. This made Isaac feel proud that his father's business has survived the test of time as well. And, of course, there was the "when can we expect you to come and visit" line, as all letters from my sisters end with. The fact is the way we are both feeling right now, we do not see traveling anywhere in our near future. I'm not even sure my heart could endure another fast stage ride to Doylestown and back. But things can and often do change, so I will not use the word *never*, as it is such a harsh word. Perhaps, *not right now* is a better answer.

CHAPTER 126

Jacob stopped by to visit with us. We so enjoy his company, and he seems to be spending more time on our farm than that of his father. Well, Jacob had a smirk on his face, and he started to tease me about losing one of my most favorite people on June 14. I looked at him as if he had three eyes, and as nicely as possible, I asked which best friend of mine passed away ten days ago. Well, good night shirt, it was Benedict Arnold! I honestly have no love for this man even if it is the Christian thing to do. Arnold is a traitor and turncoat among other things. Jacob said that Arnold took ill in January and finally passed on the fourteenth in London. He was sixty years old and leaves his wife and several children. I didn't let Isaac or Jacob know, but I did say a tiny prayer for Benedict that he rest in peace, wherever he may be. Can one rest in peace in hell?

Progress on the cabin for Abel and his family is moving along nicely. Since all crops are in, the men are able to find some extra time to work on the house. Sonny did not expand the root crop area this year but figured out a way to get more yield from the same amount of acreage. He also decided to try planting squash this year under Albert's fruit trees. This area will give the plants plenty of room to spread out and hopefully bring forth a generous amount of squash.

This beautiful weather has finally brought Isaac and me out of our melancholy mood that we seemed to have suffered with the entire winter. We even decided to take a short walk ending up at Eli and Sarah's house. Eli seems to be doing a bit better. Sarah told us that Edward has met a young lady from Asbury named Sadie Everett. Sadie is from Easton and now lives in Asbury where she tends to her great aunt, Lavinia Everett. I believe that we once met Lavinia at a hoedown on the Harte farm years ago. Edward seems quite serious, and the two have been spending all their spare time together. This is heartwarming, as Edward is around thirty years of age, and one would think that he should have found his soul mate by this time. Many a young lady has had their eye on him, but I guess the spark just wasn't there until he met Sadie.

CHAPTER 127

The harvest was excellent. This year, we were able to provide two wagons of produce to Earl Simon. Albert and Toby handled the first wagon, and Jacob and Abel drove the second team. The Cole family did not have any deliveries to make in the Weehawken area, but Albert was familiar with the path of travel, and they did fine. The squash crop seemed to be a big hit with Earl. This made Sonny happy too as one just never knows if their ideas will prove to be successful or end up fizzling out.

The new cabin needs just a few finishing touches, and the family can move in. Kit is so excited and made some really nice curtains from material salvaged from used bedding from the Mineral Springs Hotel. Abel promised her someday that she can pick out her own fabric and make pretty curtains, but for now, what she has made suits them perfectly. Little Elisha is a chubby, happy baby and such a joy to be around as he never stops smiling. Perhaps his grandma has him a bit spoiled, but one can never give a baby too many hugs and kisses.

The pigs have been slaughtered, and the springhouse is boasting of lard, ham, bacon, scrapple, and souse. Jacob and Ellis went hunting this past week and shot a nice-size doe. The meat was immediately butchered and shared with all of us. Sonny turned their portion into venison jerky that is still in the smokehouse being processed. The men seem to take a liking to this method of preparing the meat, but I prefer a nice roast. With the help of Sarah, we turned a large portion of the venison into mincemeat, as we had extra suet, currents, and apples. Tulia once told me to add some walnuts, so we included a few handful of them too. After we got it cooked, we divided it between our two families, filled a couple of stoneware crocks, covered them, and placed them in our root cellars. Mincemeat pie is always a welcome treat no matter what time of year.

CHAPTER 128

Eli and Sarah stopped in on their return home from Lavinia Everett's burial. Lavinia passed two days ago of old age, as she was seventy-two years old. The burial took place in the Methodist-Episcopal Cemetery in Asbury. Daniel Everett, Lavinia's nephew and father to Sadie, is in charge of overseeing his aunt's estate. The contents of the house will be disposed of, and the home placed up for sale. Edward wasted no time in asking Mr. Everett for his daughter's hand in marriage. The couple will marry as soon as the home is sold. Until then, Sadie will continue to live in her great aunt's home and help with the cleaning out and sale of the property. After Edward and Sadie marry, they will live with Eli and Sarah.

Eli said that he is feeling better and was out helping to stack firewood that Edward was cutting. He is not ready to do the chopping but enjoyed neatly stacking the wood. Sarah was a bit annoyed because she believes Eli is doing too much too soon. I have to agree with her, but try telling that to a man. Just the same, it is great to see Eli outdoors and enjoying the beautiful fall weather.

Joseph, Emily, and the children stopped by a few nights ago for a short visit. Joseph said that he saw several men milling around on the property across from Case's Store. About an hour later, the four men came into the store and asked where they might get some lunch. Joseph suggested the Mineral Springs Hotel if they wanted a hearty lunch, or Creveling's Tavern Stand for a quick bite to eat. Without seeming like he was prying, Joseph asked the men what they were doing, and they said that they were searching out a site to build a small tavern with limited lodging, where several animal pens could be erected in the back. A place where droviers could stay for the night, and their animals would be secure in the pens when they were herding their livestock to the markets.

The men also mentioned the possibility of a toll road being constructed from Morris Town to the Delaware River in Phillipsburg. So, perhaps, the scuttlebutt we heard earlier this year may, in fact, come about. Or perhaps, these men are just speculating and hoping if the fancy road does materialize, they will be a few steps ahead of any competition wishing to fill their pockets with gold. Over my wretched body will I pay to ride on a road with a smooth surface; actually, I will not pay to ride any road, whether smooth or bumpy. Stupid newfangled ideas!

Chapter 129

Yet another Christmas has come and gone. The New Year celebrations have passed as well, and 1802 seems to be slipping by even quicker than other years. Isaac and I turn sixty this year, a chilling thought. I'm not sure how we got to this age so quickly without even noticing the years drifting by. Perhaps it was the joy that we found in each other and our family that caused us to forget about marking our path toward destiny. Whatever it was, we are grateful to our Lord for getting us here safely and giving us the gift of children and grandchildren. When it's over, we will not be remembered for what riches we have acquired but for what good we have left behind. Our children and grandchildren are the pride and joy that keeps us moving forward even when we wish to sit for a spell. They will be the goodness that we leave behind, our legacy for eternity.

The sale of the Lavinia's home was finalized in mid-January. Sadie visited with Lea and Kit inviting them to come to Asbury and look over the household goods once belonging to her great aunt. The two young ladies were uneasy but accepted Sadie's offer, and the trio traveled to Asbury with Edward handling the horse and wagon. It took a bit of prodding and encouragement, but Lea and Kit accepted many wonderful and very useful items that will help make their daily chores a bit easier.

Edward and Sadie were married the end of March. Traveling to Easton was no easy feat with the cold weather and thawing roads. Mr. and Mrs. Everett are lovely people and went all out to host a beautiful wedding for their only daughter. The couple were married in the Fourth Street Presbyterian Church, and a reception was held at the Hotel Easton. The bride looked stunning in a very nicely made pink woolen dress. Our family traveled together in two large wagons.

Eli and Sarah traveled behind in their carriage as they planned on staying the night at the Hotel Easton. James and Ellen had offered to put Isaac and me up for the night, but we politely declined as there is no bed like your own bed.

Our Good Friday service was just beautiful, as it was held in front of our church. Just as the sun was setting, the sky gave us a spectacular display of pinks, oranges, and reds. Easter Sunday service was held at sunrise. This was equally as beautiful as we braved the early morning chill to have the service along the side of the church. Again, we watched in awe as the sun rose over the mountain and shone down upon our small but mighty church. The entire valley had to hear us lifting our voices in praise, "He lives, he lives, Christ Jesus lives today!" We also attended the eleven o'clock service, along with those who earlier needed to tend to their chores and could not come and praise the Lord. The rest of the day we all went to Pieter and Lilia's home for a tasty ham dinner. All the girls brought their favorite holiday foods and desserts. It was just a wonderful day of sharing and being a part of each other's lives.

The little ones are growing so quickly, and it appears that they all get along well, at least for now. The men also questioned Isaac about Congress establishing the United States of America's first military academy at West Point on March 16. The academy is slated to open on July 4 of this year. I was not as pleased with this subject, as reminiscing about the war can often be painful for Isaac. Today he didn't seem to mind and said that his unit had not reached West Point but did spend many days along the Hudson, building a fort along the mouth of the river. He continued to say that we need a strong military to maintain a solvent nation. We never again want to enter into a war on our own soil, or for that matter, on any man's soil. If the presence of militiamen shows our strength, then build as many installations as need be. War is hell, and don't ever let anyone tell you that war and conflict will solve problems; war causes separation, injury, and death. If war becomes necessary to achieve peace, it is still hell here on earth.

CHAPTER 130

September has brought the welcomed relief of less humidity. My garden seemed not to have suffered from the relentless heat of the summer. Sonny told Isaac that the root crops appear to be doing well, and the squash weren't bothered by the intermittent dry spells. The harvest should be right on schedule, and Earl Simon should expect at least two wagons of produce delivered to Weehawken about the first week of October. Jacob, Toby, and Abel seem pleased that they will accompany Albert to make the delivery. Jacob asked if Ellis could also travel with them. Albert agreed, thinking it would be a learning experience. I'm not so sure that Anna felt the same, but Ellis will be on board one of the wagons.

Sarah came for a visit. As we shared tea and cookies, she told me that Edward and Sadie are expecting a little one due to arrive sometime in May. She and Eli are so pleased and look forward to helping to care for the baby's needs. Sarah also said that this news appears to make Eli very happy.

A few days after Sarah's visit, Tulia stopped by and told me that Lea and Toby were expecting a child about mid-April. This was wonderful news as well, as I know how Lea prayed for a child and now God has answered their prayers. Tulia and Sonny are so pleased and look forward to this new arrival too.

I would not be surprised to hear of a marriage proposal between Jacob and Hannah in the very near future. They are both nineteen and ready to take the next step to become husband and wife. Jacob seems to be content to stay on the farm, not sure which one, as he seems to be at our farm more than his father's. He enjoys helping his uncle Albert with the orchard as well and can be found assisting

Edward often. So perhaps we should call him Jacob the Drifter. As Lilia says, just as long as he is home for supper, all is fine with her.

Isaac and Eli delivered a load of split firewood to our church this week in preparation for the long cold winter closing in on us. Sonny and Toby insisted on loading the wagon and wanted to accompany the men to the church to help unload and stack the wood. Both Isaac and Eli protested, and off they went on their own. It was no one's fault but their own when they struggled to walk the next day. Serves them right, bullheaded men!

CHAPTER 131

"Come to me, all who are weary and heavy-laden, and I will give you rest" (Matthews 11:28). God called Eli home two days ago, November 15, 1802. The pain and sorrow is so raw, I am having trouble finding the words to pen this entry. Edward and Donald, the hired hand, had just finished the morning chores when they saw Eli approaching the barn. Both men greeted Eli with a wave and a hello. Eli lifted his right arm to wave, but as he was doing so, he just collapsed to the ground. Edward and Donald ran to Eli to help him but immediately saw the blank look on Eli's face. Donald quickly mounted his horse and rode as fast as possible to Aunt Peggy's house. Being early in the morning, Aunt Peggy had not yet started her morning rounds and was by Eli's side as quickly as possible. Sadly, Aunt Peggy believed that Eli was already gone by the time his body met the ground. She believed that he died from some type of heart sickness she called edema of lungs.

On Donald's return to Eli's farm, he stopped to relay to Isaac that Eli had stumbled or somehow fallen to the ground and was not well. Isaac immediately climbed on the closest horse's back and rode off to be with Eli. In a panic, Sonny hitched his mule to his wagon and took me to be with Isaac. There was Sarah and Isaac sitting on the ground, both hugging Eli's lifeless body. The scene was a mixture of confusion, sobbing; and what do we do next? Aunt Peggy stepped in and said that she would help with final arrangements. Edward, Isaac, Donald, and Sonny carried Eli into the house, placing him on his bed. Aunt Peggy offered to prepare Eli's body for burial, but Sarah and I said that we would wash and dress him.

Much to our surprise, when Eli fell ill a few years ago, he secretly met with Pastor Kent of the Mansfield Woodhouse Presbyterian

Church. Eli asked permission to purchase burial plots within the church's cemetery. Pastor Kent met with some church officials, and they gave their approval for the sale of four plots; plots for Eli and Sarah, and plots for Isaac and me. Eli said that he wanted to be by his brother's side through eternity; knowing that I wanted to be near baby Ester and Catherina, he decided to get permission for us to be buried there. What a heartfelt thing to do. Isaac and I were speechless but sincerely grateful.

The funeral was today, and the cemetery seemed to be overflowing with people wanting to express their condolences to Sarah, their children, and Isaac for their tremendous loss. I can't seem to shake the constant feeling of helplessness. Why Eli? Why this manner of death? How can this be, Lord? Eli was beginning to feel like his old self and getting back into his daily routine. He seemed to have so much left within to give, and now he's gone. There was also much concern for Sadie who is with child. We pray that she can endure this sadness and heavy burden and safely bring this new life into this world.

CHAPTER 132

Life continued on as usual. The harvest was successful. Our spring-house, root cellar, and smokehouse are well-stocked for winter. Sonny, Toby, and Abel visited Edward several times to help with their harvest in any way they could. Yes, life does go on, but without Eli.

Christmas and New Years were met with profound sadness. We all tried to keep a happy face for the children and not allow them to see our pain. Children are so much smarter than we often give them credit for, and they could see through our false smiles. I guess they played along with the adult game so as not to upset us and cause us more grief. Sarah describes herself as feeling numb all of the time. The pain of losing Eli is sheer agony. Isaac is suffering but won't give in to his pain. The burden he is carrying within will surely cause him both physical and mental anguish. I see no joy in his eyes, just the pain of loss. Jacob has tried to get his grandfather to open up and at least share some of the good time that he and Eli enjoyed. Bringing up pleasant memories may lift some of Isaac's pain, but he wants no part of it. The feelings of guilt that he was not with his brother in the end are constantly in his thoughts. They say that time heals all wounds. I sure hope that it can help ease Isaac's pain, and the sooner, the better.

Jacob asked Wesley Convey for his daughter Hannah's hand in marriage. Wesley said he would be pleased and honored to have Jacob as a son-in-law. The wedding is set for the middle of June. We are so pleased for Jacob and Hannah, and this announcement has been long in coming. Since Hannah and Jacob will marry on June 13, Jacob had a long discussion with Isaac about perhaps putting an addition on our home and living with us. Both Hannah and Jacob said that they are committed to aiding us in our old age. Reality has just hit; we are old. Just when and how did that happen? Anyway, Jacob will pay for all materials and bring in help to build two rooms on the back of our home, lift the ceiling, and increase the size of the loft. Wow, that's a lot of living space! Isaac asked me what I thought, and I could find no reason to say no. He agreed and thought it just might be what we need right now in our lives, as what happened to Eli lays heavy on his mind. The building will begin in about two weeks.

So far, 1803 has the promise of two births and one wedding. This ray of sunshine is so badly needed. The cloak of sadness still lays heavy on our hearts with the loss of Eli. Sarah seems to be a tiny bit better, but Isaac has sunk into a deep depression. I pray for peace of mind and heart for all of us. May brighter days be on our horizon.

The winter has been quite mild and now that we are halfway through February; perhaps Old Man Winter will give us all a break this year. Since the berry bushes and nut trees gave us an average harvest, perhaps we will escape the severe cold. I can accept some of winter's chill and fields blanketed with snow is good for our crops, but it doesn't have to be three feet deep.

Sarah and I attended our annual quilting party again this year. The old biddies that gave us grief for worshipping at the Thatcher Church said nothing to us this year. Perhaps it was because of Eli's death and his burial within the cemetery walls of the Mansfield Woodhouse Church? Perhaps they have wised up and realized that we can praise our Lord wherever we wish. Who can say for sure, but the event was enjoyable, and as always, the dessert was yummy—peach pie with fresh whipped cream. Late summer, Lizzie Bryan cooked up several batches of peaches, sealed them in glass, and kept them in her root cellar to be used for special occasions like her quilting bee. Peaches in February is a real treat!

We had a pleasant surprise at church this Sunday: Ruby attended with her parents Amos and Jasmine. Goodness, she looks so refined and stylish, the look of a true city girl. She is visiting back home for a few days and will return to Carteret before the week's end. Ruby said that she really loves all of what the city has to offer and is unsure if she will come back to live in Asbury. She is working in a small dress shop and loves that she can create a fancy dress from an assortment of fabrics that she never even knew existed until she started her apprenticeship in another local dress shop. And, yes, she has a special someone she hopes to soon bring home to meet her parents. I sincerely hope that Amos and Jasmine stay put here in the Mansfield Woodhouse area. Should they return to Carteret, this area will lose an honest, hardworking couple that showers people with nothing but kindness.

CHAPTER 133

The Lord has shone down upon us and presented us with two beautiful healthy babies. Lea birthed a girl on April 7 they named Mandy. Every time Tulia cuddles the little one, she sheds tears of joy and praises the Lord for this wonderful gift of life. Sadie birthed a son on May 10, and after much soul-searching, they named him Eli. Sarah rocks the little one, singing a lullaby and seems to find much-needed joy in her life. Little Eli will be baptized sometime in June.

The large addition being added to our home is really quite impressive. I guess once a person sets their mind to something, there is no stopping them. The group of men that show up for a few hours late each afternoon and on Saturdays is amazing. Toby and Abel join in to help as well, and the men don't seem to take this as a huge endeavor but a time of fellowship and stepping up to help a family member or friend. I am sure that Jacob has and will offer his help on any projects, large or small, should they arise. It is also a good chance that the work will be completed, and the couple will move into their new rooms on their wedding day. Lilia, Anna, and Elizabeth have stepped up and provided food and drink to keep the men happy and nourished. To see my family working together along with their friends brings so much joy to my heart. I pray to God that these relationships will continue through the rest of the days of their lives. Family and friends are truly gifts from God.

Pastor Kent stopped by for a visit earlier this week. He did not pass judgement on us for attending Thatcher Methodist-Episcopal Church but just wanted to see how Isaac and I were doing since the death of Eli. Isaac spoke only when directly addressed. I rambled on with Pastor Kent about our children and grandchildren. I also said that Eli's death has left a huge hole in our hearts, one that we are not sure can be mended in this lifetime. The pastor seemed to understand and prayed with us. After he left, I prayed to God to not allow Isaac to lose all hope. Please, Isaac, call upon the Lord to rescue you from your despair. Please, Lord, show me the way to help my husband find peace and happiness within his heart and soul, amen.

CHAPTER 134

Hannah looked absolutely beautiful in her wedding dress of light-pink cotton, trimmed with rose-colored ribbon and buttons. A rose-colored ribbon also held her pretty dark hair in a braid. Jacob looked so handsome, and the pride I felt in my heart spilled out onto my face. Our first grandchild was marrying! It seemed that just yesterday, we were rocking him to sleep. Leon and Sarah Convey did a wonderful job hosting the wedding on their farm. The weather was a bit warm, but not as humid as the week before, so we didn't seem to mind the heat. I forgot to ask who made the wedding cake that was really delicious, and we were even treated to some chocolate drops.

The joy of being together should have been wonderful, but I was sincerely concerned for Isaac. As I sat at the wedding looking at my husband, I could see how he had aged since Eli's passing. He looked like an old man with no sparkle in his eyes or joy on his face. I felt pangs of fear within my body telling me that he could be the next victim of the grim reaper. Oh, Isaac, snap out of it and come back to me, our family. We love you and miss you. The just-married couple took up housekeeping in their newly finished rooms within our home. Hannah and I worked out a schedule of sharing household duties, with her wanting to take on the lion's share. This arrangement of the two of them coming to live with us just may be a blessing.

Back in March, Sonny discussed enlarging the area for the root crops to a full three acres. He believes that we are ready to handle the planting, tending, and harvesting of more produce. If his estimate is correct, we may be delivering three full wagons of vegetables and apples to the Simon and Son, dealers of fresh fruit and vegetables. Isaac just told me that the additional land has been tilled and the crops planted, including the squash that seemed to thrive below the apple trees in Albert's orchard. The prospect of a larger harvest pleases Earl Simon as he always claims he will gladly buy as much as we can deliver. Sonny and Isaac also discussed thinning the sheep and pig herds, as more time will be needed to maintain the root crops. Pieter and Albert said that they would increase their herds to make up any loss we may encounter by us keeping just enough sheep for their wool and pigs to be used for slaughter. In a few weeks, the boys, Sonny, Toby, and Abel, will herd the animals over the hill to Pieter and Albert's farms. The lambs and piglets need to be sold before most of both herds are shepherded to their new fields.

Baby Eli was baptized this past Sunday, and he was as good as gold during the ceremony. Since Hannah is helping me in the kitchen, we invited everyone back for our Sunday family meal, including Sarah, Edward, Sadie, and little Eli. It was quite a houseful but a joy as well. Our older granddaughters took turns tending to little Eli's every need. I teased Sadie that the long nap the infant took was partly from the handling he suffered when we passed the baby as he received an abundance of hugs.

CHAPTER 135

It was Monday, July 11, 1803, Hannah and I were placing the wash over the paddock fence to dry when we heard shouts and screaming coming from the hillside orchard. Today was the day that the sheep and pigs would be herded over the hill to Pieter and Albert's farms. It was decided that the sheep would go first, as there were more of them. Goodness, our shepherds were Pieter, Jacob, Albert, Ellis, Sonny, Toby, Abel, and Isaac. The flock of sheep were herded up the orchard hillside, when near the top, one of our large rams turned around and started to run back down the hill. With his head down, he butted Isaac in the chest, causing him to fall backward and land on a large rock.

As Hannah and I rounded the house to see what was happening, we could see the men running toward something on the ground. Then fear struck: it was my Isaac. I started to run toward the orchard, but Hannah stopped me because the sheep were now running amok, and the last thing we all needed was for me to be injured as well. I began to pray so loudly that I wasn't even sure it was my voice that I was hearing. I could see Jacob begin to run down the hillside and out our lane in the direction of Aunt Peggy's farm. Ellis, Sonny, Toby, and Abel managed to regroup the sheep and got them to the top of the hill and into one of Pieter's fenced fields. Toby and Abel returned without Ellis and Sonny. Soon, we saw Sonny, Ellis, Anna, and Lilia coming down the hillside; Ellis appeared to carrying a blanket. Minutes later, Isaac was being carried down the hillside on the blanket to our home.

Hannah and I met the group at the bottom of the hill. Isaac was laboring to breathe, pinkish blood was coming from his mouth, and his color was terrible. I held his hand as the men carried him into our house and placed him in our bed. Isaac tried to squeeze my hand as I assured him that everything would be fine. Aunt Peggy arrived and said very little as she examined Isaac. She believed that the headbutt from the ram crushed Isaac's chest and punctured a lung, which is why he had pinkish blood coming from his mouth. Isaac had also apparently struck his head on the rock when he landed and could also be suffering from a concussion. She also said that there was little she could do but gave him something for pain. Oh Lord, how can this be? We all formed a circle around Isaac and prayed for some divine intervention. Sonny, not so sure that divine intervention would solve this problem, set out to notify our children. As my children arrived, one by one we sat silently with Isaac; James was the last to arrive. We all laid hands on Isaac and prayed like we'd never prayed before. Isaac entered the gates of heaven just hours after he was injured.

The July sun beat down upon us as we stood in the Mansfield Woodhouse Cemetery, sobbing over Isaac's grave. Isaac was honored by a military funeral, and the amount of people who came to say their last goodbye to my husband crowded the cemetery. No words of comfort could ease my pain and agony. The love of my life, father of my children, had now gone home to be with the Lord. The only shred of comfort I was able to gleam from all of this horrible sadness was that Isaac, baby Ester, Catherina, and Eli were together again in eternity. Then the hatred started to surface. Why did we come to Mansfield Woodhouse? Why did we decide to raise cantankerous, unpredictable animals? Why did I not protest Isaac assisting in moving the sheep over the hill to our son's farms? Why? Why? Why? So much anger that I couldn't keep it inside, venting on anyone or anything near me.

My family allowed me to continue my rant over a week and then sat me down, opened my Bible, and prayed with me. Strange, how I could find no scripture that helped my aching heart. Perhaps I wasn't really reading the Holy Book but just staring at the pages? Aunt Peggy stopped by several times throughout the first few weeks, but her medicine did nothing for my broken heart. Poor Sarah, I just grabbed onto her and cried that I had not really understood her pain, and I will be forever sorry for not being there for her. After all, unless one has lost their soul mate, how would one even get a shard of pain that separation causes by death? Life is unfair.

A few weeks after Isaac's death, his will was probated. Isaac left his estate to our children, who in turn were to see that I will be forever cared for. This was a standard will with the exception of a few more paragraphs. Sonny and Tulia would be granted the right to live freely on our farm until death takes them. This also applied to Toby, Kit, and their spouses and all children born to them. Abel was also relieved of his debt to Isaac for gaining his freedom from Perry Coleman. Sonny said that he felt truly blessed by the kindness that Isaac had shown them. The gift of never again worrying what the future will bring was heaven-sent. Abel cried tears of joy for the forgiveness of his debt and tears of sadness for the loss of Isaac, his true hero.

CHAPTER 136

It's been two months since the loss of the love of my life; Isaac was my whole world. They say life goes on, but does it? My world has been turned upside down, and it is difficult to even feel the warmth of the sun on these beautiful September days. I did take a walk over to visit with Tulia earlier today. We enjoyed a cup of tea and some honey cake. She was minding Mandy, and I got to snuggle with the baby as well. Now, that did lift my spirits and allowed me to forget my troubles. Tulia encouraged me to come and visit with her more often. I think I just might take her up on her invite.

Having Jacob and Hannah living with me has been wonderful. She is such an amazing young woman and kind of reminds me of my much younger self. She is a bundle of energy and gets our daily chores completed in quick time. She also handles a horse and carriage and has taken Sarah and me to our old biddies' events. She has even taken an interest in the loom at Sarah's house, wanting to try her hand at making a blanket. Several afternoons each week we visit with Sarah; Hannah works the loom while Sarah and I work our lips.

I got a letter from my sister Vivian updating me on all the news from Doylestown. Lydia seems to be having difficulties getting around but is in good spirits. Solomon is well and enjoying his retirement, fishing almost every nice day. Vivian ran into Isaac's sister Julia, and she appears to be doing well. Doylestown continues to push toward Philadelphia. It seems as if lots of folks from Philadelphia are moving to Doylestown as they consider the area to be more of a country setting. Well, it sure won't be country for long if they keep moving out of the city to my little hometown, bringing their big city ideas with them. This is probably the same bunch that brainstormed toll roads. Good grief!

I seemed to have paid no attention to the crops and upcoming harvest. I think, as best I can remember, we had sufficient rainfall at all the right times. The corn in the lower field is starting to dry from the ground up; this is a good thing and right on schedule. I can no longer go around the house and look up toward the hillside orchard at trees laden with ripened fruit. I tried, really I tried. Even as we travel to church, I keep my eyes on the road ahead, fearing a ghost peeking out of an apple tree, taunting me with memories of something I truly wish to forget. They say that time heals all wounds; please, time, pass by quickly and rid me of the empty spot in my heart.

CHAPTER 137

Our sons, sons-in-law, and grandsons continued the tradition of the annual bird hunt started years ago by Eli and Isaac. In addition to the bird hunt, a group also went up on Scotts Mountain and shot a nice-size buck. They were hoping for an elk but were pleased with the deer. So in addition to two geese, one duck, and a grouse, we will also have a venison roast for our Christmas meal. When the men butchered the deer, they passed three nice-sized roasts along to Sonny, Toby, and Abel. The three were asked to go along on the hunting adventure but declined, saying that perhaps next year. I think they wanted everyone to honor Isaac and Eli and share memories without outsiders.

Christmas was again hosted by Jason and Elizabeth. We welcomed baby Eli to his first Christmas, but it was all so very sad without Isaac and Eli. Abigail gave the grace and although choked up, said that both her father and uncle were with us, not in body, but in spirit. It was difficult, but by the grace of God, Sarah and I managed to make it through the day without too many tears. By the time I got back home, I was totally exhausted and went right to bed.

Hannah has the mother-to-be glow. Her tummy is really showing, so probably within a few weeks, she will be in confinement. The little one is expected to arrive early May, and Jacob is so excited. Actually, I am as well, as this little one will be my first great-grand-child. I pray all goes well for not only Hannah but the baby too. Hannah will be attended to by our favorite midwife, Aunt Peggy. Our first little one for 1804, all so very exciting. Hopefully, a new beginning for all of us.

The weather has been typical for January. I am not fond of snow, but the sleet that continued for a day and a half made conditions absolutely miserable. Even the ropes that are supposed to guide us to and from our outbuilding couldn't keep us from slipping and sliding. One has to be extra careful when doing anything outdoors. The poor animals have been confined to their winter shelters, as it is too dangerous to allow them out even for a short time. Once the sun melts the layer of ice, the animals will be allowed to briefly venture out into the paddock. Who can say when that will happen as the sky seems to have been gray since early last week? A bit of sunshine would surely make all of us happy.

CHAPTER 138

My children surprised me with a sixty-second birthday get-together. The weather has been quite nice for March, and the roads were drying up, so all of my family, Sarah, Edward, Sadie, and baby Eli, attended as well. Goodness, Hannah kept this surprise from me and, even with her growing tummy, managed to get things in order and make room for all of us right under my nose. Tulia baked a wonderful cake, and Elizabeth and Abigail brought cookies and punch. What a joyful time to be all together. My children again cast ballots, voting for either a girl or boy when Hannah delivers the little one in about six weeks. The boy ballots won out, but this was all in good fun, as all we really want is a healthy baby. (Silently, I thought Aunt Peggy may have Hannah's delivery date wrong. However, if she does carry until May, may the Lord have mercy on all of us, especially Jacob. The wrath of a pregnant woman is shared with all who are near.)

After everyone had left for the night and I was snug in my bed, tears started pouring down my cheeks. How I missed Isaac as within a few weeks, he too would have been sixty-two years old. We were supposed to grow old together. I am truly grateful for my children and grandchildren, but I miss my Isaac.

Good Friday and Easter Sunday services were again held outside of our church. I thought it was very chilly, as Easter was in early April this year. Hannah did not attend services, but Jacob came with me on Good Friday. I hitched a ride with Sarah, Edward, Sadie, and baby Eli for the regular service on Easter Day. After the service, we went to Pieter and Lilia's home for our Easter celebration. Jacob brought the very pregnant Hannah. Goodness, it was noisy but joyful as well. If this family continues to grow, we will need to build a larger place so all of us can fit in at once! Many of my older grandchildren now have a special someone they have taken a fancy to who attended as well. Elbow room was tight, but no one seemed to mind, and all of us had a wonderful time.

Yesterday, I was walking to Tulia's house for a short visit when I met up with Kit. Kit shared the news that she and Abel are expecting their second child sometime this fall. Wow, this will be our second baby for 1804 and certainly joyful news. When I mentioned that I just spoke with Kit to Tulia, she said that she was both pleased and excited for the couple too. She continued to say that it was Isaac's bold move to purchase Abel from Mr. Coleman that made all of this even possible. Tulia said that Isaac was probably the kindest man she ever met, next to her husband, Sonny. What a nice thing to say, and her words made my heart swell with pride for my Isaac. He was certainly a good man and a man who believed that slavery was pure evil.

CHAPTER 139

I am not enjoying this spring weather. This constant cough has kept me up at night, and my ribs hurt as well. Aunt Peggy was here and gave me some cherry bark to make a tea with. This should have helped to relieve my cough, but I found no relief. Hannah asked that I keep drinking it anyway as at least I will be getting extra liquid into my body. I worry that I will pass along my cough to her, and in her delicate condition, she does not need an illness to cause her to feel even more uncomfortable.

With lots of pillows propping me up so I can breathe a bit easier, I find it more relaxing to be in my bed. I guess yesterday I napped on and off for the best part of the day. Today, my ribs are sorer, and my breathing seems to be a bit more difficult. Hannah just brought me my lunch in bed, chicken soup. What a sweetheart. She also told me today was April 10. That made me think, April 10? Oh my goodness, this is Isaac and my wedding anniversary! Today we would have been married forty-two years. Isaac, my love, we'll be together again soon. I promise.

The Journal of
Hannah Deremer

April 15, 1804–May 30, 1804

CHAPTER 140

Grandma was a fighter. She teetered between life and death for three days. Finally, the high fever from pneumonia became too much, and she could no longer fight. She entered the gates of heaven surrounded by her loving family. How much more sadness can this family endure? Please, dear God, bring strength and wellness to all of us.

Mariah Plumley Deremer, Jacob's grandmother, was laid to rest next to her husband in the Mansfield Woodhouse Presbyterian Cemetery. This fulfilled her desire to be not only next to her husband but near to baby Ester and Catherina for eternity. Sonny asked to be a pallbearer, along with Grandma's sons-in-laws and grandsons. The heartbreak from Grandma's death is almost unbearable. It seems as if God has cast a cloud of gloom over this family, but we all know that this is not true. As Grandma often quoted from Ecclesiastes, "To everything is a season, a time to be born and a time to die." I keep repeating this verse over and over again, seeking to find some peace from my sorrow. How I prayed that she would be here to welcome the birth of my baby, her first great-grandchild. As I sobbed uncontrollably, Jacob tried to console me, telling me that both Grandpa and Grandma are still with us, just in spirit, not body. This made me cry even more. I guess dealing with a pregnant woman who could realistically give birth at any time was extremely difficult.

I broke protocol and attended the funeral. I really didn't care as I truly loved this woman from the bottom of my heart. I chuckled at the fact should any one dare pass judgement upon me for attending in my extreme condition, Grandma would handle things from her new home in heaven. As I think back, all the old biddies that Grandma complained about attended her burial. Perhaps their friendship was strained, but they still cared enough to come and say their goodbyes. Uncle Albert said that he had no clue of all the lives his mother must have touched. The family was approached by person after person all saying the same thing that they were glad they knew Mariah Deremer, and that she was a friend to all. Lizzie Bryan dropped off a couple of shoofly pies knowing that it was one of Grandma's favorites. After the funeral, the family gathered around, and each enjoyed a sliver of the pie. With so many, we weren't even sure each could get a sliver, but the Lord saw to our needs, and we honored Grandma with shoofly pie. Grandma, we love you and will miss you forever.

CHAPTER 141

From his pulpit, Pastor Banghart addressed the congregation, "The Methodist-Episcopal Church celebrates two sacraments—Holy Baptism and Holy Communion. We are gathered at the Thatcher Methodist-Episcopal Church this morning to celebrate the sacrament of Holy Baptism. Baptism marks the beginning of our lifelong journey as disciples of Jesus Christ. The New Testament tells us that Jesus was baptized by John. In the Book of Matthew, Jesus commanded his disciples to teach and baptize in the name of the Father, Son and Holy Spirit. We are here today to obey the commandment of Jesus."

Pastor Banghart looked at me and asked, "So I ask you Hannah Deremer, who are you presenting for Holy Baptism?" I joyfully replied, "I present Mariah Lilia Deremer for Holy Baptism." Pastor Banghart took our daughter and made the sign of the cross, using holy water upon her tiny head, proclaiming, "I baptize you Mariah Lilia Deremer in the name of the Father, the Son and the Holy Spirit." The pastor gently gave me back our sleeping daughter. Next, Pastor Banghart turned and asked, "I ask you, Jacob Deremer, who are you presenting for Holy Baptism?" Jacob proudly stated, "I present Isaac Pieter Deremer for Holy Baptism." The pastor took our son and again made the sign of the cross and baptized baby Isaac. When Pastor Banghart gave our son back to Jacob, a tiny smile came across our baby's face. I saw this as a sign from heaven that all is well.

The twins endured the "pass the baby" routine as we continued our fellowship enjoying cake and punch. The kind wishes were overwhelming, and the fact that we honored Jacob's grandparents by naming our twins after them was received with praise. Finally, our cranky little ones wanting to be fed encouraged well-wishers to say their goodbyes. My mother and I prepared our babies for their ride back home. As Mama gently tied the ribbons on their little bonnets and sweaters, she commented that it was a bit nippy outside, even if it was the end of May. I found myself smiling as I reminded my mother that its blackberry winter. Special, but sometimes bittersweet things can happen during blackberry winter. Just ask the old folks, they'll tell it's so.

ABOUT THE AUTHOR

Brenda Heinrich Higgins was raised in the village of Broadway, Warren County, New Jersey. This is the same village where her mother, grandmother, and great-grandfather were born and raised their families. Brenda is a wife, mother, and grandmother who now resides a few miles from her roots. She loves Northern New Jersey with its serenity and change of seasons. Brenda is a fifty-three-year member of the Broadway United Methodist Church and is also a member of several historical organizations. Her passion is genealogy and local history and shares this hobby with her husband.

CPSIA information can be obtained
at www.ICGtesting.com
Printed in the USA
LVHW041057280620
659165LV00002B/119